GOLD SPUN

GOLD SPUN

BRANDIE JUNE

CamCat
Books

CamCat Publishing, LLC
Brentwood, Tennessee 37027
camcatpublishing.com

Hardcover ISBN 9780744301663
Paperback ISBN 9780744301748
Large-Print Paperback ISBN 9780744302325
eBook ISBN 9780744302431
Audiobook ISBN 9780744302868

Library of Congress Control Number: 2020951243

Book and cover design by Maryann Appel
Map illustration by Rebecca Farrin
Audiobook narrated by Kathleen McInerney

For Mom, my biggest cheerleader.

And for Erica,

my best friend and favorite

artistic partner in crime.

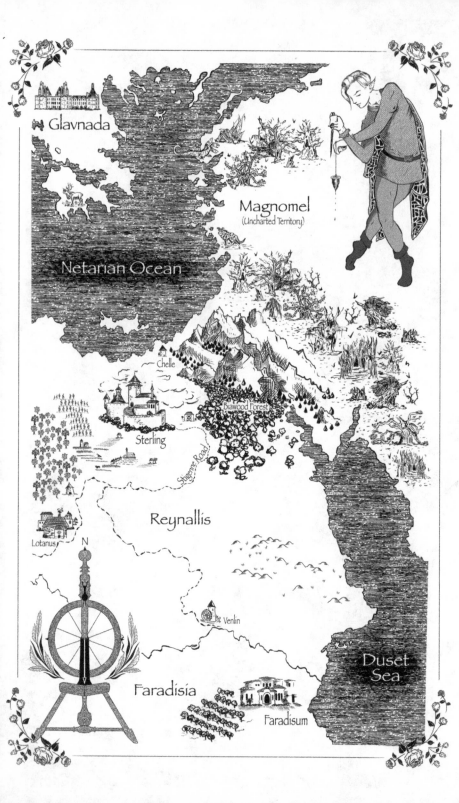

"In a certain kingdom once lived a poor miller who had a very beautiful daughter. She was moreover exceedingly shrewd and clever; and the miller was so vain and proud of her, that he one day told the king of the land that his daughter could spin gold out of straw."

–Grimm's Goblins (1876)

By Jacob & Wilhelm Grimm,
translated by Edgar Taylor

Prologue

Prince Casper leaned against the ornately carved marble railing of the balcony as he finished the last of his coffee. In his five years as a royal hostage he had developed a taste for the very sweet cinnamon coffee so common in Faradisia, but always wondered if he would still enjoy the strong, bitter tea of Reynallis when he was finally given leave to return home.

If he was ever allowed home.

It had been weeks since his brother, King Christopher, sent him a letter. When Casper first arrived in Faradisia, his brother had written almost every day, praising Casper's courage and keeping him updated with news of home. Casper knew his brother was occupied with ruling Reynallis, aware that his focus was now directed at keeping their country safe from the dangerous fay. Still, he could not help the feeling that he had been sacrificed and forgotten.

Casper stared at the vast landscape of Faradisia, long rows of citrus trees and wide stretches of grassland that were only green during the few weeks of rain. The sole movement in the serene valley was a lone man on horseback, galloping toward the palacio. As he neared, Casper could make out the official orange and white garb of a royal messenger. Casper idly wondered what news the messenger was bringing, though he knew King Jovian would never share sensitive information with Casper. The Faradisian king treated Casper with great courtesy, but never forgot that Casper's first loyalty was to his home country.

Straining his eyes towards the horizon, Casper imagined that he could see all the way to Reynallis. It was foolish, he knew, but it was his habit since he came to King Jovian's palacio. He had been fourteen when he first arrived as an 'honored' guest. Not wanting to shame his brother or his country, Casper only allowed himself to cry in the very early hours of the morning, long before even the servants would come to wake him. He would creep out on his balcony and stare to the north, his heart aching for home. He had not shed any tears in years, but he still looked towards Reynallis every morning.

Sighing, he set down the slender porcelain mug, wondering what activities the day had in store for him. Though it was mid-winter, the southern kingdom of Faradisia enjoyed mild winters, a brief respite from their sweltering summers.

Perhaps Lord Gerreld would want to hunt game or the ladies of the court would be interested in organizing a picnic by the hot springs. He might be afforded the finest luxuries the country had to offer, but his time was dictated by the whims of the Faradisian nobility, and his every move was subtly watched by half a dozen guards, even though he had never given King Jovian the slightest reason to doubt him.

As if reading his thoughts, King Jovian himself burst into his room, his rich orange and white robes flaring out behind him.

Casper startled, nearly knocking over his cup. The king never came to Casper's quarters, rather summoning Casper when he required an audience with the Reynallis prince.

"King Jovian," Casper managed, giving a short bow to the king, as he smoothed on his diplomatic grace. "I am honored by this unexpected visit." But the smile slid off his face as Casper approached the king, noting his grimace.

"Prince Casper, a messenger arrived this morning from Reynallis. I thought it only right that I be the one to tell you." King Jovian paused. For a wild moment, Casper hoped that Christopher was sending for him, that his clever brother had finally found a way to keep peace with Faradisia and summon him home. But the question died on his lips as he noted the deep furrow in King Jovian's forehead. Casper swallowed hard, a sudden knot of fear making him sick. He had to fight the desire to cover his ears.

"I take it the news is not pleasant," Casper said, forcing his words to remain calm even as his mind whirled, trying to figure out what could be so important that the king himself would deliver it.

King Jovian briefly looked away before fixing Casper with an unblinking stare. "No, it is most grave."

"The treaty?" Casper could not imagine his brother would do anything to destroy the peace he had worked so hard to create, but it was the only matter so important that the king would personally deliver the news.

The king shook his head. "This is not about the treaty."

"My family?" Casper's whisper was more of a prayer. He wished the king would correct him, but King Jovian only took another step towards Casper, confirming his fears. "King Christopher was killed a fortnight back."

No, not Christopher. The floor dropped away from Casper, the rush of emotions making him dizzy. He stumbled to a chair, almost falling into it. King Jovian stared at him for a moment. Casper knew he was breaking protocol to sit while the king stood, but he did not think his legs would work as commanded. King Jovian gave a small nod and took a seat next to Casper, letting the slight go. Casper almost wanted to laugh, that it was mad that he was thinking about etiquette breaches right now. But it was easier than allowing himself to accept the king's words. Anger, confusion, denial, and pain all swarmed inside him, making him want to scream. King Jovian sat by, staring at Casper with his shrewd eyes as Casper forced himself to regain some control. His brother would not want Casper to show weakness, even now. Casper inhaled deeply. *Pretend to be in control,* he reminded himself.

"What happened?" Casper's voice was even, if a bit husky.

"There was an attack by the fay off the Stigenne Road near the Biawood Forest. King Christopher was traveling back to your capital, but he never made it to Sterling."

"But it is too early for Christopher to be heading to Sterling. He never travels to Sterling till spring," Casper argued, as though that would bring his brother back to life.

"The messenger informed me that the fay had sent word they wanted to initiate talks of peace. Your brother was heading to Sterling early to commence such talks." King Jovian slowly reached into his pocket. "But unfortunately, it was a falsehood on the part of the faeries. They ambushed him."

Casper had never seen a fay, but knew with certainty they all had to be malicious and cunning if they had outwitted and murdered his brilliant brother.

Casper swallowed hard, praying the rumors he had heard about the fay were not true. If the Mother was merciful, Christopher died with a sword in his hand, fighting. Were the Mother truly merciful, though, Christopher would still be alive. He had to know. "And how did my brother die?"

King Jovian apprised Casper, seeming to weigh his words carefully. "The envoy told us dark magic was used. King Christopher appeared to have choked to death on his own blood." Casper imagined the scene, tasting bile in his throat. He needed to take care not to vomit in front of this king. "This was found pinned to your brother's body." King Jovian pulled out a folded piece of parchment from his robes and handed it to Casper.

Kill ours and we strike back. We do not forget.

Shock and fury warred inside Casper as he numbly held the death note in his hand. A few drops of dark rust stained the parchment. *My brother's blood.* The very thought of the fay's dark magic made him want to burn down the entire Biawood Forest, and all the fairies that lived beyond it.

"It does not make sense. We didn't kill any fay."

"The fay are a deceptive folk. They have no qualms about lying if it serves their purpose." King Jovian put his hand on Casper's shoulder, almost a fatherly gesture, but it felt wrong, awkward, and he moved his hand away.

Casper crumpled the note in his fist, wishing he was squeezing the neck of the fay that killed his brother instead. He silently vowed to never show mercy to the fay. They did not deserve it. *Someday*, he promised, *he would avenge his brother.*

"We will have preparations made for your departure."

Casper looked up from the crumpled parchment to the king, feeling a sudden rush of gratitude. "Thank you, Your Highness, for granting me leave to attend my brother's funeral." It was not the homecoming Casper wanted, but at least he could say goodbye. He wondered how long the king would allow him to stay in Reynallis.

King Jovian shook his head. "You misunderstand, Prince Casper. Your sister will not be taking the crown."

Casper stared blankly at the king, not sure he understood. "But Constance is next in line." The fact of it was so ingrained in Casper, that he had never questioned it. His memories of Constance were more faded than those of Christopher; she had stopped writing him years ago. But the pain of being disregarded by his sister would be no reason for him to betray his country. King Jovian had treated Casper well enough, but he would never abandon Reynallis. "If you are suggesting I seize the throne, you deeply misunderstand me." King Jovian was clever, and perhaps thought Casper would be a more pliable king, having grown up in Faradasia.

King Jovian's raised eyebrows were the only indication of his surprise, or possibly his irritation, at Casper's accusation. "Prince Casper, you are in shock, so I shall forgive any accusations. Princess Constance has decided to *decline* the crown. You are to take your place as king."

All of Casper's diplomatic practice and training abandoned him. "You are jesting."

King Jovian rose, and this time Casper scrambled to his feet as well. "I do not jest, Prince Casper. You are free to return home. The situation from the initial agreement has clearly changed." *The hostage exchange*, Casper thought. "And I assume you shall send my niece back home when you reach Sterling," King Jovian continued.

"Arrangements will be made for your immediate departure. I imagine you will want to reach Reynallis with time to prepare for your coronation."

"My coronation . . ." The word did not feel real to Casper. Coronations were held on the longest day of the year, and the summer solstice was in less than six months. There was no way he could mourn his brother and prepare to become a king in so short a time. "What reason did Constance give for passing on the crown?" Casper had never imagined anything would happen to his brave and brilliant older brother, but if it had, he assumed his older sister would be crowned queen. She might not care for him, but surely, she still cared for their country. Casper recalled her sharp tongue and efficient manner. Constance was no dormouse to scurry away from responsibility.

"The messenger offered no reason. Perhaps you should ask her yourself when you return home." King Jovian took several steps towards the door. "I will give you some time to collect your thoughts and ready for your travels." Right before leaving, he turned back to Casper. "And might I be the first to say to you, long live the king." And then King Jovian was gone, and Casper was left with his ocean of crashing emotions.

Once he was sure he was alone, he allowed himself to cry. *Home. King.* Casper wondered how he could possibly ever fill the void Christopher had left behind.

Chapter One

y Chace's den, we are so screwed, I thought, stomping off
the Stigenne Road and onto a lesser known path in the
Biawood Forest. I had been so sure of the day's success,
certain we could sell our cure-all tonic within the day and have
enough coin to feed us for weeks.

Admittedly it was only a simple mixture of water, cinnamon,
and molasses, but it transformed into a miracle elixir by the time I
was done selling it. We had spent the last of our meager coins on
those blasted green glass bottles.

I cringed as I thought about how I would break the news to
my brothers. When my brother Jacobie, only eight years old, had
asked where I was going this morning, I'd gleefully told him I was

off to scout the Spring Faire in Sterling and find us the perfect spot, promising to be back before midday. The sky was still inky with cold, bright stars, and my breath plumed around me as I instructed him to go back to sleep. As I left our tiny encampment, really only a rickety wagon, a crippled old donkey and the four of us in our thin bedrolls, Jacobie turned over, his soft snores soon joining those of our brothers Devon and Finn.

Only, once I reached the town square, I found another family selling miracle tonic. They even demonstrated its efficacy by curing a cripple boy's limp. I was certain the boy was their son and had no such limp. We had planned to perform the same trick with my brother Finn.

A city might be interested in one cure-all tonic merchant, but they became immediately suspicious when two set up. One time we had tried to sell our 'miracle' elixir in the same market as another party selling an almost identical bottle. People demanded a test to show which elixir was real and who was selling them snake oil. Neither tonic cured the sick villagers, and we were run out. My brothers and I barely made it out of that town, and to this day we avoided that village.

I kicked at the nearest tree in frustration. The thick birch trunk didn't care, but a sharp pain shooting up my foot had me unleashing an especially colorful string of curses as I hopped up and down in rage.

"Are you in distress?"

Whirling around, I started to see an elegant young man leading an equally fine horse. I silently scolded myself for crashing through the woods like a wild boar and thus not even hearing the approach of this stranger. I was a poor girl alone in the woods and well aware of what some men thought themselves entitled to. Still too far from camp to yell for my brothers, I took a quick step back, but my foot flared with pain, causing me to stumble and fall on my behind. The young man's lip trembled, and I had the feeling he was holding back a smile.

"I'm fine," I muttered, struggling to my feet.

"Here, allow me." The young man advanced toward me, his hand outstretched. I was about to push his hand away when I saw the glitter of gold on his finger. I held out my hand, allowing him to pull me up as I gently slid his ring off, dropping it into my pocket before he noticed.

Standing, I bit back a cry from the dull pain that still radiated from my foot and appraised my rescuer. He did not look ready to pounce on me the way drunken tavern men tried, but he was also far too richly dressed to be a pilgrim or even a merchant come for the Spring Faire. And he was not hard on the eyes; with a strong jaw, and hair and eyes the color of obsidian. He was young, probably only a few years older than me, but held himself with the erect posture of the nobility. Of course, the costly blue velvet riding outfit also called out his wealth. The steed he led, a sleek midnight-black horse, was adorned with the finest saddle and bit I had ever seen.

My daft brain was shocked by in the incongruity of seeing a lone nobleman in the midst of the Biawood and I spoke before thinking. "What are you doing here?"

His eyebrows shot up. "Excuse me?" I couldn't tell if he was amused or offended.

"I only meant that you're clearly highborn, and we don't see many nobles wandering the woods. *Alone*." My surprise made me sound foolish, and I scolded myself. I needed to stop talking and get away from this nobleman before he realized he was one golden ring short.

He laughed, a warmth filling his dark eyes. "I imagine I am an odd sight in these woods," he looked around at the surrounding trees, "but I seem to have lost my way. I was going for a ride, wishing to experience a bit more . . . freedom."

Freedom to wander around the woods? I had to school my face from betraying the mockery I felt well up when I thought about how ridiculous the highborn behaved. All the money in the world, and they go and get lost in the Biawood. That's not how I would enjoy such wealth. But instead, I smiled brightly, dipping into a deep curtsey to feign awe.

"Well, you are in luck, because I just came off the Stigenne Road. And you are not far off. You'll be able to see the road just south of that cluster of elms." I pointed him in the right direction, wanting to ensure his quick departure.

"Ah, wonderful, thank you." And without another glance, the nobleman jumped onto his horse and set off towards the Stigenne Road. I watched till he was out of sight, a grin slowly spreading on my face as I pulled the ring from my pocket. It was heavy, possibly even pure gold. It was a signet ring, the flat surface engraved with three roses, thorns, and vine intertwined. I slipped the ring on my finger, happily thinking that the morning had not been a complete waste after all. Not wanting the nobleman to find me once he discovered my theft, I detoured deeper into the woods, much farther from the Stigenne Road.

Rumors told that the fay of Magnomel came into the Biawood this close to the border, but I decided baseless gossip was less dangerous than a wealthy man with a fast horse. My return trip to camp would be a longer but safer journey.

Halfway to camp, I heard the distant sound of running water. It had to be a stream. Feeling thirsty, I veered toward the sound for a victory drink. The stream was narrow enough to jump over, but still flowed briskly with freshly thawed snow. I knelt by the water, splashing my face and drinking deeply, the cold filling my stomach and radiating through my body.

"I still think we should kill it," a voice said nearby. It was male, with an irritating whine.

"And miss our chance for the reward, I don't think so." This second voice was deep and harsh, like grit grinding.

"We can bring it in dead, Garin. It'd be safer."

"The Crown pays for live fay, not corpses, Acel. They says they can't question a corpse."

I stopped, stunned. *Would the fay leave Magnomel and enter Reynallis?*

Sterling had flyers posted with the gruesome image of the Fay Queen Marasina and claims that the fay drank human blood. I had been preoccupied in town, but now I wondered if there really were fay here in Reynallis. *Leave, leave, leave,* my commonsense shouted. *But I just want to see it,* my curiosity answered back.

Crouching low enough to the ground that I could smell the damp moss at my feet, I crept into some bushes and peered through. There was a small clearing in the woods where two men had set up camp. Their various supplies, sleeping rolls and a tiny cooking fire were off to one side. The whiny man, Acel, was tall and wiry with a rat-like face. His companion, Garin, was stout and as solid as a tree trunk. While Acel couldn't stay still, almost hopping from foot to foot in anxiety, Garin stood his ground, firm in his footing and his argument.

I couldn't see the fay, but when Acel gestured to a tree, I figured the faerie must be tied up there. It was just outside my range of sight, and I tiptoed around the clearing to get a better look. I was almost angled right to see the fay when I snapped a twig underfoot. I froze, fear of detection shooting up my spine.

"Did you hear that?" Acel hissed.

"All I've been hearing is your incessant yelling," Garin growled back.

"No, I think I heard a noise, over here," Acel said, getting louder as he approached my hiding place. I leaned back against a large oak tree, the only cover I had, and held my breath.

"We're in the middle of the bloody forest you idiot," Garin snapped. "Probably an animal or something. We're too far from the Stigenne Road for travelers."

"Yeah, fine. I guess so," Acel grumbled as he returned to Garin. I let out the breath I was holding. I should leave, but . . .

Cautiously, I leaned around the tree and looked out at the clearing. I now had a perfect view.

I gasped.

I was staring at a faerie. I almost couldn't believe it, but there he was. And he looked nothing like the monsters the flyers warned about. He was stunningly, painfully beautiful. His hair was gold—a true gold, not simply golden blonde, and it shone in the morning light. His large, almond eyes were deep, emerald green and his skin was pale, almost luminous. He had delicate, carved features, looking both elegant and otherworldly. He angrily shook his head and I saw his ears, which tapered to fine points. The only thing common about him were his clothes, which were travel-worn and dirty.

I would have expected the creature to shoot fire out of his mouth or control the minds of his captors with his dark fay magic, but he didn't look evil. His hands and feet were bound with thick rope, and another rope was tied around his chest. I checked to see if that rope was binding him to the tree, but it was not. He struggled against his bindings without success while the two men stood over him, arguing.

"Do you even think we'll get the reward?" Acel asked, pacing in tight circles. "More like the guards will think we are working with the fay."

"Then what do you suggest? We can't just leave him here. And we could use the reward money."

"We have to get rid of him. It's the only thing," Acel immediately responded.

"Just let me go and I will be gone. I shall never bother you again," the faerie said. Despite his predicament, he sounded calm. For a moment I shivered, hearing dark music in his voice. There was a power to his voice, hypnotic and dangerous. I forced myself to pay attention to the men. At the moment, they were the real danger.

"Don't listen to him," Acel snapped. For a fearful moment, I thought he was talking to me, but I realized he was speaking to his companion who had taken several steps toward the faerie. Garin shook himself, as if he had been entranced.

"I can make it worth your while to let me go. Is it gold you want? I can give you all the gold you desire." The faerie's voice was melodic, and I found myself leaning in to hear him better.

"How much gold?" Garin asked. There was suspicion in his voice, but also eager greed.

"Enough to have you living like a king."

"He's a liar," Acel hissed. "They all are. He's a fay. They'll say anything. He wouldn't be roaming the woods if he had enough gold to live like a king."

"A liar? Me? Never."

Acel kicked the faerie in the shin. Hard. The faerie let out a cry of pain. I winced thinking about my own sore foot.

"And they say humans are such a civilized race," the faerie spat out.

"Shut your mouth or you'll get another one."

"Maybe we should gag him. He might curse us and turn us into toads or something." Garin was smiling, but it wasn't kind.

"If I could have turned you into a toad, I would certainly have done so by now." Despite his calm tone, I could see fear and anger in the faerie's large eyes. It suddenly seemed very wrong that he would be killed or imprisoned just because he was fay.

I knew I should leave. This was not my problem. And what if the fay were actually dangerous? I should turn around and pretend I had never seen any of this.

But . . . what if the reward amount for a faerie was truly as high as the flyer had claimed? Maybe the amount was not a joke after all. How many months could I feed my family if I turned in this faerie? It was insane to even consider it. But a sum that great, and we could actually start life fresh, maybe even buy a new mill to replace the one we lost in the fire.

It could mean the end of a life of petty crimes just to eat. A thrill ran through me, the same nervous excitement that filled me every time I started a scheme. It felt like a challenge that I decided to accept.

I crept over to the small cooking fire. The two men were busy arguing and didn't notice me. Close to their fire was a small bundle of their supplies, a bottle of spirits and some food. I leaned over and opened the bottle. The alcohol smelled strong and sour, but I wasn't planning on drinking it. I silently poured it on a rolled-up blanket that was leaning on a nearby tree. I laid the blanket on top of the food and supplies, and carefully pulled one end of the blanket into the fire. Then I disappeared back into the trees.

Back on the other side of the encampment, I crouched near the faerie but stayed hidden. I didn't have to wait long. The alcohol-soaked blanket quickly caught fire. Soon, the whole thing was burning. Acel noticed the fire first.

"The fire," he squealed, running to the blanket and stomping on it. Garin followed, and soon both men were busy trying to extinguish the flames.

Now or never, I thought.

I slipped through the trees until I was inches away from the faerie. This close, he was even more beautiful, with a face that looked like it had been carved in glowing marble. I was stunned for a moment, until he spoke.

"If you are trying to steal me to claim a bounty, be warned: I am very dangerous." His green eyes narrowed. This close, I could see his pupils were not round, but rather cat-like slits.

"Yeah, you look very dangerous," I whispered, not wanting to draw the attention of his captors. "And you can come with me unless you'd like to stay with these kind gentlemen."

Without a word, the faerie lifted his wrists up to me. I pulled out the dagger sheathed in my boot. But instead of freeing his wrists, I began to work on the bindings at his ankles. Keeping only his wrists bound was a weak protection, but I didn't see another alternative.

"Free my hands," he hissed.

I ignored him, working on the rope around his ankles. Despite its size, the rope was cheap and poorly made. My blade cut it quickly. Once freed, I silently helped him to his feet. It was apparent he had been bound for a while in the stilted way he rose, wobbling slightly on unsteady feet. It was all the more difficult with his hands still bound together.

"We have to move," I whispered, not wanting to draw the attention of his captors. He glared me, raising his bound wrists, but I shook my head. He muttered something under his breath without resisting me while I led him away from the clearing. His legs were too stiff to navigate the bumpy ground, so I tried to shoulder most of his weight as we staggered towards the trees.

"Hey, what's going on?"

I snapped my head around to see Garin staring at me across the clearing. The fire was little more than a smolder.

"Run," I yelled.

Chapter Two

I threw my arm around the faerie as we dashed into the trees. I led us in a diagonal path, trying to shake Acel and Garin from our trail, but we didn't have enough of a head start and they were closing in. For a guilty moment, I thought about leaving the faerie to save myself. But I kept my grip on him.

"Get back here girl and give us our faerie," Garin yelled. Not wasting the time to turn around, I kept pushing the faerie to move faster. "Pox on you," Acel cried, but he sounded winded. Maybe we could outrun them.

Just as we were getting some distance from our attackers, my foot stuck in an upturned root. I slammed into the faerie and we both went crashing to the ground.

By all the Mother's maids, we were in for it.

"Untie me!" he demanded.

I saw our window to escape closing and made my choice. I whipped out my dagger and quickly cut through his bonds. As soon as the rope fell away, the faerie snatched my dagger, his fingers quick and strong.

"Give that back!" I snapped, as he and I both scrambled to our feet. I cursed myself for trusting a faerie, even for a second. Before I could grab my dagger, Garin and Acel were upon us.

"I wouldn't move if I was you," Acel said in his nasal whine. He held a knife, a jagged, nasty-looking thing, and pointed it at me. I swallowed hard.

"Don't like it when someone takes what's mine."

"I don't belong to you," the faerie snarled, but Acel didn't look away from me.

His shrewd eyes were cold and calculating. I'd seen that expression in the Faradisian soldiers who burned my village in the Southern War. A shudder of fear squeezed me tight and I had to force myself to breathe.

"She's not much to look at, but we could have some fun with her," Garin said, just to my right. I didn't look away from Acel, but the fear in me intensified. I tried to stand my ground, but I could feel myself trembling.

Acel laughed, a cackling sound. Struggling to buy time, I slowly raised my arms in the air, hoping they weren't shaking too much.

"Look gentlemen, I think there has been some sort of misunderstanding. This is my brother." I gave a little laugh, but it sounded hollow.

"That thing isn't even human. Do you take us for fools?" Acel asked.

"Actually, I kind of do," I said, lunging toward Acel. I grabbed the wrist of his hand holding the knife and shoved it away. Most crooks don't expect their victims to attack and aren't ready for it. Luckily, Acel was like that. Surprised, he stumbled backward as I pushed him to the ground. He got in one swipe of his knife before he tumbled down. My foot gave a swift kick to his groin. When he yelped in pain, I jumped on him and punched him once, in the face. A sharp crack sounded as blood began to pour from his nose.

Then I was hurled off my feet and thrown backward, hitting the ground with a crunch that sent my head spinning. I looked up to see Garin almost on top of me. Something whizzed past, and I saw my dagger embedded in Garin's shoulder.

I turned to look at the faerie, but he was already running toward Acel. Garin growled in pain and red bloomed from the wound. For a moment, he looked like he was trying to decide if he wanted to attack the faerie or me, but he started toward me again. The faerie left Acel and darted out behind Garin. He pressed at the knife wound. Garin yelled in pain and surprise. Then the faerie wrapped his bloody, slender fingers around the large man's neck.

"*Morir sange.*" I didn't understand what the faerie had said, but Garin looked dazed. He took a few unsteady steps and stopped. He started clawing at his throat, as though he couldn't breathe, even though the faerie was no longer touching him. Frothy blood started to form at his mouth and run out his nose. He dug his nails into his neck, scratching it so more blood was running down his shirt, as though he could remove whatever force was choking him. But it did no good. He dropped to the ground.

I stared at Garin, feeling both relief and horror as blood continued to pour out of his mouth and nose, and soon, streams of dark blood ran from his eyes and ears, staining his blotchy face crimson. After a few minutes, the large man stopped struggling. He twitched a few times, and his eyes went glassy. The faerie looked at me, but I couldn't read his expression.

"What did you do?" I was too stunned to move, grateful he took out Garin, but alarmed at the new danger facing me.

"Stopped him. Stopped his blood," the faerie said, speaking slowly as though I did not understand what death looked like.

"You killed him," I said, stating the obvious. *Were the fay stories true? Would the faerie start drinking Garin's blood or eat his heart?*

"Would you rather I had let him kill us?"

"Are you going to kill me?" I asked, staring into his emerald cat-eyes. I wanted to look away, see what happened to Acel, if he were still a threat. I wondered if the faerie had used the same dark magic on him. I wanted to run far away from here, from this dangerous creature, but I was too afraid to move. I cursed myself for getting involved.

"You are human." He said it as if it was an insult. "But you did free me." Now he sounded resentful.

Despite his words, I did not feel relieved. He had not actually said he wouldn't kill me. Blood dripped from his hands. I spared a quick glance to Acel, who was unmoving, no longer moaning in pain.

"Did you kill him, too?"

"Yes." I had to fight a sudden urge to be sick. My blade was no longer sticking out Garin's shoulder, but I didn't want to go see where it had fallen. There was dark blood covering the man's shirt, though how much was blood from the shoulder wound and how much was blood he had choked up, I couldn't tell. Acel's face wasn't much to look at, either. I focused again on the faerie, the real danger.

"Are you upset? They might have also been humans, but they meant me great harm, and you too."

"No, not upset," I lied. I wasn't upset they were dead, but I was upset that I let myself get into a situation where I was alone with a monster who could kill just by touch.

"I owe you for my rescue," the faerie said, taking a step toward me.

"Don't come near me." I jumped backward, desperately wanting to get away from this creature. I felt a sudden, searing pain in my right leg, where Acel's blade had grazed me. I'd hardly felt it in the heat of the struggle, but the hot flash of pain made me realize it was far more serious. I inhaled sharply but refused to look away from the faerie.

"You're hurt. I can take care of that," he said, taking another step toward me. I saw a glint of steel and realized he had taken my blade from Garin's shoulder.

"No!" I yelled, unable to conceal the terror in my voice. "Don't touch me!" I tried to take another step, but my right leg buckled, and fiery pain shot up my leg. I gasped and collapsed. My leg was soaked in blood.

I didn't hear the faerie approach, but suddenly he was kneeling next to me, concern on his beautiful face. I was surprised at how quickly he moved. "You've been stabbed, let me see your leg." He gently pulled the fabric of my trousers up, holding my dagger in his other hand. The fabric was drenched in blood. *My blood.* The cut was much deeper than I'd initially thought. I stiffened at his touch but was trapped, sure I would start choking blood the moment he touched me. He must have sensed my anxiety, because he said, "I won't hurt you."

He moved carefully, as though I were a wild animal he didn't want to frighten. His fingers were cool on my skin, his touch light. After a moment, I realized I was not choking. I wanted to laugh or cry, feeling relieved but still terrified. I wondered if this creature would change his mind.

His fingers were sticky with blood. *Do not pass out*, I commanded myself. I gritted my teeth and forced myself to focus on breathing. I closed my eyes and took deep gulps of air.

Suddenly the faerie stood up. I started to tear at my trousers, knowing I would need to create a tourniquet to stop the blood.

The faerie loomed over me. For a moment I thought it was my end. I struggled, trying to stand, the pain and blood loss making black spots appear in front of my eyes. I knew I was no match for the deadly fay.

He suddenly turned the dagger on himself, slicing a shallow cut on his hand. A shimmering, viscous liquid oozed out. It was a pale gold, almost silver. With a start, I realized that it was his blood. My surprise had me rooted to the spot, and before I realized what was happening, the faerie had knelt down, pressing his bloody palm to the cut on my leg.

His touch felt icy and numbed the fiery feeling that had been in my calf. The throbbing eased and soon I couldn't feel anything. The faerie gently removed his hand and I forced myself to look down and examine my leg. It was still bloody, but no longer bleeding. Instead, a puckered pink line ran across my skin, like that of a fresh scar. The golden fay blood had been absorbed into the wound, and all I saw was a gentle glow to my skin. I tentatively touched the scar, it was tender, but without pain.

"How?" I asked, bewildered.

"Fay blood heals. At least, it does for those with the gift to use it." He smiled, the first time I had seen him do so. He looked pale and tired, but the smile lit up his face, making him look positively radiant, even if his pearly white teeth were too sharp and his eyes had a strange glow. A film of sweat gleamed on his forehead, and I wondered what this magic had cost him.

"Thank you," I said, unsure what else to say. Even sweating and disheveled from our escape and fight, he looked as lovely and deadly as the paintings of angels I had seen in our church when I was young. Though lean, he was well muscled and stronger than he appeared. His emerald eyes assessed me intently, but I had no idea what he was thinking. I felt suddenly and ridiculously self-conscious of my dirty, straw-blonde hair and dull brown eyes. I chided myself, knowing this creature wouldn't care what I looked like. I'd be lucky if he let me live. But why heal me if he meant to kill me?

The childhood stories I had heard in my village of demonic fay ran through my head, stories of creatures that were so beautiful they lured unsuspecting villagers into a false sense of trust and then used their dark magic to torture and enslave them. Though he had saved my life, just as surely as I had saved his. But I still didn't trust him.

And then I remembered other stories, ones my father used to tell us about the fay. In them, the fay were dangerous, but not evil. They just wanted the right to live their lives in peace. In an unusual story, a faerie prince had even fallen in love with a human girl. My father was the only one in our village to tell such stories about the fay, but maybe he was right. I wanted to say something, ask this faerie why he was in Sterling, when faeries were forbidden to enter the kingdom of Reynallis.

Instead, I said, "You should leave. Reynallis doesn't allow fay within its borders."

"I owe you for my life, or at least my freedom," the faerie said slowly, as though each word weighed on him.

"I wasn't going to free you."

The faerie didn't look surprised. "But you did."

"I don't want anything from you." I just wanted this encounter to be over. Part of me wanted to stay with this faerie, as if his beauty was so intense, I was intoxicated by it. But the rational side of me wanted this boy, no, not a boy, *a deadly faerie*, to go away. I would be far safer away from this creature. No amount of gold was worth staying with a creature that could kill by touch.

"You are a strange human. Almost decent."

"You must have met some awful humans if I'm to be considered decent. Look, fay, uh, sir, you know, I don't know what to call you."

"Pel," the faerie said, and he gave me a small smile and a nod. I tried not to think of how lovely his face looked when he smiled. His smile was striking and a bit unsettling with his pointed teeth.

"Pel, I'm Elenora Molnár. Call me Nor." I put out my hand to shake his. He just looked at my hand, so I withdrew it. "You should probably stay away from all humans."

"You aren't going to try to turn me in for a ransom?" Pel asked. He was smiling again, and I realized he was mocking me.

"Not after what you did to the last people who tried to do that."

"You are indeed an odd human." Pel's look was appraising and I felt like I was being examined.

"Just one with better survival instincts." We stood there for a minute, neither of us speaking before I broke the silence. "What are you doing out here?"

Pel looked away at first, then turned to stare at me with those sparkling green eyes. "Passing through."

Before I could ask him where he was going, he yanked at a tear on his tunic. He pulled a thread loose and drew it out, unraveling a small patch of his shirt as he wound the thread around his hand. Satisfied, he ran the thread through his hand, turning the dull thread a copper as our mixed blood soaked on it. He then began to twist the thread back and forth between his fingers. After a while, the thread no longer looked copper, but glittered in the afternoon sun. I stared, transfixed, at this new magic. In his hands was now a length of delicately spun gold thread.

"Is that—"

"Spun gold. A specialty of mine." He gave a pointed glance at my hand. "I've heard humans are quite fond of gold." I glanced at my hand, seeing the noble's signet ring glinting on my finger. I had completely forgotten I was wearing it.

Without thinking, I reached out for the thread and he dropped it in my hand. It was not simply a golden-colored thread, but an actual thread of gold. I pulled at its end and saw a spidery-thin wisp of golden strands.

"How?" I asked, mesmerized by the gold. I'd never seen anything like it. I glanced at his shirt, but it was still the color of undyed wool.

"Trade secret."

I should have counted my blessings and left right then. Between the ring and the thread, I possessed more wealth than my family had seen, even before the Southern War. But he had so easily transformed wool to gold. I decided to see if I could goad him into making some more for me.

"One thread? That's the value of your life?" I asked, quirking up an eyebrow. I waited expectantly, knowing I was being too greedy, but unable to stop myself. "After all, I did just save you from some terrible fate that probably involved a dungeon, or worse."

Pel fixed me with an unreadable expression, his cat-eyes staring at me.

Something dangerous crossed his face, and his lips curled up in a feral smile, one that instantly reminded me what sort of creature I was dealing with. I immediately regretting provoking this fay, and tried to take a step back, but Pel was so much faster than I. He was on me in a moment, his slender fingers tight around my wrist.

"I didn't mean—" I started, panic rising within me.

"I know not if you are merely foolish, greedy or both, but you shall have your wish human," he said, wrapping a loop of the thread around my wrist, tying it off before pulling free the rest of the thread, which he let drop into my hand as he released me.

I took several shaky steps back, but he made no further move towards me. I looked down at my wrist, the loop of golden thread forming a delicate bracelet.

"I don't understand."

He laughed, a sweet, musical sound that played at mischief. "You asked for more Nor, so there it is."

"There is what?"

"How you can call on me for the debt I owe you. Put a drop of your blood on the thread that encircles your wrist. That will summon me, and I will come and repay my debt."

"Wait? My blood? That's wrong!" I had to repress a shudder. I yanked at the golden loop around my wrist, desperate to pull the thread off. "Come to think of it, I am actually perfectly grateful to have just the golden thread."

"I work in blood magic. Fay blood heals and human blood . . . well, that has many uses." He gestured to the two dead thugs.

"So, you didn't just kill them by touching them?" I asked, startled.

"No, I needed blood. Their blood." He paused before adding, "In order to stop their blood."

"Well, I now see why so many people think fay are scary demons," I said, my fingers still fumbling with the thread on my wrist.

"Do I look like a scary demon?" He stared at me intently. I looked up into his beautiful emerald eyes, green as fields on a summer's day.

"You are beautiful," I said without thinking, then blushed deeply. Was I mooning over some deadly fay? "But aren't the most dangerous creatures the beautiful ones?"

"They usually are." He looked like he wanted to say more but decided against it.

"This won't come off." The thread was so thin, I couldn't understand why I was unable to yank it off my wrist. I bit it, but it held fast.

"Ah, gold you have, but can never spend." He smiled and winked. "Elenora Molnár, you should know that all faerie magic comes at a price. Consider yourself lucky that the trick I played on you was so small." With that, he carefully untied the rope that was secured around his chest. As he adjusted his cloak, I realized the purpose of the rope.

He had wings.

I gaped at him, not having the words to say anything. His large wings were dragonfly-thin and translucent, their opalescent surface shimmering in the afternoon light. Acel and Garin must have tied the rope around him to prevent him from flying away. Fully outstretched, his wings were around three feet in both directions. They seemed too delicate to lift him, but he flapped them a few times, rainbows splitting the air, and then he took off, easily navigating through the tree branches and up into the sky. All without saying a word or even turning back to me. I watched him, flying high into the air until he was little more than a speck against the clouds.

I left the bodies where they were. No one would care if two criminals had been killed in the woods. I briefly considered saying a quick prayer to the Mother for them, as the only human witness to their deaths. But remembering how they had wanted to 'have some fun with me,' I decided against it. I carefully wound the rest of the golden thread into a small spool and headed back to my camp. The entire time I picked at my new bracelet, but it held fast.

Chapter Three

S topping by the stream, I washed most of the blood from my hands and leg. But there wasn't much I could do about the bloodstain on my pants. I fiddled again with the bracelet, but it held firm. I contented myself knowing that between the ring and the rest of the gold thread, secured in my pocket, there was plenty for us till I figured out how to remove Pel's 'trick.' Pushing down my sleeve, I made my way back to camp.

"Nor!" Jacobie yelled, spotting me first. He ran over, slamming into me with a massive hug. I swung my little brother around a few times, again grateful that the wound on my leg had healed. I set him down.

"You're back!"

"Of course, I'm back, you little nut," I said, patting his head.

"Why were you gone so long?" Devon asked, giving me a stern look. Even though he was only two years older than me, he had an annoying habit of trying to act like a parent.

"Because I was scouting the city."

"Did you get us something to eat?" Finn asked, pausing from packing up our meager supplies. At thirteen, he was a sapling of a boy, always hungry and thin as a beanpole.

"Sorry, we didn't have enough coin." I tried not to wince, remembering the fake crippled boy. Finn looked painfully disappointed but didn't say anything.

"But I'm hungry," Jacobie whined, and I had to look away from the forlorn expression on his small face.

"And that took all morning? That's not like you, Nor."

"Sterling is a big city, Devon." I didn't know exactly why, but I didn't want to tell my brothers about Pel. I tried to convince myself that they would just worry too much.

"Nor, your leg," Finn cried, seeing my bloody pants.

Chace's den, I thought, trying to think of some plausible excuse. Finn reached out to examine my pants. Jacobie and Devon were also staring at the bloodstain. Jacobie's eyes were wide, filled with fear. I worried he'd start crying.

"It's nothing," I insisted, but no one believed me. I batted Finn's hand away when he tried to touch my pants.

"What happened sister?" he asked, voice high with anxiety.

"I'm not hurt. It's not even my blood." My three brothers looked at me skeptically.

"It's not," I insisted, desperately trying to think of some sort of lie to appease them. I quickly decided a half-truth would serve me best. "I was attacked, on my way back to camp."

"Who hurt you?" Devon asked. My older brother looked ready to track my attacker and murder him.

Too late for that.

"They're long gone," I lied, trying to ease the tension. "And this is their blood, not mine, so no need to fuss over me."

"What happened, Nor?" Devon asked, still using his serious-parent voice.

"I was, well, I . . ." Nervously, I fished around in my pockets, fingering the signet ring as my hand closed on the spool of golden thread. Recalling the young noble in the woods, I decided to alter the truth of the morning a bit. "I picked the wrong pocket. This man caught me, and we had a bit of a fight. I had to use my dagger. But he came out for it far worse than me. And look what I got for my trouble." I pulled out the golden thread, displaying that and the ring. They shone in sun and my brothers came in close to see my new treasures.

"Nor, is that gold?" Devon asked, stepping to me. His eyes were entranced by my sparkling prizes.

"Yes!"

"So pretty," Jacobie said in awe. "Can we buy sweets?"

"If we're careful, this much gold could last us months, maybe even a year." Devon was already making the calculations in his head.

"We can buy sweets and food and new clothes," I added, catching my brothers' excitement.

"We won't even need to sell elixir today," Finn said, staring at the gold.

"Which I should mention is no longer a possibility." I let them know about the family already selling 'miracle' tonic.

"All the extra luck then that you found gold," Devon said. "With this much money, we could replace the wagon and get new supplies for whatever job we want to do next. Get some fresh straw for Stony."

Our donkey perked his ears at the mention of his name. Something about replenishing our supplies stuck with me. Something about the straw.

"And buy sweets," Jacobie repeated, making sure his request wasn't forgotten.

"And actually have some money put aside for leaner times," Finn added, always practical.

The fragments came together like pieces of a puzzle, and I realized I had our next plan. "I got it!" I practically yelled, halting my brothers' enthusiastic chatter. "We're not going to sell the gold, not yet anyway."

Three sets of brown eyes looked at me as though I had lost my mind.

"I have an idea. One that will let us fill our pockets and keep the gold."

"What are you talking about, Nor?" Finn asked, his tone as wary as his look.

"I have a new plan for the market faire. We're going to need straw. A whole lot of straw."

I quickly explained the plan, excitement building within me as I mapped out details. The familiar rush of nerves and anticipation that came with every new job flowed through me. It was a feeling I craved; one that made me feel alive. I demonstrated what I would do with the gold thread, slipping it seamlessly up my sleeve.

"That's a terrible plan."

My next words died on my lips as I looked into Finn's hard face. He usually supported my schemes but now crossed his arms, a disapproving frown pulling down his thin lips.

"What?" I asked, stunned and hurt.

"It's reckless, Nor. Sometimes you go too far, and you are putting us in danger for no reason. We already have plenty of gold now."

"You sound like Devon," I countered.

"I think this is a fine plan, so leave me out of this," Devon said, stepping away from us.

"Sorry, Devon," I muttered, still glaring at Finn.

"Come on Jacobie, let's pack up camp while Nor and Finn finish their spitting match." As Devon pulled Jacobie away to gather up our things, I could hear my little brother asking why we were fighting. Devon said something about us having the temperament of stray cats.

Low enough that my other brothers wouldn't hear, I stepped towards Finn and said, "Seriously, Finn, what is the matter? It is a good plan."

"It's not a terrible plan," Finn said, but then stalled, as though searching for the right words. Though only thirteen, he had always been a studious boy, probably the smartest of all of us, at least when it came to book knowledge. Though our father was a simple miller, he had known how to read and write, something he had taught us. We had even owned several large books, mostly about medicinal plants and herbs, and Finn had read every one several times.

"Nor, your story doesn't make sense," his voice as low as my own.

"What do you mean?" I could not quite meet his eyes. He was far too good at reading people.

"You haven't gotten caught picking a pocket for years. You're too good."

"I got lazy, it happens," I said, still looking away. If anyone could call out my lie, it would be Finn. "Let's get to work. Besides, does it even matter how I got the gold? The important thing is that we are going to be rich."

"Fine," he said, throwing up his hands in defeat. I could tell he didn't believe my story, but I didn't say anything. "We'll go along with your plan, because we always go along with your plans. But I don't like being lied to."

I tried to laugh, as though such deception was a jest, but it stuck in my throat. I considered telling Finn the truth, but instead turned and began to pack up my meager supplies. I deserved to keep the memory of Pel to myself.

I had so little that was only mine.

It was well past dark when the four of us headed to some of the farms on the outskirts of Sterling. The farms were about an hour's hike from our camp in the Biawood Forest. Far enough outside Sterling, they were not enclosed within the city walls. Hopefully, the farms would have barns full of straw. Each of us carried a burlap sack. Devon even had two.

"Do you think this will really work?" Devon asked as we approached the first farm, little more than glowing windows in the distance.

"Of course," I said. *It has to*, I thought.

"I'll race you there," Jacobie challenged us as we got closer. I could make out a large, dark barn a good distance away from the warmly lit farmhouse.

"I don't know, little brother. My legs are so much longer than yours, it wouldn't be fair," Finn said, and despite the dark, I could hear the smile. *At least his temper had cooled.*

"Yeah, but I'm super-fast. Like really, really fast."

"Then you're on." And before Devon or I could say anything, my two younger brothers sprinted toward the barn.

"Do you think that's safe?" Devon asked, staring after our brothers.

"Don't worry, the barn is far from the house. No one will see them," I reassured him. As I watched Jacobie and Finn, I grinned. "But maybe we should hurry up. I'll race you."

"I don't think so."

"Afraid you'll lose, big brother?"

"That's not why . . ." Devon started, but I took off running after Finn and Jacobie, suddenly feeling giddy. I glanced back once, warmed that Devon was playing along and running, trying to catch up. He was usually faster than me, so I pushed myself hard, focusing only on my brothers and the approaching barn. As I got close, I slowed, seeing Finn and Jacobie had reached the barn and were playfully throwing straw at each other.

The barn smelled of clean straw and warm animals, and I noted two horses in stalls. They did not seem to care about us intruding in their barn.

"*You lost. I won. You lost. I won,*" Jacobie sang in triumph.

"But you're the one covered in straw," Finn countered, and dumped a heap of straw on Jacobie's head. Jacobie peeked his head out of the straw, wayward stalks clinging to his hair, making his blonde hair even more unruly than usual. There was a mischievous look in his eye before he retaliated by pulling out Finn's legs, forcing him to fall into the straw.

They were both laughing, and I couldn't help but join in. Even Devon smiled to see such a ridiculous sight. For a moment, it felt like old times, my brothers just being silly children. I wished we had more times like that.

"All right you demons, let's get to work," Devon finally said, opening one of his sacks and heaping straw into it.

"Make sure to spread the straw around," I added, "so it doesn't look so obvious that we took some." I filled my sack quickly, and then took a moment to practice the sleight of hand I would use to create the illusion of turning the straw into gold.

The rough straw kept catching on my sleeve when I tried to palm it.

"You're messing it up," Finn complained, still holding his grudge from earlier.

I shot my brother a sour look before grabbing a handful of straw and flinging it at him. Most of it missed, but a few stalks settled on his head.

"Just saying how I see it," Finn retorted.

"Not helping."

"You need something to distract people . . ." Finn's voice trailed off as he started exploring the barn. I tried to ignore him, but my too-observant brother was right.

"How about this?" Finn called. He had climbed onto the second story of the barn.

"What are you doing up there?" I asked, making my way up a roughly carved ladder.

"Look Nor," he said, proudly gesturing to a piece of furniture in the corner. I stepped closer to see what he was pointing at. The moonlight cast a dull glow on a rickety hoop of wood.

"A spinning wheel?"

"Exactly! You can spin the straw into gold. It will give you a reason to hunch over. And you can use it to block people's view while you palm the straw."

My brother was beaming.

I looked closely at the spinning wheel. It was a relic, warped and cracked wood. But a gentle push on the wheel, and it spun. It was a strange idea, but not a bad one. Somehow, it felt fitting with such an outlandish plan. Turning to Finn, I smiled, especially happy to have Finn aiding my plan instead of fighting it.

"You might just be brilliant, little brother."

"I know."

Devon helped us take the spinning wheel down. Finn and I carried it between us, each with bags of straw in our other hands. Devon and Jacobie carried the rest as we made our way back to camp. I felt ignited even as we sweated the long trek back.

I lay in my sleeping roll late into the night, staring up at the trees and the sky. The night was lit with an almost full moon and dotted with sparkling stars. I traced my finger over the imprinted crest on the signet ring, and briefly recalled the handsome young nobleman, before slipping my finger further down my wrist, feeling the gold thread bracelet. It was oddly warm. I gently tugged at it, but as Pel had said, it stayed coiled around my wrist. Eventually, my eyes closed, and I dreamt of strange, graceful boys with sparkling, emerald cat-eyes and ropes of shimmering gold.

"Rise and shine," I called out. The morning was crisp, and dawn's early light was just shining above the trees. I had already been up for an hour, practicing palming the straw with the aid of the spinning wheel.

"Nor, I'm hungry," Jacobie said, already wide awake.

"I know, and tonight we'll eat like kings. How about you be a good boy and wake your brothers?"

"It's gonna be hard," Jacobie said with all the seriousness an eight-year-old could muster. "They sleep like rocks."

"Then you should probably go jump on them," I encouraged, as I began putting together a simple breakfast with our meager rations. I heated up water to make a thin gruel as Jacobie pounced on one brother and then the next.

"Would a *please wake up, dear brother of mine* kill you?" Finn grumbled, as Jacobie moved on to his next victim.

"It's not his fault you lot are so difficult to rouse in the mornings," I said, laughing.

"Aloisia's sake!" Devon swore.

"Good morning," I called out to Jacobie's latest conquest.

"I blame you for teaching him to do that," Devon said as he yawned.

When my brothers were up, I served our small breakfast and reviewed the plan again with them. My nerves were alight with the anticipation of a job, and I practiced palming the gold thread.

We finished packing the straw into the wagon, hitched up Stony, and took to the road. The early hours were still fresh with dawn, and the coolness was invigorating. I inhaled the woody smell of pine mixed with that of the fresh straw as we made our way down the Stigenne Road.

"There are so many people," Jacobie said, as we reached the gates of Sterling. Merchants, entertainers, and pilgrims were still making their way to Sterling for the Spring Faire. I briefly wondered if Pel were anywhere around but was quickly consumed by thoughts of the job ahead.

Occasionally, we saw black ribbons tied to gates or public buildings, old memorials for the late King Christopher. The ribbons were weather worn, more tattered brown strips of fabric than dignified memorial tokens, but I guessed no one wanted to be seen taking down a tribute to our late king. Not that I cared. From my experience, the ruling class did little more than burden the rest of us.

After all, it was kings who had started the Southern War. I would never accept that my parents and sister had died for royal disputes. I pulled off one of the ribbons and let it flutter to the ground.

"Finn, you go on ahead as lookout. Stay somewhere you can't be seen with us but not too far off in case there's trouble. Jacobie, you'll stay with us and arrange the straw when we set up."

"With you sister, there is always trouble." Finn patted me good-naturedly on the back.

"Very funny. When the guards come, I'll be sure to point them in your direction."

"Till dinner," we all said. It was a motto in our family, around from simpler days when our mother would let us play till dinner. Now it was our slogan that by dinner, we would be back together.

"Devon, you all right?"

"Yeah," he said, keeping his focus on the road ahead. "We've just never done a job like this before. Makes me nervous," he added in a hushed voice so as not to be overheard.

"Every job we do was new the first time," I said to reassure him. Before a job, especially a new one, Devon got anxious. I got excited.

"Of course, but I promised Rilla I'd look out for you all, right after mother died and right before she . . . well, it isn't easy when we try something new."

I gave Devon's arm a comforting squeeze. Rilla had been our older sister, taking charge of us after our parents died in the war. Willowy and delicate, she hadn't lasted much longer, succumbing to a terrible cough that shook her whole body. I forced myself to push away the memories. "Don't worry, big brother, we'll be fine."

Devon smiled, but the furrow in his brow never left. We walked the rest of the way in silence, making sure the straw didn't spill out of the wagon.

As we passed through the large iron gates into the city of Sterling, a new flood of anticipation and nerves washed over me.

"It's showtime," I whispered to my brothers.

Chapter Four

"Straw into gold! Get the only source of mystical straw in the world. It will turn to gold after spinning it!" I yelled to the crowd. "All the gold you desire," I added, remembering Pel's words.

We had set up our wagon in a small, open area on the north side of the faire, making sure we were far from the elixir family. It took little time for me to arrange the spinning wheel. Devon settled Stony while Jacobie arranged the straw into a more presentable heap.

Now I just needed to attract the crowd, which was slowly starting to gather as I called out the miracle claims of the straw. Even this far out, the streets were busy with people.

"What are you going on about girl?" an old woman with wispy gray hair asked me. Her clothes were worn and threadbare and there was a slight tremor to her hand when she pointed at me. I felt a stab of guilt knowing that if I did my job, this woman would be wasting her coins on a hoax. *But it's her or my family,* I reminded myself sternly. I plastered on my most charming smile and beckoned to her.

"I bring extraordinary wares to the Spring Faire, granny," I said, slowly starting to reel her in. "We have an enchanted lot of straw. It can be spun into pure gold." I paused, waiting for her response. I smiled as her curiosity piqued the interest of those around her and more townspeople stepped in closer to hear our discussion.

"Straw into gold, I've never heard of such a thing," the old woman responded. "What do you take me for, telling such tales?"

I answered loudly enough for anyone nearby to hear while pretending to whisper, as though I was carefully confiding in just her. "I take you for a wise woman who would certainly not buy something without proof." Though she was not yet persuaded, I could see she appreciated the compliment. I continued, "This is no ordinary straw. It was blessed by an old druid who knew ancient earth secrets. It was collected in holy fields during a lunar eclipse and thus imbued with strange powers. You can do amazing things with it, but you must be strong of mind, able to completely concentrate on transforming the straw."

The old woman eyed me warily. I took my cue and proceeded, slowly and confidently, to sit down at the spinning wheel. I made a big show of focusing on the wheel, as if willing it to obey me. If folks believed their concentration would transform the straw, then they would sit stupidly at their spinning wheels for long enough that we might depart Sterling with their coins in our pockets.

"Brother," I finally said to Jacobie, my voice deep and serious, "fetch me some straw."

Jacobie, chosen for this role because people tended to trust small children, carefully handed me several stalks of straw, treating each one as a cherished treasure. Reverently, I set them up to the spinning wheel as though it were wool I was about to spin into yarn. I started a low chant, just a noise to distract the onlookers, and deftly let out some of the golden thread that I had been palming. I slowly let out more and more of the thread while palming part of the straw, not minding the scratchy feeling of it sliding up my arm inside my tunic.

I carefully threaded the spindle of the spinning wheel, my foot keeping a steady pace on the pedal to keep the wheel spinning. Golden thread started to collect on the spindle.

Soon, there were gasps and cries of surprise. I pretended to pay them no mind, appearing too focused on my chanting and spinning. I didn't stop until I felt the tail of golden thread slip through my fingers before it wound onto the spindle. By then, I had slid the rest of the straw stalk up my arm.

I sat for a moment, as though the trance of concentration was hard to break. The murmurs of the crowd grew louder, the commotion building. I could have laughed, thinking about how gullible people were. Finally, I opened my eyes and stood up, my chanting over.

"Look, if you like," I told the crowd, gesturing to the golden thread. It sparkled in the morning light, enticing the onlookers. I gave a very slight nod to Devon, who quietly stepped closer to the spindle. We didn't want anyone trying to swipe it.

"Well, by the Mother's maids," the old woman said, her milky eyes round with interest. "You truly have made gold out of straw."

"I must warn you," I said, "that it will only work for the pious. You must have perfect concentration or the straw will not reveal its hidden treasure. It is not for the weak-willed." I imagined townsfolk trying to stare down straw on their spinning wheels and thinking the fault was theirs.

"How much?" asked a young man. He was scrawny but puffed up with overconfidence.

I smiled inwardly but kept a serious demeanor on my face and announced the price. It was outrageously high. Some people huffed and left at the idea of such a crazy sum. But many of them stayed. I reminded them that the price was far lower than the value it would have once it was transformed into gold. And I was only selling it because I didn't have the strength of mind to transform all of it.

Immediately, townsfolk started clamoring to buy the straw, afraid they'd be left out. I picked up the spindle and played with the gold thread, making it glitter in the sunlight. Devon managed the transactions, trading straw for coins. I felt a thrill as our pile of straw diminished and our coin purse grew heavier. This had to be the most successful con we'd ever run.

I didn't notice Finn pushing his way through the crowd, trying to signal to me from a distance. I should have been paying attention. If I had, I would have noticed the man riding up, flanked by an entourage of royal guards and nobles. His imposing steed parted the crowd—a sleek, midnight-black horse. It was the same horse I had seen the day before. Too late, I looked up, seeing the young nobleman from yesterday. But he was no longer a lost young man in the woods, an easy mark. Now he sat tall in a fine and very expensive riding outfit. Everything about him marked his wealth and power. He led guards and nobles, men and women in costly garments, all admiring him. Who was he?

Then all the townsfolk began bowing and it clicked into place.

"All hail Prince Casper, the future king," I heard the old woman call out reverentially. Soon, everyone was chanting that.

I've stolen from the prince, I thought painfully.

I quickly dropped into a deep curtsey, praying Prince Casper would not recognize me from the woods as I hissed at Devon and Jacobie to bow. I couldn't see Finn anywhere, and desperately hoped he had managed to slip back into the crowd.

I stared hard at my feet, willing the prince to continue on his way.

"And what do we have here?"

I looked up to see the prince had ridden right up to our wagon. The sun was behind him, making me squint to see. *We are in serious trouble.* I sent a quick prayer to Chace, the god of chaos, and Aloisia, his sister and goddess of order, that Finn had had the good sense to get out of here.

"I asked you what your wares are, or didn't you hear me?" the prince asked. His voice was stern, but not cruel.

"Nothing, Your Highness," I said, making my voice as meek and humble as I could. The tremor in it was real enough. "Just a poor straw merchant."

"She's selling magic straw," the old woman said. I had to fight the impulse to lash out at the crone.

"Magic straw, you say?" The prince dismounted with an ease that revealed his strength and strode over to me. I tried to keep my eyes averted, but he had such a commanding presence that I couldn't help but stare at him. I was reminded that Prince Casper was strikingly handsome, ruggedly so, with strong features and dark eyes. He held himself with a posture that was reserved for the overly confident and extremely wealthy.

"It's, well, you see," I said, fumbling for an explanation. It wasn't like me to lose focus like this, but I felt overwhelmed by his looming presence. "It can turn into gold!" someone in the crowd cried out. I turned, trying to see who had spoken but couldn't identify the voice. Whatever slight chance I had to give some plausible excuse, was gone. I was as good as dead.

"Is that so?" Prince Casper asked, looking directly at me. He sounded amused, but the question was doused with a cold threat. I was pretty sure the prince did not appreciate swindlers in the capital. I prayed that he might not want to make all his subjects look like idiots for believing me. But then his eyes narrowed, taking me in as recognition dawned in his black eyes. "*You!*" he hissed, the word an accusation.

"There was a misunderstanding," I started, desperate to come up with an explanation that wouldn't end with my arrest.

"Don't be so modest girl," the old woman said with a kind smile. I wanted to smack her. She gestured at the spinning wheel. "This girl was showing us how to do it. She'll make us all rich as kings." The nobles, a cloud of silks and velvets behind the prince, snickered, and the woman immediately realized her mistake. "Pardon me, Your Highness, I meant no offense." She quickly dropped into a curtsey as deep as her old joints would allow.

"No offense taken, good woman," the prince said, and I noticed no threat in his voice when he spoke to her. "We could all use some more gold, I am sure." He directed his gaze at my hand, and I suddenly felt the weight of his ring. He knew what I was, and the hatred in his eyes made me flinch. Then he looked back at the crowd and his eyes softened.

"Our great kingdom could use an additional source of gold to supply us with the funds to protect ourselves from the fay. At any moment, the Fay Queen Marasina could decide to invade, and where would that leave us? The fay armies have dark magic on their side." His voice was deadly serious, and shocked cries rang out from the crowd.

I thought about Pel. Not all the fay were the monsters I had been led to believe they were, but I knew better than to argue with my sovereign. At this point, I was just hoping he wouldn't have me hauled off in chains.

"And that is why we need to have a strong army," Prince Casper continued. "The fay kingdom of Magnomel is too close to our borders for us to ever let our guard down, even for a moment. Their murder of my brother is proof that we must always stay vigilant!"

I nodded along with everyone else in the crowd. Maybe the prince would get so distracted by preaching about the fay, he'd ignore the reason he came over to my wagon.

"Yet rebuilding our army has not been possible, not even after five years of peace. Our coffers were depleted in the Southern War. Think of how gold spun of nothing but straw would benefit the entire kingdom—how it could be used to fortify our military and give them a fighting chance against our enemies."

My head shot up. Prince Casper was staring at me, a satisfied smile on his lips. He looked like a cat cornering a mouse.

"I would happily give you the rest of my straw," I finally choked out. "Anything to help against the fay." *And while you are carting a wagon of ordinary straw back to your palace, we'll be getting far away from Sterling.*

"Oh, I don't think so." His eyes lingered again on my hand.

"And you dropped this in the woods," I added quickly, starting to pull off the signet ring. "I am so grateful to be able to return it, Your Highness."

"No," he said, his hand shooting out to stop me. "I think you should keep it." His grip around my hand tightened as his smile broadened. Louder murmurs and gasps came from the crowd.

"Prince Casper, only royalty may wear the Famille De Rose ring." An older nobleman in yellow and black velvet had stepped towards the prince, putting a warning hand on his shoulder.

Prince Casper removed the man's hand, but his smile never wavered. If anything, it grew sharper. "Clearly, this young woman is an expert at conjuring gold."

"Not at all," I stammered, feeling the trap closing in. There was no getting out of this one. I quickly glanced around, desperately hoping not to see my brothers. It would be far better if they weren't here. Devon and Jacobie were still by the wagon. *Damn.*

"You should have seen it. It was a miracle," the old woman said enthusiastically. I tried not to cringe.

"You would be an asset against the fay," Prince Casper said, looking smug. "Certainly, you would want to do anything you could to aid your kingdom against the fay. After all, with Reynallis devoting so many of our resources to protect the Sterling border, we wouldn't want to be caught unaware. There is nothing I hate so much as my subjects being taken advantage of in a devious deception." Whether anyone in the crowd could tell if he was talking about me or the fay, I could not surmise. But he and I both knew he saw through my deceptions. *Chace's den, my lies are piling up around him.*

"Do not fear, girl. If you do this one, simple task for me, one you clearly do so well," he said gesturing to my gold thread, "then you can keep my ring."

"If I can spin gold, why would I need you to let me keep a gold ring?" I spat out. I was too terrified to be polite and already as good as dead.

"Clever girl," the prince said, appraising me. "But as Lord Arnette pointed out, only royalty may wear that ring," he said with a smile.

"What?" I asked, sure I had misunderstood his implication. The crowd let out gasps of awe and shock.

"Prince Casper, you can't be serious," a young noblewoman in a blue and silver gown said, her voice lilting with an accent. She and the rest of the prince's retinue looked visibly disturbed by the idea.

"A room full of gold would aid our military efforts immensely. A fitting reward for such a dowry would be the realm itself. A woman able to protect our kingdom would deserve to be queen. Do this, ensure the safety of Reynallis, and—" He paused, piercing me with a look. "I shall make you my queen."

The crowd of townspeople erupted into cheers, thrilled at the notion. Prince Casper smiled and waved to the crowd, encouraging them on. His smile was brilliant, and the crowd was eating it up. When he looked back at me, his smile never faltered, but his eyes were steely.

He was determined to make an example of me. He knew he'd never have to marry me because I couldn't spin gold, and this way he could impress the crowd. I hated to admit it, but it was a clever move.

When the cheers and shouts of 'long live the prince' and 'to our future king' died down, Prince Casper jumped back up on his mount with little effort. He extended his hand to me, and it took me a moment to realize he wanted me to ride with him. *That will seal the illusion*, I thought.

The royal guards closed in around us, making escape impossible. At best, maybe my brothers could get away if I didn't make a scene. I stepped toward Prince Casper, feeling defeated, but someone tugged at the hem of my tunic. I turned to see Jacobie, looking up at me with wide, scared eyes.

"Are you leaving?" he asked, his eyes bright with tears.

"I have to go," I told him, trying to make my voice gentle.

"But I don't want you to go," he cried, tears now running down his cheeks, leaving dirty smears on his face. "Mama and Papa left. Rilla left. And they never came back."

I pulled him into a tight hug, wishing I never had to let go. "Don't cry sweetie," I said, forcing my voice to stay level. "I'll come back as soon as I can," I lied. I looked at Devon, standing a few feet away, looking more distraught than when our father left for the war.

"I'll go with you."

"No, you won't," I said with a tone that brokered no compromise, even from an older brother. One of the prince's guards was already taking hold of Stony, ready to lead our donkey and his wagon of 'magical' straw back to the palace. "You'll get Jacobie out of here and protect our brothers." I needed Devon to understand there was no hope for me, but he could still protect the rest of our family. I rushed towards him, pressing the golden thread into his palm. "Take care of them," I said, blinking hard at the tears that threatened to spill out.

The prince's voice interrupted. "We can invite your brothers to come with you. They'd be honored guests in at the palace." I turned to see the prince, smiling and looking perfectly like a benevolent ruler. "In fact, it would be a good idea if they came with us."

"Absolutely not," I shot back. Seeing the look of shock on the faces of the prince's entourage, I quickly lied, "My sister is quite ill. They need to go home and tend to her." Even Devon looked surprised that I would mention Rilla.

"Of course," said the prince, but I could tell he didn't believe me. But I didn't need him to believe me so long as he let my brothers go.

"If you come along willingly, we can probably manage without your brothers." Again, I heard the threat in his voice. If I ran or tried to escape, he would go after my family. For all I knew, he'd send solders after my brothers to hunt them down.

I heard Jacobie crying, but forced myself not to look back at him, lest I started crying too. Instead, I stepped toward Prince Casper, took his outstretched hand, and leapt into his saddle. The close proximity to the prince was terrifying, and I sat rigid. The velvet of his tunic pushed into my back and in an oddly detached way, I noted he smelled of expensive soap.

"She's good with horses too," the prince joked to the amusement of the crowd. Close to my ear, so only I could hear him, he added, "When I expose you for being a fraud, I will make an example of you. I do not take kindly to thieves in my kingdom." With that, he turned his horse around and gave it a kick that spurred it back to the palace.

Chapter Five

Prince Casper didn't say another word as we rode. I tried to formulate a plan, but nothing came to me. I was drowning in a sea of red and gold uniforms, surrounded on all sides with royal guards. Each one had a long sword that dwarfed my small dagger—which I remembered I didn't even have. Pel had never returned it. I was no match for a single guard, assuming I could even get off Prince Casper's horse. My only comfort was knowing my brothers had escaped. I prayed they had the sense to flee the city.

The further we got from the main city, the more my panic rose. The bustle of the city was fading as we approached the area where the nobles lived. Vast manors spread out; luxuriously appointed homes with high, intricate wrought-iron gates surrounding them. But even these impressive homes were dwarfed as the Rose Palace came into view, the sight turning my blood icy.

I hadn't realized I was squirming, until I felt Prince Casper grip my wrists, his hold iron tight. Taking a quick glance back at him, he didn't deign to look at me, keeping his cold black eyes focused on the palace.

I stared ahead, watching as my beautiful doom came into view. I had assumed that Rose Palace was only a pretty name for the place, but I was wrong. An enormous rose garden opened before us, leading to a path that ran to the castle. Early spring roses in whites, pinks, oranges, and yellows, planted in intricate patterns interlaced throughout the garden. The sweet perfume in the air was cloying in its intensity. I suddenly felt like I was in an ornate tomb. *I'm going to be buried here.*

The palace was an imposing structure, comprised of towers, turrets, and domes. Reaching up from the ground were thousands of climbing roses, as though they were trying to envelop the palace and pull it into the ground. Blood-colored roses bloomed from within the vines; a splattering of red against the green and white. I was sure that in different circumstances, the palace would appear beautiful, but it reminded me of the blood on Garin when Pel had forced him to choke to death. Bile rose in my throat, almost gagging me.

All too soon I found myself at the entrance to the palace. Two immense doors loomed in front, built from a white wood with intricate rose carvings deeply etched into each. Prince Casper jumped off the horse and held out his hand, impatiently motioning for me to dismount. I considered taking the reins and trying to make a run for it. But we were surrounded by his entourage, and for every glittering noble there were at least five royal guards. An attempted escape wouldn't last long. I jumped off the horse, avoiding any help from the prince.

"What now?" I demanded, my mind already racing. There had to be a way out, if only I could find it.

Around us, the guards and nobles were dismounting. The guards were mostly staying close to the prince, but many of the nobles headed directly into the palace. The young woman who had spoken to Prince Casper after he declared his intentions for me approach us. She did not look pleased.

"Prince Casper, you cannot seriously mean to do this," she said, in what I now recognized as a Glavnadian accent. Her chilly blue eyes raked over me as though I were a dead mouse the cat had dragged in. I stared defiantly back at her. I didn't want to give this stuck-up noble anything else to gloat about. She was pale with snowy blond hair and delicately defined features. Rumors were that the cold of that northern country of Glavnada made the people there frosty, and her cold demeanor certainly wasn't changing my mind.

"Lady Ilana," the prince said, turning on the charm, "of course I am serious about this."

"You would marry an ordinary commoner? I did not think such a thing was possible, even in Reynallis." It almost pleased me to see her pale face flushing pink in anger.

"Any woman who could turn straw into gold is certainly not ordinary," he said with a smile. In response, Ilana turned, storming into the palace. I deflated, reminded of the real danger I was facing.

"I guess some people just don't believe your magnificent claims." Prince Casper finally turned to me.

"And you're one of them."

"Ah, but I have to demonstrate you are a *liar*," he said, spitting out the last word. "Only a tyrant dispenses justice before proving a subject guilty. I will not start off my reign as a tyrant. Come on." He linked his arm in mine, wincing as he did so. To onlookers, it would look as though he were kindly escorting me. He reached over and gripped my wrist with his other hand, and the vicelike grip was so tight, I started to lose feeling in my fingers.

The inside of the Rose Palace was just as magnificent as the outside. Glittering white stone walls reached high up into golden domes. Shiny marble tile gleamed in the light. And there were roses everywhere. Every surface boasted huge bouquets of fresh-cut flowers, and the rose image infused everything.

Magnificent tapestries of climbing rose vines adorned the walls. Rose shaped black tile were inlaid among the white marble of the floor. There were paintings of roses, and arranged in porcelain vases were delicate, spun-glass roses—so fine I was sure they'd break if I touched one.

"Hurry up," the prince snapped at me. I had stopped, momentarily distracted by the splendor around me. His grip was still tight on my wrist, and I quickly resumed walking as he all but dragged me along.

"I've never seen anything like this," I said, unable to keep all the awe out of my voice.

"Yes, my great-great-grandmother had a thing for roses." We passed through a hallway of royal family portraits. I could see the resemblance to Prince Casper in the dark hair, black eyes and strong faces of the past royals.

"Casper, what in the Mother's name are you doing?"

Prince Casper skidded to a halt, almost causing me to fall over. I righted myself to a see a young woman in a red gown, a few years older than Casper. She looked furious, her raven hair cascading in waves as she rushed toward us down the hall of portraits.

"Oh sister darling, how delightful to see you. My expedition to the Spring Faire went well. I hope I find you in good spirits," Prince Casper said, releasing my arm for a moment to kiss his sister on the cheek. I rubbed at the place on my wrist he had held me, red marks forming where his hand had been.

"Don't *oh sister darling* me, brother," she snapped, pushing him away. "Lady Ilana just came to me in tears saying that you were about to marry some commoner you met in the town square because she claims to be able to spin straw into gold." She looked at me for the first time, her eyes judging and finding me wanting. "This girl, I assume from the look of her."

"Yes, sister. This is . . ." Prince Casper paused. "I don't think I ever got your name," he said to me. I stood in mute resistance. "Tell me your name," he demanded.

"Elenora, Your Highness." It wasn't worth the risk that he'd go after my family to punish me if I misbehaved. But I withheld my last name, not wanting to give him another lead to find my brothers.

"Elenora, isn't that a fancy name?" Princess Constance said, clearly surprised.

It was a fancy name for a commoner, but my father had liked beautiful names and had chosen mine. Not that I would tell these royals that.

When I didn't say anything more, she turned back to Casper. "So, you are planning to wed a commoner whom you just met today and whose name you did not even bother to learn? What are you playing at, brother? You haven't even been home for a fortnight and already you are making such messes. I thought getting lost alone in the woods was foolish, but now you are busy offending the nobles."

"You could have taken the throne, remember?" Prince Casper countered, his voice daring her to argue. "You still can, if you are willing to make certain sacrifices. King Jovian wants to know when we will be sending his niece home." I recalled that Princess Constance had abdicated the throne. I wondered why, what 'sacrifices' Casper was referring to, and how any of it related to the Faradisian king.

"Do not bring Flora into this," Princess Constance almost yelled at her brother. "You can't possibly believe this girl actually makes gold. Why are you doing this?" I had a fleeting hope the princess would talk her brother out of his crazy charade.

"There was a crowd of townspeople who all claimed they had seen her do it. They were quite adamant about it."

Princess Constance just stared. I felt my face growing hot. I hated being talked about as though I weren't right there in the room with them. "It was really a misunderstanding," I said, making my voice meek. If I could get the princess to see reason, perhaps she could convince Prince Casper to let me leave. "I did not mean to cause problems. Please, I promise you'll never hear from me again if I could just leave."

"I was not talking to you," Princess Constance snapped, the commanding sharpness causing me to shut my mouth. She turned her attention back to the prince. "Commoners are easily fooled. I'm surprised you were taken in."

"I don't believe it," Prince Casper said defensively. The corners of his mouth raised in the smallest of smirks. That scared me more than all the yelling.

"At least you haven't lost every bit of your sense," Constance said, sounding only slightly mollified. "Then why go through this farce of an engagement?"

"Because that is how I get my subjects to believe me. They saw her turn straw into gold with their own eyes. I have to prove she's nothing more than a fraud. Otherwise they'll make a martyr out of her."

"You are trying to be too clever. Christopher would never have been so devious."

I realized they were speaking of their brother, the late king. His death was the reason Casper was taking the throne. It was just my luck that of the two siblings, our future monarch was into such a public demonstration of justice. My odds might have been better with Constance, if only because she saw me as so far beneath her as to be insignificant.

"Not devious, only practical."

"I know you want to prove yourself a worthy king, but the nobles will see right through this pantomime of justice." She reached out to touch her brother's hand, but he yanked it away. She visibly stiffened. "No one in court cares about some nobody criminal, and you are going to make a fool of yourself for dragging her here just to lock her in a room filled with straw."

"Then it's a good thing I don't need your approval for how I decide to rule," he shot back at his sister. "In fact, she won't be faceless to them." Casper lit up with an idea. "She will be my honored guest at the feast tonight. I'll have her sit at our table."

"Um, what?" I choked out, sure I misheard. "Really, that is not necessary." But neither of the royal siblings were paying any attention to me.

Princess Constance let out a snort of disgust. "Christopher would never have done something so ludicrous." Without another word, she turned on her heel and marched off. Prince Casper watched her go long after she turned a corner.

Turning to me, he wrinkled his nose. "You smell horrid."

His comment about my smell stung, even though I knew it was true. Hot baths were not readily available in the woods and it had been too cold to bathe in the streams. Still, I thought about how he smelled so clean, and suddenly felt a flush of embarrassment, despite hating him and not caring what he thought of me.

I tried to pay attention to the grand rooms and hallways we hurried down, mentally drawing a map of how to exit the palace the moment I found a chance to escape. But there were too many hallways and corridors, and I soon lost track of direction as Prince Casper towed me along. Finally, he led me into a large parlor room, filled with velvet red chairs and a crackling fire in a massive stone fireplace. He let go of my arm and went to one corner of the room and pulled a thick rope, which I assumed was connected to a bell in the servants' quarters.

"Sit," he commanded. I didn't have the energy to argue, so I collapsed into one of the rich chairs. It was a relief to stop being herded around by my arm. I rubbed feeling back into my wrist and hand, avoiding eye contact, mostly staring at the thick rug on the floor, which, naturally, was embroidered with roses.

After a few minutes, a servant dressed in the deep, red livery of the palace enter the room. He was shorter than Casper and looked to be about forty, bald, and sporting a fine mustache, carefully groomed.

"Your Highness has returned." He smiled, bowing deeply to the prince. "And you have a guest," he added. His eyebrows raised in surprise for a moment before he schooled his features back into that of polite attentiveness.

"Yes, Jock. That is why I rang for you. This young woman, Elenora, will be joining me for the feast tonight as my personal guest. She needs to be cleaned up and provided with more appropriate attire for the evening. Can you have those arrangements made?"

"Certainly, Your Highness," Jock responded, as though clothing strange girls was a normal request. Maybe it was.

"Once you deal with her, have hot water brought to my rooms for a bath and lay out my clothes— probably the most regal and uncomfortable ones you can find. I cannot be late to the celebrations."

"Certainly, Your Highness," Jock replied with another bow.

"And one more thing," added Casper. "Assign a guard to her. One who won't let her out of his sight. For her safety, of course."

And so I don't try to escape.

"As you command, Your Highness. Milady, come with me, if you please."

I stood, about to follow Jock into a new form of torture, when Casper leaned over to me. "Be very good," he said.

Anger bubbled up in me. "And if I decided not to go along with your act?"

"Then I instruct every guard at my disposal to find your family. There were a lot of witnesses that can identify at least two of your brothers. And I have no doubt that with the right resources, we can find out if you truly have a sick sister." Cold chills prickled my spine. I nodded, afraid to say anything, and then, with dread, stepped out the door to where Jock was patiently waiting for me.

Chapter Six

J ock led me through a labyrinth of hallways and staircases. I
was completely disoriented, but if I were lucky, he'd lead me to
a guestroom with a window large enough to climb out.

"This is one of the few guest rooms I knew would be available
and unoccupied at the moment," Jock said as he opened the door.

"It's enormous," I gasped, taking in my surroundings. I couldn't
believe that such an immense space simply existed as a spare room.
It was such a waste.

"It's actually one of the smallest rooms," Jock said, giving me
a wink.

"Small?" I asked. The main parlor was almost as wide as my
family's old house. I stepped into an elegantly decorated room with

pale blue walls and white scrolling accents that reminded me of frosting. The chairs and small end tables matched, upholstered in a fine blue cloth and engraved with the same accents.

"Perhaps a bit more space than you are used to?" I couldn't read his tone, unsure if he was trying to be friendly or mocking me. "I will send up a maid to start the fire," he said, gesturing to the fireplace in the center of the room. "And she can bring up the water for your bath and clothes." Unlike the prince, he didn't betray the slightest disdain at my appearance.

"Thank you," I said, not sure what else to say.

"I would never presume to ask you where you are from, but if Prince Casper has taken a shine to you, then you must be special." Jock gave me another wink, as though I were in on a friendly secret. It made my heart sink. "And I will send a guard up here shortly," he added. The cold fear rose in me. One night in luxury so I could be humiliated and probably executed. *I have to come up with a plan,* I thought desperately.

Jock left without another word. I explored my temporary prison, wandering around the rooms, hoping to find something that would trigger an idea. The parlor was only the beginning. A door to the left led into an immense bedroom, also decorated in blue and white. There was a canopy bed in white Aspen wood with pillars that reached the ceiling and thick, soft blue blankets covered the mattress. Another fireplace, this one almost as tall as I was, was situated on the far wall. There was another door that led into a smaller bathing room with a porcelain claw-footed tub and a delicate vanity with a curved silver mirror and matching stool. I jealously marveled at what life must be like for those rich enough to consider such rooms 'small.' In the bedroom, I paced around, looking for any inspiration to aid an escape. By the fireplace was an iron poker, but I doubted that would help me much against a legion of royal guards. There was one large window, elegantly framed in white lace. *Perfect.*

Except one look out the window showed I was several floors above the ground. A fall from this height would probably kill me, or at least break my leg. From this vantage point, I could see the vast layout of the rose gardens. It would have been a breathtaking sight, but I could only think about how this place was merely my decorated prison.

"Milady?" I heard someone asking from the parlor.

A maid, a few years younger than me, was carrying a large bucket of steaming water. Her auburn hair was pulled into a tight braid and freckles dotted her face and hands. She was a tiny thing, struggling under the weight of the bucket.

"Let me help you with that," I offered, stepping toward her. She immediately shrank back, almost sloshing water over the side of the bucket.

"No milady, that wouldn't be proper."

"All right then," I said, raising my hands in surrender and backing up. "I'll just stand over here, being proper or something." I felt useless as she carried the heavy bucket into the bathing room, and I heard water pouring into the tub.

"I'll be back with more water," she said, hurrying out the door.

A few minutes later, there was another knock. I opened the door, expecting to see the young maid. Instead, a massive royal guard stood in the doorway. He was a good head taller than me and appeared to be made out of tree trunks.

"Lady Elenora?" His voice was surprisingly soft.

"I'm no lady," I said, but he did not look amused. "Please, just call me Nor."

"Nor?"

"Umm, yes, that's my name."

"I am Sir Yanis. Jock assigned me to watch you while you are a guest at the Rose Palace." He sounded sincere, and I wondered if he realized I was more a prisoner than a guest.

"Well, thank you," I said awkwardly. "I'll let you know if I need any, um, protection."

"You seem new to this," Yanis said, but with warmth in his voice.

"And what gave it away?"

"You don't seem very comfortable with my presence, if you don't mind my saying so. And your attire is . . . unusual for a guest of the palace."

"Right," I said, looking down at my travel-worn clothes.

"And I saw you at the festival," he added, looking a bit sheepish.

"Oh." He probably knew that I was here to perform miracles.

"Can you really do it?" he asked. His brown eyes were bright with curiosity. He reminded me of Finn, not so much in looks, as Finn was a slight slip of a boy while this young man was massive and all muscle. But he had that same eagerness for knowledge.

"I certainly hope so," I said. "Else I fear things will go rather poorly for me."

"Don't worry. I heard old Granny Marrion say you could do it. And if she believes in you, I'm certain you can." Granny Marrion must have been the old woman from the faire. *Of course, she believed me. It's easy to believe miracles if you see them.* "And let me just say it is an honor to guard you. That much gold will save our kingdom from the evils of the fay. It will rebuild our army to the strength we had before the Southern War."

I nodded, trying to look convinced.

We hadn't been strong enough in the Southern War when my father, a miller by trade, had been conscripted. We hadn't been strong enough as a nation to protect him from death at the hands of a Faradisian solider. They seemed more monstrous than the fay, at least compared to the only fay I had ever met. I recalled Pel's fingers on my leg, cool and gentle as he healed my wound. I slipped my fingers up my sleeve, feeling the gold thread still wrapped around my wrist. Too bad this one bracelet of gold wouldn't be enough to buy my freedom, if I could even figure out how to take it off.

Wait, would it? Pel's instructions about calling on him to redeem the debt he owed me came back in a rush. It was a long shot that he could help, but I was grasping at straws at this point. *Terrible pun.* But remembering his words about using blood to summon him made me shudder. More likely, it was only another one of his dark fay jests.

"Lady Elenora?" Yanis asked, concern in his voice.

I blinked at him.

"Sorry, I was distracted. This is all so new to me," I added, trying to make my face a mask of young innocence.

"Of course, milady. I grew up on farmland myself, came here to join the royal guard for a more exciting city life."

A farm boy, I thought. *That might be useful.* If he was from some poor village, perhaps he had plenty of mouths to feed back home and I could bribe my way out. Pel's bracelet might hold fast, but I still had Casper's ring. "That sounds like quite the change," I agreed, preparing to broach the subject. I twirled the signet ring around my finger.

"Indeed, it was," Yanis nodded enthusiastically. "But I'd say the biggest change was waiting on others, not having servants wait on me." Yanis misread my dismay, as he was quick to add, "Not that I mind, milady. It is a great honor and privilege to serve at the Rose Palace."

"Servants?" I asked weakly. "But you said you grew up on a farm."

Yanis laughed. "Sorry milady, I did not mean to cause confusion. My father owns lands to the west of Lotanus. He has three hundred acres, and all converted into farmland during my grandfather's time. Did you know that sweet corn and figs do especially well there?" Yanis grinned with pride. "My family is particularly known in those parts for our fig jam."

"Fig jam?"

"Indeed. The recipe is a family secret. I'll have to write to my brother back home to send some jam here for you to try."

"You are too kind." I swallowed hard. "But you decided to come to Sterling for a position as a royal guard? I cannot imagine the pay here is better than the profit of three hundred acres of fig jam."

Yanis straightened, looking almost offended. "I did not come here to seek riches, milady. I truly do consider it the highest honor to serve king and country." The utter sincerity of his words convinced me that this was not a man to be bribed. Why I had to be guarded by such an honorable man was a shame. I stopped twirling the ring, its weight feeling heavy on my finger.

"You seem to be doing an admirable job."

Yanis beamed. "The palace can be a bit overwhelming at first, but you'll learn your way around."

"Oh, I don't think I'll be staying here long," I blurted out. *I'll either escape or meet the end of a hangman's noose*, I thought.

"Won't you? Prince Casper said he's to marry you after you turn the straw into gold." Yanis looked so genuine, I almost laughed.

"Right, I forgot. It's been a long day."

Yanis looked unsettled, but I was saved by the maid coming back at that moment. She had another bucket of hot water with her, and she was struggling even more to carry it.

"Can you help her with that?" I asked. It seemed ridiculous that an ox of a man should stand by when a slip of a girl was lugging heavy buckets.

"Really, I'm fine," the girl pleaded, but looked relieved when Yanis took the bucket without asking and easily carried it to the bath. He seemed uncomfortable in the intimate bathing room and exited as quickly as he could.

"I'll be right outside if you need me. Please let me know if I can do anything to assist you." The look in Yanis's open, honest face was so earnest, I was about to ask him to send word to my brothers. Maybe I could give him a sealed letter to tell my brothers to flee the city while they still could.

"Actually . . ."

"Yes, milady?" Yanis stood tall to attention, making him look once again the guard that he was. The *royal* guard no less.

"Sorry, nothing." It would have been beyond foolish to ask him—maybe even a death sentence. I had to watch myself.

"Very well milady. I'll escort you to the prince's chambers at half past six." Yanis hurried out.

"I think one more bucket should do it, milady," the girl said, and I turned back to look at her. She looked so tired.

"This is fine. Plenty of water to wash up in," I told her. The tub was far from full, but there was enough water that I could easily clean up.

"If you're certain," the girl said uneasily.

"Yes, I am."

"Then I shall help you wash."

"Oh no you won't," I snapped, regretting it instantly when she cowered. "I mean I don't need any help washing up," I said, trying to make my voice gentle. But really, were nobles so pampered they needed help bathing themselves? No one but my family had seen me naked, and I didn't feel like changing that now.

"Why don't you find whatever I'm supposed to wear tonight?" I asked, hoping to distract her.

"If you insist," she said, dipping into a quick curtsey before scurrying out of the room.

Climbing into the massive tub, I appreciated the hot water despite myself. It was a luxury I was rarely afforded, though I scrubbed myself quickly, afraid the maid would come back and try to help. I was just drying off when she returned.

"Milady, I have your dress." Her timid voice came from the bedroom.

"Thank you. Just set it down and I'll put it on." I pulled on a dressing gown; the fabric finer than anything I had ever owned. I almost wished I could wear it to dinner.

"But don't you want help to do your laces and buttons?"

"I think I can manage to get dressed by myself," I muttered, striding into the bedroom. But I stopped when I saw the array of items on the bed. It wasn't just a dress. It wasn't even close to just a dress. Instead, there was a frothy lilac gown placed next to a stack of petticoats, a corset, stockings, and dainty satin shoes that I was sure I would not be able to walk in. I surveyed the pile, feeling a rising horror.

"I don't really need to wear all of that, do I?" I tried to keep desperation out my voice.

The maid was clearly too scared to contradict me, but also wouldn't say no, so she just stood there, mute, her large puppy-dog eyes looking worried.

I sighed, defeated.

"I guess I do need your help." The girl visibly relaxed. "But I should at least know your name if you're going to help me dress."

"I'm Annabeth, milady," she said with a curtsey.

"Don't call me *lady*. I'm Nor. Just Nor. And I think you can tell that I've never worn something so elaborate," I said, gesturing to the pile of clothes on the bed.

Annabeth smiled for the first time. It was a small smile, but genuine, and lit up her tiny face. "I did get the feeling you were a bit . . . different, from most of the ladies here. It would be my pleasure, Lady Nor, to serve you. I'll have you looking like a princess."

The mention of a princess reminded me of Prince Casper's challenge, one I was sure to fail, and I felt a stab of anxiety. But I reminded myself that I had spent the last six years surviving. This was simply one more obstacle. I simply had to find an escape. I let out a deep breath.

"Then let's get started."

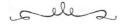

I had never worn anything so uncomfortable. The soft linen shift and creamy silk stockings had felt fine on my skin, but then I was weighed down by layers of petticoat skirts and squeezed into a corset with stays so tight I thought I might pass out. When I objected, Annabeth insisted that it be this tight or the dress wouldn't fit. I wanted to argue that she should just get me a bigger dress, but I couldn't spare the breath. And almost as bad as my inability to breathe was the way the corset pushed up my breasts, forcing them almost to my chin. I wanted to push them back down, but the corset had not the slightest ounce of give. Once the gown was draped over my head, Annabeth began working on a long string of tiny pearl buttons down the back. She had been right; I would have never gotten myself into this dress on my own. Why did nobility feel the need to wear clothes they couldn't even put on without assistance?

"Almost done, Lady Nor."

"Just Nor. I'm no lady," I wheezed.

"It wouldn't be right for me to address you so informally, Lady Nor," Annabeth said, helping me into the satin slippers. I didn't dare tell her Nor was actually my nickname.

"Fine," I relented as she laced up the slippers. They were delicate shoes embroidered with lace and pearls. *Completely impractical*, I thought. Though the heels were short, they were taller than the boots I was used to wearing. It took me a few practice steps before I could walk without leaning against the wall.

"Am I done?" I asked, unable to keep a whine out of my voice. I felt ridiculous.

"Almost. Please have a seat and I'll do your hair."

"What do you have to do to my hair? Can't I just comb it?"

"I should put it up, Lady Nor. There isn't much time before Jock will be back for you. It wouldn't do for you to go with your hair like that." My hair had mostly dried from the bath but looked like a pile of unkempt straw. And I really didn't want to think about straw right now.

"You sure get pushy with this stuff," I grumbled. Immediately, Annabeth recoiled, the look of fear back in her eyes. Any of the confidence she had when dressing me was gone.

"I didn't mean to offend you, milady," she said meekly.

"No, you didn't offend me," I said, softening my voice. "I've just never needed help getting dressed. It makes me self-conscious. But that's not your fault. Please, do my hair. At least I can pretend to look presentable."

Annabeth began to gently comb out the knots in my hair. It was actually soothing and reminded me of how Rilla, my older sister, would comb my hair and sing to me when I was younger. I felt a pain in my chest and forced away the memories.

Annabeth hummed while she worked, something I didn't think she realized she was doing. After a while, she began pinning up my hair into a simple but elegant knot.

"I'm done, milady," Annabeth said. I was surprised my hair had taken far less time than getting me dressed. Annabeth must have misunderstood my shock, as she was quick to add, "It's nothing fancy, I'm afraid. I didn't have much time. But it should suffice." She gestured to a full-length silver mirror on the other side of the bedroom. Warily, I extricated myself from my seat, careful not to trip in the slippers. I managed to make it to the mirror with a minimum amount of wobbling. Mentally bracing myself, I looked at my reflection. The sight made me want to scream.

Chapter Seven

"**I**'m a cupcake."

"Is that a good thing?" Annabeth asked cautiously.

"Would you want to be a cupcake?" I snapped. I was covered in frothy purple frills and cream-colored lace. I looked ridiculous.

"Maybe a tasty one?" Annabeth ventured.

The skirts were so big and round from the layers of petticoats that I might have been sitting on a ball of lilac satin. The fabric was gathered in a nauseating number of shiny silk bows. Worse still, was the way the way the neckline dipped far lower than I would have liked, displaying too much of my pushed-up cleavage. I felt like a dressed-up sausage.

I might be going to my demise this evening, but even I had standards.

"Get me out of this," I demanded, awkwardly clawing at the buttons securing the lace collar at the back of my neck. I failed miserably. Despite the copious amounts of fabric on the sleeves, they were surprisingly tight. I could only flap my arms uselessly. I imagined this was what the world's fanciest chicken would look like.

"Lady Nor, please stop," Annabeth cried, reaching for my arms. "You'll tear the lace."

"That's the point," I snarled. "I refuse to look like some rich brat's nursery doll."

"But this was the only gown available on such short notice," Annabeth pleaded, still attempting to stop my destruction.

"Then I'll go in my trousers. By Chace's den, I'd rather go naked than wear something like this!"

"Is that so?"

Annabeth and I both whipped around at the sound of a male voice. Prince Casper was standing in the doorway, looking immeasurably smug. His dark eyes sparkled with unspoken mirth. He looked handsome, which made me even angrier. He had changed and washed, and now appeared every bit the prince of folktales in his red and gold uniform. A thin gold band circled his brow, and it shone in the lamplight. I felt even more humiliated in my outlandish outfit.

"Your Highness," Annabeth said as she immediately dropped into a curtsey.

"Do you always just barge into women's rooms?" I demanded, curtsey be damned.

"I wanted to make sure you would be ready, and not getting into trouble." Prince Casper looked mildly surprised to be so affronted but recovered quickly. "Besides, this isn't your room. And I heard yelling."

"I'm certain you did. I am being attacked by the world's ugliest dress." I swatted at one of the cursed bows. "I believe it's trying to devour me."

"I think you look charming," Casper said, clearly amused. I could tell he was trying to keep from smiling.

"And I think you have terrible taste." I balled my fists by my side but reminded myself there were terrible consequences for smacking a prince.

"Come, it is time for my feast," he said, offering his arm.

"You have got to be kidding me. I am not parading around in this."

"I don't kid." The amusement from Casper's voice vanished, and I sensed the steel underneath it. My stomach turned in fear, as I remembered I was speaking with the person who could have me executed any time he wished.

"Can I please just wear my clothes? I promise I won't look any more foolish than I do now." *And I'd be less likely to trip wearing my boots*, I thought.

"Those rags you were wearing? They were filthy. And they stank. We've had them burned."

I looked around. In the distraction of getting dressed, I hadn't looked for my old clothes. I didn't see them in the room. I turned to look at Annabeth, who blushed and cowered under my glare.

"They were very dirty, milady," she said in way of apology.

I sighed, defeated. "I am going to tread on your feet all the way there," I warned the prince.

I managed a few steps toward Casper before tripping on my own skirts, tangling one of the slippers in the petticoats. My heel twisted, and I went flying forward. I threw out my arms, sure I'd hit the floor. Instead, Casper moved with unexpected speed, catching me before I hit the ground. His arms were strong as he held me up. I felt an unexpected thrill before coming to my senses. I stood, careful not to fall over again, and quickly disentangled myself from the prince.

My traitorous pulse took a moment to slow. Thinking about how much cleavage this dress displayed, I felt heat rise in my cheeks. I looked at Casper and he looked a bit surprised too.

"Thank you."

"Yes, well, be careful," he said. Did he sound flustered?

"Your crown," I said. In the rush of movement, the gold circlet on his head had shifted slightly and sat askew on his forehead. I moved to adjust it, before snapping my hands back to my sides.

"I'm not used to wearing this yet," he admitted. He adjusted the circlet till it sat upright on his brow, the gold contrasting with his dark hair. "It's heavier than it looks, made of pure gold. It used to give me headaches."

Gold, I remembered with a sinking feeling. Suddenly, I no longer felt flushed or even embarrassed. I only felt dread. "Guess you'll be getting a lot more gold," I deadpanned.

At my declaration, Casper became serious, and for just a moment I missed the person he'd been when he entered. Smug, but more of an amused boy than my future judge and executioner.

"Right," he said coldly, and stiffly offered his arm. He recoiled a bit when I took it, and I wondered if he was thinking of how he despised me for deceiving his subjects and stealing from him. I was a fool to think, even for a moment, that he was anything except my enemy. Had my brothers' safety not been at stake, I might have refused to move, and simply allowed his guards to lock me in the dungeon, or wherever they planned to keep me after tonight. Instead, I followed him out of the room and braced to meet my fate.

Yanis and two other guards, whom I could only assume were Casper's own personal guards, fell in place behind us, walking silently, watching our every move. Yanis had a better game face than I did, as he didn't even crack a smile when he saw my new attire. Casper strode through a labyrinth of hallways and staircases. I struggled to keep up, careful to keep my balance in the dangerous slippers. The too-small shoes bit into my toes with every step I took.

Casper stopped before a pair of massive oak doors. He stood for a moment, looking tall and regal, every bit the king he would soon be, as he waited for the guards stationed on either side of the doors to open them.

The room beyond took my breath away. It was an immense dining hall, filled with rows of long, elegant tables and ornately carved chairs. Seated in each chair was a richly dressed lord or lady, more nobility than I had ever seen in one place. It was a sea of fine silks, velvets and lace, all in stunningly bright house colors. Beads and jewels glittered from the light of the many crystal chandeliers that hung from the high ceiling. Royal guards in Reynallis red and gold uniforms stood silently at attention along the long walls, surveying the guests. Massive tapestries of climbing roses and vicious victories from ancient battles hung on the walls. In between the tapestries were wrought iron windows with panes of thick glass. At the far end of the room was a raised table, larger than the others. Behind it was an immense stained-glass window depicting one huge rose, illuminated panes of gold, yellow and crimson glowing in the evening light.

Suddenly faced by so many nobles and guards, my stomach dropped. These were people I had tried to avoid all my life, people who carelessly dictated the lives of poor and insignificant folk like me and my family. With the arrival of Prince Casper, all heads turned to look at us. A herald seemingly jumped out of nowhere and announced the prince's presence. Chairs scraped along the floor as everyone stood before dropping in bows and curtseys in the presence of their future king. Terror gripped me as my feet turned to stone. Casper moved to take a step forward, but I couldn't get my legs to work.

"Come on," he hissed. His voice was sharp, but he never lost the smile he showed to the crowd.

"I can't," I whispered, hating the fear in my voice.

"Nonsense, it's just dinner."

"I don't think I can," I repeated, still unable to move.

"You have to do this. Think of your family." There was a pressure in his voice that was equal parts urgency and threat.

I closed my eyes and allowed myself a long breath. I thought of my brothers, of responsible Devon, bookish Finn, and wide-eyed Jacobie. I couldn't give Casper any excuse to go after them. I opened my eyes and steeled myself. Who were these people to frighten me? What could they do to me that Casper wasn't already planning to do after I failed to transform straw into gold? Why should I care what they thought of me? With that, I managed to take a step. I felt Casper breathe a sigh of relief.

All eyes were on us as we slowly crossed the immense room toward the raised table at the back. I could hear murmurs in the crowd. No one else was wearing anything with quite as many bows or skirts quite as puffy, I noted with irritation.

After what felt like forever, we reached the royal table. Princess Constance was seated to the chair left of center, looking radiant and angry as we approached. Next to her was a beautiful Faradisian woman with dark skin and black hair braided in a complicated arrangement. Her soft curves were wrapped in a gown of deep sunset orange, embroidered in white. I was surprised to see a Faradisian at the court at all, much less at the table of the royal family. After the Southern War, I assumed they would have stayed far from Reynallis royalty. But Casper had mentioned something to Constance about King Jovian's niece.

Casper smiled at his sister, ignoring her scowl as he climbed the steps to the table. I followed along, taking extra care not to trip. Servants stationed behind the table rushed to pull out chairs for Casper and myself.

Casper remained standing, and in a booming voice addressed the crowd. "Lords and ladies, nobles and knights and guards of the royal court, I am pleased to see you all in attendance of the Spring feast. It has been five years since I have attended the festivities, and I am grateful to be home. While we will never stop mourning my brother, our great King Christopher, I swear by the crown that I shall do everything in my powers to be a wise and just ruler, as Christopher would have wished. Though tradition dictates that my coronation take place on the longest day, I am not waiting till midsummer to begin my service to this great kingdom. Already, I am at work to fortify Reynallis against some of our greatest threats. The fay who murdered my brother will never set foot on our soil without the fear of death!"

A loud cheer went up and Casper smiled, looking triumphant, and perhaps a bit relieved. He sat, practically pulling me into the seat beside him, and the entourage of nobility returned to their seats. Servants poured into the hall, filling wine glasses and bringing out platters of food.

"Not a terrible speech, brother, but a touch over the top."

"I'm doing the best I can, sister," Casper said tightly. "Would you prefer to take my place?"

"You're doing fine," Constance replied, her voice softer. But then she looked over at me and her eyes grew cold. "Though I maintain that parading this criminal around like your honored guest is unnecessary and unwise."

"I don't know what you're talking about. The lady is my betrothed as of this afternoon."

"Please stop," I said, my voice quiet.

"Are you trying to cause a scandal?" Constance asked her brother, ignoring me.

"Are you?" he asked, looking pointedly at the lady sitting next to Constance, the beautiful Faradisian woman. She looked at Casper and I saw hurt in her doe-like brown eyes.

"Casper!" Constance hissed.

Immediately, regret filled Casper's face. "I'm sorry Lady Flora," he said. For the first time this evening, he sounded truly sincere. *I was right*, this lady was the Faradisian king's niece.

"No apology needed, Your Highness," Lady Flora replied. Her voice was soft and musical.

"I shouldn't have spoken like that. My sister was just needling me."

"She can be quite the nuisance," Lady Flora said, smiling fondly at Constance.

"Flora!" Constance exclaimed, but she was smiling.

"Well, I think you're worth the trouble," Lady Flora replied warmly and gently placed her hand on Constance's.

"Then maybe my sister can explain to King Jovian why his beloved niece refuses to return home."

"He has done well enough without me for five years, he can do well enough a while longer," Flora said, and though her tone was light, I noticed she squeezed Constance's hand. Despite myself, I wanted to know what was not being said, but their conversation was put on hold by the arrival of the food.

I had been so anxious crossing the great hall, I was sure I wouldn't be able to eat a bite. But the aroma of the baked cod with lemon, tiny broiled potatoes with salt, steaming broth soup, and fresh bread immediately took my attention away from the royal siblings. My stomach growled, and I remembered I had not eaten since this morning, and that had been only a thin gruel.

I also knew I needed to keep up my strength for tonight. I would find a way out of the mess I was in, even if I had to scale the walls of the palace to do so. And it was easier to have a clear head with a full stomach.

Famished, I ripped off some of the bread. Its golden crust opened to reveal soft white bread inside, far finer than the heavy, grainy bread I was used to. It reminded me of bread we used to eat when I was small and my father still ran the mill. Unable to resist, I held it to my nose and breathed in the warm, yeasty scent before I dunked it into the broth and greedily gobbled it down, licking crumbs off my fingers.

Then I noticed everyone at the table was staring at me. Flora looked concerned, Casper amused, and Constance disgusted.

"You couldn't have found a thief with some table manners?"

I was suddenly angry, having these nobles judge me on how I ate, considering it was their wars and their taxes that made it so my family was lucky to ever have enough to eat. I shoved a huge bite of fish into my mouth to avoid making a rude remark.

"You might want to slow down," Flora said, but unlike Constance, there was kindness in her words. "This is only the first course."

I swallowed the rest of the fish, nearly choking. "There's more?" I asked, genuinely astonished. The food on our table alone was more than enough for several meals.

"Of course," Flora said. "This is just to start the feast."

"I haven't seen this much food since before the rationing."

"We haven't enforced rations since the Southern War," Constance said. I couldn't tell if she was confused or righteous.

I didn't want to tell her that not enforcing rations meant nothing to our family since the war left us too poor to buy anything. Or that our family business, running a small mill in the southern city of Venlin, was destroyed during the war and we had no money to fix it. Or that the war took both my parents and my older sister soon after, so we were a bunch of orphans doing the best we could to survive. These royals didn't deserve to know my life. Instead, I simply said, "Not all of us emerged from the war this fortunate." I gestured to the spread of food on the table. The three of them sat, stunned at my statement.

When a servant with wine came to our table, I covered my goblet with my hand, requesting water. I didn't need my head foggy with drink. But I ate my fill of the different courses, enjoying the roast chicken, steamed crab, fresh fruits, piles of baked vegetables, and additional bread that came with every course. Though there were many forks, spoons, and knives laid out next to my delicate porcelain plates, I ignored them all and stuck with one fork and knife for the entire meal, declining to hand them over to the servant who came to clear plates between courses, much to his chagrin. I was tempted to pocket several pieces of silverware but decided not to risk it.

Throughout the meal, I plotted options to escape the palace. I might never have been in direr straits, but I had been in rough situations before, and had always made it out. *But my brothers had been with me then*. I pushed that thought aside. Maybe I could use one of the dreadfully uncomfortable hair pins Annabeth had used to pick the lock of my door.

I was starting to feel I could handle the situation by the time desserts were brought to our table. I was full but still managed to eat a chocolate mousse and raspberry tart, while drinking some of the strong tea a servant poured into a delicate teacup. The cup was beautiful, but far too small for my liking, and I had the servant refill the cup twice more.

As I was finishing my third cup of tea, Casper stood and cleared his throat. All voices in the great hall hushed as the future king made his second speech of the evening.

Chapter Eight

“I wish to make an announcement that will affect the entire realm,” Casper said in a loud voice that echoed across the great hall, silencing the crowd. “It is about this stunning woman.” I detected a note of sarcasm in his smooth voice, as he continued, “Lady Elenora has shown the good townsfolk of Sterling that she has the exceptional ability to transform straw into gold and generously offered to lend her services to aid her country at this vital time!”

A muffled cheer went through the crowd, and my face grew hot as I felt the inquisitive stares of everyone in the room. I spied Ilana in the crowd, a familiar face, but not a friendly one. Her hair was intricately done up, and she wore an even more elaborate silver and blue gown, which unlike my puffed-up monstrosity, draped elegantly around her. She glared at me as though she might be able to kill me with a look.

"Lady Elenora will spend tonight spinning an entire room full of straw into gold. With that much gold, our military can be fortified and Reynallis shall be stronger than we have been since the Southern War. Our might will keep us safe from ever-increasing dangers of the fay and their cruel kingdom of Magnomel!"

As he spoke this, he grabbed my hand, pulling me to my feet. My massive skirts hit my chair, sending it sprawling at the same time my foot slipped on one of the traitorous heels. I stumbled, much to the crowd's amusement. I could hear snickering throughout the entire hall.

Only Casper's firm grip on my hand prevented me from tumbling backwards. "Don't you want to wait till tomorrow to disgrace yourself?" he jeered at me in a whisper while still smiling at the crowd. Loudly, he continued, "What could we possibly do to repay such a gift to our kingdom? There would be no adequate payment, short of the kingdom itself." Those words dropped like a stone. In stark contrast to the cheers in the town square earlier that day, the laughing immediately ceased and the court went silent, probably wondering if their future king had gone mad. "So as a reward for restoring Reynallis to its former wealth, I offer my hand in marriage to Lady Elenora. An engagement contract will be finalized as soon as she produces the promised gold as her dowry!"

The court began murmuring, a loud buzz. There were too many voices, and I couldn't tell if they were pleased by this new arrangement or offended by it. I spotted Ilana again, and her stare was even deadlier than before.

She rose with a cold grace.

"And what if she is a fraud?" Even in the noisy hall, Ilana's voice rang out clearly. The other nobles also seemed to want that answer and eyed their prince expectantly.

"Well, I didn't think it necessary . . ." Casper started, and for a moment his confident demeanor slipped. *He has no plan for me even though he knows I'll fail,* I realized with a small flame of hope. Perhaps I could convince him to let me go once I was out of the public's eye. But just as quickly the mask was back on, Casper standing tall and serious in front of the crowd. "But for deceiving my subjects," Casper paused, his suddenly cruel gaze fixed on me, "for deceiving me," my pulse began to race in a very unpleasant way, "the punishment would be nothing less than complesile." Casper let the words sink in. Indeed, the crowd had quieted, I on the other hand, had no idea what a *complesile* was. I imagined it had to do with thumbscrews and dungeons. I would make sure one way or another I would not be around to find out.

"And now, lords and ladies, we shall leave you for the evening. I shall personally escort my future bride to her chambers, where she will tirelessly spin straw into gold. If I am engaged come tomorrow night, it shall be because our kingdom has become rich again. Power and strength to Reynallis!"

"Power and strength!" the crowd echoed back, excited by Casper's speech.

As he pulled me along, out of the dining hall, Yanis and the other personal guards fell in behind us. Everyone in the great room rose and bowed as Casper passed by them. It took all my concentration to keep up with his brisk stride without tripping over my ridiculous outfit. As we made our departure, I caught a last glimpse at the royal table. Constance looked concerned, but Flora was smiling. Seeing me staring at her, she offered a small wave.

"So, what is complesile?" I asked as we entered the hallway.

"Complete exile, of course," Casper said, still tugging me along. "You and yours would be ordered to leave Reynallis, never to return on pain of death. Your records and histories destroyed."

"Well, that's a relief," I said, my anxiety starting to lift. "I was worried you were planning to lock me in a dungeon or something terrible." Maybe exile would come as a shock to noble families, but for somebody like me, who belonged nowhere, it meant nothing. I was sure my brothers and I could slip away to some tiny village in the south and be forgotten by this prince and his court.

Casper stopped, so suddenly that I ran into him. His face was grave. "You do not understand, Elenora. A complesile means every one of your family must leave Reynallis immediately. Any member of your family caught in Reynallis would instantly put to death."

My blood turned to ice at his words. My brothers had been seen by a dozen nobles and at least twice that many guards. And if I couldn't find them in time, then their very lives would be in peril. All because of me and my greed.

It was a circular room at the top of a high tower, and I could immediately tell it was a prison. There were no decorations or tapestries on the walls, simply some utilitarian lamps that had been lit prior to our arrival. The walls and floor were bare stone, with none of the elegant rose carvings I had become accustomed to seeing throughout the palace.

The sparse room was piled with the straw from our wagon. There was a simple cot for a bed and a plain chair by the sole window in the room, both barely visible under the heaps of straw. Next to the cot was a chamber pot and a plain pitcher of water sat beside the chair. The whole room smelled like a barn from all the straw. At least it smelled like a clean barn.

The only other object in the room was a spinning wheel. It sat in the middle of the room, shining in the lamplight. The one we had commandeered for our scheme must have been left at the faire, as this one was new. It was a work of art, a finer spinning wheel than I had ever seen. The entire thing gleamed of brightly polished wood and there was a small stool to match. I ran my hand along the wheel and the stool, feeling the smooth wood beneath my hand. I traced my fingers up to the needle and pricked my finger, not realizing how sharp it was. A tiny marble of blood welled up on my finger.

"I shall leave you to it."

I turned to face the prince. I could probably only make one request. And even that was if I was lucky.

"I need work clothes."

"Pardon me?"

"I need something I can work in, not this puffed up costume piece. I can't even sit on the stool without knocking over the spinning wheel in all these skirts." Casper looked like he was actually considering my offer. "Please," I added sincerely. If I had any chance of escape, it would be far more likely in clothes I could actually move in. I didn't add that he owed me that much after having my own clothes burned.

Casper turned, and without another word left the tower room. I heard the heavy stone door close and its lock shut. I wondered if I might be able to pick the lock and reached for one of the hairpins Annabeth had used in my coiffeur. I pulled out a slender silver pin and examined it. It was tiny, but sturdy, and I thought I could make a go of it.

I was at the door when I remembered Yanis was standing guard on the other side. I paused, frustrated, and sighed, at least as much as I could in the tightly corseted dress. Pacing over to the window, I looked out. The chill night air of early spring was refreshing after the stuffy atmosphere of the dining hall. It was long past dark, but the moon was almost full, casting everything in a silvery light. I looked down and saw the ground was a dizzying distance away. A fall from this height would kill me. I should have claimed to weave rope into gold, then at least I'd have a room full of rope instead of straw.

The gardens in front of the palace were dark, but I could see lights coming from the town. I imagined there would be plenty of festivities going on there, with people enjoying the Spring Faire late into the night. I looked out to the east, into the pitch blackness that was the Biawood Forest. I hoped my brothers were getting far away from Reynallis and its vindictive future king. I felt a sudden pain in my heart, realizing I might never see them again.

The door was suddenly unlocked and flung open. I looked to see Casper in the doorway, flanked by his two guards and Yanis off to the side. But what intrigued me the most was the bundle of cloth Casper was holding.

"Take this," he said, holding out the bundle to me.

There was a simple tunic and a set of trousers that looked roughly my size. They were far plainer than the elegant court attire, but finely made of a soft linen. I reached to unbutton the dress, but the tight fabric of my sleeve allowed me only a few inches of movement.

"I need help," I said weakly.

"What?"

"I can't get out of this dress on my own," I said, heat rising in my cheeks.

"You can't expect me to, you know, help." I saw a blush in Casper's face that must have mirrored mine.

"I don't want your help," I snapped, "but I literally cannot get out of this dress." I flapped my arms around, attempting and failing to get to the buttons on my back.

"If you just unbutton the back, I can manage the rest on my own. I promise not to bite." Growing up with three brothers and a sister, I had never been modest, but asking a stranger—asking the future king—to help me undress was madness.

"I really shouldn't," Casper said.

"Are you scared?" I knew I shouldn't be goading the prince, but I was terrified he'd flee, leaving me in this awful gown for the night.

Without another word, Casper stepped toward me. For just a moment I was taken in with his handsome features. With his high cheekbones and determined eyes, I could have mistaken him for a prince from a folktale come to save a princess. Except I wasn't a princess.

He stepped around behind me. He was so close I could feel his warm breath on the back of my neck. A thrill rushed through me, as I felt a tug on the back of the dress as he loosened the tiny buttons holding the bodice together.

"The corset too," I said. "I can't get to that either." Casper didn't say anything, but I felt a pull at the tight laces, and soon the straining stays of the corset felt loose against the shift. I took in a huge gulp of air, thrilled to have full use of my lungs again. My breasts were finally released from being squeezed up towards my chin, and the relief was immense.

"I think you should be able to take it from here," he said, practically jumping away from me. I almost smiled to see how studiously he was staring at the floor. *Almost*.

"Thank you," I said, wiggling out of the dress and pulling the corset off. I was still fully clothed in the shift and petticoats, so it was ridiculous the way Casper refused to look at me. Even the guards were staring straight ahead, determinedly not paying attention to me. It was silly, as I was wearing more layers now than I ever had worn at home, but at the same time I was beginning to feel far too exposed in front of Casper.

"Yes, well, I will be leaving now," Casper said, still unable to look at me. Before I could say anything else, he had fled through the door. The guards closed it behind him. Any humor I felt at the situation vanished as I heard the lock click into place.

Chapter Nine

I t took a while to get out of the rest of the ensemble, undoing the ties of the petticoats and stripping off the silk stockings. Eventually I managed to extricate myself from the clothes and left them in a discarded heap. I pulled on the shirt and trousers, and since there was no way I was voluntarily wearing those slippers ever again, I remained barefoot. The stone chilled my feet as I paced the room, considering my options.

Even from the soft lamplight, the gold on my wrist sparkled, far brighter than the prince's signet ring, which only gave off a soft glow.

I considered Pel's words in the woods, wondered if he would really come here if I summoned him or if it was only another faerie trick. The idea of doing anything related to fay blood magic made me uneasy, but I was short on options.

I looked around the room for something to pierce my skin. *The spinning wheel.* I went over to it and quickly jabbed my finger on the sharp needle before I could change my mind. My finger stung from the impact and a small bead of blood welled up on my finger. I rubbed it on the thread tied around my wrist, smearing the blood in the process.

At first, nothing happened. But then the gold grew warm on my wrist. And it didn't stop heating up. It got hotter and hotter until I was sure it was burning my skin. I yelped and tried to pull off the thread, but it held fast. The thread was glowing brightly, almost white.

And then, just as suddenly, it stopped.

I gasped, clutching my wrist and fell to my knees. The gold was now cool on my wrist, but there was an angry red band where the skin had burned. I glanced at the door, afraid Yanis might have heard, but the door didn't budge.

I went to the pitcher of water by the cot and splashed water on my wrist, quietly cursing myself for being such a fool. Of course, Pel had played another trick on me, and a painful one at that. There was no strange and beautiful faerie coming to rescue me from the tower. The burn was already blistering and throbbed slightly. My heart started to race when I thought about what would happen in the morning.

I eyed the dress and petticoats piled high in the corner. Maybe they could prove useful. I grabbed the lilac silk and tore a long, thin strip off the skirt, ripping off the stupid little bows while I did so. There was a satisfaction to destroying the dress. At least I would never have to wear it again. I pulled off two more strips and began to tightly braid them together. As I did so, I walked over to the window, wanting to better gauge the length of rope I would need.

Looking down from the window, I could tell I would need a lot of rope. I scanned the sky, determining how much night was left. The feast had taken up far too much time and there were maybe five or six hours till dawn. I was pretty sure Prince Casper was not a late sleeper. I tore another strip off the dress, braiding it into my makeshift rope.

I don't know how long I worked at the rope, an hour, maybe two, but finally there was very little left of the satin skirts; most transformed into a heap of lilac cords, all braided together. I looked around my prison, trying to find something sturdy to tie the rope to, but neither the cot nor the spindle looked like it would stay mounted when I made my escape.

Finally, I settled on one of the wall sconces. I carefully tied one end of my new rope to the metal.

I dropped the rest of the satin rope out the window. There was a significant gap between the end of the rope and the ground, but I would just have to jump. Gingerly, I pulled on the rope, testing that it would hold. I was not completely convinced, but time was running out, so I climbed out the window, holding on tightly to the rope. The wind hit me as I braced my bare feet against the cold, outer stone wall.

Starting down the tower wall, I carefully lowered myself one step at a time, praying to Aloisia that the knots would hold. After a few feet, I encountered some of the climbing rose vines. Though I tried to push them away, it was impossible to avoid all of them. The branches were full of thorns, cutting and scraping me with every move I made. I gritted my teeth and kept going. My progress was painfully slow, the ground still too far below.

I heard the snap the moment before the rope went loose in my grip. I was falling. I screamed as I dropped the rope and scrambled against the side of the tower, desperate to grab hold of any bit of stone. Thorns and rose vines whipped around me, but I didn't care. A drop from here would kill me.

Desperately, I jammed my fingers against the stone wall, finding a tiny purchase in a chink in the stone, and clung to it, halting my fall. I had only a small handhold on the wall in which to hold myself up. My breath was ragged, my heart pounded in my chest. I flung my other arm against the wall, desperate to find another handhold. The stones were too slippery, covered in moss and vines. My hand ached, my fingers growing numb. I tried to think, but all that came to mind was that I would lose my grip and fall to my death. I tried to adjust my grip, but my hand slipped.

I fell.

I screamed and flailed as thorns and leaves whipped by me.

And then I stopped.

Impossibly strong arms were holding me up.

"I find you in the strangest situations."

I looked up to see golden hair and glittering green eyes.

"How?" I stared at Pel, completely bewildered. Then I gasped.

Beyond his face, I saw his wings, those delicate dragonfly wings, gently flapping back and forth, making the moonlight passing through them shimmer. His limbs were long and his movements liquid. He radiated light and power as he rose higher in the air, carrying me as though I were a doll, up to the tower window. He managed to fly through the narrow window and still land gracefully on his feet before gently setting me on the stone floor.

I wanted to say something but had completely forgotten how to speak.

"I didn't expect you to summon me so soon," he said. His voice was melodic, like the sound of brook or the notes of lute. "Or in such a dramatic fashion."

"You came."

Pel's lip quirked up slightly. "You sound surprised, Nor. It was you who summoned me."

"I am calling in my favor," I said, forcing myself to stop admiring the way the lamplight made his iridescent skin glow or how it highlighted his cheekbones and jaw.

"In addition to saving you from falling to your death?"

"Yes," I said, my face reddening. "Well, that was an accident." I looked over at the wall where the sconce had been. It had been pulled off the wall. The sconce and the satin rope were now lost in the climbing rose vines.

He ripped a strip of fabric from one of the petticoats and dipped it in the water. For a moment I wondered what he was doing until he returned to me, kneeling beside me before wiping my face with the cloth. His touch was light and gentle, and my heart fluttered before he handed me the cloth. It was pink with my blood. Nothing deep, but still, I was scraped up from head to toe from the rose thorns. I took the damp cloth and began to dab at my wounds.

"What, then, *do* you request of me, Nor?" I couldn't read Pel's expression. In the lamplight, he almost glowed.

For a moment, I thought about asking him to fly me to freedom. With his wings, I knew he could. But as the words were on my lips, I stopped myself. If I went on the run, then Prince Casper might send soldiers after me to ensure he made an example of me. And I wouldn't be the only target. I'd be putting my brothers in danger too. The threat of the complesile still rang in my head. Was there no way this could end other than with exile and our lives in danger?

I had been willing to take the chance and run when I had no other option, but looking at Pel, I realized I had another choice. It was a crazy idea.

"I need you to transform straw into gold."

"You need me to do what?"

"It's a long story, but the prince believes I can spin straw into gold. If I don't turn all this straw into gold by morning, I'm done for," I gestured to the piles of straw around the room. "You can transform it, just the way you did the thread."

"Why does a prince think you can spin straw into gold? Is that a common request from human princes?" He stared at me, perplexed.

"Not exactly," I said. "I might have tried to convince some people in the village that I could turn straw into gold, and the prince saw this and decided he needed proof."

Pel studied me. "And why were you trying to convince people you could turn straw into gold?"

"Because I wanted to eat," I said defensively. "Because I wanted to make enough money to provide for my brothers."

"So, you did it for personal gain?" There was no accusation in Pel's voice, simply curiosity.

"You could say that."

"I have heard humans crave material wealth above everything else, including the good of others."

"It wasn't like that," I almost yelled, before remembering Yanis on the other side of the door. "I needed to feed my family," I hissed. *But yes, it was exactly like that*, my conscience argued.

"And the gold I gave you wouldn't have fed them? The ring on your finger wasn't enough?" There had been surprise and even admiration in Pel's emerald eyes when I had rescued him. That was gone now, replaced by a look of disappointment.

"Are you going to help me or not?" I demanded. Shame made me lash out.

Pel looked at me coolly. "No."

"What?"

"I said no."

"You can't say no," I said, desperation creeping into voice. Maybe I had overestimated his magic. "You turned wool thread into gold. This can't be that different."

"The cost is too high." Pel's voice was softer, tinged with sadness. I didn't care. I was out of options.

"But could you do it?"

Pel sighed. "I would ask you to change your mind."

"No, I need this."

"Because you saved my life, I will help you," he stated, his voice devoid of emotion. "Whether or not I want to," he warned.

I winced but plowed through. It didn't matter what he thought of me. "So you can do it?" I asked, gesturing to the straw around me.

"This is a lot more than one small thread. I could fly you out of here. Wouldn't that be easier than transforming a room of straw?"

"I can't leave," I finally said. "If I do, the prince will hound my brothers. I'm not a good person, but family is family. So, either you help me make a room full of gold or you leave—because I don't have any other options." I prayed he wouldn't call my bluff.

"You have quite the heart for a greedy human," Pel said, but there was no admonishing tone in his voice. He surveyed the room, shaking his head at the heaps of straw on the floor. "It's a lot of straw."

"I could throw some out of the window. Would that help?"

"It might," Pel said, considering me. "You do know all magic comes at a price."

"I learned that when you gave me this," I countered, holding up my wrist with the gold thread around it. "But I'll pay it, whatever it is." I had no idea how I'd pay for anything, but that was a problem I would deal with later.

"I'm afraid you'll have to. We both will. If you are sure you want me to do this."

"I am," I said.

"I was afraid you'd say that."

Chapter Ten

Pel stepped toward me. Before I realized what was he was doing, he pulled a small, familiar weapon from his belt. It was my dagger. With unnatural speed, he grabbed my hand and slid the blade across it.

"What are you . . . ?" I yelled, but Pel wrapped a hand around my mouth, motioning to the door. I nodded and he released me. Remembering Yanis, I quieted my voice, but not my tone. "What, by all the Mother's maids, are you doing?" I hissed. The cut on my hand was shallow but stung as a shiny red line of blood formed across my palm.

Pel snatched up a piece of straw with one hand and with his unnatural speed wiped it across my bloodied palm. The blood smeared across the yellow straw. As I was thinking that I had made a huge mistake by summoning a demented faerie, Pel started to spin the straw in his hands. As he rolled the straw in his palms, the blood absorbed into the straw, which turned pink as the blood soaked into it.

"What?" I asked but stopped. The pink straw was losing its color as Pel continued to roll the straw in his palms. Soon, it had lost almost all its color, as though he were working with a piece of thin glass, not a stalk of straw. I forgot the pain in my hand as I watched him mold the straw. The more he spun it between his hands, the longer and thinner it became, till it was almost as fine as the gold thread he had given me in the woods.

As he worked the straw, or at least what had been straw, color returned to it. Slowly, so slowly that I didn't notice at first, the straw lost the glassy transparency, but absorbed the color of the lamplight and glowed from within. The straw took on more and more of the lamplight as it became a fine, twisted cord that blazed in Pel's hands.

"Put your hands out," he commanded. Mesmerized, I obeyed without thinking. He draped the cord across my open palms. The moment he let go, the light left it, dispersing in a moment of glimmering shards. When the air had cleared, the cord in my hand no longer glowed but still glittered in the lamplight. I cautiously held it up and inspected it.

"Gold," I breathed, barely believing the miracle. I felt a sudden thrill of hope that died the moment I looked up at Pel. He was pale and tired. A light sheen of sweat had formed on his brow. "Are you all right?"

"It takes a certain amount of energy to transform one material to another," he said. There was a touch of fatigue to his voice and I wondered how much it had cost him to transform the straw into gold.

"So, you're an alchemist," I said, trying to piece together what I had just seen. There were plenty of human alchemists. Their mission was to figure out how to transform base metals into gold, but so far, I had never heard of anyone actually doing it, much less with a piece of straw.

"Something like that," he said. "But I'm not like what you call an alchemist. I can transform materials, but only with life magic."

"Life magic?"

Pel gestured to the cut on my palm. "Blood."

I looked down at my hand, feeling dread well up in me as understanding took hold. I quickly dropped the golden cord, thinking about how it had my blood in it. I remembered how he had spoken of human blood having 'many uses' and how his hands were already smeared with blood when he had transformed the thread in the woods.

"You use blood magic to transform things?" I asked, feeling sick. All the stories of the fay drinking human blood came back to me. I had assumed they were just old peasants' tales, but perhaps there was more truth to it than I initially believed. Pel had used Garin's own blood to kill him, after all.

Pel studied me, the lamplight making his strange cat-like eyes glow. "All magic has a cost. And the cost for me to transform something is that I work with a material that has a life force behind it. Blood is the strongest element for that."

I considered screaming for the guards. Could they get here before Pel would use his dangerous magic on me? But that was ridiculous. Why would he have come all the way here and shown me what he could do if he wanted to harm me? He could have done that in the forest.

"So now you know the extent of what you're asking," Pel said, his musical voice low and serious.

I looked around at the room full of straw. There was no way he could transform it all, not if he looked this tired after one piece. And that was the easy part, I didn't even want to think about how much blood he would need.

"Can you do some of it?" I asked, already weighing how much I could throw out the window.

Pel stared at me with his dark gemstone eyes. "You realize that it is human blood that transforms. Not fay blood," he said finally, looking pointedly at me. "You'd be the one to pay the price."

I gulped.

"I understand."

"Then we better get started," Pel said.

I nodded and searched the room for a container for my blood. Just the thought made me queasy. I reminded myself that the alternative would be worse. I picked up the pitcher of water and was about to dump the contents out the window.

"No. Pour the water on the clothes," Pel said, gesturing to the pile of petticoats. "You'll want to clean the wounds when we're done. I won't have the energy to heal you."

"Right," I said, turning back to the discarded clothes. I poured the water out on the linen shift and the cotton petticoats, trying not to think about how they would be my bandages before the night was over.

"You're certain about this?" he asked, his brow furrowed in concern.

"I don't think I've ever been less certain about anything. But I don't see another option, at least not one that won't put my family in danger."

"And the danger you'd be in if your prince found out you used fay magic?"

"I'll just have to make sure he never finds out." I braced myself for the next part. "Give me my dagger."

Without a word, Pel handed me my dagger. I held it out to my wrist, and took a deep breath, preparing to slash the flesh.

"Don't cut yourself there!" Pel snapped. The horrified look on his face surprised me. "That's a bad place to make a cut."

"I didn't realize there was a good place to cut myself."

"It can get too hard to control the blood flow if you cut yourself there. My whole trip here would be a waste if you bled to death."

"I'd hate for my death to inconvenience you," I said sourly. In truth, I felt so nervous the blade was shaking in my hand.

"Here, let me help," he said, stepping toward me. I was torn between wanting to flinch away and relieved that I wouldn't be the one stabbing myself. I silently handed Pel the knife.

Gentle as air, Pel ran his fingers over the inside of my arm, tapping the vein on the inside of my elbow. "Hold this," he said, handing me the empty water pitcher. Nervously, I took it. "Now look at me," he commanded. I did so, staring into his deep green eyes. I didn't think I could look away, even if I wanted to. He stared right back at me, even when he stabbed my arm.

I bit the inside of my lip to keep from crying out. The pain was sharp, a quick puncture to the inside of my arm. Blood ran down my arm and into the pitcher. I allowed myself only a glance at the red stream of blood, wondering how much blood I'd have to lose for this to work.

Pel carefully pulled the pitcher from my hand and set it on the floor, putting my hand into it so the blood flowed into the container. My arm hurt, but not as much as I thought it would.

"Create a fist and breathe in," Pel directed me. "Open your hand when you exhale. That will help the blood flow. Understand?"

I nodded, too dumbstruck to say anything. Pel seemed so at ease doing this, I wondered if he had collected human blood before. I tried not to think about it and hoped his plan wasn't to let me bleed to death.

Not waiting for me to finish the job, Pel picked up a large piece of straw and gently brushed it across my arm, smearing it in blood. He began rolling the straw, turning it pink and glassy. I started to feel nauseated, thinking about my blood in his hands, but I forced the bile down. I glanced at the cut, but watching my blood run down my arm made me lightheaded, so I averted my gaze. My eyes settled on one of the lamps, and I focused on the flickering light. I still squeezed and opened my hand, slowly breathing in and out as I tried not to think about our gruesome work.

"How much blood do you need?" I asked, still looking at the lamp. The flame danced back and forth, and I tried to concentrate on that.

"Depends how much straw you want me to change for you. I don't need much blood on the straw, but I need some and there is a lot of straw here." Pel's voice was soothing, which surprised me, considering his grisly undertaking.

"That's all right, we'll just throw the rest out the window," I said, feeling suddenly giddy. The image of pompous Prince Casper walking under the tower and being rained upon by a straw shower suddenly struck me as funny. Maybe I was starting to crack under the pressure. The metallic smell of my blood was getting stronger, and I had to fight down the sick feeling.

I risked a glance at Pel. He looked tired but was still diligently working with the straw, though the straw in his palms no longer resembled straw. It was now a true gold and he was winding it into a fine cord. I was mesmerized. Once he set down the coil, he picked up another piece of straw and wiped it on my arm. He looked carefully at my arm as he did so. I didn't look down but saw concern in his eyes as I felt the scratch of the straw.

"What's wrong?" The pain in my arm had diminished to a dull throb, but I kept clamping and opening my hand as he had instructed.

"The wound has almost closed. You're not bleeding very much."

"Usually that's a good thing." I risked a glance down. The pitcher had a few inches of blood, a thick garnet liquid that made me suddenly sure it would be a very long time before I would ever touch red wine. Pel was right, the stream of blood from my arm had slowed to a trickle.

Pel examined the pitcher with a detachment that made me nervous. "More blood would be ideal."

"Ideal? As if any of this were ideal," I retorted.

"Would you like me to leave?"

"No, please don't. Bloodletting sounds great. I may even buy some leeches after this. Just do it for fun. Here, give me that. It's mine anyway," I said, reaching for my dagger. After a moment of hesitation, Pel handed me the blade. Before I could think better of it, I slashed at the neat puncture in my arm. The clotting was torn away, and I screamed in pain as a fiery burn ripped through my arm.

"Lady Elenora, are you all right?" Yanis yelled from the other side of the door. Pel and I froze in fear, and I held my breath, praying he wouldn't open the door to check on me. I forced down the rest of my scream though the pain in my arm was making me see spots.

"I'm fine," I called back, forcing the tremor from my voice. "It's part of the process," I managed to call to Yanis. "Don't come in. No matter what you hear."

"Yes, milady." We waited, but my guard didn't say anything else.

I slumped to the floor, barely managing to keep hold of the pitcher. The cut on my arm was deep and jagged, but at least the blood was flowing again. If I bled out before the end of the night, at least I wouldn't have to face the prince in the morning. The air in the room had a coppery tang.

"You don't look so good," Pel said, his voice hushed.

"I don't know about fay anatomy, but humans generally aren't supposed to lose a lot of blood," I croaked.

"Should we stop?"

"No, I'm good," I lied. "Just keep making the gold."

Pel hesitantly pulled another piece of straw. I tried to focus on the lamp, but found it difficult to stay focused, my mind wanting to wander. I felt like I was floating.

"Tell me a story," I said. I turned to face him, careful to look only at his face.

"A story?" His eyebrows raised in surprise, though his attention remained fixed on his work.

"Yeah, something to distract from all this," I said, then added, "Please."

"Once upon a time there was a stupid thief who rescued a faerie, but then got very greedy and demanded a room full of straw be turned into gold, and probably died of exsanguination in the process. The end." Though Pel didn't look up, the corners of his mouth lifted in a small quirk of a smile.

"You are a terrible storyteller," I chided, but I, too, was smiling. "You should have at least said the thief was beautiful." My lightheadedness was making me foolish.

Pel looked up at me then, though his fingers never stopped winding the straw. "She is." He quickly ducked his head back down towards his work.

I would have flushed if I had had enough blood to spare. "You're just being kind because you're bleeding me dry. I bet fay women are absolutely breathtaking if they're anything like you." *What made me say that?* I had to be losing a lot of blood. Suddenly, it seemed very funny, and I started giggling. I giggled so hard I got the hiccups which just made me laugh harder.

"Nor, are you all right?" Pel asked, eyeing me as though I had just lost my wits, which I might have. "You are very pale; I think maybe that's enough blood."

"It's just *hic*, so funny to think that *hic* I would be flirting with some *hic* beautiful and deadly faerie."

"All right Nor, let's close that wound," he said, tearing off the hem of a petticoat.

"Are you *hic* sure? I want the stupid prince to *hic* have all the gold *hic* that he needs to leave me alone. I could do this *hic* all night." I tried to stand to prove my point, but suddenly felt myself break into a cold sweat. The room tilted, blackness bloomed in front of my eyes, delivering me into darkness.

Chapter Eleven

I woke up with no idea where I was. There was a cold compress on my forehead. Water from the cloth trickled down my face and into my hair. It felt refreshing. I stared at the stone ceiling and recalled that I was locked in a tower bleeding out so a faerie could make gold. I tried to sit up, but immediately my head began to swim, the room rocking sickly back and forth.

"You'll want to lie down for a while," Pel said as he helped me back down to the cot where I had been lying. I noted that he had pulled up the stool from the spinning wheel and was sitting beside me, a translucent piece of straw in his hands.

As I lay back down, I noticed that my arm was wrapped in a bandage made from the petticoat. The bandage was stained red but had stopped the bleeding. My arm stung, but the pain was manageable.

"Do you have enough?" I asked, gesturing to wound on my arm.

"I'll make do with what we have," he said, focusing again on winding the straw. "I don't have the strength to heal you, not with so much transformation magic to perform."

I took a steadying breath and willed away the dizziness. "Clearly, your stories are so bad they cause fainting." Pel let out a surprised chuckle and I smiled, feeling a thrill at making him laugh. "But seriously, can I help?" I asked. I looked out the window. We had only a few hours of darkness.

"If you feel well enough to sit up, you can prepare the straw," he said, focusing again on his work.

"You mean . . ." I trailed off. The thought of smearing my blood on the straw made me queasy all over again.

"What did you think I'd ask you to do? Make us some tea?"

"Oh, I could kill for a cup of tea. Do the fay drink tea?"

"Everyone drinks tea."

"Well, if I didn't have an illegal faerie doing dark magic here, I could probably ring for some." I sighed, thinking about how nice a hot cup of tea would be about now. I focused on deep breaths in hopes of getting rid of my nausea.

I slowly sat up. I felt mildly lightheaded, but not about to fall over or pass out again. I carefully picked up a piece of straw from the piles around the room. Pel had quite a few golden coils at his feet, but there was hardly a dent in the straw. It would be best if I could do something to speed up the process.

I inhaled the straw's clean smell, trying to get the coppery smell out of my nose, and then I dipped the straw into the pitcher. I forced myself not to retch as the piece of straw came out of the pitcher dripping with blood, *my blood*, and the metallic tang filled the air again.

"What are you doing?" Pel hissed. "You'll waste it."

"What do you mean? I was trying to help," I said defensively.

"The magic only needs a little bit of blood to work. You don't have to drench it. It will go faster, but we'll run out of your blood much quicker." He finished the coil he was working on and reached out to take hold of the straw I was holding. I handed the stalk off to him, careful not to let it drip on me.

Immediately, he began spinning the straw in his hands. I thought his hands would be stained a grizzly red, but they seemed immune to the blood, with it all sinking into the straw at an amazing speed. It took less than half the time it normally took him, and the straw was another sparkling coil he casually tossed in the pile with the others. I looked up at him. He didn't look quite as tired as he normally did after finishing a golden rope.

"You weren't kidding about fast," I commented. "How did you learn to do this?"

"Lots of practice. The skill runs in my family, but it still requires a lot of training and study."

An image of Garin choking flashed before me, but I was quick to push it aside. Garin had been trying to kill us.

I turned and picked up another piece of straw, desperate to be busy. I carefully dipped my thumb and pointer finger into the pitcher. The blood had cooled but was thick and starting to congeal. I tried very hard to imagine that it was just ink. Ink that smelled like death.

I grabbed the closest piece of straw to me and rubbed my fingers up and down the stalk of straw. Red smeared to pink across the stalk.

"Like this?" I asked. Pel looked over, almost approving.

"Yes, that should work." He took the straw and began working on turning it to gold. I did this over and over again, creating a pile of rust-stained straw next to Pel. We worked in silence for a while, Pel concentrating on the transformation, and me staining fresh pieces of straw and trying not to vomit. I had to be careful not to bend my bandaged arm or it would start bleeding again. The pain was an ache that wasn't debilitating, but enough to be distracting. The more straw I marked with blood, the less the room smelled like a fresh barn and more like a battlefield.

But I had to admit that the pile of golden ropes on the ground was stunning. The ropes were tight-twisted coils and glittered in the light of the lamps. There had to be more gold here already than in the Reynallis royal vault. Albeit, the vault was probably pretty depleted. Still, it was an impressive sight.

After a while, Pel stopped working. I figured he needed a break. He sat back on the stool and stretched out his fingers. His pale hands were free of any blood, long and slender and almost glowing in the lamplight. He wiped sweat from his brow, and I noticed the dark circles under his eyes. I wished I could offer him something, but even the water was gone.

"Who are you really doing this for?" Pel asked. It was the first time he'd spoken in a while.

"What do you mean? I was ordered to by the prince." I stifled a yawn. Now that we were in a routine, even a grisly one, my adrenaline was seeping away, and fatigue began to set in.

"But are you really doing all of this for your prince? Is it to fill the royal coffers? Or is it for your family? Or is it for yourself? Are you trying to become a hero?"

"Oh, trust me," I said with a laugh, "I am no one's hero."

"Come morning, you will be. Thanks to you, a war-torn country suddenly will have a room full of gold."

"I hadn't thought about it." I honestly had not. I had been too consumed with thoughts of escape to even consider what would happen if I succeeded. I wondered if Casper would let me leave the palace once I fulfilled my end of the deal. "It's funny, actually. The prince said he'd marry me if I did this."

"So, is that why you summoned me and called in your favor? You want to be a royal bride?"

I laughed at that so hard it came out as a snort. "I don't think he'll go through with it. Can you see me as a princess? I am definitely not royal material."

"You seem brave. And resourceful. Those are important qualities in a ruler." Pel sounded so serious, it caught me off guard.

"I've had no choice in life but to be resourceful. And I'm not brave. I'm just a survivor. If I'm lucky, Prince Casper will see this room full of beautiful gold tomorrow and pardon me. Then I can return to my brothers and continue my life of trickery and crime."

"You have strange goals for your life, Elenora Molnár."

"Says the boy working with blood like it's fresh dough."

"We each have our own gifts," Pel said as he picked up another piece of straw. I stared at him for a while. Macabre magic or not, he looked beautiful at his work. His lithe fingers expertly worked with straw, moving it so fast sometimes I couldn't even see the transformation.

His eyes were focused on his work, and I noted that he had the longest eyelashes I had ever seen on a man. They were a shade darker than the gold of his hair. He looked too dazzling to be real, as though he should be living in legends. Foolishly, I felt very self-conscious about my own dirty blonde hair and calloused skin.

I prepared all the straw that I could until I ran out of blood. Pel looked exhausted but didn't complain. He was hunched over on the bench, and every now and again he started to nod off, only to jerk his head up a moment later. His hair hung limply and his bloodshot eyes formed an eerie contrast with his gold-silver blood. Despite his fatigue, he kept his fingers twisting the straw, working it into gold.

Knowing I couldn't give up more blood, not if I wanted to see the next morning, I carefully collected what little clean straw there was and threw it out the window, hoping the straw would get stuck in the rose vines. It wouldn't take much to realize that there was a small pile of straw around the tower, but I hoped that Casper and the court would be far more concerned with the pile of gold inside the tower to care. If anyone asked, I'd claim the cast-aside straw had not been suitable for transformation.

As I watched Pel spin the straw, I thought about what he had said to me. *You seem brave and resourceful. Those are important qualities in a ruler.* Was there any chance that Casper would want to wed me after this was over? The idea was absurd.

I looked around the room, trying to see if I could do something to make myself useful.

"Can I do anything?"

"Not really," Pel said, concentrating on a piece of straw that was beginning to turn translucent. Then he paused and looked up at me. His eyes were tired, but there was a trace of a smile on his lips. "Why don't you tell me a story? See if you are any better at it than I am."

Chapter Twelve

"I was going to tell a tale about the stupid thief, but you already know that one. Let me see . . ." My father had told us beautiful stories about the fay, about them being wonderful and magical beings. I was transported back to the days before the war, when I was younger and my family was whole and safe. After a day working our modest mill, my father would come home, and we would all eat around our large, wooden table. Then my mother would pour cups of hot cider and we'd sit by the fire listening to my father's stories.

"Once upon a time," I started, "there lived a young maiden who lived in a faraway village. She was the most beautiful maiden in the entire village. She had hair the color of burnished copper and

eyes the soft brown of doe." I swallowed hard, remembering how
my father would always describe the young maiden as my mother,
making her blush and giggle as he lavished praise on her in his
fictional tale. "Every eligible man in the village had asked for her
hand, many doing so *twice*, but she had turned them all down,
saying she would only marry for love, and she was in love with
none of them. But her beauty never made her idle or vain. She
was studious and performed all her daily chores with a smile and a
song, her voice as sweet as a nightingale. Early in the morning, as
the sun was just rising, she would go deep into the forest to forage
for mushrooms, nuts, and berries, all the while singing her beautiful
song."

"Hopefully she didn't try hunting in the woods. Sounds like she
made quite the racket."

"Hold your tongue. Do you want me to tell the story or not?"

"I am your attentive audience, oh masterful storyteller."

I sighed but continued. "One day, while she was collecting the
first blackberries of summer, a faerie prince heard her singing. It was
so lovely that he had to see who could make such a lovely song. He
hid behind a bush to spy on the maiden, but as soon as he saw her,
he was overcome with love for her. He stepped out from hiding and
declared himself to her. When the maiden saw the faerie prince,
she too was deeply affected by his handsomeness, for all the fay are
beautiful to behold—" I stopped, an embarrassed heat flushing me
as I realized the double meaning of my words. I had been so lost in
retelling the story exactly as my father had, that I only now realized
what I was saying to an actual fay, and a very handsome one at that.
Pel quirked up an eyebrow, a smirk burgeoning at the corner of his
lips, obviously amused. I hurried on through the next part. "And she
fell deeply in love with him."

"That was fast."

"People always fall in love quickly in folktales. Do you know any stories where the couple take a few years to get to know each other? And hush, I'm busy distracting you from your tedious toiling."

Pel did look worn out, dark copper circles forming under his eyes, and I thought his hands might be shaking ever so slightly. Despite his fatigue, he looked up at me and smiled, the amusement still plain on his face. "Then by all means, milady, do continue to distract me with tales of unrealistic love."

I ignored his comment but continued with the story. "So, the faerie prince took the beautiful maiden back to the fay kingdom to make her his bride. The journey was a happy one. The lovers rode on pure white horses during the day and when they made camp in the evenings, the stars shone brightly as they listened to the lovers speaking of their future long into the night. The pair faced many an obstacle on their long journey to the fay kingdom, but they conquered each one, and every trial only brought them closer together.

"Finally, they reached the prince's kingdom. Side-by-side they rode to the palace, a grand thing created from living trees and spun glass.

"But instead of welcoming their son and his bride-to-be with open arms, his parents were furious that the prince would think to take a mere mortal girl as a bride and a future queen of the faerie realm.

"'You must abandon that girl if you wish to be prince,' his father, the faerie king, declared to his son in front of the entire royal court.

"'Kill her. She knows the secret way to get to our palace. She will surely tell other humans,' the faerie queen added, her voice full of hatred.

"The prince and maiden trembled in fear, for they both knew the faerie prince had powerful parents. But not for a moment did the prince think of carrying out his mother's awful decree and they stood with courage in their hearts, hand in hand, before the king and queen.

"You shall not harm her. She is my love and you will have to kill me first,' the prince loudly declared. The entire court erupted in an uproar.

"You cannot tell me what I can or cannot do. I know far better than you what is right for our people,' the queen yelled. As she did so, she shot lightning from her palms toward the maiden. If the girl had been struck, she would have died instantly, her heart stopped by the magic bolt. But instead, the prince, sensing what his mother would do, flung himself in front of the maiden and took the force of the blast. They were both hurled to the far end of the hall. But the prince did not die. Instead, he used all his strength to create a brilliant light, so bright it blinded the entire court. While the fay court couldn't see, the prince and the maiden fled. They traveled back into the woods and to the maiden's home.

"The journey was arduous and the pair were saddened by the exile. They had to travel slowly, since the prince was badly injured, but the maiden tended to his wounds, and eventually he recovered. He glamoured himself to look like a human man so they could live in peace in her village. They were quickly wed and soon the maiden, now a wife, gave her husband children, and the couple spent their days farming and their nights warmed by the hearth with their adoring children surrounding them. Content with his life such as it was, the prince never used his magic again."

When I paused at the end of the story, I noticed Pel staring at me, his eerie green eyes unreadable.

"Where did you hear that tale?" His voice was serious, devoid of the earlier humor and mockery.

"My father told me the story. He used to tell us children lots of stories before . . ."

"It sounds very similar to a story we have."

"Really? What happens in that story?"

"Nothing I want to discuss," Pel said. He didn't snap, but his voice held finality. I wondered if I had accidentally offended him. Perhaps implying a faerie would live like a human was repellent to him. We sat in silence for a while, no noise in the room save for the quiet sound of Pel twisting straw.

As he worked through the pile of bloody straw, the metallic, butcher smell diminished, but the earthy barn smell didn't return. Instead, all I could smell was the cold night air, fresh this far from the city. Finally, Pel spoke up.

"I think that's all I can do," he said, dropping the last golden coil on the pile, which had grown substantially during the hours he had been here. There were heaps of golden ropes scattered throughout the room. A surreal sight.

"How are you feeling?" I asked. Pel looked like he had aged ten years in this one night. Sweat ran down his face and arms, soaking his tunic. My elation at the huge pile of gold soured into guilt at what I had put him through. I should have tossed more straw out the window.

"I've been better," he admitted, though even he seemed impressed with his work. I noticed there wasn't a drop of blood on him, unlike myself, with my blood-soaked bandage and red-stained clothes. Even in this state, he looked unnaturally handsome. I had to stop myself from drawing closer to him.

"Can I get you something?"

"A glass of wine and side of mutton would be lovely," he said ruefully, but he smiled, a tired smile. "Just don't ask me for any more favors little *ladriena*."

"What's *ladriena*?" I asked. The word sounded musical on his lips.

"It means thief."

"Oh." Actually, it didn't sound that nice. I looked out the window. The sky was just starting to lighten, and I worried there wasn't much time.

Pel followed my gaze toward the window. "I should be going."

"Are you sure you're strong enough to fly?" I wished I could offer him some food or something to drink, but even the water I had poured on the petticoats had long-since dried.

For a moment Pel wavered, but then he mustered. He flexed his translucent dragonfly wings. I wanted to touch him, run my hand through his golden hair and caress his high cheekbones and kiss his rose lips. What was I thinking? I barely knew Pel; luring humans into their trust had to be some natural fay talent.

Besides, tonight was likely the last time we'd ever meet.

"I will be fine."

"You look fine," I said before thinking. "I mean, you look tired, but strong." I bit my lip to stop myself from babbling on.

Pel grinned, though it had a hint of sadness about it. "Goodbye, Elenora Molnár. You are an unusual human."

"Will I see you again?" I hated myself for asking but couldn't help it. I looked at the golden thread around my wrist. My wrist still bared an angry red burn line, but it was thin.

Pel's eyes followed my gaze. "Nor, you know how to call on me." He lifted his eyes to meet mine, his strange green eyes burning with something I couldn't name. "I shall come if you so desire."

For an intense moment, I considered asking Pel to take me with him, away from this tower and a plotting prince, and back to the freedom of the woods. *Do not think about running away with a faerie*, I chided myself. "Just in case I need more gold?" I had meant it to be a joke to break the tension, but instead I sounded petty and greedy, and it made me wince.

Pel's bright eyes clouded, and it stung to feel his disappointment. "I've fulfilled my debt to you, Nor. Nothing short of calling my true name would command me to do such labors again."

"And what is your true name?" I asked, my curiosity overtaking my sense of shame.

Pel smiled, his sharp teeth giving it a wicked gleam. I was reminded how wild he looked. "I cannot risk telling you my true name. For a faerie must obey any command that comes from someone using that appellation. We keep our true names hidden. But perhaps we shall meet again."

Pel gazed at me, and again I felt caught in the sparkle of his eyes. Quickly, he leaned over and kissed me on the cheek. His lips were petal-soft and he smelled of the forest after a rain, green and fresh. Before I could react, he backed away and jumped out the window. I saw his wings flash back and forth, shimmering in the pale light of the fading moon, holding him aloft and taking him back toward the Biawood Forest. I watched him go, getting smaller and smaller till he was just a spec on the horizon. A tiny dark spot against the lightening sky. I absently touched my cheek where he had kissed me.

I sat down on the cot, finally feeling the overwhelming fatigue I had staved off while Pel had been with me. I wanted to just lie down and sleep. I figured I could squeeze in a tiny nap before the prince came calling. Chace only knew what chaos that would unleash. But as I was about to lie down, I noticed the pitcher, empty, but still stained with a film of blood on the inside.

I threw the pitcher against the wall. It shattered into fine white shards of jagged pottery. *Perfect*, I thought. Then I lay down on the cot. Though my mind was buzzing with all the events of the last day, fatigue soon won over and I drifted into a deep and dreamless sleep.

Chapter Thirteen

I awoke to the sound of the heavy door to the tower being unlocked. The early morning light was streaming in through the window, and I guessed it was just after dawn. I wasn't sure what to expect, but I jumped to my feet, rubbing the sleep from my eyes. I immediately felt lightheaded and had to brace myself against the wall.

Instinctively, I reached for my dagger, only to remember it wasn't there. Pel must have taken it with him. Not that it would have done any good against a bunch of royal guards.

"Good morning, Lady Elenora, and do you have a pile of gold to—" Casper said as the guards opened the door for him. He stopped midsentence as he took in the room. The piles of golden coils glittered in the morning light. His mouth actually hung open in surprise.

"Why good morning, Your Highness," I said, using a curtsey to cover a yawn. I rose from it carefully, hoping to avoid a dizzy spell. I looked at his face in mock dismay. Even this early he appeared every bit the handsome and regal prince. He was dressed in a red velvet tunic and his black hair was neatly combed beneath his golden circlet. It was annoying how perfectly put together he looked. In contrast, I likely looked more like the images of the fay from the flyers in town; something monstrous with hair sticking out and bloodshot eyes. "What is the matter? Not enough gold for you?"

"You did it. You actually did it!" he shouted. He knelt and picked up a rope of gold, testing it in his hand, confirming it was real.

"You sound surprised," I chided. I sensed my confidence return, as though this were any other scheme I was selling. "Wasn't this what you wanted? Like I told the villagers, it was straw that could be turned into gold." *Slow down*, I warned myself.

"Varin, go fetch Master Dauvet," Casper instructed. His guard gave a curt nod and vanished. Casper was still on his knees, staring at the room of gold.

"Who is Master Dauvet?"

"The court alchemist." Casper didn't even look up at me, too mesmerized by the piles of glittering cord.

"What? You don't trust me?" I said, forcing my voice to remain light. In truth, a knot of anxiety formed in my stomach, as I wondered if the alchemist would find something wrong with the gold.

What if fay gold was different than real gold? *Could I really trust Pel?* He toiled all night to save my life, but still . . . I ran my fingers along the golden thread around my wrist and felt comforted knowing it hadn't changed back into woolen thread. I kept my face blank, revealing nothing.

Casper looked up and I was surprised to see hope on his face. He didn't say anything but began counting the coils on the floor in earnest. I should not have expected anything different and yet, realizing that I was scratched and bloody while this prince just cared about how much gold he now owned had me biting back some smart retort about greed that would undo all the work to get my freedom from this place. Instead, I clenched my fists at my side, only stopping when I noticed my bandage was starting to seep blood. Casper was still counting coils when Master Dauvet arrived. With his disheveled hair and thick glasses, the alchemist looked like he belonged in a university rather than court. There was a bright curiosity to him that made me think of what Finn might look like in a decade or two. He carried a square slate with him, made from some black stone as thick as my thumb.

"Your Highness," Master Dauvet said, bowing low as he approached. He was slightly out of breath and sounded both excited and suspicious. "So, it's true," he said, his eyes, already enlarged from the glasses, grew insect wide as he took in the sight of the room. "I heard your speech last night, but I'll admit I didn't believe that straw could be transformed."

"Is it really gold, Anton?" Casper asked, rising and handing a golden rope to the alchemist.

Master Dauvet studied it for a while. Running the glittering rope of gold through his fingers and even biting down on a small section of it before he carefully scraped an edge of the coil against the stone he was holding. He looked puzzled. "That's strange," he finally said, sounding distant and staring transfixed on the slate before him.

"What is it Anton?" Casper asked, his voice instantly wary.

I wanted to back up, to run. I could barely hear the alchemist over the pounding of my heart.

"Here." Master Dauvet said, showing his tablet to Casper. I leaned in to see. There was a scratch mark on the stone from the golden coil, as bright as if Pel has created a small line of gold directly on the stone. Next to it, I saw several other scratch marks, ones I hadn't noticed before. They were metallic in hue; varying from dull rust to burnished copper.

"What does that mean?" I asked before I could stop myself.

"It can't be real." And there it was. Master Dauvet might as well have issued my death sentence.

"Then what is it?" Casper asked, wariness creeping into his voice.

"No, you misunderstand me," Master Dauvet said. "It is gold, but it's so pure. Note the color on the touchstone," he indicated his slab, "and see how the others aren't as bright? It tells how pure the gold is. Even the purest, most refined gold has some level of imperfection, however slight. But this gold has none." There was an excited gleam in Master Dauvet's face, and I wondered if it was lust for the gold or the secret to creating it.

A hush fell over the room as Casper took in those last words. I started to breathe again; unaware I had ever stopped. A faint trace of apprehension hung in the room, but this prince couldn't imprison me for creating gold that was too pure. At least, I hoped he wouldn't.

Finally, Master Dauvet broke the silence. "I shall assess further in my workshop to confirm, but this may be the purest gold in the known world."

"You did it, Elenora," Casper said, quietly. He appraised the heaps of gold on the floor, and I could sense him calculating the wealth. "You have made Reynallis a rich country again." I had made *him* rich, not Reynallis. I didn't imagine he was about to send this gold to poor peasants, but wisely kept my mouth shut.

"So how did you do it?" Master Dauvet asked. His eyes were shiny with manic energy.

"As I said in the market faire, it's the straw, not me. Blessed by an ancient druid and sown in a field of holy land," I added smoothly, remembering my tale from yesterday. "I just had to concentrate, but the magic itself was in the straw."

"Oh," said Master Dauvet, his face falling. Then he brightened. "Where is this holy land? We shall go and get more immediately. Perhaps other things would grow there as well. We could have trees of golden apples and a ground full of golden potatoes!"

I thought of Pel's worn-out face and my own exhaustion, the smell of my blood covering the straw. Maybe he was right about human greed. "Isn't this enough?"

"It is everything you promised," Casper said, his voice still full of awe. I noticed he couldn't pull his eyes away from the shining coils.

"Yes, of course," Master Dauvet said, trying to placate me. "This is wonderful, truly wonderful. It's miraculous even. But if we knew where the straw came from, then Reynallis would always be well-funded. Perhaps I could even discover the key to the transformation in the straw. Then we could take that and transform anything into gold." I saw his eyes alight at the idea.

"There is no more straw, not like this," I snapped. It was kind of true. I had used up my one favor from Pel, and I wouldn't ask him to do more.

"But even if you don't have any, perhaps you can just tell us where it came from? We can send expeditions out. You would be doing your country a great service."

Think quickly, I told myself. "I would happily tell you where it came from if I knew, but alas, I do not. My father was the only one who knew where to find this straw. He told me that he would confide in me the secret of its source when I was old enough, but sadly that day never came. He died fighting in the Southern War." At least that much was true. I hoped I would not be interrogated about my father after he died serving the crown. "This was all the straw we had left before he died."

Master Dauvet's face fell in disappointment. I thought he might ask more about the straw, the blessed land, and my father, but he surprised me by gently putting his hand on my shoulder. "Your father must have been a brave man and he was an honor to his country and the crown." As if he couldn't help himself, he added, "And now that we know that transformation into gold is possible, we will continue your father's glorious work. Perhaps we can track down his sources or I can find the key in this gold." Master Dauvet suddenly stopped, looking a bit ashamed.

"My father would have been pleased," I lied, suddenly ashamed I had brought my late father into this.

"Yes, Anton, take as many samples as you need," Casper said, handing over several golden ropes to the alchemist, as if he hadn't heard a word I said about my father and the war. "Do whatever tests you see fit to the gold or start expeditions for holy straw or blessed land. Notify me immediately if you make any progress."

I swallowed hard, wondering what the alchemist might discover about the gold.

What if he could detect the blood or the fay magic? I couldn't think about it right then and decided to change the topic. "I am very tired," I said truthfully, and a yawn easily came on cue. I wasn't a pretty sight and felt extremely weak, probably a side effect of the blood loss. "Being up all night working on the straw required great concentration."

To my surprise, Casper nodded, truly looking at me for the first time since he entered the tower. "You look awful."

"I didn't exactly have time for my beauty sleep last night." I had an inkling that I looked terrible, disheveled and covered in scratches, but it still stung to hear him say it. I had never felt the contrast between his royal appearance and my ragged one more acutely.

"I didn't mean it like that," he said, sounding genuinely apologetic. "You just look so pale, and your arm!" he cried, noticing the bloody bandages on my arm. I tried to hide my arm, but I just ended up exposing more of the scrapes I'd received from the rose vines.

Casper was immediately by my side, examining my cut arm. "And you're covered in cuts. What happened?"

"It's nothing, only an accident," I said, glad I had thought this might happen. I pointed to the shards of the pitcher. "I was very tired, scratching myself to stay awake. Then I tripped. I broke the pitcher and cut my arm in the process. I'm probably pale from blood loss." I gave a small smile, as if I did this sort of thing all the time. I hoped the lie would hold.

"Why didn't you call for help? We could have had the royal physician sent up here immediately." Casper gently touched my arm, and I felt a thrill go through me. He seemed so concerned. I forced myself to remember that only the night before he'd been ready to expose me as a fraud in front of the entire court. And he threatened my family. I pushed his hand away.

"I'm fine." But the moment I said it, I was attacked by a bout of lightheadedness and had to sit down or risk falling down.

"You need medical attention and rest. We can discuss everything else later. I can't have my bride-to-be collapsing. Come on," he said, extending his hand to help me up.

Bride-to-be? Is he seriously planning to continue the charade? I bit back a scoff. Silently refusing his assistance, I cautiously got to my feet, taking a slow step to avoid losing my balance. He looked uneasy but did not touch me again. Though I noticed he was never more than an arm's length away from me, as though ready to catch me should I fall. I would be certain not to.

Anton and the guards bowed as we passed. Yanis's brows knit in concern, but he didn't say anything, simply followed behind us. I felt lighter leaving the tower. It had been my prison and I would be happy to never set foot in that room again, not for all the gold in the world. We made our way carefully down the twisting steps and onto the main hallway. Our progress through the palace was slow. I hadn't realized just how weak I was. Casper led me to my rooms from the day before, stopping frequently to allow me to rest against a wall or pillar.

"Rest," Casper commanded when we reached the rooms.

I didn't want to obey anything he told me to do, but the bed looked so inviting and I was so tired that I did not bother to object. The walk from the tower had exhausted me, and simply climbing onto the bed was a struggle.

"Here, let me—" Casper stepped forward, as though to help me on the bed, but I waved him away.

"No," I muttered, finally pulling myself onto the bed. The mattress was so soft and the blankets warm. I would have happily drifted to sleep for a few days, but his words rang in my head. "You weren't serious," I said, though I was already fighting to stay awake. "You called me your bride-to-be. You didn't mean that, did you?"

"Elenora, we can discuss all of this later. For now, just rest. I'll have a physician summoned and a servant bring you something to eat and drink. You may have just saved Reynallis. For that, you deserve to sleep." Hesitating slightly, he held my hand and kissed it. His lips weren't petal-soft like Pel's, but they were warm and strong, and I couldn't deny the thrill that ran up my arm. But I yanked my hand away. It was a weak gesture, but I saw a look of pain flash over his face before he pulled on his mask of courtly grace. It gave me a small sense of satisfaction. "You need to recover. We shall talk later," he said, his words stiffer than before. He turned and left the room.

Chapter Fourteen

When I opened my eyes, it took me a moment to recall where I was. I sat up and immediately felt a sharp pain in my right arm and looked down at clean, fresh bandages.

The room was dark save for the glow from the fireplace, but I remembered that Annabeth had let down the thick, velvet curtains over the windows to block out the light. I had no idea what time of day it was or even if it still was the same day.

Resisting the urge to lay back down and sleep, I pulled off the covers and carefully climbed out of bed. The plush rug beneath my feet staved off the chill of the tile floors and the fire in the fireplace offered pleasant heat after the cold in the tower. I stood there for few minutes, enjoying the warmth.

"Milady," Annabeth said as she entered the room. She smiled broadly at me and gave me a low curtsey, which looked incredibly awkward, as she was carrying several logs for the fire.

"Here, let me help you with those," I said. She recoiled slightly, and I stopped, remembering her inability to accept my help. "How long have I been asleep?"

"Most of the day, milady. It's nearing sundown. I'm glad you're awake. I need to get you ready," Annabeth said, putting the logs down by the hearth.

"Ready for what?" I asked, alarmed. Nothing good had come from Annabeth getting me ready.

"Dinner with his highness, Prince Casper," Annabeth said, sounding almost giddy with excitement as she pulled open the curtains, letting in the evening light. "I imagine you are very anxious to see your betrothed."

Not if I could help it. "News travels fast in the palace."

"Oh yes, everyone is talking about how Prince Casper is taking a commoner for a bride and how she has saved the country by spinning straw into gold so Reynallis will be rich and prosperous again. It is such a deep honor to serve you," Annabeth said in one long breath. Her face had split into a huge grin and she curtseyed again. "So, let's get you ready. I have your gown in the other room."

"Oh no," I said, backing away and thinking about the horrid purple dress. "I am not going to be paraded around like a giant cupcake."

Annabeth smiled. "Don't fret, milady. I promise you that will not happen again. After last night, you are a treasured heroine of Reynallis and our future queen. That makes it far easier getting you better clothes."

"I would still prefer a tunic and trousers."

"That would not be appropriate for the future queen." Annabeth sounded horrified.

I groaned. "For someone who is here to serve me, you are awfully pushy." I knew I sounded petulant, but I didn't care.

"I am making certain you look your best for court. You don't wish to make a fool of yourself. We're all relying on you."

"Relying on me? Who? For what?" I didn't like the sound of that. I didn't need more people depending on me right now. Or ever.

"You're one of us. You will be a queen of the people from the people." In a conspiratorial tone she added, "You know the people better than any high-born noble ever could. Do you understand that?" There were actual tears in Annabeth's eyes, and she was smiling as though she were gazing at a saint and not a petty crook. I wasn't sure what to say. The responsibility I suddenly felt grew a lot heavier. A desire to run welled up in me, almost as strongly as it had the night before.

"I don't think I can do this."

"But I promise you the dress won't have bows," Annabeth pleaded, misunderstanding my distress.

"No," I said, forcing myself to appear calm. "No bows, no gowns. I will not be dressed up to suit a prince who must have only been jesting about marrying a commoner."

"But milady, the prince would never break a promise."

"We'll see about that." And before Annabeth could object, I marched out of the room.

Sir Yanis was waiting outside and raised an eyebrow when I emerged, but upon my request, he escorted me to the prince's chambers without a word regarding my attire.

"We are here, milady." Yanis opened an immense oak door, highly polished and carved with the usual climbing roses.

As I stepped in, Yanis gave a quick bow before heading out. I envied that he got to leave, but I mustered my courage and continued into the room. In front of me was a massive parlor, bigger than all of my rooms combined. Furnished in the traditional red and gold, the room felt regal but warm with a bright fire burning in a large stone fireplace. There were rose stained-glass windows, large oak tables with matching chairs upholstered in red velvet, and a scattering of plush settees in red and gold brocade. Against the far wall was a bookshelf lined floor to ceiling with massive leather-bound volumes. I was awed by the extensive room but, looking around, noticed it was empty.

"Uh, hello," I called out tentatively, right before Prince Casper entered the parlor from what I could only assume was his bedchamber. I hated to admit, but he looked good, very good. He wore a fine black tunic ornately embroidered in gold and a jacket of red velvet with matching gold embroidery. His dark hair was combed back and the gold circlet on his head glittered. He stood tall, and I half expected a white steed to come charging into the room to take him off to a quest involving dragon-slaying and maiden-rescuing.

Most surprising was his smile. I wasn't used to Casper smiling at me, not a genuine smile anyway, and it took me off guard. My traitorous stomach did a flip that had nothing to do with being hungry. But as soon as he saw me, his smile slipped off his face as his brows knotted in confusion.

"Why are you still wearing that?" he asked, eyeing the tunic and trousers with distaste. "I gave orders for you to be provided with appropriate clothing."

"So you did, but I chose the apparel *I* deemed appropriate," I shot back.

For a tense moment, Casper and I stood facing each other. This was the first time I was actually alone with him since our chance meeting in the forest. Casper's expression was unreadable, and I wondered if I had gone too far in my defiance. Perhaps I should have worn the dress.

Finally, he spoke. "I think we have gotten off on the wrong foot." There was no mockery in his voice. "I meant to supply you with court attire, not force you. I shall make note to provide you with more options in the future, so you can find something more to your liking." Before I could ask him what he meant about the future, he gestured to my elbow. "How is your arm?"

"Sore, but it's healing." I rubbed self-consciously at the bandage.

"Would you come with me?" He offered his arm and waited. It was the first request he made to me that did not sound like a veiled threat or demand. I stepped closer and took his arm. Even under the silk and velvet, I could tell his arm was strong and muscular. This was not a prince who simply sat around. Not that I wanted to think about his muscles. I felt my cheeks flush again. I cursed them, but they refused to cool down.

"There aren't any roses," I blurted out upon entering the private dining room. The décor was done in muted greens and browns, not the vibrant reds and golds of the parlor. The large, elegant table was adorned with a pair of silver candelabras and two place settings next to each other, leaving most of the table bare—except for the roast duck with boiled potatoes and gravy, a vegetable tart, some white rolls still steaming with heat and a plate of yellow butter, as well as an opened bottle of wine and a pitcher of water next to two crystal goblets. While the spread was nothing compared to the feast of the night before, it was more than I was used to eating on the best of days. My mouth watered at the fragrant smells of the fresh bread and roasted meat.

"Are you hungry?"

"Famished," I said, realizing it was true. My stomach growled to reaffirm the sentiment.

"It's not much, but I thought it would be a good idea for you and I to have a quiet dinner to discuss matters in private."

"Not much?" I asked, my eyes as wide as the porcelain dinner plates on the table. "This amount of food would have lasted my family for a week, two if we were careful."

"I think you would get tired of it after the first few days," Casper said, chuckling as he pulled out a chair for me. I stiffened, unsure if I was more surprised at his new chivalry towards me or aghast at the casual manner he treated food. "Did I say something wrong?"

"One gets a lot more tired of starving than eating leftovers," I said, sharper than I intended. I knew I should hold my tongue, but he was so infuriating.

"That was inconsiderate of me," Casper said, his voice serious. "I wasn't thinking."

Before I could stop myself, I added, "Well, you need to think about that if you are going to be ruling this kingdom. Most of your subjects are living meal to meal. Regular folk are not waited upon with roast ducks whenever the mood strikes them." I clamped my hand over my mouth, suddenly horrified by what I had said. Criticizing my future king would not bode well for my personal future. "I'm sorry, Your Highness," I whispered. I looked at Casper, terrified he would suddenly demand that I be *complesiled* immediately.

To my vast surprise, he looked thoughtful, worried even. "You're right Elenora. I don't think about my subjects enough. I am not used to thinking of myself as their future king."

"You're not?"

"No. I wasn't supposed to be king."

For long moment, the two of us stared at each other. I knew Casper had not been first in line to the throne, but somehow hearing those words felt like a private confession. I had always assumed monarchs were eager to claim their power, but Casper now appeared as an uncertain young man, his eyes pleading that I understand. I almost pitied him.

Chapter Fifteen

"I am a second son and a third child." Casper paused. He seemed to have lost some of the confidence and easy charm he usually displayed. "I *was* a second son. I grew up knowing Christopher would be king and the crown would pass to his child. And even if something happened to him—" a look of pain flashed across his face, and I remembered King Christopher had died only a few months prior. But in an instant Casper's face was once again composed. "I had assumed Constance would take the throne." There was a slight hardness in the way he said his sister's name.

"Why are you telling me all of this?"

"Because you should know what is going on. I believe we need to understand each other to make this union work."

"Union?"

"Marriage. Two people get together, say some vows and kiss."

"Yes, I know what marriage is," I said, annoyed. "But I didn't think you truly would marry me." Just saying the words out loud sounded ludicrous.

"To be honest, I wasn't. I didn't think you could actually create gold. For that, I am truly sorry, Elenora. I thought you were stealing from my subjects with a made-up story, just as you stole my ring." He gave a pointed glance at the ring on my finger. Feeling caught, I quickly moved my hand under the table. He sighed. "I may not have planned on being king, but I truly do care about the people of Reynallis. And I told those people I would marry you if you spun gold, so I shall."

I laughed. "Oh, you can't be serious."

"I am completely serious, Elenora." The sincerity in his tone was startling.

"No," I said, getting to my feet. I stood too quickly, and a wave of dizziness came over me. Casper rose, but I waved him away, pressing my palms against the table to steady myself. "You threaten my family and parade me around your court to humiliate me. Don't mock me further. I did what you asked. You have your gold. I am leaving." When the world stopped spinning, I turned to go. My stomach growled loud enough for Casper to hear. I didn't care. I turned back and grabbed several of the rolls, still hot, before heading to the door.

"My ring."

I was only a few steps from the door. *Damn.* I had hoped he wouldn't remember. It was the only compensation I would be getting from this harrowing ordeal. "You said I could keep it," I shot back.

"But that was under the assumption you would marry me."

"You can have your stupid ring back." Grudgingly, I trudged back, pulling off the gold signet ring and reluctantly thrusting it on the table.

"Elenora, why don't you sit down and we can discuss this?" Casper gestured to food. "You would at least get a fine meal out of it and the opportunity to turn down a prince. Please."

My stomach growled again. "Fine," I muttered, dropping back into my chair.

I tore into the duck, eating an entire leg of meat within seconds. It was seasoned with a tiny bit of spice I couldn't name, and perfectly plump and juicy. I had never had better, and the food helped clear my head.

"Now, about our betrothal," Casper started.

I downed a large gulp of wine. "Why would you want to marry me?"

"Because I never lie, Elenora." Casper's gaze met mine, and I saw complete conviction in his dark eyes. "I find deceivers foul creatures. I said I would wed you if you created the gold, and so I shall."

I did not mention that he would thus find me a foul creature, but instead countered, "I don't think I'm queen material."

I thought Casper might argue, and maybe hoped he would. Instead, he laughed—a hearty, rich sound.

"Of course, you're not."

"Excuse me?" I said, suddenly annoyed he was so enthusiastically agreeing with me.

"What I mean, is you're not ready to be a queen *yet*. I doubt you've received training for it."

"There weren't a lot of queen lessons for war orphans," I snapped, before realizing what I was saying.

"You're an orphan?" Casper asked, his voice soft and serious.

"Yes." I wasn't sure why I kept talking, but perhaps some part of me wanted Casper to understand what common people had gone through. That or the wine was loosening my tongue. "My father was a miller, but he was enlisted into the Southern War. He died fighting. My mother . . ." I paused, looking for the right words. "There was a bad raid on Venlin, my hometown, near the end of the war." I stared down at my hands. For a moment, I recalled my mother's eyes, staring but not seeing. I forced the image away and willed the tears back. "We lost my sister soon after from an illness we couldn't afford to treat."

"I'm sorry."

Taken aback, I stared at him. He was being sincere. I wasn't sure what I had expected him to say, maybe that my father died an honorable death serving his country or some other meaningless platitude.

"I won't pretend to know what it was like for you, but I do know what it is to be without parents and to lose a sibling."

I had forgotten that Casper, despite being a prince and even a future king, was also an orphan, and not much older than I. His brother had been king since the end of the Southern War, and King Christopher had only just died. Reynallis lost a king, but Casper lost his brother, which I thought was far worse. Their mother, Queen Natalia, had died before I had even been born. Their father, King Charles, had been killed fighting the Faradisians. The realization struck me that Casper had lost his father around the same time I had lost my parents. A strange and sad connection.

"You needed the gold and I created it. You don't have to marry me because of it." I said, suddenly wanting to change the subject

"The people need hope. I saw how desperate the people are as I traveled through Reynallis after my release from Faradisia. I had been held there as a royal hostage after the war. I was treated well, but it was a reminder of the tenuous treaty between us and them."

"I didn't know you had been a hostage," I said, feeling painfully ignorant. Honestly, my family had not cared about a royal second son, not when we were trying to recover from a devastating war. But bits of conversation from the day before started to make more sense. I had not thought to question why Casper had only recently arrived in Sterling.

"For the last five years." Casper must have read into my shocked expression. "It was part of the treaty. Royal hostages were required to ensure peace."

"Your brother sent you to live with the enemy? How could he?" I exclaimed, horrified at the very idea.

"It was a required cost for peace."

"But he was your family," I persisted. "Wasn't there another way?" I could not imagine ever turning my brothers over like that, no matter the cost.

"He did what he had to," Casper snapped, but his voice softened as he continued. "At least he wrote; he didn't pretend I was dead because it was easier to move on that way." Casper closed his eyes and took a deep breath.

"Did your sister . . . ?" I let the words trail off when Casper opened his eyes, the hurt plain on his face, making him look unusually vulnerable.

"Her letters stopped after the first year."

"I'm so sorry." I couldn't think of anything more adequate to say. I found myself wanting to comfort Casper. The world might betray me, but at least my family never would.

"It's fine. I was treated well in Faradisia," Casper said, a bit too briskly. "And once Christopher died, King Jovian allow me to return home." Casper took a few sips of wine as I tried to process all that he was telling me. "People love weddings," he finally added, abruptly shifting back to the topic of marriage. "They are the very epitome of hope."

"Don't you want to marry someone you love?" I blurted out. After what his brother and sister had done, I figured he'd want someone who loved him.

"Love is not the first priority for a royal marriage. And I hear it often comes in time," Casper said, but I could tell he was evading the question.

"You gave this a lot of thought over a single night."

"I didn't sleep much last night," Casper confessed. "Truth is, I haven't slept much since leaving Faradisia. I had not even returned to Sterling when I started getting reports of border raids from the fay." Casper's face darkened. "The faeries killed my brother. If they can kill a king, then no one is safe from them."

"What?" I asked sharply, a quick flood of panic filling my stomach. *Does Casper know about Pel? Is this another elaborate set up?* I cursed myself for forgetting what this prince was capable of.

Casper misunderstood my fear.

"I'm not trying to frighten you, but you should be aware of the situation. It's why I am so desperate to fortify our eastern borders. We have never had good relations with Magnomel, but the fay never launched organized attacks before." Casper added, "I promise, we will have the fay raiders taken care of soon. I've put a bounty on any faerie caught in Reynallis. We can question those we catch, and I am confident the rest will scurry back to Magnomel. I will not tolerate such assault on my people." Casper's eyes were ablaze, and I saw true passion there. He might not have wanted a crown, but he would do everything to protect his people. *He already has*, I thought, remembering that a much younger Casper had left his home to ensure peace.

I thought about Pel's emerald eyes and sly smile. I thought about how he came to my aid in the tower and the smell of the forest and dew he'd brought with him. I couldn't tell Casper about him. And I couldn't protect Pel from being caught if he wasn't careful. I didn't believe Pel could possibly be one of the raiding faeries, but in my mind, I could still see the blood choking the life out of Garin in the woods.

Pel could so easily kill. But he wouldn't have helped me if he were a heartless killer, I reminded myself. But did he know who was raiding our country? Did he know the fay who killed the king?

"But let us not dwell on the problem of the fay. It shall be taken care of now that you have replenished the gold supply to pay for soldiers. Back to the important matter of agreeing to marry the charming and roguishly handsome prince who has just proposed to you." Casper's brilliant smile was back, and I sensed his confident mask returning, though he eyed me carefully, waiting for my response.

"Is that how you propose?" I asked, unable to think of a real answer.

"I didn't think I would have to. But I could get on bended knee if you prefer. Or serenade you with love ballads, but I will warn you, I'm an awful singer."

I felt overwhelmed. I had merely hoped to escape with my life, nothing more, and now Casper was genuinely offering me a crown. "Can I think about it?"

Casper's smile dimmed. "Elenora, I promised to wed you in front of the entire court and half the city of Sterling. Think of how it would look if you refused."

"Maybe you should have asked me first before making such an announcement," I spit back. "You might be a prince, but I'm not going to marry you simply so you don't look a fool."

"Elenora, that's not what I meant." But I snorted, knowing that was exactly what he meant. He studied me for a moment, carefully laying out his next words. "I doubt anyone else will give you a better offer. I can give you a throne, plus I can provide well for your family. I know your parents are gone, but you have your brothers. I can ensure them great futures."

"And are they safe?" I asked, suddenly praying for a good answer. I hadn't dared to even mention my brothers in front of Casper, but I was desperate to know how they were.

He looked guilty. "I did not send any guards after them. And I am sorry I threatened them. But I promise you, I can give you and them a better life."

I hadn't thought about what this would mean to them. If I were suddenly rich and powerful, if I had the ability to not only spare them from the crown's punishment, but to actually give them the life of nobility, was there any reason strong enough not to?

"If you agree to marry me, the brothers of the future queen will be given lands, titles, wealth. If you wish to provide for them, there is no better way."

"Are you trying to bribe me?"

"I certainly am. Is it working?"

"Maybe," I admitted, considering these possibilities. Devon would never have to worry about taking care of us, Finn could be the scholar I knew he should be, and little Jacobie would never again cry because he was hungry. I could make all of that possible. And why not? I felt a pain knowing that it was too late to help Rilla. If she were still alive, I could imagine her in rich velvet dresses, smiling in the carefree way she used to before our parents died and she took ill. She had always been so beautiful, and with wealth added to that, she would have drawn the eye of every nobleman in Reynallis. I would never be able to help her now, but I could do something for my brothers.

"I want to see my family."

"Of course. I will send word immediately throughout the kingdom that they are to be welcomed guests at the Rose Palace. *Real guests.*" He colored slightly, and I wondered if he was thinking about his initial 'invitation' for me to come to the palace.

"You realize I don't know the first thing about being queen." It was madness that I was even considering his offer. But if I could pull this off, it would be the greatest scheme of my life. It would also reap a lifetime of rewards.

"You know how to negotiate, so that's a good first start. And Constance and Flora can teach you the rest."

I grimaced. "Your sister hates me, and not even a room full of gold will change that."

"She might, but that doesn't mean she won't make an excellent teacher. She was raised to be a princess. By the Mother's maids, she could have been a queen."

"Why did she choose to pass the crown to you?" I asked, curiosity getting the better of me as I recalled the royal siblings' argument.

"Being king or queen means there are certain expectations one must yield to. Constance could have been queen, but that would have required her to find a husband and create an heir." Casper trailed off. I didn't push him for details, but I remembered the soft looks Constance gave Flora when she thought no one was looking. I felt a bit warmer to Casper. I was impressed despite myself that Casper would take such care of his sister after her neglect of him.

"You are taking on a lot in her place," I said, but Casper only waved his hand, as though assuming kingship was no monumental task.

"Elenora, you said you would consider my offer. I want you to be my queen. Please say you will."

"What happened to having some time to decide?"

"It has been minutes," Casper complained. "I am a royal prince. I am used to getting what I want."

"It's a grand offer, but I need more than a few minutes, even if it's just to figure out that I'll never find a better offer."

"Can I just tell you that you won't?" he asked, giving me his most charismatic smile. He was a hard one to say no to, but I persisted.

"I need more time. You have no idea how strange this is."

"All right, but I will warn you now, the longer you stay here, the more charming I'll become." With that, he reached for my hand. His hands were soft and warm. I realized that my own tanned hands probably felt terrible, roughly calloused. He moved closer to me as he slipped the signet ring back on my finger. He was so close to me; I could smell him. He smelled of cinnamon and cloves. It was a rich, almost spicy smell, though nothing like the forest smell of Pel. But he was still intoxicating, and so close.

"I have no doubt," I said, a bit weakly. I felt the familiar rush of starting a new scheme, but this time, I would have to fool an entire kingdom.

Chapter Sixteen

asper meant what he said. The next morning, I awoke to see
my room filled with roses. Dozens of vases, all overflowing
with sweet smelling blooms at the height of perfection in
all shades of pink, orange, white, peach, and of course, red. It was a
sight to behold, but rather overpowering on the olfactory senses. I
sat up in bed and started sneezing.

"Milady, are you all right?" Annabeth asked. She had been
tending to the fire and looked up in concern.

"It's a lot of flowers," I confessed once the sneezing stopped.
I sniffled slightly. The cloying scent of so many roses somehow
reminded me of the smell of blood in the tower. I stifled that
thought.

"I know, isn't it beautiful? Prince Casper insisted that your chambers be filled with the most perfect blooms," Annabeth replied, clearly missing the note of derision in my remark. "And we all had to be ever so careful not to wake you while bringing in the vases."

"Yes, very beautiful. The prince is indeed extravagant with his gestures," I reluctantly agreed. "Perhaps next time he could wait till I had woken up and had a very strong cup of tea before trying to woo me. They may be a bit much for one room. I'm used to fresher air," I added, thinking about nights spent outside under the stars.

"Oh, don't fret, milady, there are more in your parlor and in the bathing room." Annabeth smiled broadly and I had to withhold a groan.

"I may have trouble getting around with so many vases to trip over," I said, pulling myself out of bed. I had to mentally pry myself from its embrace. After all, strong tea would not come to the bed.

"Here, milady," Annabeth said, handing me a brocade dressing gown that I slipped on over my nightgown. "Your breakfast is laid out for you in the parlor. Then I can help you dress." She paused, looking at me expectantly.

I sighed. If I were to play the role of future queen, I would need to look the part. "Fine, I'll wear a gown." Annabeth looked delighted. I narrowed my eyes at her. "But no bows."

"No bows," she agreed solemnly. "Now, you should eat. I was told to have you ready to meet Lady Flora in an hour."

"They aren't wasting any time," I said, making my way into the parlor. Just like my bedchamber, roses adorned every free space, and I nearly knocked over a vase of creamy blossoms while getting to the table. But all thoughts of roses faded when I looked at the breakfast laid out before me. There was a silver pot of steaming tea with a saucer of cream and a small jar of sugar. A plate was piled high with hot biscuits, and there was butter and jam, honeyed ham, fried eggs, fresh figs and a creamy bowl of porridge with maple syrup.

"Is this all for me?"

"Of course it is, milady. I didn't know what you would like, so I wanted to ensure there was enough variety to suit you."

"This is far too much food," I protested. If I kept eating meals like this, I would surely double or triple in size. I wondered how Casper managed to stay as lean as he did. Probably lots of riding around rescuing damsels in distress. Or whatever it was that princes did. "Would you like some?"

"Oh, I couldn't," Annabeth said. "It wouldn't be right."

Annabeth refused to eat anything, but I made her promise to take her pick once I was done, and ensure the rest went to servants who would appreciate the good food. I devoured my breakfast, trying not to dwell on thoughts of my hungry brothers as I ate mouthfuls of hot ham and sweet biscuits. It almost worked. I ate far more than I needed and felt too full but immensely satisfied. I'd have to show more restraint in the future. There was still plenty of food left untouched on the table. I hoped Annabeth would enjoy some of it once I left to meet with Flora.

After breakfast, Annabeth gleefully led me to the bathing room. True to his word, Casper made sure I was provided with a variety of dress options. Laid out on the chair next to the vanity were three gowns, one sky blue, the second a rich brown, but it was the third that immediately drew my eye. It was an ornate, raw-silk dress in gray, shot through with silver. Even I had to admit it was a stunning gown, and far more elegant that the lilac monstrosity I had destroyed. Tiny seed pearls were sewn into the embroidery on the hem and sleeves, and silver lace trimmed the low neckline. On the vanity was a pair of silver hair combs set with pearls alongside a matching silver necklace consisting of thin silver threads beaded with more seed pearls. A pair of matching gray slippers had been placed next to the dress. Fortunately, their heels were far shorter than the ones from the first night.

I stood, staring at the dress, too stunned to speak.

"Gifts from his highness," Annabeth said, grinning. "He seems set on impressing you." Silently, I pointed to the gray dress. Annabeth nodded in approval.

I noted that the dressed laced up the back, tied by a silver ribbon. With dismay, I saw Annabeth pull out petticoats and a corset from a large dresser. *To play the part you must look the part,* I reminded myself. "Please make sure I can breathe this time."

When Annabeth had me dressed and looking as respectable as possible, I examined myself in the large silver mirror. I didn't recognize the girl who stared back. She appeared as a lady with her straw-blonde hair tied up in intricate braids and her wide brown eyes flecked with gold. I had never noticed the gold in my eyes before, but I had never had such a fine mirror to examine myself in, either. I was used to looking like a boy in comfortable but shapeless tunics and trousers, worn hand-me-downs from Devon, but between the corset and the fine tailoring of the dress, I actually had a waist, hips, and even some cleavage, though thankfully not the bulging amount from the night of the feast. The dress was cut lower that I would have liked, with silver lace covering my chest, but Annabeth assured me it was all the fashion right now. The necklace twinkled in the morning light.

The lady in the mirror might be the type who would live in a folktale and marry a prince. But where was I? What happened to the miller's daughter who got by on wits, luck and sleight of hand? And would anyone care if that girl was gone? What had she been good for anyway? Conning old women out of their meager pensions? My brothers were the only ones who would care, and I tried not to dwell on the anxiety they must be going through. I would make sure to get word to them . . . just as soon as I knew what I was doing.

Yanis was again waiting outside my door. He nodded with quiet approval, and I could tell he also was happier to see me in something other than a blood-stained tunic, before he led me through the obstacle course that was the palace.

"How long does it take one to get a sense of direction in this place?" I finally asked after we had gone through so many corridors and stairwells that I was completely lost.

"Only took me three months, milady," Yanis answered. "But I am a quick study."

"Wonderful," I said, following him along. "Someone should make a map of the palace." Yanis chuckled. At long last we finally stopped in front of a large oak door at the end of a corridor. I couldn't differentiate this door from all the others we had passed, but Yanis seemed confident that we had arrived at the right place. He took up his post by the door and gestured for me to go inside.

Plastering on a smile full of confidence I did not quite feel, I pushed open the door and entered an elegant parlor. In the center of the room was Lady Flora arranging silver cutlery on a table that had been set for two. Unfortunately, Princess Constance was occupying the other seat. The two were deep in conversation. I hung by the doorway, waiting for them to notice me.

"I see no reason you need to bother yourself with my brother's whims on this," Constance said, picking up several pieces of the flatware and examining them.

"It is no bother to me to spend a few hours with the girl. I worry she might feel out of place," Flora said, her voice calm and serene.

"Because she is; she does not belong here," Constance retorted. I felt my cheeks burn as I realized she was referring to me.

"All the more reason to help her." Flora gently pulled the flatware from Constance's grip and laid the spoons and forks back in their places on the table. "And besides, he is to be king. I do not wish to defy my future king over such a minor task."

"*Your* future king?" Constance asked, her voice no longer harsh, but with something that almost seemed hopeful.

"Maybe," Flora said carefully. "If my uncle can be persuaded that I need not return."

"We will persuade him. He must see you are not held here against your will." There was a warmth in Constance's voice that she reserved for the Faradisian woman alone.

Flora looked away and saw me standing by the door. She let out a slight gasp, and I felt a flush of embarrassment, as it must look like I was eavesdropping. Probably because I was. But Flora recovered quickly, giving me a gracious smile. "Welcome, Lady Elenora."

"Lady Flora, Princess Constance," I muttered while giving a clumsy curtsey. "I didn't want to interrupt."

"Of course not," Constance snapped, her gaze following Flora's. I saw no kindness in Constance's eyes. "Flora, I suggest you count the silver before she leaves." Constance abruptly stood, sweeping past me in a rustle of velvet skirts. "I doubt you have what it takes to stay at court long." And then she was gone.

Flora waited for a breath before saying "The Princess has a lot on her mind right now. Please, don't take it personally. Come in. I am so glad you could make it," Flora said, looking up at me and smiling warmly. Flora was stunningly beautiful in a deep turquoise dress that complimented her complexion and polished pieces of turquoise braided into her rich black hair.

She set down the spoon she had been placing and came over to me, giving me air-kisses on both cheeks. I returned the air-kisses, feeling acutely self-conscious.

"Thank you for helping to, umm, teach me about all this," I said, gesturing vaguely around. "I don't have to tell you how new it all is to me." Constance probably was right about me, I thought, looking bewildered at all the utensils piled around the plates.

"Do not worry. I have wonderful etiquette. I promise you will pick it up in no time."

"You're from Faradisia?" Flora stared at me, and I feared I had accidentally offended her. "I'm sorry. Did I say something wrong?"

"Oh no," Flora said, collecting herself. "Yes, I'm from Faradisia."

"Why are you here?" I asked. As soon as I said it, I realized it sounded bad, but Flora did not look upset.

"I was sent here as a hostage."

"A hostage?" I gasped, looking anew at this girl. First Casper and now Flora? How many hostages were still being held from a war that ended years ago? "But the war has been over for so long." It had been awful to leave my home, but at least my siblings had been with me. And here Flora was all alone, long after peace had been declared.

Flora laughed, a musical little laugh as though I had said something amusing. "I was sent here after the war as a permanent guest of the court of Reynallis to ensure that Faradisia keeps to the peace treaty. I am a member of the Domus Ante Solis family. My uncle is King Jovian."

"I'm so sorry," I said, not sure what else to say.

I recalled the note of hurt in Casper's voice when he had told me of his time as a hostage, even if he had been 'treated well.'

"Oh no, I didn't mean to make it sound like a bad thing. Keeping the peace is of the highest importance. And I love it here." She looked towards the door and smiled. I wondered if she was thinking about Princess Constance. Perhaps Flora truly did want to stay. "Now please, come and have a seat. I have our first lesson laid out for you."

I followed Flora to the table and sat down. A cream-colored linen tablecloth had been laid over the table and the two place settings looked like someone had elegantly piled every piece of cutlery and flatware they possessed. Several plates were stacked on top of each other, with the smaller plates on top. There was a silver goblet, but also a delicate crystal glass. A small bowl sat above the plates and it was all surrounded by silver forks, knives and spoons of various sizes.

"I don't want to sound rude, so please let me know if you already know this," Flora said cautiously, "but do you know the correct order to use your utensils and plates? You seemed a bit *overwhelmed* at the Spring feast."

"That is the nicest way anyone has ever told me my behavior was an utter disaster," I said with a laugh. "But seriously, who needs a dozen spoons to eat a meal?" I couldn't help but calculate the cost of so many silver utensils. So much wealth wasted. No wonder the coffers had been empty.

"In the Rose Palace, many spoons are needed. And forks and knives," Flora informed me. "But do not worry. It is not very difficult once you get used to it. And if you forget, just work your way from the outside in. Now, this is the bread knife, and that's why it's on this tiny plate. It is the bread and butter plate."

And so it went. For someone who could seamlessly palm a coin and remember almost every face in a crowd, I turned out to be a painfully slow learner when it came to fancy table manners and etiquette. Flora was patient with me, never scolding but kindly reminding me I was using the wrong wine glass or that the fish fork was not to be used during the meat course. I couldn't see the practical point in it, and as such, had an awful time trying to commit the intricate rules to memory. After a few hours, I was finally able to identify at least some of the cutlery and the basics of serving tea.

When Flora started explaining the crests and mottos of the noble families, I perked up. I knew that the three intertwined red roses on a gold background was that of the royal house, as that symbol was etched into the signet ring I wore. I was interested to learn that Flora's family's crest, House of the First Sun, was an orange sun on a white background. But after another dozen or so noble family crests, I started to lose focus and they blurred together in a mass of lions, eagles and bears.

A knock at the door startled me so much I spilled the tea I had been pouring. I mopped up what I could as Flora's maid answered the door. Sir Yanis was standing outside.

"Pardon my interruption," Yanis said with a bow, "but I was instructed to take Lady Elenora back to her chambers so she could rest before dinner."

Eagerly, I set the teapot down and stood up. "Thank you, Lady Flora. I am certain I shall be far less of a disaster now."

"My pleasure," Flora said, also rising and seeing me to her door. "You will have a wonderful chance to show off your new skills tonight."

I gulped. I hadn't thought that I would need to eat in front of the court tonight. I had rather been hoping for another private dinner with Casper or ideally a plate of food in my room. Foolish thought, I knew. Why would I have been taking lessons all day just to sit in my room?

As if sensing my discomfort, Flora added, "And don't worry. If you don't know what to use, just look at the person next to you."

"Oh, I'm not worried. I know it will be delightful," I lied, as I followed Yanis out the door.

Chapter Seventeen

I allowed a servant to pull out my chair before I sat down next to Casper. Under the pretense of adjusting my skirts, I took several steadying breaths and slipped on a mask of confidence, the same face I used to sell 'magic' elixir or read fortunes. It was all about convincing those around me that I knew what I was doing. And I could use any advantage at my disposal with tonight's audience.

We were in a smaller dining room than the feast hall, though it was still a massive room with six or seven large tables, all full of nobility in a dazzling array of finery. Gazing down at my own silver gown, I wondered if it ever became ordinary to dress like this every night. Casper still sat at the head of the main table, with me to his left and Constance to his right, her annoyance clear in the way her lips formed a tight line every time she glanced my way. Flora sat next to her, looking lovely and serene, and I was relieved there was at least one kind face at the table.

But next to her sat Ilana, unfortunately stunning in an ice-blue dress that set off her eyes. She smiled pleasantly, but I could sense the venom behind it. Next to her was an older man, the one who had pointed out that I was wearing the Prince's ring at the market faire. He wore a blue doublet embroidered with a yellow eagle and velvet jacket. I imagined he had been very handsome in his younger days, and while still attractive, was letting himself go as his gut suggested.

This is going to be a very long night, I thought, but I fixed on a smile anyway, wearing it as defense.

"Good evening, Lady Elenora," Casper said, as I sat down. "I hope you had a pleasant day with Lady Flora." For just a moment Casper looked concerned, and I wondered if he thought I might eat the food with my fingers or slurp the soup. *I should*—it would serve him right for setting me at a table with Ilana. But I thought about Flora, noting that my behavior would reflect on her tutelage, and reluctantly nodded my head.

"Lady Flora was very instructive and most patient with me. I'll admit that I am not used to having so many forks at one sitting. Usually, one is enough for me."

"Oh dear," Ilana said. Her voice was light, but her eyes steely. "You will have a lot to learn. *You poor thing*. I can't even imagine how awful it must have been growing up under such unfortunate circumstances."

My blood began to boil at her mockery of my life, and her feigned concern. "Well, it is the life of many of the subjects of this great kingdom, and far better than many," I said, staring straight into her cold blue eyes.

"Lady Elenora was an excellent pupil," Flora said, cutting in. "I am sure she will feel at ease here in no time."

"Only thanks to your tutelage, I would wager," Constance said, giving Flora an affectionate pat on her hand.

Delightful, I thought. *The food has not even been served and I have already been attacked by two people at the table.* As if sensing my distress, Casper's hand found mine under the table and gave it a reassuring squeeze. His hand was soft, but strong. I hated to admit it, but the small gesture did calm me a bit.

"Where are my manners?" Casper suddenly asked. "I don't believe you have been properly introduced to everyone. You know Princess Constance and Lady Flora. This is Lady Ilana Oleshin, of the House of the Silver Star in Glavnada, and Duke Samuel Arnette of the Aigles En Vol House. Samuel was a good friend of my father and has been a trusted advisor to my family for years."

"It is a pleasure to meet you, Duke Arnette," I said, focusing on the duke and not Ilana.

"The heroine of Reynallis, the pleasure is all mine, I assure you," he said with a genuine smile, which further eased my nerves. "You clean up well. Compared to the faire." Though there seemed no malice in his words, my cheeks flamed. I would bet the tower room of gold that he never had to wonder where his next meal was coming from. "And please, call me Samuel. Casper and Constance are as dear to me as my own children, and I hear you will be officially joining their family. The Famille De Rose ring looks quite good on you." He gave an exaggerated wink, and I shot Casper a desperate look.

"Nothing has been officially announced Samuel," Casper said smoothly.

"What do you mean, *nothing?*" the older man said, laughing. "You announced it to the entire bloody court two nights ago. You're not getting cold feet, are you Lady Elenora? Has Casper scared you away already? He's not so bad," Samuel was smiling, and I knew he was joking, but I felt a knot of anxiety to be questioned about Casper's proposal. I wanted to be sure I could pull off such a deception before accepting his offer. I wasn't there yet.

"What a glowing account you give of me," Casper said, with his effortless charm. "Lady Elenora has had to go through a lot of changes over just a few days. I would like to give her some time to adjust to this new life before we move forward with any . . . future plans." I smiled at Casper, the knot of anxiety uncoiling slightly.

"Very well, but I'd advise to get it all settled before your coronation. It's only a few months till the summer solstice, and your subjects want the stability of knowing there is a future queen by your side. Too many have been questioning if you will live up to Christopher's legacy." The duke gave an affectionate pat to Casper's shoulder, something that seemed almost fatherly concern.

"I am doing my best," Casper said, but I noticed the tightness in his words.

"Of course you are," Duke Arnette agreed, oblivious to Casper's discomfort. "But your brother, he ended a war, brought peace to Reynallis. He was larger than life. And that is a lot to live up to."

"Sometimes I still cannot believe he is truly gone," Ilana said wistfully. "There will never be anyone quite like him."

For a moment, I saw Casper's confidence mask slip as he bit his lip and quickly squeezed his eyes closed. Why did no one notice what these comparisons were doing to him?

"King Christopher was not some sort of god," I quipped, not sure why I felt the need to defend Casper. All eyes turned to me, a mix of shock and surprise, probably because none of them expected that I, a lowly commoner, would dare contradict them. That thought goaded me on. "Well, he wasn't. The poor still struggled to eat, and coin to fix the cities' war damage never came as promised. So maybe stop acting like Casper is living in the shadow of some perfect king. Can't you see it makes him nervous?"

"Elenora, I don't need you to defend me," Casper snapped. I turned to him, startled by the anger in his words. "My brother was a great king."

I bit back a number of sharp retorts. *Fine*, I fumed. *I won't help you, you royal brat.*

"I think it is such a wise idea to take things slowly," Ilana said. Her voice was sticky-sweet, making me want to punch her. She was clearly enjoying our fight. "There must be so many new things and customs strange for you, as a commoner, to learn now that you are in the palace."

"I shall manage," I said, feeling defiant. "After all, you seem to have managed learning Reynallis customs, which must be new and strange for a foreigner. I might be common, but at least I have the advantage of growing up in Reynallis. I don't know what I'd do if I had to learn all the ways of Glavnada. Is it true that you eat raw reindeer meat in the winter?" I asked, smiling sweetly.

"Of course not," Ilana retorted, her face growing pink. I enjoyed my tiny triumph, until Casper kicked me under the table.

"What?" I asked, but before Casper could say anything, the doors to the dining room flew open. Master Dauvet burst in.

"I had an idea," Master Dauvet stated to the room at large. The alchemist looked like he had fallen into a haystack before barging in. Straw clung to his clothes and stalks stuck out of his hair at haphazard angles. I kept my face neutral, but my heart hammered. Could he have discovered my deception?

"What is going on?" Constance demanded.

"Your Highness," Master Dauvet added, dropping into a hasty bow, which caused bits of straw to go flying. "Pardon my intrusion, but I came up with a theory to test the straw."

"And it couldn't have waited till after dinner?" Constance asked, not amused.

"It's all right, sister. I instructed Anton to come see me the moment he discovered something about the straw," Casper said, trying to appease his sister.

Around me, there were murmurs, whether of excitement or irritation I wasn't sure. The knot of anxiety reformed in my stomach, tighter this time.

"I thought I might try to recreate the situation that caused the straw to be, shall we say, malleable, in the first place." He pulled out a fistful of straw from his pocket. "Here!" he said, as proudly as if he had pulled out a pocket full of gold instead.

"So you have straw?" Constance gave voice to the bemused feeling in the room.

"Not ordinary straw," Master Dauvet insisted. "I had Father Geoffroi bless the straw. He used the book of the Holy Family and prayed over it. Maybe this straw can also be transformed." Master Dauvet held the straw out to me.

"I don't know if that will work . . ." I quickly interjected, leaning away from the straw as if it could reveal what a fraud I was.

"It couldn't hurt to try," Casper said, eyeing the straw. "After all Elenora, what's the worst that could happen?"

You could find out I was making up everything and working with your enemy, I thought, but didn't say. Instead, I took the straw from Master Dauvet. Everyone in the room stared intently at me. *It's just another deception, another show*, I reminded myself, but my hands shook slightly anyway. I closed my eyes, as though concentrating on a task I might actually be able to achieve. It was easier than looking into the expectant faces. I began to twist the straw between my fingers, mimicking Pel's movements from the tower. I took several long breaths, drawing out the moment, all the while twisting the straw with my fingers. Finally, I opened my eyes and forced myself to look surprised that there was still straw in my hands. I sighed, forcing myself to sound defeated, before handing the mashed straw back to Master Dauvet.

"I'm sorry, but it just won't work," I said, making my voice sound contrite.

Master Dauvet's face fell as he took back the straw, but he added, "No worries. This was only the first of many experiments."

Stifling a groan, I took a long drink of wine. "But hopefully the gold now in Reynallis's coffers will suffice," I said, annoyed that my work from the tower could be overlooked so easily. Well, *Pel's work*, really.

"It certainly will," Casper cut in quickly, looking at me intensely with dark eyes. Then he smiled. My stomach did a flip that had nothing to do with the straw.

"Then I shall leave you to your meal. Please pardon my interruption," Master Dauvet said, and quickly left the room, trailing straw in his wake. The conversation shifted to a discussion of repairing war-torn Reynallis with my gold. Even Constance looked happy about the idea.

"We are planning to start right here in Sterling."

"That's unbelievably selfish and an awful idea," I said before I could think better of it. My mind flashed back to my childhood home—burned fields and smashed buildings. I had been in the south of Reynallis last winter, the villages there had never recovered from the ravages of the war.

"How dare you," Constance snapped, her eyes filling with anger. Everyone was staring at me, most agog with surprise at my multiple rude outbursts. Flora looked concerned and Ilana was smirking.

"I'm sorry, I didn't mean . . ." I started, but then I stopped. "No, actually, I'm not sorry. The war wasn't fought in Sterling or anywhere in the northern territories. Have you been to the cities near the southern borders? That's where the real fighting happened. I've seen it. I *lived* it. People in those towns need assistance far more dearly than here. Five years later and people still live crammed together or in the streets because homes were destroyed. If you want to make a show of being a leader, go ahead, but if you really want to restore Reynallis, then maybe you should start where she's actually hurting."

My eyes were burning with tears. I knew I was making a scene and that I should have just kept my mouth shut, but I couldn't. The hypocrisy of the nobility pretending to care when they simply wanted to polish their already shiny city sickened me.

I stood abruptly, trying to ignore the stares of those at the table and the courtiers around the room. Not sure what else to do, I fled the room.

I ran blindly down the hallway. There had to be a way out of this Chace-forsaken palace. Tears were streaming down my cheeks and a panic was starting to well up within me. Not only had I embarrassed myself, but I had insulted the crown prince. I doubted he'd still be so willing to make me his queen, room of gold or not. I desperately needed to escape.

Turning quickly down a mirrored hallway, I slipped on the sleek marble title and went sprawling on the floor. I yelped as pain shot up my wounded arm. Struggling to my feet, I continued on, eventually finding a small corridor that led outside the palace and into the rose garden. I let out a breath and immediately felt better in the openness of the outdoors. I made my way past the rose garden till I reached a small grove of maple trees. I did not want to be easily found should Casper send guards after me.

I stomped through the trees as I inhaled the crisp spring air. My heartrate slowed as the intense anger seeped out of me, replaced by my old disappointment in the noble classes. What had I expected of them after all? That because a commoner had given them a room of gold that they would suddenly care about us? Did I really want to become like that?

Maybe I didn't have to. I pulled out one of the silver combs in my hair, the tines sharp enough that when I jabbed it on the pad of my thumb, a bead of dark blood welled up. I quickly wiped the blood along the band of gold on my wrist and waited.

Soon the familiar burning lit up the gold, though it was not as intense as the night in the tower. And almost as quickly the heat was extinguished. I sat on a nearby stump and waited, wondering if Pel would indeed show, and what I would say to him if he did.

"You summoned me?"

I startled at his voice. He had been so silent I had not heard him approach, but turning, I saw he was right behind me. He seemed to glow in the moonlight. My heart ached at his beauty.

"Did the little *ladriena* miss me already?" Pel's eyes sparkled.

"Hey, you don't need to call me that. I haven't stolen anything, at least not today."

Pel gave a mocking bow, but his lips quirked up in a crooked grin. "My apologies, Nor. I must have been woefully mistaken."

"Indeed, I gave up a life of crime and deception yesterday." My voice grew bitter as I added, "I traded it for lessons on excessive flatware and listening to preening nobility complimenting themselves on their self-serving interests. I should never have trusted them, not for a moment."

Pel studied me with his green cat-eyes. "Come with me, Nor. Let me take you away." The playful mockery was gone from his voice, replaced with a deep sincerity. I took a step towards him. He stretched out his dragonfly wings, like spider-spun crystals in the moonlight. "I could fly you far away from here."

"Where would we go?" I asked, almost ready to flee the petty court. This close to him, I smelled his fresh forest scent. It reminded me of nights under the stars and cool-running streams. There was a wicked edge to his grin, his white teeth so sharp that he looked feral. After a day confined in palace walls, I drank in the wildness that was Pel.

"Magnomel."

The dangerous word broke whatever spell his offer made. I backed up too quickly, slamming into a tree branch, but I barely felt it. "You were escaping Magnomel," I argued. "No humans ever return from the faerie kingdom."

"That's not what I—" Pel started but stopped abruptly. His voice became gentle, the same coaxing he used when I was injured in the woods. "True, I am avoiding Queen Marasina, but she does not have eyes in all of Magnomel. I can take you somewhere out of her reach. You would be safe, I promise. And you would be free to be yourself, not having to hide your beautiful spirit to satisfy some ungrateful prince. Come with me, Nor. Let me show you." Pel reached out his hand to mine, his long, slender fingers so inviting. Part of me wanted nothing more than to weave my fingers with his, escape with him into the night. I allowed myself a few seconds to enjoy the fantasy before I pulled back.

"I can't Pel, not right now."

Pel looked as though I had struck him, hurt clear in his slitted eyes. "Is the prince's wealth worth so much to you?"

"No," I snapped, stung. "My brothers. They would never be able to find me. Right now, there are royal guards seeking them, to tell them I'm at the palace. I need to get my family back together."

Pel's features softened, the hurt replaced by a thoughtful look. "And once you are reunited with your family?"

"Then . . . I don't know. I would have to think about it."

"Always weighing your options, little *ladriena*. You are a crafty, clever human." But Pel's lips twitched up.

"Someone needs to have a plan."

"I am sure you have many plans, Elenora Molnár." Pel moved towards me, faster than should be possible. His petal-soft lips were on mine, the kiss making my pulse race. He tasted like honey and berries, sweet with something sharp underneath. The kiss only lasted for a moment, but my lips tingled, even as he pulled away. He paused, studying my face. "I hear your little prince is about to become king."

"He is," I said slowly, still dazed from the kiss.

"And when will that be?"

"The summer solstice. It's tradition in Reynallis to have coronations on the longest day of the year." I studied his beautiful face, feeling a strange sliver of suspicion. "Why do you ask?"

"Because I need to know how much time I have."

"Time?"

He smiled, such a dazzling smile that I felt lost in it. "I won't press you for an answer now, Nor. But I promise I will be back for you. And I will be back before the prince is crowned."

As he flew off into the night, the longing to be with the strange fay boy did not leave me.

I leaned against a large aspen tree, stalling my return to the palace. I dreaded the confrontation with Casper but saw no way around it.

This can be temporary, I reminded myself. Once my brothers were found, when my family was reunited, then I could decide what to do. I rubbed the gold around my wrist. It was a strange comfort to know Pel would be returning. He was right about me, always weighing my options. Eventually, with no better plan, I made my way back to the Rose Palace.

I was passing by the rose gardens when I saw Casper approaching. Spotting me, he strode over to meet me. I took a fortifying breath, preparing for him to yell about the scene I had caused. Maybe he would call off the engagement. Maybe he would take more drastic measures; I had seen the results of Casper feeling humiliated before.

The yelling never came.

"There you are." He sounded slightly breathless, as though he had been running. "I have been looking all over for you. Are you all right?" His concern took me by surprise.

"Do you care?" I hadn't meant for such a sharp response, but I said it without thinking.

Casper seemed to brace himself. "Let's take a walk."

"Are you going to punish me?"

Casper laughed, but then saw I was serious. "What? Why would you say that?"

"I insulted you in front of the court. I'm pretty certain I'm not supposed to do that."

Casper sighed, running his hand through his dark hair. "I can send you to the dungeon if you like, but I thought a walk in the gardens might be more pleasant."

I had barely glanced at the gardens when I first ran out, but now I had time to study them. The gardens were a lovely sight, even at night, the soft scent of roses and grass pleasantly fresh. The moon was bright, just starting to wane, and gave us plenty of light to walk among the hedge mazes and blooming bushes. In the moonlight, everything was silver and gray, a softer version of the explosion of color during the day.

"What does this place look like when the roses aren't in bloom?" I asked as Casper led me down a stone walkway lined with climbing white roses.

"I wouldn't know."

"Huh?"

"The royal family usually winters further south, in Lotanus. We have a winter palace there."

The mention of the south brought back the conversation from dinner, and I stilled, anxiety coming back in waves. As if sensing my apprehension, Casper led me to a small stone bench and sat down next to me.

"I'm not angry with you," he said, taking hold of my hands.

"You're not? Why aren't you?"

"Because what you said wasn't a bad idea." My eyebrows shot up in surprised. "I'll admit that it was rather lacking in tact, well, it was entirely tactless. And I can't have you scream at me and run out of the room every time you have an opinion that's different from mine. But that doesn't mean I won't listen to what you have to say."

I stared at him, completely at a loss for words. Whatever I had thought he might have said, this certainly wasn't it.

"You might be shocked to learn that I can be a reasonable person. Have you considered that?"

"I haven't much experience with reasonable nobility," I admitted. "And two days ago you threatened me and my family. You will have to understand that I do not yet trust you."

Casper sighed, pinching the bridge of his nose as if a headache might be forming there. "Elenora, I am sorry about my behavior, I truly am. And I don't expect you to forgive me right away, but I need you to understand that was different. I thought you were stealing coins from the people, tricking them out of the money they needed to survive. I was sure you had stolen my ring, not just found it. I thought that was proof. You must see how that is different from you disagreeing with me."

I swallowed, feeling my face heat with shame. I hoped Casper wouldn't notice in the dark. He had been completely right about me while I might have misjudged his character.

Maybe he was too removed from the common people to see what they needed, but if he was willing to listen to a commoner, wasn't that something? And who was I to judge him? I had been conning people out of their coin and he was trying to protect them.

"So, you will send resources to rebuild the south?" I finally asked, trying to distract myself from my own guilt.

"I will see what can be done," Casper said, looking a bit uncomfortable.

"But you said—"

"I said I'd listen to you, and I will. But it's not that simple."

My temper flared. Being angry with Casper felt better than feeling ashamed of myself.

"All your pretty speeches about listening to me and wanting to help your subjects mean less than little if you don't plan on any action to follow it up."

"Reynallis has a bigger threat than Faradisia now, and I need to consider present danger first," Casper shot back. His voice was hard, but I sensed fear behind it.

"What do you mean?"

"There have been more fay raids on the northeast border, even since I spoke to you about it last night. Queen Marasina has refused any negotiations and the pressure is growing daily. The Biawood Forest is little protection against Magnomel, and if the fay attack, Sterling would be the first city to fall. How would it look for a kingdom if their capitol city falls? Our peace with Faradisia and our alliance with Glavnada would all be compromised if we appear weak, not to mention what would happen to the townsfolk of this city. People don't understand how dangerous the fay are, but they are more devious and treacherous than any human could be."

"You really think they are such a threat?" I asked. I thought about Pel's soft lips on mine. I could still taste the honey. But I also remembered Garin's death. It wasn't simple.

"I honestly do. The faeries attacked my brother on his way back to Sterling from his winter in Lotanus. They killed a king in an unprovoked attack. Reynallis is in a vulnerable state right now; technically without a king until my coronation this summer. The fay used to stay in Magnomel, but lately there have been a lot of skirmishes along the border. I fear they are testing the waters. And if things get worse, we'll need a way to defend ourselves, and to fight back."

I had to admit that Pel had been deadly, but only when his life was threatened. But why was he in Reynallis when our kingdom was so unfriendly towards the fay?

The thought came unbidden and left me with an uneasy feeling. He had mentioned wishing to avoid his queen, but not why.

I would have to ask Pel when he came—assuming he didn't change his mind about returning.

"Do you understand?" Casper asked. I stared at him blankly, too lost in thought to have heard the beginning of his question.

"Sorry, what?"

Casper looked troubled. "I said that is why we can't simply send all our resources to the southern border, because there isn't a pressing threat there. I need to see what protection and defense we need to provide to the northeast border, but then I promise to review the needs of the south. Do you understand that?"

"Yes, of course," I said quickly. All my anger had turned to apprehension, and suddenly I felt too hot, despite the evening chill.

"But know that I do appreciate your thoughts on the matter, even if your expression was a bit . . . brash," Casper said. He was leaning in closer to me, and I noticed that he hadn't let go of my hands. "In fact, I rather respect your passion. I think together we could do a lot of good for the kingdom, if you would consider marrying me, Elenora."

"Nor."

"Pardon?" Casper was a mere breath away now, the moon bathing him in a silver glow. I could smell the spices of his soap; it was a heady scent.

"Call me Nor. Everyone I care about calls me Nor. Elenora always felt so formal."

"It would be my pleasure. *Nor*," he whispered, his hot breath tickling a delicate part of my ear. My name sounded like a prayer on his lips, or a promise.

I knew I should say or do something. Too much had happened lately, and I wasn't thinking logically. I should have asked for more details about the faerie raids or even changed the subject entirely and asked if there were news about my brothers. Casper let go of my hands and caressed my cheek, his hand soft against my skin. Gently, he tilted my chin up with his hand. I let him, staring into his handsome face. There was apprehension in his dark eyes, but also need, and my own heart quickened.

I realized I wanted to kiss him. I wanted him to kiss me. The line between the part I was playing and who I was became tangled, and I couldn't tell which one was truly me. I suddenly needed space, needed air. I could not go around kissing princes and faeries. I rose, so quickly I almost stumbled back.

"This is happening too fast. I'm not ready."

Casper looked at me, the desire so naked on his face that I almost lost my resolve. Then he closed his eyes and I stared at the delicate veins on his eyelids, forcing myself not to focus on his mouth, on lips that I wanted to kiss. But quickly his hunger was gone, replaced by the cool prince who was not ruffled by anything, certainly not by me.

"Of course, Nor. I did not mean to rush you."

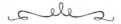

Late that night, I stared at the ceiling in my room. I had never cared much for anyone outside my family, and now I felt my heart pulled in two very different directions. I only wished I knew which path to take.

Chapter Eighteen

"Why Lady Elenora, I am so glad to see that the dress is such a magnificent fit on you," Ilana said as she poured the tea.

"You were too kind to gift it to me," I said through gritted teeth as I tried to subtly scratch at the itchy material. I had been at the palace for several weeks, yet it seemed I was still to be made a fool of. The thick woolen sleeves constricted my movements, and the dress, maybe ideal for icy Glavnadian winters, was already making me sweat in the warm spring sunshine.

Lady Ilana had prepared a tea party and invited me, along with Constance, Flora and a dozen other ladies of the court. Yesterday, a messenger had delivered a large wrapped parcel. Unwrapping it, I discovered a thick brown woolen tunic and skirt, richly embroidered with green and yellow flowers. Along with the bulky garment, there had been a note, sealed with blue wax stamped with a shooting star. I broke the seal, even more surprised with the note than the gift.

Dearest Lady Elenora,

It would be my greatest pleasure if you would join me and some of the ladies of court for tea tomorrow at noon. I believe we got off to a terrible start, and as a peace offering, please allow me to gift you with this traditional Glavnadian dress. It is a Glavnada custom to give a gift when offering peace. Please do me the honor of wearing it at tomorrow's party.

Most sincerely,
Lady Ilana Oleshin

I mentioned the gift to Casper during a walk in the gardens, something that had become a daily ritual after that first time. "Can you believe she gave me a dress? As a peace offering?"

Casper smiled. "See? I knew you would begin to fit in, and the court would accept you."

I frowned. "I don't know. Lady Ilana has never been fond of me. I was actually thinking of skipping the party."

Casper stopped walking, and holding my shoulders he looked at me, his dark eyes serious. "I do not think that wise, Nor. Lady Ilana would take it a slight against her and against the ladies she invited to the tea."

"Why should I care what offends her?" I grumbled. "She never bothered to hide her disdain for me."

"Because, Nor," Casper said with long practiced patience, "she comes from a powerful family. We need to be diplomatic with Glavnada. The ladies she invited are also from rich families in Reynallis."

"So?"

"You want us to restore Reynallis, to be able to do more public works in the south, right?"

"I don't see what that has to do with—"

"So, you need to make friends with nobles who pay the taxes that will fund the works. Make sure they support these projects so they will spare the laborers and craftsmen we will need to build these public works."

"I thought I gave you a room full of gold so I wouldn't have to kiss up to nobles," I muttered, annoyed that I had to play nice with Ilana.

"Yes, and that's a good start, but we need to start circulating money if we want to keep the economy going. Besides, Nor," and there was a twinkle in Casper's eyes, "you are a tremendous show woman. I saw the way you brought in a crowd at the Spring Faire. If it is easier for you, think about it as a part you are acting."

He smiled then, looking as though we were sharing some devious joke. I smiled back, but my conscious ached. He had no idea how good an actress I was, or how deceitful. "Very well, I'll go to the tea party."

But I could tell that Ilana's gift had not been sent in kindness. As soon as Annabeth pulled the wool over my head, it began to itch. The tunic was too tight, restricting my ability to bend my arms, and the skirt was far too large. Annabeth quickly took up the hem, but we had to use a wide sash as a belt, tying it in the back to even keep the garment from falling off me. And once I joined the tea party, set out on delicate white tables and chairs in the rose garden, I felt immediately self-conscious. All the other ladies were in light, gauzy dresses, fanning themselves with decorated lace fans. Only I was in thick wool, as though I was ready to sip tea on an iceberg.

"I do hope you are not too warm in it," Ilana said, snapping me back to the present as she poured my tea. I could hear the light tittering of several ladies, though they tried to hide themselves behind their fans.

"Not at all," I demurred, though I was already starting to sweat. The damp only seemed to make the itching, burning sensation worse, and I fidgeted in my seat, trying to scratch my back against the chair without making a scene.

"And how do you like your tea?" Ilana's smile was pointy, and I met it in kind.

"Sugar. Thank you," I said as she spooned several heaps into my cup. I was sure the tea would be too sweet, even for my new-found fondness of readily available sugar.

"The embroidery is lovely," Flora said, politely studying the green and yellow flowers on the skirt. "What kind of flowers are they?"

"Thank you, Lady Flora," Ilana preened, as though she had done the needlework herself. "They are chrysanthemums, the national flower of my country."

The ladies continued their chatter as I picked up my delicate teacup. I had to strain against the sleeve of the tunic in order to bend my elbow enough to bring the cup to my lips and ended up leaning forward the last few inches. I rewarded my efforts with a large swallow of tea.

But my mouth filled with hot saltwater. I gasped in surprise, inhaling the awful stuff. I began to choke, sputtering and spitting out the nasty liquid, most of which went flying on my dress. Tears filled my eyes as I coughed out whatever was left in my lungs. Constance, who had been seated next to me, wiped her cheek with a napkin, her mouth souring though she didn't say a word. With a nasty feeling, I was sure some of my spit had landed on her face.

"Lady Elenora, are you all right?" Flora asked, concern in her voice. She, along with everyone in the garden was now staring at me.

"Salt," I gasped out, still trying to catch my breath. But the movement from all the coughing seemed to intensify the prickling feeling all over my body. I felt like my skin was covered in ants. I raked my nails along my sleeves, trying to scratch at the skin.

"Oh dear, whatever is wrong Lady Elenora?" Ilana asked. She had stopped pouring tea for the ladies, and I could see she was trying to suppress a smile.

"You put salt in my tea." My words were little more than a croak, my throat raw from the hacking coughs. My skin was still crawling. I needed it to stop. I pushed to my feet, knocking over my chair in the processes. I started to scratch all over, desperate for some relief, but unable to get the stinging to abate. I could hear the ladies laughing, but I did not care. I was going mad in my own skin.

"Here, let me help you," Ilana said, coming towards me before I could stop her. I tried to wave her away, but the movements were weak, I was too busy tearing at my skin. "You don't stand a chance commoner," she hissed in my ear. I felt a tug at the sash around my waist but managed to push her away.

"I don't need your help." I stumbled away from Ilana, who looked like a kicked puppy, as though I had hurt her feelings. I had to leave. Another few steps and I felt a loosening around my waist. The sash had fallen down, the heavy skirt with it. I was still in layers of petticoats, but the ladies gasped and giggled as though I had completely exposed myself. The burning in my skin doubled, humiliation searing through me as the laughter grew while I practically hopped around, digging my nails into my arms, my chest, my legs.

"Come on." A steady hand took my arm. While still scratching, I looked up to see Flora by my side, Constance next to her. Flora's face was a study in concern, and while Constance did not seem to share Flora's worry, she did take my other arm. Too miserable to protest, I allowed them to lead me away from the party. All the while they held tightly to my arms to prevent me from clawing my skin to shreds.

I slid into the milk bath Constance had ordered the minute we reached my rooms, an order Yanis and Annabeth had hurried to obey. Constance insisted on immediately removing the wool dress, and with some difficulty she and Flora were able to yank it off of me. My need for modesty was shoved aside as I was almost dropped into the tub by Annabeth in nothing but my shift before she poured a freshly retrieved pitcher of milk on my head. But all my protests died on my lips as the cold milk hit my skin, calming the burning sensation with remarkable speed. I gasped in relief as I slumped against the tub, too tired and sore to fight. My arms were covered in splotches of red rashes.

"Ground vermillion bean, as I suspected, on the inside lining," Constance said, studying the fabric. Her nose wrinkled in disgust and she dumped the garment on the floor. She studied her own hands before going over to the water pitcher and rinsing them off.

"The worst of it was in the lining, but Flora, you should wash your hands. You too," she indicated Annabeth. "Anyone who touched this dress."

Flora and Annabeth followed suit, looking as confused as I felt. "What is vermillion bean?" I asked.

"A plant native to Glavnada. Dried and ground, it can be a very potent itching powder." Constance was all matter of fact, seeming not at all surprised to find out I had been ambushed by clothing, as she neatly dried her hands. The other two women in the room were more affected, Annabeth almost covering her mouth with her hand in horror before remembering she needed to rinse her hands.

"You don't think that was done on purpose, do you?" Flora looked as aghast as Annabeth. I was gratified that at least a few people cared if a gown tried to murder me.

"Of course I do. Lady Ilana has hated Elenora since the first day Casper made that ridiculous offer of betrothal. Nobility would never stoop to marrying a commoner in Glavnada, and Ilana must see the impropriety of it. Especially as I do believe she was hoping to become the future queen of Reynallis."

"Still, such open hostility," Flora murmured.

"Hardly open at all. She would deny all charges if confronted. Place the blame on whatever merchant was commissioned to make the dress or claim it was contaminated on the ship that delivered it."

"But she tried to kill me," I protested. My skin had cooled, but the angry red welts still ran the length of my arms.

"Don't be so melodramatic," Constance snorted. "Vermillion bean is uncomfortable, but hardly fatal. I imagine she simply meant to humiliate you in front of the court. Show you that you cannot possibly think to hold a place here." Constance turned her gaze on me—cool dark eyes, so like her brother's. I flushed to think about how I was facing a princess while sitting in a bathtub drenched in milk. "And maybe she did you a favor. This court really is no place for you." That sparked my anger.

"Now Constance, really. Perhaps we should speak to Casper. I am sure your brother can do something." Flora put her hand on Constance's arm.

"No," I said, too quickly. They both stared at me. "I don't need Casper to fight my battles, not if I plan to *stay* at court." I did not add that I had not decided if I was going to stay, but I wanted it to be my choice, not because I was run off by some snobbish noblewoman. "I will deal with Lady Ilana." I sat back in the bath, letting the cool milk sooth the scratches and welts on my arms. I stared at Casper's signet ring, still on my finger as I started to formula a plan, one that would teach Ilana that I was no weak-willed commoner she could bully and intimidate.

Chapter Nineteen

I waited for five days to enact my revenge. Five days of cowering away from Ilana whenever I passed her. Making her think she had won. She preened and gloated to other ladies at court, and I even overheard her saying that it was simply a matter of time before the 'street filth' left the palace. That was fine with me. I wanted her to slip into the easy overconfidence of a mark that thinks she's won.

News of my humiliation had made it to Casper, of course. Rumors and gossip flew as quickly through the court as fire through tinder, though I pretended to ignore the extra-long stares or the quiet laughs hidden behind gloved hands. Casper had been immediately worried, then incensed, which I found surprisingly satisfying. When he threatened to send Ilana away, back to

Glavnada, I silently relished the idea, imagining her embarrassed in front of the entire court. But Constance's chiding came back to me and I shook my head.

"It's only harmless fun," I assured Casper. "No need for you to bother with it." *And I can fight my own battles*, I silently added.

On the fifth day, the sky was overcast and the air chilled in the way that meant we were in for a spring thunderstorm that night. I could almost taste the storm brewing as I sat at the little desk in my parlor, rereading a letter I had forged in Casper's elegant script.

My darling Ilana,

Though I have tried to keep it hidden, my love burns for you like an all-consuming fire. If you hold any love for me, now is the time to prove it. Too soon I shall be crowned king, with no choice but to marry that commoner, unless I know for certain your love and loyalty to me. Meet me in the cover of dark this night at the gazebo in the rose garden. Wait for me there. I shall come to you, wearing a cloak as dark as midnight. But if I do not see you there, I shall know your heart has no room for me, and I will never again ask you to be queen.

With ardent love,
Casper

I folded the letter closed and poured melted wax to seal the forgery. I pressed Casper's ring into the smooth surface of the wax, waiting for it to cool before pulling the ring off. Left in the wax was the perfect impression of the royal crest; three roses intertwined with vines.

Annabeth, my only confidant in my scheme, peered over my shoulder. "Is it ready, milady?"

I blew on the cooling wax, testing that it was cool and solid to the touch. I handed the note to her. "Indeed it is." Looking at Annabeth's eager, freckled face, the excitement I had been feeling dimmed. "Are you sure you want to do this? It would be dangerous if you get caught."

Her small face grew serious, her hands set resolutely on her hips. "No one disrespects my lady. Not on my watch." A mischievous, infectious smile split her face. "Besides, who else could deliver your note unnoticed?"

"You mean *Prince Casper's* note," I said, grinning back at her as I handed her the note and watched her scamper out of the room. Now I just had to wait.

The storm was even worse than I expected. The winds picked up just before sundown and howled all night. Rain splattered against my windows until sometime near midnight it turned into the hard, banging clatter of hail. I did not sleep much, the anticipation of facing off with Ilana making my nerves jangle. I watched the lightning illuminate the sky and wondered if Ilana was suffering in the gazebo or had given up. Either way, this victory would be mine.

An hour before dawn I climbed out of bed and wrapped myself in a dark navy cloak, pulling the hood down low. I slipped quietly through the halls of the palace and into the gardens. The rain had eased up to a light drizzle, a soft mist covering the grounds. The air smelled fresh and clean, and as my boots crunched on small piles of hailstones, I prepared myself.

Ilana was seated at a bench in the gazebo, a thick fur cape wrapped around her. She immediately noticed me coming, her eyes initially lighting up. She rose, though the movement was stiffer than her usual grace. She pulled down her hood, and I saw what a mess she was. Despite the cape, she was drenched, her hair a knot of ivory wet tangles and her eyes puffy and bloodshot, dark circles under them. But despite that, she smiled at my approach. I almost pitied her but remembering the laugher of the court ladies as my skin itched and burned, any trace of sympathy died.

Her smile was immediately replaced by something grim when I pulled down my own hood, revealing my identity.

"Why Lady Ilana, what a lovely surprise to see you out here this fine morning," I said cheerfully.

"What are you doing here?" she snapped.

"Maybe I just needed a breath of fresh air." I hummed softly as I plucked a rose from a nearby bush, careful of its thorns. Ilana let out a frustrated noise and craned to see over my shoulder, as though Casper might be on his way.

"He's not coming. He doesn't even know you're here."

Ilana turned her chilly blue eyes on me. "What do you know?"

I made my voice deep, a mocking imitation of Casper. "My darling Ilana, though I have tried to keep it hidden, my love burns for you like an all-consuming fire."

Ilana's pale face went purple in anger. "You!" she hissed, the pieces coming together in her mind. She lunged at me, but I was far more adept at brawling than she was. I easily jumped out of the way, sticking out my boot to catch her ankle and she went sprawling onto the muddy ground.

"I will get you for this," she spat.

"No, you won't. In fact, you won't even speak of this to anyone." My voice was calm, but there was a steely edge to my words.

"And what makes you think that?" she asked, getting to her feet and scowling at the new mud stains on her clothes.

I steepled my fingers. "Because now we're even. The score is settled. Whatever you have against me, we're done. You leave me alone and I shall do you the same courtesy."

"Oh, this is just the beginning, the prince shall hear—"

"Hear what, exactly, Lady Ilana? That you were so delusional to think he loved you? That you actually believed you would marry a prince, and so desperate to believe that fairytale that you waited all night, in a thunderstorm no less? You would be the most pathetic soul at court. People would talk. And they wouldn't stop talking. You should be thanking me that I at least had the courtesy to do this in private. But try anything against me again, and you will not be so lucky. I think you would be wise not to test how resourceful or devious I can be."

Lady Ilana had started crying, which seemed to make her angrier. I almost felt sorry for her but knew this was the one chance I had to kill this rivalry. I did not want to worry about her next attack.

"You know nothing about my love," Ilana hissed, almost to herself.

"What does that mean?"

She leveled her watery blue eyes at me. "Nothing," she snapped. She wiped her eyes with the sleeve of her cloak, slowly taking in my offer, my threat. "So no one knows about what happened tonight? No one at court? Not even Prince Casper?" With impressive speed she regained her composure, her haughty demeanor back in place.

"No one," I confirmed. I trusted Annabeth to keep it secret and did not want Ilana's ire to reach the girl.

Ilana made a noise that was somewhere between a sigh and a laugh. She seemed to relax for a moment before remembering who she was speaking to and tensing back up. "At least that is a relief. And you promise it shall stay that way?" She glanced towards the palace, as though needing proof a swarm of courtiers were not about to descend upon us.

"As long as I find no more unpleasant surprises from you," I said, wanting to make my point clear.

She narrowed her eyes at me. "And if I don't agree to this little treaty?"

I smiled then, a feral grin that I knew made me look a little unhinged. It was one I had used to worry my opponent in the few times I found myself in a brawl. "You know, as a poor commoner, I have a lot of connections to the wrong sorts of people, if you catch my meaning. People who could do so much worse than vermillion bean. Folks who are masterfully adept at making things look like an accident."

My bluff had the desired effect. Ilana's eyes grew wide in horror, so much so that I almost wanted to laugh and confess that not every commoner knew a horde of assassins they could call upon. I was still deciding if I was amused or offended when she spoke.

"Very well, Lady Elenora. I think we have an arrangement. We are done."

"I'm delighted to hear that," I said, dropping any menace from my voice. I held out my hand to shake, but she kept her hands tight at her side, carefully stepping around me, as though any contact with me would contaminate her. I did not mind. So long as she did not poison my food or hire an actual assassin, I would consider this a victory. I sat on one of the benches in the gazebo, watching the sunrise turn the sky from murky gray to watery yellow. I felt empowered in a way that had eluded me since I had come to court. My tactics might be unconventional for a royal court, but I was proving my doubters wrong. I could survive in this court. A small part of my mind wondered at her reaction, the way she seemed

more concerned that no one discover what happened than learning
that Casper did not love her. *Why had she spent all night in the rain
if not to prove her love?* But I pushed the thought aside. I did not
need to care about Ilana's motivations so long as she did not try to
sabotage me again.

I rewarded myself with a detour into the kitchen. Early into my
stay at the Rose Palace I had made a point to befriend the kitchen
staff, and Madam Marie was always delighted to see me, plying me
with treats. Today she presented me with a large sticky bun, which
I ate on the way back to my rooms. The hot pastry tasted of butter
and cinnamon and was studded with plump currants. It was a warm
delight after my cold morning. I was licking my fingers clean of the
cinnamon and sugar as I opened the door to my room.

"There you are." Casper was sitting in my room, fully dressed, and
clearly waiting for me. "I wondered where you got off to this morning."

I stared down at my sticky fingers. "I had a craving for pastry,"
I said, which made Casper chuckle. "What are you doing in my
room?" I suddenly was on high alert, wondering if Ilana had gone
to him. But no, he was smiling, a bright, eager smile.

"I have a surprise for you."

"Is this really necessary?" I asked as I leaned on Casper's arm. He
had insisted I close my eyes, so as not to ruin the reveal as he guided
me down a hallway. I felt both excited and foolish.

"Most definitely," he said, and I could sense the smile in his
voice. "All right, now stay there." I could hear him opening a door.

"What's going on?" I asked, but suddenly something slammed
into my waist. I stumbled backward, catching myself before I fell.

Whatever had slammed into me was holding me tight.

"Nor!"

My eyes flew open. Jacobie was gripping me in a tight hug. In the room in front of me, Devon and Finn looked on, smiling. They were dressed in fine clothing that I knew must have come from the palace. Before I could stop myself, my eyes filled with tears.

"Nor! We missed you so much," Jacobie said, not letting go of me.

"I missed you all very much too," I said, hugging him back. My brothers all rushed to me, and for a blissful moment I was simply caught up in their arms and their love. It felt like the piece of myself that had been missing had made me whole again.

We all stood there for a long time, holding each other. I let happy tears stream down my face, not wanting to disengage in order to wipe them away. When we slowly separated, all of us were still smiling. I hastily wiped at my eyes.

"Nor, we were so worried about you," Devon said. "I should never have left you." There was guilt in his voice, and it pained me to hear him talk like that.

"No, you did the right thing," I reassured him. "After all, look at how well it turned out for us."

"That's right," Finn agreed, taking in our surroundings. "Who'd have thought our sister would be a guest of the royal family? We've been evading guards for weeks. We were sure we'd be arrested!"

"We had no idea they were actually trying to invite us to the palace."

"I'm glad they finally did get you the message. We can all be together again," I said, grinning like a fool.

"And we heard the strangest rumor that there was a prince in love with our sister," Devon said, with a knowing smile.

I blushed and looked at Casper. He was standing off to the side so as not to intrude on our family reunion and looked a little out of place. I briefly wondered if I had broken protocol with my display of familial affection, as I thought about how I had never even seen him hug his sister. But Casper stepped forward, and suddenly was the shining, handsome prince, full of confidence.

"That rumor is completely true," Casper said, and I felt my blush grow even hotter.

"You will have to tell us everything that happened since that day at the faire," Finn said. For a moment I thought he was changing the subject after sensing my embarrassment, but he was looking too intently at me. I could sense Finn, my clever brother, wanted to know more about the gold, but was too smart to ask in front of Casper.

My smile froze on my lips. With adjusting to palace life and missing my brothers, I hadn't actually thought about what I would tell them when I saw them.

I felt a pang of guilt thinking about Pel but pushed it down. Of course, observant Finn would be the first to wonder how I had pulled off a feat of gold. Fortunately, it seemed like no one else picked up on his suspicion.

"Nor, you look just like a princess," Jacobie said.

"You think so?" Casper said, addressing Jacobie. His voice was warm and friendly.

"Oh yes!" Jacobie shouted.

"Do you think she would want to be my princess?" Casper asked, and turned to me.

"What are you doing?" I asked as he pulled something out of his pocket and got down on one knee. My brothers went silent. Casper held a glittering golden ring. In the center was an intricately cut ruby. I felt like I had swallowed a live moth.

"You have my ring, but I thought you might also like one specially made for you. Nor, I want to ask you again, will you marry me?" Casper looked a bit nervous, which was an endearing sight on his usually confident face. "I know you wanted time, and while it has only been a few weeks, I hope that has been enough time to convince you that I will be a good husband for you. And that you would be a wonderful queen. You can do more for Reynallis and your family on a throne. I want to give you that throne."

I felt slightly deflated, but I wasn't sure why. Perhaps if he had said he loved me I would have said yes. Even though I could do more as queen than I ever could as a poor orphan and small-time criminal. My brothers were all shocked into silence. I looked back at Casper. He might not speak of love, but he respected me enough to listen to what I had to say. That might be a good start to a marriage. Unbidden, Pel came to mind. I saw his stunningly beautiful face promising me a life of freedom. I wish I had asked Pel if he loved me. My heart again felt pulled in two very different directions.

Gently, I closed Casper's fingers around the ring. I saw the hurt cloud his eye. "I'm not saying no," I clarified. "I'm only saying not yet."

Casper pulled on his charming, princely mask, the one that was never hurt, though I still felt there was pain in his eyes even as he smiled. "No rush, Nor. I am sure you wish to spend some time with your brothers."

"Thank you," I said, genuinely relieved he was not going to push for an answer this morning.

"Now, I know you had a craving for pastry, but if you can manage to eat some more, I had a breakfast laid out for us."

"Breakfast!" Jacobie cried in delight. "I love breakfast!" We all laughed, the mood suddenly lighter. Whatever I decided, I now had my family back with me.

Chapter Twenty

"Empty your pockets."

"I don't have anything in my pockets."

"Empty them," I repeated.

"But Nor . . ." Jacobie whined.

"Now." Two silver spoons dropped to the floor. I sighed, picking them up. "Jacobie, you can't do this anymore." It had only been a few days since my brothers had been in the palace, and we had just finished a lavish welcoming meal to celebrate our reunion.

The boys ate their fill with excited contentment. The meal had gone beautifully. Until, with my ex-pickpocket's eye, I saw Jacobie swipe a teaspoon. I waited until the meal was over and then cornered him in the salon connecting our bedrooms. Devon stood by as I reprimanded Jacobie for what I would have encouraged only a few months ago.

"But they gave me five spoons," Jacobie argued, incredulity lacing his words. "FIVE. Who needs so many spoons?"

"I know, but things are different now." I waved the spoons at him. "These need to be returned." I had found that sneaking silver back to where it belonged was as delicate an art as stealing it in the first place.

"But what if things change again? It was good before and it got bad. What if that happens again?" he asked. My heart pinched at the worry in his voice.

"Then we revert back to a life of pretty crime," Devon interrupted before I could respond.

"Agreed," Finn said as he entered. Ready for bed, he wore a nightshirt, but had put his jacket on over it. I noticed the bulging pockets.

"Please tell me you didn't steal the silverware too." I looked pointedly at his pockets.

Finn reddened. "No," he mumbled, and pulled out two rolls, squished and covered in a fine coating of wool. "Just in case," he added.

"Brothers," I said, grabbing the rolls, "you can't go around taking bread and spoons anymore." But my brothers weren't looking at me, instead, their gaze had shifted to the door. I turned to see Casper his mouth slightly open.

"Am I interrupting?" he asked, looking almost as uncomfortable as I felt.

"No," I insisted, whipping my hands behind my back. A flush rushed to my face.

"I didn't mean to—"

"Not interrupting—"

"I just wanted to make sure everything was acceptable with the rooms."

"They're perfect."

"I didn't mean—"

"It's good."

"If we ever have to leave, can we take the extra spoons? No one needs five spoons at supper." Everyone turned to Jacobie. I cringed. Perhaps the future king was going to have second thoughts about marrying into the Molnár family.

Instead, Casper laughed. It was a surprised laugh, but not condescending, as I had feared. "If I ever tell Nor to leave, you shall have all the spoons in the palace."

"All of them?" Jacobie asked, his eyes wide, calculating the wealth of spoons in the Rose Palace.

"Indeed, all of them. Though that means I shall never be able to tell Nor to leave."

"No?"

"Definitely not. I am far too fond of soup." Casper smiled and I laughed. I felt a flood of relief and warmth toward the prince, toward *my* prince. I felt a little stab of hope that, although my family was definitely unusual for the palace, we might find a place for ourselves here.

The next few weeks flew by as the weather warmed to full summer and preparations were made for Casper's upcoming coronation. My brothers adjusted to life at court. Devon and Finn stopped stealing food after I introduced them to Madam Marie and the kitchen staff. Madam Marie let them know they were always welcome to stop in the kitchens for a treat, but I had to watch out for Jacobie, who tended to horde shiny treasures. He took after me more than I had realized.

Devon quickly found himself overwhelmed with invitations to join hunting parties, and he enjoyed the expeditions. He rode well, and with his handsome looks, he was always surrounded by admirers, which seemed to baffle him more than anything. There was a lightness in him that had been missing for years.

I was surprised how easily he shrugged off his parental worry in exchange for that of a nervous young man when the ladies of the court flirted with him. I even found Ilana complimenting his tunic once. Though she gave me a wide birth, apparently she did not extend the courtesy to my brothers. Devon's face was beet red as I made up some excuse to forcefully pull him away from the ice queen.

Jacobie finally got to play with other children his age. Casper gifted him with a wooden sword, finely carved, but blunt enough not to do too much damage. To my amazement, noble parents encouraged their children to befriend my brother, and though I knew the reason was to create alliances with the potential future queen's family, I was still pleased that my little brother was not ostracized for his low birth. It seemed that nobility was ready to overlook our modest origins when enough gold was provided. I still had to subtly check his pockets to make sure he had not acquired someone else's golden watch or pearl bracelet. It was a strange experience to suddenly have to convince my brother not to steal after spending so many years teaching him to do just that.

But Finn was another story. He loved the library and devoured books on topics from local wildlife to mathematical theories of the sun and stars. I was pleased to see that he was so happy, except when he started to develop an interest in alchemy.

Devon and Jacobie accepted that I had pulled off some miraculous feat without much fuss. As expected, they questioned me about it as soon as we were alone together. By then, I had created a story, though it seemed a weak one to me. After my arrest, I had been trying to escape the palace when I found a locked door hidden behind a tapestry. In it, was a forgotten room full of gold. I carefully took the gold back up to the tower. Jacobie was young enough to believe my story and while I wasn't sure if Devon believed me, he seemed content not to question me further. I had usually been the one to plan our deceptions, so he must have figured that this was not different, only on a larger scale. My brothers were all too happy with our new lot in life and distracted by the activities and pleasures of the palace to think much about it.

Except for Finn. Whenever we were alone, he would ask me how I did it. Every time I would make up a new answer, much to his annoyance.

I dreamed the gold and it became real.

It really was holy straw.

I figured out the secret to alchemy, but I forgot it in the morning.

None of the answers pleased him, and once I caught him reading a book on alchemy, but he shut it quickly when I approached him. Another time I saw him speaking with Master Dauvet. They were leaning over a book in the library, speaking in hushed tones. They immediately stopped talking when they noticed I was there. I tried to ignore this. I didn't want Finn to discover the truth, but I knew he wouldn't find it with the alchemist.

Sometimes I wondered why it was so important for me to keep Pel a secret from them. More than once, I wanted to simply confess everything to my brothers, not wanting any more secrets between us. I felt guilt for not telling them, but I told myself it was to keep them safe. The less they knew about the fay, the better. Part of me, a selfish part, wanted to keep my experience with Pel all to myself. I wondered if I would ever see the magical boy again. But as the days and weeks went by, I slowly concluded that Pel did not want to return. And I was not going to summon him if he did not want to return.

The pain that came with knowing Pel didn't want to return eased as I realized I was developing genuine feelings for Casper.

My favorite place in the palace was Casper's study. It had started with my interest in studying his maps, beautifully detailed drawings of Reynallis, the roads and cities, maps that laid out Faradisia and Glavnada, and the wide oceans surrounding the coast. Magnomel was included in some of the maps, but without much detail. Instead, the page went blank, an unknown with demonic-looking creatures seemingly intent on threatening would-be explorers. I did not tell Casper that I had met a faerie, and that he looked nothing like the nightmare creatures on the map. I simply enjoyed studying the maps, thinking about where I had traveled and where I might like to visit.

Casper encouraged my interest, explaining which goods were traded between which cities and describing his future plans for national improvements once he became king. And when I learned he had spent very little time traveling Reynallis, between the Southern War and his years in Faradisia, I realized I could give him valuable information about life in many of the cities in our kingdom. My brothers and I had lived nomadic lives, constantly traveling lest we get caught in a scheme. I had always been too busy trying to survive to appreciate that I now had a wealth of first-hand knowledge about much of Reynallis. I worried Casper would think such things trivial, but he listened with rapt attention as I imparted my homegrown wisdom. I told him how the port city of Tolpin had the best crab pies and that in the south many shops closed for several hours at midday in summer, as it was so hot most people would take long naps after lunch, working late into the cooler night instead. Before I knew it, spending time with Casper in his study became one of my favorite pastimes. I began to believe that maybe we could continue to work together and rule a country. And with every day Pel did not come to see me, the idea felt more and more like a possibility.

I struggled to truly look and act like a lady of the court. Much to Constance's chagrin, tea parties still put me on edge, and when Flora insisted on teaching us to paint, my attempt at a still life of roses was so laughably bad that even Flora cracked a smile. Jacobie's childish paintings looked more realistic than mine. And when Constance tried to teach me embroidery, I made such a mess of a brocade that I cussed in a very unladylike manner, much to the princess's horror.

"If Constance comes looking for me, I will have to hide behind a stack of books, or possibly just jump out the window," I told Casper as I slipped into his study and settled myself on a desk by an open window. An early summer breeze fluttered some of the papers. His desk was covered with reports and foreign correspondences.

Casper looked up from the document he was reading and smiled. He seemed happy to see me, but I could see dark circles under his eyes and wondered how many late nights he had spent in his study instead of in bed.

"And what is she trying to get you to do now?" he asked, rubbing his eyes.

"Embroidery," I said, scrunching up my face in distaste. "I think I would prefer a slow and tortured death before trying to sew another flower." I dropped the silk embroidery I had been working onto the desk.

He actually let out a laugh. I wondered if I should feel indignant that he didn't even try to say my work was any good, but with how tired I had seen him lately, I was too happy to see him laughing.

"It's a good thing I'm not trying to marry you for your needlepoint skills."

"Good thing indeed," I agreed. Casper had stopped outright asking me to marry him, instead hinting around the idea. I had yet to give him an answer.

"Milady, shall I dispose of this?" Jock asked, gesturing to the crumpled silk.

"Might as well get rid of the evidence." I laughed as Casper's valet carefully picked up the silk and tossed the ugly thing into the fire.

"Would milady care for some tea?" Jock asked, indicating a tea service that had been set out in a corner of the study.

"I can fetch it," I insisted, jumping to my feet. I wanted to feel like I could do something useful. Jock nodded before letting himself out of the room, discretely giving Casper and me a few moments alone. Casper's cup was empty on his desk, a dark ring around the bottom of the cup. "Care for more?" I asked, and he gratefully nodded. I took his cup over to the tea service, well, the coffee and tea service, as there was a tall silver carafe of coffee next to a white porcelain pot of tea.

I couldn't stand the foul dark coffee, but I knew Casper was fond of it, and refilled his cup, adding plenty of sugar before I poured my own tea.

"So, what is the news?" I asked Casper as I sat down with my tea. It was hot and wonderfully strong.

He sighed, sifting through various papers on his desk. "None of my advisors feel up to the task of picking out even the smallest detail for my coronation without my approval, so I am having to review everything from the seating arrangements to the musicians they propose hiring to the wines they want to serve."

I sat up. "The wine part sounds rather fun."

Casper gave me an annoyed look. "Perhaps, but I have more important things to worry about. Reports of fay raids are increasing, and I need to work with my military aides and engineers on fortifying our outlying cities. And those are only the first steps, the defensive measures."

I thought briefly of Pel, as I did every time Casper mentioned the fay, but pushed the thought of him away. The strange faerie boy was not returning, and Casper looked so worn out. "Casper, you sound like a weary old man, not a young prince about to be king."

"I sound exactly like a prince about to be king. The needs of the people come first."

At his words, I felt a warm pride towards Casper. "Very noble, Casper. But even noble kings need to take some time for idle pleasures."

"I don't think so, Nor. There is still so much I need to review," Casper said, rubbing his forehead.

I lit up. "I have a brilliant idea."

Casper eyed me with suspicion. "Coming from you, that sounds like trouble."

I grinned. "Of course it is. And you need some trouble, come on." I pulled Casper to his feet.

"Nor, what are we doing?"

"We are getting some fresh air."

"Nor, half the court is waiting for my answers on various petitions. I am sure they will pounce on me the moment I leave my study. Maybe after I finish these reports."

"No worries, I know a secret passage out of the palace," I said, prying the papers away from him.

Casper abruptly stopped walking, his feet digging into the rug. "You know of a what?" he asked, his eyes wide with surprise.

"Not exactly secret, but it's a servants' hall that exits out through the kitchens. It's a secret to you nobles." I could tell Casper was teetering on the offer, so I added, "Please. It would make me so happy."

"Fine. If it will please you."

I took his arm, leaning in towards him, close enough to whisper in his ear. "It pleases me greatly."

"Would you believe I grew up in the palace and never once visited the kitchens?" We stood in one of the lesser used doorways to the kitchens.

Casper had been more than a little bemused when I pulled him into a servants' passageway and led him through a labyrinth of nondescript hallways till we reached this exit.

"How do you even know where you're going?"

I laughed, remembering my first few days in the palace when the elaborate rooms and corridors had me turned around and lost.

"All these hallways look the same," Casper said, staring at the plain hallways. The astonished expression on his face made me laugh all the harder.

"Not at all. There's the water stain that looks like a face," I pointed to a smudged mark on the wall. "I call him Inky. It means we're close to the kitchens." And indeed, the smell of baking breads and roasted meat came wafting our way. "As soon as I could manage to get around the palace, I made sure to learn the servant passages. Finn only needed to follow his nose. And based on Jacobie's sticky fingers, I am certain he visits Madam Marie once a day for pastries."

"It's huge." The awe in Casper's voice made me grin.

"Of course it is, how do you think all the people living in the Rose Palace get fed?" I gently chided as I led Casper into the wide kitchens. Indeed, it was a vast series of rooms, large brick ovens for baking, deer and rabbits roasting on spits, long wooden tables where cooks kneaded breads and chopped vegetables. "Come on, we're going to see Madam Marie," I said, pulling Casper through the great rooms.

"You know someone who works here?"

"Someone? I know everyone," I said with a wink.

We had only made it a few steps when our presence was noticed. At first, I got a few smiles from familiar faces, before the servants noticed my companion.

There was a ripple of confusion and anxious agitation, as I could tell everyone was wondering what their future king was doing in the kitchens. Finally, Madam Marie, the respected old baker with salt and pepper hair and strong, bony hands, dropped into a deep curtsy, with everyone else taking their cue from her, bowing or curtseying as well.

I shot Casper a look.

"What did you expect?" he mouthed.

"Tell them to rise so we can get something to eat," I murmured.

"Right." Loudly, he added, "Rise, my subjects. And carry on."

Slowly, everyone stood, but no one looked away from the prince. Their wary glances told me what I had been too careless to realize, that Prince Casper's presence here was making them uneasy.

"Your Highness, it is such an unexpected pleasure to see you in the kitchens," Marie finally said, daring to step forward. She, along with everyone else, seemed bewildered as to why Casper was here, and I noticed the edge in her voice.

"Madam Marie, I told Prince Casper that he has not truly lived till he has had the pleasure of your rosemary Parmesan rolls hot from the ovens," I said, stepping towards the woman. My praise did it. The baker beamed at the compliment.

"My, Lady Nor, you are too kind. If His Highness wants some, I have some freshly made."

Casper nodded, as perplexed in this new situation as the kitchen staff. "Lady Nor?" he asked as Marie hurried off to fetch the rolls.

"I don't like to be too formal here, but the 'lady' is something everyone seems to need to add."

Madam Marie returned with a heaping plate of rolls, offering them to us. Without waiting for Casper, I took one, taking a big bite and savoring the herbs and buttery goodness of hot cheese. Casper followed my lead, and actually closed his eyes as he took his first bite, clearly savoring it.

"It is indeed a marvel in baking, Madame Marie," Casper said. Marie beamed with the royal praise.

That opened the floodgates. Suddenly everyone was asking if *His Highness* would like to try a bite of this or a piece of that delicacy.

Casper was plied with raisin pudding, toasted quail eggs, rabbit stew, almond cakes, and a dazzling variety of colorful macrons. Every time, I greeted the cook or chef by name, and Casper complimented their creation to much delight and applause. I imagined this was the most excitement the kitchens had ever seen.

But the pure bliss I saw on Casper's face when he tried one of Madam Marie's famous apricot honey tarts gave me an idea.

"If you liked that, then I know just the thing," I said, thinking of the wild blackberry bushes that I had noticed in one of the far ends of the hedge maze.

"And what would that be?" Casper asked, his eyes still closed in appreciation as he savored the apricot tart.

"It's a surprise," I said, already pulling him to his feet. "But you will have to be very stealthy," I joked.

Casper swallowed the last bite, as if wistful the delicacy was gone. "I don't know Nor, I have already been away for some time now." He looked back at the doorway we had entered but seemed reluctant to move in that direction.

"Please," I begged. "Let me show you this."

Casper looked back at me, his deep brown eyes warm as he gazed at me and his resolve weakened. "I doubt I could deny you anything at this point."

His words were surprisingly sincere, making my pulse quicken. I could almost hear my heart beating. Something about the way Casper submitted to my request pleased me in an unexpected way. "This way," I said. Impulsively, I grabbed his hand. Soft, yet strong, his fingers slightly sticky from the tart, he squeezed my hand back, and I knew he would not let me go.

Together we left the kitchens, saying our goodbyes to Madame Marie and the rest of the kitchen staff as I led him towards the doors that opened to the outside of the palace. I knew there would be heaps of treats delivered to his quarters, the other delicacies he had not gotten around to tasting.

"Don't let anyone see us," I whispered, as we snuck over to the far side of the hedge maze, the side that faced away from the palace, and was thus obscured from view by the casual observer. I padded quietly through the grass, but Casper clearly lacked my stealth, almost marching along. "You are as quiet as a lumbering bear," I teased as the two of us crouched by the side of the hedge.

"I'm not accustomed to skulking around," he said, far too loudly, but his eyes were bright as he tried to suppress a grin, the corners of his lips twitching up. "You have far more skill—"

I put my finger to his lips to shush him as I heard a group of ladies passing on the other side of the hedge, chattering about the weather. His lips on my finger were soft and hot, and I felt a desire to know what those lips would feel like on my own. I was suddenly very glad that I had led us to a secluded section of the maze, the wall of green hiding us from view. My skin burned in a way that had nothing to do with the bright summer sun. We stayed locked in silence as the ladies slowly made their way away from us. As their voices grew fainter, I started to pull my hand away, but Casper caught my fingers in his hand, keeping them by his lips. Carefully, he began to kiss my fingers, his lips lightly touching my knuckles as his thumb drew circles on a delicate pulse point on my wrist.

I inhaled sharply, shocked at how sensual such a gesture could be. Casper smiled, a wicked, delicious grin and his eyes darkened. He lowered his chin, staring up at me with a hungry expression, as if daring me to stop him. I felt frozen in place, not wanting him to stop, but feeling acutely inexperienced and unsure. When I didn't move, he gently pulled my hand down, leaning in so close to me I could feel his breath on my ear. "Nor, I would very much like to kiss you now." His voice was husky, rough in a way my polished prince rarely let himself be. It delighted me.

I tried to speak. "I . . . I . . ." My head was swimming and I couldn't form the words as I inhaled his smell, cinnamon and spice, and something that smelled deliciously like a man. Instead, I nodded, staring up at him with my own wide eyes, trying to convey what my words were failing me. Then his lips were on mine, hot and soft, melting away all other thoughts. His lips felt wonderful and my head was spinning. I wondered briefly, if my lips felt as sweet and soft on his, or if mine felt dry and chapped from hard living on the road. I resisted the urge to pull away and run my hand across my mouth to check.

Instead, I leaned into him, kissing him back, hungry for it. I wanted to get lost in this kiss. I forgot everything except his lips. He tasted of the sweet honey and tart apricot, and I ran my hand through his hair, knocking the gold circlet off his head, savoring the feel of his smooth, black hair through my fingers. He wrapped one arm around my waist, drawing me in even closer as his other hand cupped my cheek.

Behind us, someone cleared their throat.

Casper and I instantly broke apart, whirling around to see Yanis standing over us. I scrambled to my feet, trying to smooth down my skirts as heat rushed to my face. Casper stood, awkwardly reached down to pick up his crown, and put it back on his mussed hair, displaying far more dignity than I.

"Ahh, Sir Yanis, I fear you have caught us taking a break from duties," Casper said, attempting to make his voice light, but I could hear the strain. Despite my embarrassment, it pleased me. Yanis, however, did not look pleased.

"Your Highness, Lady Elenora, we have been looking all over for you." Yanis's embarrassed expression had quickly changed into one of deep concern. "The guards were especially anxious for your personal safety." Yanis looked directly at me, and I felt a small prick of guilt that I had worried my guard.

"We are fine, I can assure you," Casper said, his confident persona slipping back into place. I smiled to confirm Casper's words, but my heart ached for the passionate side of him I had glimpsed just now. I knew Yanis was tasked with protecting me, but I wish he had not found us so quickly. "We needed some fresh air."

Yanis was still a mask of distress. "And that is not the only concern. There has been another fay raid. The Captain is waiting in your study."

Captain Moureux, head of the Royal Guard, sat waiting for Casper when we reached the study. The captain jumped to his feet when we entered, giving Casper a deep bow.

"Sir Yanis informed me there was another raid. What happened?" Casper demanded. He was rigid as we waited for the answer, dread welling up within me.

"A village near the northeastern border was set aflame. No one was killed to our knowledge, but many were wounded by the flames, and many buildings burned before the fire was put out. And while the villagers were putting out fires, three children from the village disappeared. Several villagers saw some faeries running back into the forest, but none were captured." The captain, a serious man who did everything with military precision, pointed to a site on one of the study's large maps.

As Casper studied the map, I leaned over his shoulder to see exactly where the attack had happened. The village, Chelle, was small, right on the edge of Reynallis, backing into the Biawood

Forest. The forest was Chelle's only protection from the forces of Magnomel, but it was clearly not enough to deter the fay.

I sighed, wishing I had something helpful to say. I didn't. It seemed like forever ago that I had yelled at Casper for not sending immediate aid to the south, but I now understood the difficulty. With such limited communication with Magnomel and increased raids, we had to be careful not to underestimate the fay. And now three children were gone in one raid. Guilt seared through me. For a brief moment, I wondered if Pel had anything to do with this. I thought, *hoped*, that he didn't. It seemed unfair to assume all fay would partake, but I would never know. I suddenly wanted to confess to Casper everything about Pel, as though it would somehow help.

"I think morale is becoming a big problem," Captain Moureux said.

"What do you mean?" Casper asked, still staring at the map as though he could will a solution from the parchment.

"Even with the funds to recruit soldiers"—Here, the captain gave me a nod of acknowledgement, while I tried not to think that the gold he was referencing came from a faerie—"we must have enough time to train them. We're months away from having enough ready soldiers to defend our borders, and even more time is needed for us to go on the offensive. People are facing this dangerous and mostly unknown force, and they don't know what to do about it."

"Noted, thank you Captain. Please, gather Lord Arnette and the rest of the council. We will meet in an hour," Casper said, commanding without a trace of fear.

"Yes, Your Highness." Captain Moureux bowed before sweeping out of the room. The moment he was gone, Casper sunk into a chair, his earlier confidence sliding off him.

"What are you planning to do?" I asked. "Captain Moureux made it sound like he thinks we're getting ready for war."

"I don't know what to do about it." For a moment, I saw the frightened boy who never felt he could live up to the legacy left by his brother. "We are not ready for another war, and even if we train enough soldiers, we have only had five years of peace. But we cannot do nothing."

The idea of war was too big for me to start to consider. Instead, I focused on the immediate need. "What if we told the people that we are working to make things better?" The words came out without me even thinking about them.

"What, shall we go door to door and talk to our subjects individually?" Casper gave me a sad smile.

"No, of course not, but maybe it would be a good idea to go to some of these villages. Talk with the people who live there. Find out from them what they need—be it more guards or a better way to warn the villagers of an attack. I think it would do your people good to see their future king helping people. People like me, we rarely see nobles working to make our lives better. I always assumed the royal family simply lived a life of luxury off in their palace." I sat back and looked at Casper. It was a hard truth I had told him, but I hoped he'd understand that I only meant to help him.

"Maybe some goodwill trips would be useful." His eyes alighted as he considered the idea. "I, *we*, couldn't meet with people individually, but maybe a town hall in select cities and villages. Summer solstice will be here soon, and then I shall be coronated. Perhaps we start the trip after that."

"Why wait?" I asked, the excitement of the idea growing. "Why not go to Chelle now?" I studied the map again. "It would be a journey of only a day or two. We could bring supplies, maybe some soldiers to help them rebuild their village. They could stay on to protect Chelle from future attacks." I paused as childhood memories surfaced. Softly, I added, "When my home was burned to the ground during the war, I would have given anything for someone to have come to our village with aid." I had to stop, taking a few deep breaths as a stinging behind my eyes threated tears.

Casper reached out for my hand, and gently squeezed it. I looked up from the map to see him staring intently. I held my breath, afraid he would dismiss my idea, telling me it was impractical or inappropriate for royalty to go tramping off to a poor, ruined village so close to the border. Instead, he gave me a warm smile. Something quivered in my stomach and I held onto his hand.

"I think that's a wonderful idea, Nor."

Chapter Twenty-One

As the carriage sped down the road, I nervously twined my fingers around my skirts, willing us to arrive faster, while also dreading what we would find. Finally, Casper gently put his hands over mine, stilling their anxious movements.

As we neared the village, I smelled the damage long before I saw it. I expected to see plumes of dark smoke and bright, bloody fire reaching into the sky, but instead, all I saw were gray clouds. The main fires must have been extinguished. But I smelled the smoke. It was not the clean, delicious smell of fresh branches in a cookfire, but an acrid smell of destruction. Our village had smelled the same way so long ago. I could taste the ash in my mouth, and it stung my eyes. Suddenly, it was like the last six years had never happened.

I was a girl of eleven, back in my childhood village. My mother was screaming at me to get out of the house. I wanted to find a toy, a wooden doll my father had made me, one I slept with every night since he'd left for the war. Our thatched roof had caught the fire that was spreading throughout Venlin, and smoke was filling the room. Rilla had gotten my brothers out. Mother was trying to pull me out of our house. Though the smoke, thick and bitter, was choking me, I stubbornly didn't want to leave the doll. But my mother dragged me out of the house, thrusting me at Devon when we were free of our blazing home.

The night sky was lit with orange fire not only from our home, but from every building in Venlin, including our beloved mill. I had never felt so afraid in my life. Streaks of yellow flames ate up every place that was familiar to me. Faradisian soldiers in uniforms of orange and white ran throughout the village, setting more fires and looting whatever small caches of goods they could find.

"Go!" my mother cried at us; her voice hoarse from the smoke. "Get to the forest. Go deep in the woods and hide."

"Mama," I wailed, not wanting to leave her, but Devon yanked me toward the safety of the trees as Rilla took Finn and carried Jacobie, who was only a toddler back then. Despite the smoke and ash, he wailed almost as loudly as me. Finn stayed silent, his eyes wide and frightened.

"I'll be right behind you," our mother promised.

It was the last time I saw my mother alive. I had been too young to realize everything the soldiers wanted to take that night.

"Nor, are you all right?"

I looked away from the window into Casper's concerned face. I had been so lost in memories that I hadn't been paying attention, realizing only now that we had arrived and the carriage had stopped.

At Casper's worried look, I touched my face. My fingers came back wet with tears.

"Do you want to stay in the carriage? I can take care of everything in the village."

"No," I said, sharper than I intended. I fiercely wiped away my tears with the sleeve of my dress. "I can actually do something this time."

"What?"

"Nothing." I took a steadying breath, telling myself I wouldn't cry in front of the villagers.

Casper sat, quietly giving me the time I needed to compose myself. When I felt ready, or as ready as I could, I nodded, and he gently knocked on the carriage door, summoning a footman to open it.

The sight around me was as bad as I had feared. The buildings were now blackened husks, the cores burned out by malicious flames. I looked around at the skeleton of Chelle. The smell alone made me want to gag. I was grateful that I had eaten little that morning. Ash floated on the air like strange, hot snow, coating everything in a fine, gray powder.

"Where is everyone?" I asked.

"They are in the city square," a middle-aged man answered. Other than the royal guard, he was the only other person around, and I immediately realized he was the representative from Chelle. His hair was dark brown, streaked with gray, but I wasn't sure if it was naturally aging gray or the ash that had fallen on his clothes and skin.

"And you are?" Casper asked, looking at the man.

"Francois Aloys, Your Highness," the man said, giving us a deep bow. "Thank you, Your Highness, and to you, Lady Elenora, for coming to the aid of our humble village." Looking at the destruction around us, I feared that anything we could do for this man and his village would be too little and far too late.

"Lead us to the city square, Master Aloys. The sooner we are there, the sooner we can set repairs in motion." Casper had a deeply concerned look in his eyes. "Do tell us what you witnessed during the attack."

"Thank you, my merciful king," Francois said again, bowing low. Casper did not correct the man but held his arm out to me. I took it, allowing Casper's strength to seep into me as we made our way to the village square. Master Aloys relayed the details of the attack. It was not until after the fire was controlled that he even learned of the missing children. Passing blackened and burned buildings, I had to force myself to keep walking.

"Are you all right, Nor?" Casper whispered into my ear as we strode past a church, delicate stained glass shattered on the ground in colorful shards. Stained glass did not come cheap. It must have been the most expensive building in all of Chelle.

"It's just . . ." I stammered, cursing myself for being so weak. I forced myself to stare ahead, but caught a glimpse of their mill, the top of the large waterwheel smoldering, even though the lower half of the wheel was still submerged in the water of the small river that ran through the village. I shuddered, remembering my last look at my home before Devon pulled me away. *I was a small child then,* I reminded myself. "It brings back memories of the war," I finally confessed, hating the way I shivered when I mentioned the war. Casper put his arm protectively around my shoulder but didn't say anything else. For that, I was thankful.

The village square was merely a clearing away from buildings, so there was little to catch on fire, making it the safest place for the villagers to gather. I saw several hundred people, all looking ragged and frightened, covered in soot and ash. I fought an impulse to run away from these desperate people. Part of me wanted to confess that I was nothing more than a fraud and could not do a thing to help them. What struck my heart was the hopeful way they looked at us. On a silent cue, they all began to bow as they gazed upon Casper.

"Subjects, rise," Casper said, his strong voice carrying across the clearing. No longer did he sound like a second son, or even a hesitant suitor, but a commanding prince. "This day marks a great tragedy for Reynallis, as suffering of her people is a blow for our country. I know you are enduring the consequences of this unprompted act of aggression by the fay. But take strength knowing that you do not suffer alone. Reynallis protects its own. We shall come together and overcome the malicious designs of the fay. Where they intended to tear us down, we shall rise.

"I have instructed royal guards to bring supplies, which shall be distributed to everyone in need. And in addition to immediate needs, I shall meet with the village leaders, so that we may work to not only aid Chelle, but to rebuild and protect it. Chelle will stand stronger than ever." As his voice carried, I sensed the crowd rallying, eagerly taking in the words of their future ruler. I realized that the young man I was falling for actually could be king.

A cheer went up from the villagers, and I clapped along with everyone else, swept up in their enthusiasm. Casper held true to his word, as wagon upon wagon began to arrive, stocked with immediate necessities such a fresh water, food, blankets, and additional supplies. Everything was divided among the villagers. And Casper did not leave it there. He met late into the night with the village leaders, Francois Aloys amongst them, discussing the best tactics to rebuild the village and fortify it from the fay. He seemed desperate to not only aid the people but ensure they could protect themselves before we left.

And then they came out, one by one. The injured, the lame, those who would never be the same. People with terrible burns, their skin melted. They walked painfully, some limped, supported by family members. These were the people who had paid dearly, weeping with relief at getting food and clothing.

Unable to sit still, I helped the soldiers distribute supplies, passing out blankets and clean clothes. I got lost in the work, and hours slipped by. I was glad to have something to do, and continued to work without stopping, even as the ash in the air stung my eyes and burned my throat.

"Will you find my sister?"

I looked up from dispensing wedges of hard cheese to see a grubby girl of about five or six looking right at me as I handed her a small chunk cheese. I crouched low to get to her level.

"Did you lose your sister?" I asked, making my raw voice as gentle as I could.

"Grace!" a woman yelled, coming toward us. The woman looked haggard, rushing toward the little girl. When she noticed me, I saw her pale visibly. "I am so sorry, milady," the woman said, grabbing the girl and dropping into a low curtsey. "My daughter doesn't realize who she speaks to."

"Mama, the pretty lady will help us find Rosie. Won't you?" Grace struggled in her mother's arms to reach out to me.

"Is Rosie your other daughter?" I asked the woman. She rose, staring at me with red, puffy eyes.

"Aye. She was taken," she said, her voice low and filled with pain.

"I am so sorry." I wanted to say more but could not think of anything adequate to tell this woman. I prayed her daughter was somewhere in the crowd of displaced townspeople, but I knew she would have been united with her mother long ago if that was the case. The woman didn't respond, but tears started to stream down her face, forming wet tracks on her sooty cheeks.

"I would do anything to get her back. Children lost to the fay . . ." the woman's voice trailed off.

Children lost to the fay are never returned, I thought, but did not dare to voice the common saying. Even as far south as Venlin, villagers would say that. I couldn't bear not saying anything to this poor mother, but I did not want to provide her with false hope.

"Soldiers will search the area," I promised. "I will have them comb through the surrounding forest."

"Thank you, milady," the woman said, but her voice was flat and hopeless. She didn't believe the soldiers would find her daughter any more than I did, though it broke my heart to admit it. I desperately wished I could summon Pel again, ask him where the stolen children were taken. But I knew it would not be safe for Pel here. If he even came. These people's lives had been destroyed by the fay, and I didn't trust that they could be made to understand that Pel was a different sort of faerie. Unable to watch the woman's pain, I left her quickly, promising to get soldiers to search the woods. She curtseyed again. Sir Yanis had accompanied us, and I pulled him aside to make the request. He promised it would be done, but I could tell from his tone that he also did not believe we would find the children.

Well past midnight, I forced myself into the village square, finally eating a supper of bread and cheese and a mug of ale. I approached Casper, who was still in deep discussion with the leaders of the village.

Everyone looked tired, but as I approached, I heard them in a lively debate on the advantages of an aqueduct versus a dam for the village. I carefully balanced the food and ale in one hand and gently tapped Casper on the shoulder. He turned, looking exhausted, but pleased to see me.

"Sorry to interrupt," I said to him and the group at large. "But it is getting very late. Perhaps discussions could resume in the morning?"

"Lady Elenora is correct," Casper said, rising slowly. The rest of the group also got to their feet, dipping into deep bows. "Master Aloys, let us continue this in the morning."

"Of course, Your Highness."

I led Casper away to a small collection of tents on the edge of the village, as far as possible from the smoke.

"When was the last time you ate?" I asked as we approached the tents. The thought of laying down, even on the hard ground, sounded like a glorious relief after this day. Casper's pause revealed that it had been a long time since his last meal. "Here, eat this," I said, giving him my half-eaten bread and cheese along with the mug of ale.

"I won't take your supper," Casper argued, but his resolve waned as he eyed the food.

"I'll get more in camp. I've already had at least three bites, which is probably more than you've eaten all day." I forced the food onto him as we continued to camp, and it made me happy to see him eat. I made a note to remember to bring him food throughout the day tomorrow, not only late at night. I wished I had packed some of the foul coffee he loved.

"Sleep," I commanded Casper, as I took him to the largest of the tents set up for us by the soldiers. My slightly smaller tent had been erected nearby, Yanis already standing at attention right outside. His somber expression told me everything I needed to know about the search for Rosie. I felt a flood of sadness, though I had not expected anything different.

"There's so much still to do," Casper said, looking like he might rush back to the village square. Casper had put on a good show for his subjects, but I could see purple shadows forming under his eyes and an exhausted weight to his step.

"And you can do all of it tomorrow." I squeezed his hand. "I'll be right back," I said, awkwardly disengaging myself from him. My bladder felt heavy, and I only now realized how long it had been since I'd relieved myself. Feeling self-conscious, I pulled away from Casper. He looked at me, surprised.

"Where are you going?" he asked, concern clear on his worn face.

"Nowhere . . . Just for a breath of air," I stammered, not wanting to explain as my face heated. I hoped Casper couldn't see my flush in the dark of the night. Of course, tonight the moon was full and brilliantly bright.

"This forest isn't safe at night. I'll go with you."

"Really Casper, I can handle myself. And I have to . . . relieve myself." I was blushing furiously, and my insides felt like they might explode. Fortunately, Casper finally understood.

"Of course. Well, I shall be right here. If you need me."

"I'm pretty sure I can do this on my own," I said, blushing harder. After all, I had a new dagger in my boot to replace the one lost to

Pel so many weeks ago. I raced into the woods, desperate to end the awkward conversation. I went deep into the forest, wanting to ensure Casper would not hear me watering the ground. But despite my embarrassment, I smiled, thinking of his concern. When I had finished, I adjusted my skirts and began to head back to Chelle. That's when I heard a voice behind me, dark and melodic.

Chapter Twenty-Two

"Don't run off so quickly, my pretty."

I whirled, nearly tripping on my skirts. As if he had materialized out of thin air, stood a young man with golden hair, twenty or so feet away.

My vision of him was partially blocked by the trees and diminished by the dark lighting of the night. The bright moon left dappled shadows on his pale face.

"Pel?" I asked, but barely had the name left my lips when the boy stepped closer. The shadows of leaves and branches jumped around his face, but I could tell this was not Pel.

"No, pretty thing. I am not my brother, though I have heard of you. You must be Lady Elenora Molnár, no?" The faerie smiled at me, but it was a cruel smile, and I felt like a small mouse cornered by a cat.

"Brother?" I couldn't think of anything else to say. I saw no warmth in this faerie's features, only a cold amusement that froze my blood.

"You didn't know? Just like Pel not to mention me." Something akin to disappointment flashed across his face. "He has spoken much about you, dear Elenora. Elrik, at your service, milady." The faerie gave me an elaborate, mocking bow.

"Is Pel with you?" I tried to look around Elrik, hoping that Pel might be nearby, but we were alone. I could sense that Elrik was not like his brother, and a terror started to well up within me. I cursed myself for going so deep into the woods.

"Oh no, sweet one. My brother is not here. But come with me and I shall take you to him." He extended a hand to me, a graceful gesture. Something about the hungry look in his strange cat-like eyes unsettled me. I had no intention of going with him.

"I should return to camp," I said, taking a step backward. "Pel knows how to find me if he needs me."

It took Elrik a moment to realize I was rejecting his offer. When I did not go towards him, a look of anger flashed across his face before he smoothed his features into something wolfish. "But we haven't had any fun yet," he said, his voice a dark silk that I might suffocate in. "And I love to have fun." Another look at his cold, sharp smile, and I was sure I wouldn't like his idea of fun.

I turned and began to run, away from Elrik. I managed only a few steps before I felt long fingers grab me. I let out a shriek as Elrik dug his nails into my arm, yanking me backward. He pulled harder, whipping me around and pinning me against a tree. Rough bark scraped my back and before I could react, he had secured both my wrists in his hands, pressing me against the tree. Despite his delicate fingers, his grip was like iron and I couldn't budge, even as I struggled.

"I don't believe a human has ever refused me. You shall learn better, Elenora." The more I struggled, the more he laughed, a confident, deadly sound.

My fear mounted as I studied my captor. While he shared a familial resemblance to Pel and his hair was the same glittering gold, his slitted amber eyes were predatory. His carved features were sharper than Pel's.

The terror in my stomach threatened to paralyze me. I thought about how he merely had to nick my skin and he could use my blood to kill me. Looking down at his hands on my wrists, I saw the thin strand of gold. I began to form an idea, as risky as it was desperate.

"What do you want?" I asked, trying and failing to keep my voice steady.

Elrik's smile widened, exposing his gleaming, sharp teeth. "I have exactly what I want." He looked at me as if I was a savory treat, something he would soon enjoy. I felt sick.

"I don't know what Pel told you. But he was mistaken. You don't want me. I'm no one."

"Nonsense. You are too modest, Elenora Molnár." He leaned in so close I could feel his breath in my ear. I shivered despite myself. He smelled of the forest, but with an acrid scent underneath, like something burning. I thought of Chelle.

"You burned the village," I accused, the words out before I could stop them.

"Obeying my queen's orders," Elrik said, his voice full of pride and pleasure.

"Queen Marasina?" I flashed back to the image of the monstrous fay queen I had seen on flyers in the town square of Sterling so long ago. Perhaps the drawing of a bloodthirsty monster had not been so far off if she had ordered the burning of a poor village.

"And she will reward me handsomely for giving her a hostage so dear to the little kingling," Elrik said, as if I had not spoken. He pressed in closer and slowly licked the side of my face. I tried to lean away, but his strong grip held me in place. He smelled even stronger of ash and smoke. His tongue was hot and slippery against my cheek. "You taste like luck and dreams. I can see why my brother fancies you."

"Did Pel tell you about how I fight?" I whispered, trying to make my voice low and seductive, though it came out as more of a rasp. But it had the effect I wanted. Elrik took the bait, leaning in closer to hear me, his ear right next to my lips.

"Oh, do tell me, pretty one." His grip on my wrists tightened. He sounded excited.

"Dirty." I bit his ear, hard as I could.

Elrik screamed in surprise and pain, his grip momentarily loosening from my wrists. I drew up my knee and slammed it into his groin. He screamed again; all his sadistic humor turned to rage.

"You *kanjia!*" he swore, but his pain bought me the distraction I needed. I broke away from his grip, pulling out the short dagger from my boot as I bolted deeper into the forest. I sliced quickly at my hand, deeper than I intended but hardly feeling the pain, as I pressed my bloody palm to my wrist, all the while still running as fast as my legs could manage. The gold around my wrist began to burn, but the sensation was welcomed.

Please Pel, please come to me, I mentally begged. He promised to return to me, and I needed him now more than ever. I knew the faerie boy who had saved me in the tower would stand a better chance against his brother than Casper.

I didn't hear anyone following me. I stilled, my back against a tree, and silently gulped air, trying to catch my breath. My lungs were on fire, the smoky scorch in my throat exacerbated by my run. The heat around my wrist had cooled, but Pel was nowhere in sight.

"Are you finished?" Elrik stepped out from the shadows, mere feet from me, though I had not heard his approach. While he seemed to still be in pain, a deep grimace cut into his face, he did not appear winded from the run.

"Stay away from me." I held my dagger out, ready to slice his throat if need be.

"Now why would I do that?" he asked, having regained some of his composure. I could see the bitemark I left on his ear, oozing a golden blood. With shocking speed, he was back on me, yanking my dagger from my hand and kicking my legs out from under me. I fell to the ground and he was instantly on top of me. Elrik forced my face down in the dirt, and I felt his knee dig into my back as he immobilized me on the ground. The more I struggled, the tighter he held onto my hands, forcing them painfully behind my back. I choked on dirt, grit and mud filling my mouth and nose.

"You cannot win against me. You should have come with me willingly. I can be a powerful ally to you in the High Fay Court if you prove useful. Or you can be a problem and I will be your worst nightmare," he said, pushing my face again into the dirt. "But I appreciate you bringing me this lovely little knife." He gently ran the blade of my knife across my cheek, not cutting the skin. Not yet. It was a caress of cold metal.

Remembering Pel's blood magic, I froze. The fight left me, and I felt myself trembling. I had practically given Elrik the dagger he could use to kill me if he had not already noticed the cut on my palm. Perhaps I had angered him enough that not even a reward from Queen Marasina would stop him from murdering me. I imagined choking on my own blood. Pel was not coming. I was about to die and would never see my brothers or Casper again. I prayed to the Mother that Casper wouldn't come looking for me. I didn't want him to meet a similar fate.

"Please, kill me quickly." I hated the way my voice shook. I waited for Elrik to plunge the dagger into me, or maybe he would cut me slowly, taking his time before allowing his magic to stop my blood. Instead, he started to laugh—a cold, dangerous sound.

"My sweet, have you not been listening? I'm not going to kill you. You are too valuable. I won't even hurt you that much."

I only had a moment to wonder what he intended to do when I felt my dagger slice into my cheek. Pain flashed bright and hot, but then he pulled the blade away. I could tell the cut was superficial, but knowing his powers, I felt no relief. His tongue was again on my cheek, licking my blood. I screamed and tried to pull away, but it was no use. He forced my face back into the dirt, choking off the scream.

"You are delicious. Far tastier than most humans. I shall figure out why that is once I convince Marasina to give you to me when she is done with you. I think I would like that."

"Chace curse you," I spat at him.

"Hush now, my sweet. It's time to go home." Elrik's voice was suddenly quiet, almost consoling. I felt his fingers on my cheek, touching the cut. "*Dormrir sange,*" he whispered, soft as a breeze.

"What are you doing?" I demanded as I felt the blood magic begin to work. The cut on my cheek turned cold where he touched it, and the chill absorbed into my blood, running ice through my veins.

"You will thank me for this someday." Elrik kept his cool hand pressed against my cheek, but he no longer restrained me. I imagined he was focused on controlling my blood. I was so cold. My limbs wouldn't obey my command to move. Elrik continued to watch me, seeming to wait for something. A slick sheen of sweat broke out on his face, and I wondered how much the magic was costing. Clearly not nearly as much as it was affecting me.

"Fight it all you want, my sweet, but you will lose. Now sleep, my pretty." Elrik smiled his feline smile, knowing he'd won.

"Noooo," I tried to say, but the word slurred in my mouth, which felt full of cotton. My heartbeats slowed. The cold sensation was growing into a numbness. Even keeping my eyes open was a struggle.

"Hush," he whispered, looking pleased. I wanted to spit at him, to claw his eyes out or bite him again, but I couldn't move. He began to sing to himself as he cleaned my knife.

My pretty, my love, don't disobey
You'll break my heart if you run away
Hey nonny nonny, hey nonney hey
One dark night I'll walk into your dreams
And tear out you heart to hear your screams
Hey nonny nonny, hey nonney hey
I'll lock your heart in a crystal jar
So never again shall you go far
Hey nonny nonny, hey nonney hey.

His song was a twisted lullaby, and I felt my eyelids grow even heavier. I might have dreamed of hollow girls and bloody hearts. I opened my eyes as I felt myself being lifted. Elrik had picked me up as easily as if I weighed nothing more than a doll. I couldn't even summon the strength to struggle.

"RELEASE HER."

A voice, warm and strong and angry sounded behind me. I must have been dreaming. Or maybe Pel had answered my summons.

"NOW!"

I felt myself spinning around as Elrik turned. Funny, the boy in front of Elrik looked like Casper.

"What a delight," Elrik crooned, his voice playful and deadly. "A baby king has come to join us. I wonder if you will be as much fun as your brother." Casper stiffened at the word brother, and I remembered how King Christopher was killed by the fay. I didn't want the same fate for Casper.

"Run," I tried to yell, but my voice came out thick and garbled.

Casper had his sword out ready for a fight. There was a fierceness in his posture and his eye blazed.

"Unhand the lady immediately," Casper commanded.

"Just till I deal with you," Elrik said, as he dumped me unceremoniously on the ground. I was too numb to feel pain from being dropped, but the moment he stopped touching me, Elrik's magic control over me started to fade.

It wasn't all at once, but I could feel my heart starting to beat faster, stronger. I struggled to sit up as Elrik and Casper faced each other. Elrik had pulled out a sword, a short and deadly looking thing I had not noticed.

"Come at me, baby king," Elrik crooned. "I just need one teeny tiny cut. It took no more than a scratch to fell your brother."

"I will kill you," Casper promised, advancing towards Elrik.

"No, Casper, run away," I screamed, finally regaining my voice. I felt like I was moving through molasses, but at least I was moving.

"I am not leaving you." He shot me a brief look, something protective and fierce, before turning his attention back to the faerie. Casper's handsome face turned dark and determined. "You will pay."

"I think you mean I shall be handsomely rewarded. The girl and the kingling. Come, let me take you away." Elrik lunged toward Casper, his movements as graceful as a dance.

"No!" I cried again. "He knows blood magic." I thought Casper might blanch at the thought, but he merely nodded, never taking his eyes off Elrik.

"Well, there she goes, ruining my surprise." Elrik mock pouted before lunging at Casper. There was a clash of metal as the blades hit, the reverberation from the swords strong enough that I felt it. Elrik's sword was shorter, but he wielded it with inhuman grace and speed. Yet Casper met him blow for blow as the blades crashed together, the steel singing as each fought for advantage.

Casper dodged a swift blow from Elrik, using the opportunity to strike out at the faerie's leg. He connected. Elrik swore as thick, golden blood stained his pants. The cut wasn't deep enough to incapacitate the faerie, but it did enrage him. Elrik began a determined offense, swinging his sword again and again, without giving Casper any time to recover in between. Finally, he broke through Casper's defenses and his fay blade swiped down. Casper jumped away, missing most of the blow, but a thin line of red appeared on his shirt and there was blood on Elrik's blade. My heart sank. I struggled to my feet, anxiety for Casper blotting out every other thought.

Without Elrik actually touching my blood, I was regaining control of myself, but I was still lethargic. It took all my strength just to stand. Lightheaded, I leaned heavily against a tree, forcing the world to stop spinning.

"You put up a good fight little king, but you are no match now that I have your blood." Elrik smiled, taking a step back and carefully licking the blade. "You taste like desperation."

"Stop it." I tried to cry out, but it came out as more of a croak.

"Nor, stay back. I won't let him hurt you. I promise," Casper said, protectively putting himself in front of me. I wanted to be warmed by the gesture, but instead my fear sharpened.

"Please don't hurt him," I begged the faerie. Elrik took a step toward us, an amused smile playing at his lips. I risked a glance at Casper, but he was still intently focused on the faerie. He feigned to his right, and as Elrik brought up his blade to meet the strike, Casper swerved, swinging his sword down hard to the left, landing the first deep cut on Elrik.

The faerie hissed and leaped backward, going on the defensive for the first time. Casper wasted no time to take advantage, and moved in almost as quickly as Elrik, getting in another good hit, this one a deep cut into Elrik's arm. Golden blood gushed out of the wounds, coating his clothes with an eerie, dark shimmer. Elrik cursed as he dropped his sword, his fighting arm now covered in golden blood.

"I will finish you," Casper promised, and he thrust for a killing blow. Elrik extended his wings. Long dragonfly wings opened behind him, glittering in the moonlight. Casper gasped, and I realized he hadn't noticed the faerie's wings in the fight. Elrik used the momentary distraction to take flight, rising several feet off the ground till he was well out of reach of Casper's sword. Though in pain, his movements were still graceful. He hovered for a moment, still in the sky save for the magnificent wings beating the air. Golden blood slid down his arm and leg, dropping like gruesome, magical rain to the forest floor.

Casper kept his sword out, ready to defend us should Elrik fly in for an attack. I wondered if he would. He might not have a sword, but his magic was far deadlier. Instead, he looked at me and winked.

"I shall be seeing you soon, Lady Elenora Molnár. Or whatever your real name is." He gave me a sly grin, as though sharing a secret, then turned to Casper. "You fight well, kingling, almost as well as your brother. You have won the battle, though not the war. I shall see you soon, too." And without any further explanation, he flew higher into the sky and then north, presumably back to Magnomel.

Casper seemed ready to follow after Elrik, but he only took a few steps before he froze, glancing back at me. I could tell he was weighing the urge to continue after the faerie to avenge his brother against the obligation to stay here and protect me. I waited for him to run after Elrik, to tell me he would return soon, but instead he rushed over to me and carefully helped me to the ground. Elrik's magic no longer controlled my body, but I was stiff and my limbs ached. I no longer felt like I wanted to sleep. I wasn't sure I'd ever want to sleep again.

I was afraid Casper might be angry to have found me with a faerie, but all I saw in his dark eyes was worry. "Are you all right? Did he hurt you? I will track him down and kill him if he hurt you."

I was shaking and to my horror, I started crying. I couldn't stop. "I'm sorry, I'm so sorry."

"Nor? What is it?" Casper was right beside me. Holding me close, his strong arms wrapped protectively around me. I could smell his rich soap, mixed with sweat. He smelled so much cleaner than the acrid burning scent that clung to Elrik.

"He burned it down. He set the fire to Chelle. He destroyed it all." I couldn't stop my sobs that were heaving in my chest. In my mind's eye, I saw not only the smoldering town of Chelle, but my home of Venlin, smoking from a raid so many years ago. Nothing had ever been safe after that.

"Shhh, Nor, shhh. It's all right. He can't hurt you."

"He killed your brother, and because I left on my own, he could have killed you." I pulled away from Casper enough to look up at his face. His expression was hard, but not scared.

"Someday I will kill the faerie that killed Christopher, but my first concern is keeping you safe."

"He could have stopped your blood in your veins. I could have lost you!" I had not let my terror take control of me when facing Elrik, but now that he was gone, all the fear washed over me anew.

"I've never been so afraid for anyone, Nor." For a moment I thought Casper was talking about himself, but he gently touched my cheek, and I watched as his hand came back bloody. I had forgotten that my cheek was cut. "What did he do to you?" And I understood the worry I saw in his eyes was for me, not himself. The realization made me feel strangely warm.

"I'm all right," I lied, willing myself to make it true.

"You looked . . . You were gone so long, and I got concerned. I decided to follow you and then I heard you screaming. When I saw him carrying you, I thought . . . you weren't moving, and I feared the worst." A tear ran down Casper's face. "I was so afraid, Nor." Casper wrapped me tighter in his arms and whispered into my ear, "I will never fail you again, I promise. I will protect you."

As I leaned into him, my body slowly began to relax. No one had promised to keep me safe, not since Venlin had burned to the ground. I let my head rest on his chest and listened to Casper's heart, a steady and comforting beat. For the first time since the day my home burned, I found someone I could feel safe with.

"I love you, Nor."

"Marry me."

Casper pulled back, enough for his eyes to search my face, seeking confirmation of my words. "Are you serious?"

"If you still want to," I said, suddenly anxious that he would see that I was more trouble than I was worth. He had not tried to propose in some time, and I worried he had changed his mind.

Casper's face lit up in a bright smile, undiminished by the sweat or dirt caking his face. In fact, it only made him appear more handsome, my legendary prince who fought the monster to protect me. I mentally said goodbye to Pel, knowing it was far better to be with someone who would be there when I truly needed him than a pretty dream. Casper kissed me, his lips searching out mine as his stubble lightly scratched my face, all of it making him feel so real.

Chapter Twenty-Three

I sat on the delicate stool in front of my vanity anxiously twirling Casper's signet ring around my finger, watching the gold glitter in the light. Our engagement ball was to commence in mere hours. *You're being foolish*, I told myself. Everyone already knew of the engagement. Yet, my stomach felt full of eels. Slimy ones that slithered around.

"Elenora, you're going to wear that ring down to nothing if you keep that up," Flora said, but her voice was comforting. She was brushing my hair the way Rilla used to when I was younger. While Flora knew I had Annabeth and didn't need such a highborn lady to help me, I appreciated her comforting presence.

I forced my hands to be still in my lap.

"Are you nervous?" Flora asked. In the mirror, I saw her concerned expression.

"Me? Nervous? What possible reason could I have for being nervous?" I tried to make my voice sound light. I suddenly wished for the rush of adrenaline that I had always felt before jobs—more excitement than nerves. This sensation was undeniably different.

"But this is what you want."

"Of course," I replied without hesitation. I wanted to ensure my brothers' futures. I wanted to do some good for Reynallis. And I was falling in love with Casper. So why was I nervous?

"Because you don't have to," Flora softly said.

I was saved from an answer by Annabeth's return. She had left to fetch my dress, which I had yet to see as it was a gift that Constance had commissioned for this event. I had been as surprised as anyone that Constance wanted to gift me a gown but knew better than to turn down the princess. And Flora assured me there would be no vermillion bean powder in this garment.

"My ladies," Annabeth said, as she entered the room and curtseyed. She sounded a bit breathless. Her face was flushed, and she was smiling widely. "I have your dress." In her arms was a very large package wrapped in linen.

"Let's see it," I said, eager for a distraction. Annabeth's excitement was contagious as she carefully set the package on the bed. Unwrapping the linen, I was amazed at what was underneath.

"It's beautiful," Flora breathed, looking at the dress.

On the bed was a gown of liquid gold, silken, radiant pools of brilliant, metallic fabric. It was by far the most beautiful garment I had ever seen, even during my months at the palace. Annabeth helped me into the dress and gave me a moment in front of the large, silver mirror.

Is this really me? Staring back was a girl straight out of a folktale. Golden skirts cascaded down to the floor, gathered in bunches along the hem that were secured with roses fashioned out of rubies and garnets. The bodice was embroidered with more ruby roses and intricate vines and leaves, leading into delicate lace sleeves. I twirled, watching the skirts billow out as the light twinkled off this magical dress.

"Elenora, you look like a princess," Flora said. I saw there were tears in her eyes and she was smiling. I floated as Annabeth finished braiding and curling my hair, adding golden ropes and strings of rubies.

A knock sounded at the door. Annabeth went to answer it and Casper entered. He looked dashing in red and gold velvet, his black hair neatly combed and the gold circlet resting on his brow.

"I came to escort . . ." he started but fell silent as he saw me. His mouth literally hung open.

"How do I look?" I gave another twirl.

"Stunning." It seemed like he wanted to say more, but he just stood there, staring. I started to blush.

"I should go check on Constance," Flora said, breaking the silence. She smiled and kissed my cheek. "Your Highness," she said as she gave a quick curtsey to Casper. "Annabeth, could you please come and help me?" Flora called out as she left the room. Annabeth was quick to follow, leaving the two of us alone.

"Do I look . . . regal?" I asked, feeling suddenly self-conscious with only Casper in the room. "I'm supposed to fool everyone into thinking I could be a proper future queen."

Casper stepped toward me, his smile back on his lips, and a look of something I couldn't quite name in his eyes. Was it longing? Very gently, he wrapped his arms around my waist, standing so close that

I had to look up to meet his eyes. They were dark and beautiful, and they sparkled in the candlelight.

"You look every bit the future queen," Casper said. For a moment, his bravado evaporated, replaced by something far more serious. "And my future wife."

I felt the eels in my stomach turn into fluttering moths as he leaned in and kissed me. His lips were soft and warm, and I breathed in his familiar, spicy smell of cinnamon and cloves, like a heady cologne. He pulled me in close, and I was reminded how strong he was. I let my hand caress his cheek and then ran my fingers through his hair, careful not to knock off his golden crown. I felt a sudden hunger. I leaned into him, looking up into his face. I carefully placed my palm on his cheek and stood on tiptoes so I could kiss him. Casper bent his head toward me, and I felt my entire body light up when his lips met mine. They were salty and a bit sweet, and he seemed as desperate as I was. I wanted to stay here forever with him, locked in my room and kissing my prince.

All too soon, he gently disengaged and stepped away. I had to resist the urge to pull him back, feeling a slight sting of disappointment. But it passed when I saw the hunger lingering in his eyes. I was immensely pleased by it.

"We should get to the ball," he said, breathlessly. "Everyone will be waiting for us."

"Of course," I agreed, though I would have much preferred to spend the evening alone with him.

"Besides," Casper said, the old charm returning to his voice, "Constance will probably send a servant to check on us if we are not down there soon, and that might be awkward." I chuckled, self-consciously remembering our first kiss in the hedge maze. He offered me his arm, and I let him lead me out of the room.

The great hall was full when we entered. Two doormen pushed open the great oak doors, and everyone in the room rose to their feet and bowed or curtseyed as Casper and I walked down the long aisle to the royal table. I thought about how different my first experience here had been.

The nobles looked at me with respect, or at least pretended to do so, instead of the curiosity and contempt that I had felt that first night. It also helped that I looked like a princess tonight and not like an overdone cupcake. I knew most of the nobility by sight and house colors, if not personally, and while I would consider few of them friends, I knew allies from enemies. The long hours in Casper's study and lengthy meetings with his advisors, had taught me which houses truly supported Reynallis and which ones were merely out for themselves.

I strode with Casper, holding my head high, and at least pretended to possess the confidence I needed. My brothers were already at the feast, next to the royal table, and I smiled to see them. Their outfits were more modest than Casper's and mine, but they were still richly attired in silk and velvet of gold and green, the new Molnár house colors. Jacobie smiled and Devon even winked as we walked past them. I returned the wink, trying to make it look regal. It didn't.

At the royal table, Constance, Flora, Samuel Arnette, and several other high-ranking nobles and official dignitaries rose to greet us.

People clapped and yelled. As the noise eventually died down, Casper and I took our seats at the head of the table as servants began filling goblets with wine and bringing out large platters of food.

"You look so lovely," Constance whispered, sounding genuine. "Perhaps I was wrong about you, and you do have what it takes to survive in court."

"Thank you for the gown, it is stunning," I said, and couldn't help but add, "and I am so relieved the fabric does not itch." Constance let out a small laugh which had Casper quirking an eyebrow in confusion.

Samuel leaned in. "Casper told me about your idea to start a tour of the kingdom after the coronation."

Casper put his hand protectively on mine. "We learned a lot about the villagers' needs." Casper locked eyes with me and added, "And about what I need to do to keep my people safe. I protect my own." He squeezed my hand. I smiled, feeling warmed by his care.

Chapter Twenty-Four

By the end of the dessert course, I thought my corset strings might break. Even after so many meals at the palace, this was an impressive feast with courses of roast meat, salted fish stew, honeyed fruits, fresh breads, sharp, pungent cheeses, tiny pastries with buttery crusts and rich custards, and so many more delicacies that I lost count. Our trip to the kitchens must have made an impression on Madam Marie, because there were several dozen apricot and honey tarts, each the size of a dinner plate. I knew I should be upset at the copious amount of food when so many in the kingdom went without, but I tried to put that out of my mind for the evening. I would have the rest of my life to help the people of Reynallis, *my people*, so I decided to allow myself one evening to set aside cares and worry. Of course, the servants were extra vigilant to ensure that my wine glass was never empty, so I was pleasantly tipsy by the time dinner had ended.

I could hear an orchestra starting to play in the ballroom as Casper extended his hand to me.

"I think it's time to dance," he said with a wink.

"Certain you want me as a dance partner?" I asked as I rose with him. Lords and ladies were already making their way into the ballroom. "I will probably trample your feet." I had been taking dance lessons from Flora, practicing with a very patient Yanis, but the thought of doing it in front of the entire court was a different story.

"I will take the risk," Casper said, giving me a wicked smile as he led me into the ballroom. "I can always step on your feet as payback."

I couldn't suppress a giggle at the thought of suave Casper trying to stomp on my feet while still dancing. My laughter died as we passed a group of ladies, Ilana prominently in their center and stunning in sapphires and diamonds. I schooled my features to give the entire group a smile, though my eyes lingered on her. I couldn't help wondering what she was thinking. She had not pulled any more stunts on me, but I was a long way from trusting her. She curtseyed with the rest of the group, a serene smile firmly fixed on her pale face. Gone was the usual venom from her stares, though I never assumed she would be happy for me. Perhaps she was a better actress than I gave her credit for. Or perhaps her love for Casper was not as strong as I had imagined.

We entered the ballroom, and the sight took my breath away. Hundreds of crystals glittered from chandeliers alight with candles. Vast ice sculptures of swans and fountains of wine were displayed on tables that lined the walls. Off to one side, the large orchestra was playing. The floor had been polished to a burnished gleam and men and women stood around the sides of the room, the center floor empty.

"Are they waiting for us?" I asked, the glow from the wine not enough to stifle all my anxiety about the dance.

"They are, so we better give them a good show," Casper said, leading me onto the center of the dance floor.

"I'm not sure . . ."

"Don't worry. Just keep your eyes on me. Forget everyone else." With that, he wrapped one hand on my waist, and held my other hand in his. I carefully put my free hand on his shoulder. Not daring to look at anyone else, I focused on his dark eyes.

"Here we go," I said as the music started to play a slow, melodic song. Casper gave my hand a squeeze before we took our first step, in unison, and began the dance. He was right. Looking only at Casper, I could forget that every noble in the court was staring at us. He twirled me around the room with an effortless grace, and I found myself keeping up easily. I was just starting to enjoy the feeling of dancing with Casper, almost floating with him, when the music came to a sudden halt.

For a moment, we continued to spin, lost in the moment. But all too soon, Casper stopped, turning to see what caused the change. I nearly lost my footing, but balanced myself quickly, only stepping on his foot once. I followed his gaze to the doors. Captain Moureux strode into the ballroom, followed by a pair of burly guards, dragging a bound and gagged man between them. The man, tall and thin, fought the guards, but they were too strong for him. I strained to see the prisoner.

"Captain Moureux, what is going on?" Casper demanded, as confused as I was about the interruption.

"Your Highness, we have caught a Magnomel spy in the palace," Moureux began but I stopped listening. The prisoner was close enough that I could clearly see his golden hair, his chiseled face, and his emerald cat eyes.

Pel!

My breath caught as I nearly yelled out his name, only stopping myself at the last moment. Casper didn't seem to notice as he was entirely focused on Moureux and Pel. The entire room was focused on them. Lords and ladies stared at Pel, fascination and horror playing across their faces.

"A faerie in the palace?" Casper asked. His disbelief was tinged with anger and perhaps a bit of fear.

"Yes, Your Highness," Moureux replied.

How had Pel gotten into the palace? Why would he even want to be in the palace?

Casper and Moureux continued to discuss the situation but I stopped listening. Pel was still stunningly beautiful, but he looked worn. There were fresh bruises flowering on his silvery skin, turning into patches of deep copper. One eye was swollen almost shut. The fight to capture him must have been brutal, but human blood must not have been spilled. If one of the guards had bled, Pel could have used blood magic and easily escaped.

Pel had stopped struggling now and stared at us. At me. His green eyes burned into me, though I could not tell if he was angry with me or the situation he found himself in. I was torn between a desire to run and untie him and an unexpected stab of betrayal. When my life had been in danger, he did not come to my rescue, but now he was in the palace. I didn't want to believe that the boy I had saved in the forest would be a spy for the fay queen. The queen who was ordering raids on our villages, killing livestock and stealing children. I thought about the night with Pel in the tower, and how he saved me from a terrible fate. But just as clearly, I recalled the night at Chelle, at the mercy of his cruel brother. Had it all been a ruse? Elrik had showed just how vicious the fay could be.

"Remove his gag," Casper demanded. I stiffened. Snakes of terror squirmed within me. If Pel told of his part in transforming the straw into gold, what would become of me? Or my family?

"Don't!" I suddenly yelled. Everyone in the room turned to face me, surprise clear on all their faces. Pel's expression changed, and I was almost sure he would be smirking if he wasn't gagged.

"Why not?" Casper asked, as shocked as everyone else at my outburst.

"Because," I said, desperately trying to think of a plausible excuse. "Because . . . I heard fay can control you with their words," I finished lamely. I expected to be laughed at, or worse, for Casper to become suspicious.

"That is no more than an old wives' tale. This faerie can't hurt you," Casper said, his voice pure kindness. He believed my fear, which made me feel awful for lying to him. But what choice did I have?

"Now remove the gag," Casper again demanded of the guards. The two holding Pel looked afraid, and I wondered if they believed that Pel could control them with his words. It wasn't that far from the truth, not if either of them had even a small bleeding cut from his capture. But Moureux nodded, strode over to Pel, and ripped off the cloth that had prevented Pel from speaking.

The terror within me was more palpable now, my heart pounding in my chest. If Pel told them the truth . . . I instinctively glanced at the doors and windows, trying to find any sort of escape, but I knew I couldn't make it, not in this crowd with guards stationed throughout. And even if I could, there was no way I would abandon my brothers here. And I couldn't leave Casper, I knew that now. I held my breath, waiting for the terrible moment to come. All of my fear from the first night in the palace came back to me tenfold. I would not only be exposed as a con artist, but one who had gotten aid from the enemy. I would be revealed as a traitor. It would destroy Casper's trust in me.

"Why did you come here?" Casper demanded of Pel, a deadly sharpness in his voice.

It took Pel a long moment to drag his gaze from me and face Casper. "I was searching for weakness," Pel said, defiance in his voice. I braced myself, sure the end was near.

"And what did you find, *fay*?" Casper asked, spitting out the word 'fay' like a great insult. But Pel did not speak again, his lips drawn into a narrow line, no matter what Casper threatened. "Take him away," Casper eventually commanded when it was clear Pel would not reveal anything.

As Pel was led away, I sighed in relief. He hadn't exposed me, though it was the perfect opportunity. I remembered his delicate, long fingers spinning straw into gold, and his kiss . . . and felt a surge of guilt mixed in with my relief.

"Nor, are you all right?" Casper asked, concern back in his voice. "You're shaking."

Chapter Twenty-Five

U nable to sleep, I laid in bed for most of the night, thinking about Pel. An hour or so before dawn, I finally got up. The fire had burned low and my tea was ice cold, but I barely noticed. I slipped into a dressing gown, tying it tight before pulling a dark wool cape around me. It was too hot for such a cape, but it might help conceal me. I took a few ruby hairpins and dropped them into my pocket.

Silently, I crept from my room, slipping between the shadows in long, deserted hallways and staircases, carefully making my way toward the dungeon. The palace felt abandoned in this ethereal time before dawn, even the most stalwart reveler having passed out by now. Once or twice I heard someone approach, a guard doing rounds or a kitchen maid collecting fresh water, and I'd crouch in a nearby alcove or empty room until the footsteps faded. I was pleased to see that even after several months of luxury, my skills at stealth had not turned rusty.

Despite the summer heat, the stairway to the underground dungeon was chilly, and I tightly wrapped my cloak around myself. The moment I entered the stairwell, I was in a different world. The walls were plain, rough stone and the air smelled of rot and stale urine. I had to cover my mouth to avoid gagging. Torches provided the only light this far below the ground, eerie shadows flickering against the cold stone walls.

I hoped I could quietly slip by whatever guard was on watch, knowing that otherwise I would have to incapacitate him somehow. Even then, I would need to be careful not to give away my identity. Pulling the hood farther over my head to hide my face, I slowly approached the stool where the guards kept watch.

Chace's fortune was on my side. The guard, a stout and scarred man, was dozing at his post. I watched his rhythmic breathing for a few minutes, making sure he was truly asleep before I crept past him toward the cells.

A long aisle stretched out before me, with cells to my left and right, most no bigger than a horse stall. Many of the cells I passed were empty, bits of dirty straw scattered on the floors and manacles bolted to the walls. The few occupied cells contained men in rags, sleeping.

I was beginning to worry I wouldn't find Pel, when I reached a cell near the end of the aisle. There he was, lying in a small pile of straw that served as his bed. As I got closer, I saw that he wasn't sleeping, but staring at the ceiling of his prison, as if he could will the stones to part. Maybe he could.

"Pel," I whispered.

Pel's head snapped toward me, his green eyes fierce. He looked wary, and I realized he couldn't see my face, still hidden beneath my hood. I pushed the fabric back, exposing my identity. The suspicion so clearly written on his face changed into amazement.

"Nor?" he asked as he approached the bars of his cell. I put my finger to my lips. Quietly, he continued, "Little *ladriena*, what are you doing here?"

"I should ask you the same thing."

"I was caught by your guards. You were there." Though he was bruised and his clothes looked even shabbier than when we met in the forest, he still looked beautiful, and I had to force myself to stay focused.

"I know why you are in the dungeon," I hissed, sure Pel was purposefully obtuse to annoy me. "I don't know why you were in the palace to begin with."

Pel's emerald eyes bored into me, and I shifted uncomfortably. I was asking the questions and he was behind bars, yet I felt like I was the one being interrogated. The image of Elrik flashed before me, and I shuddered.

"I met your brother."

A shadow passed over Pel's face, and he slumped against the cell walls.

"I know." The words almost sounded like an apology.

"He burned down a village. Stole children. Tried to kidnap me." The memory of my face pressed into the mud and dirt, the blood in my veins slowing, had me shaking with anger. "And you knew?" I had to fight not to scream the words at him.

"How did you get away?" Pel looked genuinely troubled. But maybe I couldn't read the fay as well as I read humans.

"No thanks to you," I spat, yanking at the gold bracelet, which held fast as ever. The burns around my wrist had mostly healed, but I suddenly wanted their pain. A physical pain would be easier than the emotional hurt now breaking my heart as I faced Pel. "I tried to summon you," I held up my wrist, the faint white scar all the proof I needed, "but you never came. I needed you and you never came." I found myself bitterly blinking back tears. I hated that his betrayal still pained me. "And now you are caught in the palace." The anxiety that I had been too trusting of Pel slammed into me all over again.

"Nor, I'm so sorry. I was trying to make it up to you."

"Why did he do it?" I demanded. I wanted to ask Pel why he never came but was afraid of hearing the truth, that he did not care about me. His action had made that all too clear.

"Elrik? I have no idea."

"How can I believe you? How do I know you aren't working with your brother?"

Pel looked like I'd slapped him, and I felt a wicked surge of pleasure, knowing that I'd finally gotten to him.

"I've been running away from them."

"What?" Now it was my turn to be confused.

"My brother is almost as cruel as our queen. My brother and I are from a noble family that serves in Queen Marasina's innermost circle. But I no longer want anything to do with their schemes. I don't want to burn down villages or steal children. That's why I could not come when you called me. My brother would have forced me to return to serve Queen Marasina. I'm sorry, Nor. If I had helped you, I would have only caused other humans to suffer. I am so very sorry."

There was such a heavy guilt to Pel's words that he had to be telling the truth. I knew I should not blame him for wanting to live a life free of servitude, but the evidence that he knowingly left me at the mercy of his brother stung more than I was willing to admit. Instead I asked, "Then why were you in the palace?"

"I was looking for you," Pel finally admitted.

"What?"

"I promised I would come back for you before that prince was crowned. Have you so quickly forgotten?"

"No," I whispered, taken aback that he had come for me. Even though he had not come when I was attacked by Elrik, I still remembered the spring day he had urged me to leave with him. I recalled his promise to fly me to Magnomel, right before he kissed me. The memory of his soft lips on mine made me flush despite myself. But the captain's words rang in my head. "Why would they claim you were in Casper's—I mean the prince's study?" Pel had no idea that I spent most of my days there with Casper.

"I was lost in the palace. Please Nor, believe me."

"Why say you were looking for weakness?" Part of me wanted to believe that the boy who'd saved me in the tower was telling the truth, but there were holes in his story.

Pel looked frustrated and ran his hand through his hair before answering. "I lied. What would you have had me say? I couldn't tell them I was looking for you without putting you in danger."

His words made sense, and I felt a flood of irritation at myself for believing the worst in him, even as I nursed my own hurt that he had not come for me at Chelle. But I could not wholly blame Pel for putting himself first. After all, I had done that all my life. Pel had given up everything so as to not be a part of his brother's evil schemes, and I could not resent him for what Elrik did. Pel had been doing nothing more than trying to protect himself. And now he was back here, risking his freedom to see me.

"I do believe you, Pel. But why didn't you use your magic? You could have escaped from the guards, or at least freed yourself." I gestured to the bars.

"The guards caught me unaware, so I had no chance. And these bars, they are iron. All fay magic is perfectly useless on iron."

"So the old tales about iron are true?" Out in the rural villages, people would sometimes hang iron horseshoes on the doors to keep out the fay. "I assumed that was mere superstition."

Pel gave me a defeated look. "The old tales hold a grain of truth."

"Then it's a good thing you have a friend who does not rely on magic." Quickly, I pulled one of the jeweled hairpins from my pocket and began picking the lock, forcing myself to focus on the lock and not the beautiful faerie who wanted me to run away with him. The lock was heavy and complicated, and I quietly swore for several minutes before I felt the mechanisms inside the lock click, a sweet music to my ears. The door swung open and I grabbed it, careful not to let it swing too wide and clang against the wall.

Pel looked at me with such awe-struck bafflement that I couldn't help but laugh. I quickly smothered my chuckle and looked around, making sure no one else heard. But the aisle was just as deserted as before.

"You are a human of many talents," Pel murmured, still staring at the open door.

"Come on," I whispered. "We don't have much time." I had no idea when the guard shift would change, but the longer we lingered, the more we were in danger. Pel quickly stepped out of the cell, careful not to touch any of the iron bars, his movements still full of their liquid grace. We were halfway up the aisle when I had an idea. I rushed back to his cell, this time closing and relocking the door.

"What are you doing?" he whispered as he joined me.

"If the door is left open, it will look like someone opened it for you. If your cell door is locked, well, people don't know much about fay magic. Maybe they'll think you just *poofed* yourself free or something." I continued to tinker with the lock, this time waiting for it to click closed.

"*Poofed?*" Pel asked. Despite our perilous situation, he looked amused. "Do you humans really think we can *poof?*"

"I don't know," I said, in no mood to be mocked. My nerves were fraying more and more with each second we were down here. The lock finally clicked into place, and I stood, careful to put the pin back in my pocket and pull my hood over my head. "Let's get you out of here." Giving a quick prayer to Chace, I started back toward the stairway.

Chace heard my prayers, or at least luck was on our side, as we made our way out of the dungeon. Neither the guard nor the prisoners stirred as we passed them on our way out. Through corridors that were now familiar, I carefully led Pel out of the palace, checking each corner and hallway before signaling for Pel to follow. I was starting to relax as we stepped out into the gardens. The sky was still dark, but with a hint of lightness to the east. I breathed in the rose-scented air, relieved to clear my nose of the foul dungeon smell.

We had nearly crossed the length of the garden that led straight into the royal woods, when a guard hailed us. He stood near the edge of the garden, and I cursed my carelessness. My hood was down low enough to hide my face, but it would do no good if the guards caught us.

"You," he called out. "Who goes there?"

"Run," I yelled to Pel.

Instead, Pel embraced me. I gasped as his lean, strong arms tightened around my waist. As the guard raised the alarm and ran towards us, my heart leap into my throat.

"What are you doing?" I screamed, but our sudden movement cut me off. We weren't moving forward, but up. Pel had picked me up and was flying.

"Stop struggling Nor, or I'm going to drop you," Pel yelled as we gained altitude. I hadn't even realized I was squirming till Pel mentioned it, and it took some effort to still my trembling limbs. The ground grew further away as we lifted into the sky, and the sudden height made me woozy. I never realized I was afraid of heights, but then again, I had never been so far above the ground with only a fay's iridescent wings holding me up. I looked up and saw that he was struggling.

The last time he had flown with me was the night I spent in the tower. It had been too dark and I was too scared of falling to my death to really look at his wings. Now I saw them clearly. They were large, but so delicately thin, it was a wonder they could carry even him.

The guards below were racing after us, but they were no match for Pel's flight. But one pulled out a bow and cocked it.

"Watch out!" I cried.

"For what?" Pel asked, his voice ragged from his exhaustion.

"An arrow. Coming in from the left. No, my left," I screamed as Pel veered towards, then away from the oncoming arrow. The arrow flew by close enough that I could feel the wind rush as it passed by. "We need to get further into the forest."

"You think I don't know that?" Already we were skimming over trees at the edge of the Biawood. If we could go even a bit further, I was hopeful we could lose the guards.

My relief at our escape was tempered by the terror that clutched at me as I saw the tops of trees so far away. I closed my eyes, and even then, I kept imaging myself dropping to my death. What if Pel got too tired and let me go? I focused on breathing, trying to imagine myself somewhere else, like my bedroom in the palace. I thought of the warm bed, so firm and solid, and most importantly, on the ground. Only a short time later we were slowly descending. A few feet from the ground, Pel's strength gave out and we tumbled to the forest floor. Instinctively, I tucked my head and rolled. My shoulder hit something hard, and I looked up to see a large stump. I felt sore and bruised, but nothing worse.

"Are you all right?" Pel asked. He was sitting on the ground, trying to catch his breath. He was soaked in sweat, his golden hair plastered to his head.

"Yeah, I'm fine, just a little banged up. Nothing serious," I said, rubbing my sore shoulder. "You?"

"Just need to catch my breath."

"Your wings look so . . . delicate."

"Perhaps, but they are strong. They are part of my magic, which was weakened from the iron. I shall recover."

We sat for a few minutes more, silence between us. Slowly, Pel's breathing returned to normal and my fear ebbed to a manageable level. I looked up; the sky was just starting to lighten.

"How far from the palace are we?" I asked. I wanted to make sure Pel could get away from the guards, but also started to worry about how I could return without my absence being noticed.

Pel stood and examined the way we came, though all that was visible in that direction was an ocean of trees. "It's a reasonable head start. About an hour on foot. And we have the advantage that there will be no scent of us in the woods, in case they decide to bring in dogs. We should be able to get to Magnomel by tomorrow night." He began to walk in the direction of the fay country. I mustered myself for what I had to say to him. Pel noticed I was not following him and stopped to turn around. "What?"

"I'm not going with you."

"What do you mean? Why did you get me out of the dungeon if not to escape with me?" Pel looked bewildered.

"Because I owed you for helping me in the tower. But I have to get back to the palace." I glanced up at the sky. "And I'll need to hurry if I am to get back there before I'm missed."

"Why would you go back?" Pel asked. I could see he was completely serious.

"My family is in the palace. My brothers are there. They would be in trouble if I disappeared." It was at least partially true. And it was easier to explain my familial ties than my love for a prince who had thrown Pel in a dungeon.

"We can take them with us. Go and fetch them. Or have them meet us in the woods. I can't fly all of you, but we can make good time on foot."

"Pel—"

"Nor, please. Come with me. I want to be with you. I can show you wonders you've never imagined. I know beautiful places in Magnomel, places where you will be hidden from Queen Marasina and my brother, and far from this cruel prince. You can be free. Don't you want to be free?" His green eyes seared with intensity. "We are more alike than you think," he added as his slender hands reached out and held mine, and for a moment, I let him. He kissed my knuckles, his lips like petals.

I felt the same tightening in my chest as I had the first time I'd seen him. With him, I would never have to lie. I would not have to worry about trying to run a country, or court politics, or pretend I worked miracles with straw. Or conceal what I had to do to survive. I could be myself—Nor. I wasn't sure I could ever be Queen Elenora. I was drawn to Pel, his unearthly beauty, but also his ease at being in nature.

I took a small step toward him. But I thought about Casper in his study, trying to think of ways to protect the people of Reynallis. And how his face lit up when I suggested a tour to see his subjects, to help them. I thought about the way Casper rushed to me when Eldrik had threatened me. Maybe it was selfish, but I didn't know if I could ever forgive Pel for not being there when I called to him. I relived the way Casper held me after Elrik left, and how I had felt safe and loved. I could rely on Casper. Everything else melted away in that moment. I did not want to leave Casper, ever. I could not abandon him. Gently, I pulled my hands back from Pel and stepped away from the faerie. I had made my choice.

"Pel," I said slowly, "I am engaged to Prince Casper." I held up my hand to show the gold signet ring. "You saw me dancing with him."

"The same prince that locked you up in a tower?" Pel asked. "Yes, I saw you with the prince and he put you in a fine golden dress, but he still imprisoned you. Don't you want to be free?"

"It's more complicated than that," I argued. "It was my fault I got locked up in the first place." Though the words were true, they sounded like a flimsy excuse. Pel looked at me skeptically. "You know I lied about the straw. Casper was only protecting his subjects."

"You will be living a lie the rest of your life if you go back to him." Pel pressed his lips together in a thin line. I couldn't tell if he was disappointed or angry.

"I can do more to help Reynallis by marrying him," I shot back, irritated that his words hit a sore spot in my soul because I knew they were true, no matter how much I tried to push them away. Pel only stared at me, as if he could penetrate my heart and see that I was not choosing Casper for solely altruistic reasons.

"You belong with me, Nor, not locked up in a golden cage." He extended his hands again to me, his tight grimace slipping into a hopeful smile.

Even with his sharp teeth, the smile lit up his face with a new layer of beauty.

"I can't," I said, forcing my voice to be firm. In that moment, I was sure I had two hearts. One was in love with my prince back in the palace. The other was breaking over this strange, kind faerie boy. "I'm in love with Casper."

"I see," he said, the smile slipping away. Seeing him saddened was physically painful. "I should have come for you when Elrik found you."

"But you didn't." I tried to keep my voice level but heard the slight shake.

"And if I promised to come the next time you call?"

"My answer will remain the same."

Pel studied me for a long moment, his cat eyes intense. "So, when do you marry this prince of yours?"

"We don't have a date set." Pel raised a questioning eyebrow. "But only because his coronation is upcoming, and all planning efforts are going to that. It doesn't mean I'm not serious about marrying him."

"You shall be marrying a king then, I see." There was something cold in Pel's tone now, almost bitter. "And remind me, when is his coronation?"

"Summer solstice. That's tradition in Reynallis."

Something flickered across his face, an expression I couldn't read. His head cocked to one side. He seemed to have figured out something. "I imagine coronations are big events in Reynallis."

"Yes, of course. But I don't see why you should care. It is not safe for you here." I glanced again at the lightening sky, knowing our time was running out. "You need to go."

Pel smiled then, but with such pain that I wanted to reach out to him. Instead, I curled my hands into fists to keep them by my side.

"Never forget that I offered to take you away from here. Twice. I will not offer again." He took a step away from me. "I see we all must do what we can for family and country. If I advise you to leave this golden prince before he becomes king, even if you do not come with me, will you heed wisdom, Nor?"

I shook my head. I had no doubt about my love for Casper, but I still felt my heart ache to see sadness on Pel's face.

"I was afraid that would be your answer. Goodbye, Nor."

Without looking back, Pel turned, flying deeper into the Biawood. I watched him go, taking my second heart with him.

Chapter Twenty-Six

"Well, come on Lady Elenora. What are you waiting for?" Ilana said to me from atop her horse, a lovely chestnut mare. She, Constance, Flora, and a few other ladies of the court were all sitting on their mounts, fine wool riding skirts carefully draped on one side. Only one horse, a massive black and white stallion, stood without a rider.

I cursed myself for accepting Ilana's invitation to ride. She had invited some of the ladies to go riding through the royal grounds, as an entertaining distraction from the anxiety that had rippled through the court in the days following Pel's disappearance. For my part, I had barely made it back to my rooms before Annabeth came in with the breakfast tray. But no one in the court suspected

I had aided Pel in his escape. Finn tried the hardest of everyone around me to determine the faerie's escape, making me thankful I had never told my brothers about Pel.

After chatting with the ladies, Ilana had then turned to me, and with that sugary-sweet voice, said, "I wish I could invite you as well, Lady Elenora, but I doubt you ever had the opportunity to ride before. Perhaps I could secure a little pony for you." Her smile was wide, and I could almost taste the condescension. She had not tried anything blatant since the vermillion bean powder, but it did not stop these smaller, verbal barbs.

"I can ride," I blurted out before thinking better of it.

Looking up at the huge black and white horse, who more resembled a monstrous cow than anything equine, I deeply regretted my decision. The saddle had two pommels, leather constructs that I was not at all sure how to use.

"I can't ride sidesaddle," I muttered, refusing to look at Ilana or any of the ladies.

"What was that, Lady Elenora?" Ilana asked, her voice a shade away from snide. "I didn't hear you."

"I learned to ride astride. I have never ridden sidesaddle," I said louder. Several of the ladies tittered, like annoying little birds. My face flushed hotly.

"Oh goodness," Ilana said, feigning horror. "Riding astride, that's practically indecent. It must have been very exciting."

"I think I shall just go back to the palace. You all enjoy the ride."

"Nonsense." Constance was directing her horse over to me. "You must learn eventually. Might as well take your first lesson now."

Without waiting for my response, she called for a stable hand to assist me. A young boy of twelve or thirteen, came to my aid with a small wooden stool that I climbed upon to mount the horse. When I was younger, I would simply jump onto the back of my family's horse, but then I never wore so many petticoats and skirts.

"Charm is a sweet horse, milady," the lad said, as he held the reins. The boy instructed me that I should put my legs on the left side. My left leg rested similarly to when I rode astride, but my right leg was also on the left side now, with my knee bent and both my thighs pressed into the pommel with a death grip to keep me on top of the horse.

I felt terribly off-balance. The boy handed me the reins and I carefully walked Charm a few steps. When I didn't immediately topple off the side of the saddle, I let out a breath of relief, though my thighs still squeezed the saddle grips for dear life.

"See, not that hard, is it?" Constance asked, looking at me appraisingly. In a quieter voice that only I could hear, she added, "You survived vermillion bean powder. It would be a shame to let Ilana win over something as trivial as riding a horse. Never show them your fear. Especially not if you are going to be our queen."

I grinned tightly, my legs still tightly hugging the saddle. "Princess Constance, I would almost think you want me to become queen."

Constance huffed, but I could tell it was more for my benefit than from genuine disdain. "Lady Elenora, you apparently have more determination that I gave you credit for." She glanced at Ilana, who was riding ahead of us with the other ladies of the court. "And I believe you care more for Casper than those who have been angling for a crown, no matter who they need to wed to acquire one."

I wanted to ask her more, but Flora pulled her horse up to ride beside us. "Lady Elenora," Flora said, "is this truly your first time riding sidesaddle?" From anyone else, the words would have sounded like mockery, but they were no more than polite interest coming from Flora.

"Yes, it is. My family owned a horse before the war, but we only had one saddle." I didn't add that my father had rode off to the war on that horse, and how I had never seen either of them again.

"You are doing incredibly well for your first time. You seem quite the natural," Flora said warmly.

"She is doing an *adequate* job," Constance snorted. "But your technique is lacking. We will have to get you additional lessons and make riding a regular activity. Come on, we are lagging behind." She snapped her reins, catching up to the party.

Flora smiled at me. "I think she actually complimented you." I raised an eyebrow. "No, truly. Otherwise, she would not have suggested we go riding more often."

"Am I supposed to be losing sensation in my legs?" I asked. Flora laughed and let me know that I need not grip the saddle quite so tightly. I sighed. "I guess that is as close as I'm getting to being in her good graces."

Flora stared fondly at Constance. "Give her time. I can already tell she's coming around." Flora turned to me, the humor back in her eyes. "The first year I was at the palace I was absolutely terrified of her." She smiled. "But now there is no place I'd rather be than by her side."

"How did the two of you become so close?" I asked, interested in knowing how anyone could pierce Constance's armor. "You two are so . . . different." Flora's amicable warmth was the opposite of Constance's cool control.

Flora laughed softly. "*Because* we are so different, I think. We complement each other well. We are like puzzle pieces, different but fitting together."

I bit my lip, thinking about how I fit with Casper. Pel was more like me, but Casper brought out the side of me that wanted to be a better person. "I've seen how you calm Constance, but how does she balance you? If you don't mind my asking," I quickly added, in case Flora thought I was prying.

But Flora only stared ahead, her focus on Constance. "In her own way, she keeps me calm. When I first came to Reynallis, I was terribly homesick. Oh, I knew I was doing a service to my country, but I desperately missed Faradisia. I would cry myself to sleep most nights. I assumed it was late enough that no one would hear me, but Constance found out. She researched all sorts of Faradisian delicacies and ensured they were included at every meal. She even managed to find a chef that could recreate the caramelized plum cakes that we have on our name days. It was a welcomed taste of home."

"She does seem well-versed in international cultures," I said, thinking back to how easily Constance had identified the vermillion bean powder.

Flora smiled. "Constance believes knowledge is her greatest weapon at court. You should see the way she has been poring over the peace treaty, trying to find some loophole so I can stay." Flora's hand flew to her mouth, as though she had said more than she intended.

"Now that Casper is back?" I asked. Flora nodded. "I think it's obvious that you want to stay, so why can't you?"

"Initially, it was a trade, a one-for-one arrangement. So it looks unbalanced if I stay in Reynallis. But I have not given up hope." Flora's lips quirked up. "I have never met anyone as stubborn as Constance. If there is a way, she will find it."

We rode for a while through the blooming rose gardens and the fruit trees in the royal private orchard. Summer was in full force and the air was warm and sweet with the smells of apples, figs, and pears. The sky was overcast, a hazy gray, but so far, the weather held. Riding sidesaddle at a slow pace was not terribly difficult, and I was rewarded with a sullen Ilana, disappointed that I had not failed to ride. The other ladies of the court seemed impressed and chatted with me as we rode. I was careful to smile and not let on that my thighs were aching with the strain of the ride. I silently wondered if I'd be able to walk the next day.

When we reached the edge of the royal forest grounds, the wind turned chilly, picking up in speed as the sky grew dark with a summer storm.

"We should return to the palace," Constance said, raising her voice to be heard above the wind. "Before it starts to rain." As if on cue, the clouds blackened to bruised purple and rain began to fall, remarkably hard. Some of the ladies cried out, but I didn't mind the rain. This was nothing compared to the winters I had spent on the road. I was secretly pleased to see Ilana amongst the ladies who were complaining loudest. I looked at Flora, who grinned back at me.

"You don't have a problem with the rain?" I asked.

"It's only water. In Faradisia, we don't get much rain. It's considered a sign of good luck. But we should head back."

I rode alongside Flora for a while, enjoying the rain, despite the difficulty it caused in navigating the terrain. Charm was a steady horse and didn't falter once. But I noticed some of the other ladies' horses weren't fairing so well. Ilana's mare was especially skittish.

The palace was just coming back in sight when thunder cracked close to us. Ilana's horse let out a terrible whinny and rose on her hind legs in panic. Spooked, she set off at a wild run. Ilana screamed, unable to control her. The other ladies cried in fright, and though a few tried to catch up with Ilana, her horse outpaced them all. Suddenly our rivalry seemed petty as I heard her shrieks. She was terrified.

Oh, Chace's den, so much for propriety, I hiked up my sodden woolen skirts and swung my leg around to sit astride. The saddle wasn't designed for this, but I leaned in, touching Charm's wet neck, which was warm and solid to my touch. *Let's see if I remember how to do this.* I sent a quick prayer to the Holy Family and kicked the sides of Charm, sending him galloping after Ilana. My legs felt stretched apart as I pressed my knees together to stay on.

Charm picked up speed and the wind and rain whipped into my face. But almost as quickly, I felt elation at riding a galloping horse. Ilana was still a good way ahead of me. I could hear her screams carried on the wind. She was a white blur on the brown horse. I urged Charm faster, and he obliged.

We sped along the edge of the forest, getting closer to the palace and Ilana. I gritted my teeth as the reins cut into my palms. Charm was foaming at the mouth, and horse-froth flew into my face in addition to the rain. I tried to wipe my eyes on my sleeve without loosening my grip on the reins. Charm was hot and wet, and I couldn't tell if it was the rain or his sweat. The air smelled of leather and water, and the sound of his hooves pounding down melded into the pelting sound of rain. I looked ahead, to see that we were gaining on Ilana and her horse. The horse was still running, erratically, but it was getting tired. The reins were flapping around wildly, as Ilana had lost her grip and was holding onto the saddle for dear life. I directed Charm to run up close to Ilana's horse, which he did with ease. I grabbed for the chestnut's reins, but they slipped out of my hands at first. When I was finally able to catch the wet leather, I held on firm. The mare bucked, and I had to squeeze her reins with all my strength not to let go as the leather burned into my palms. I called out to the horse and carefully slowed Charm, which, in turn, slowed the mare. We trotted and then finally came to a walk, the mare snorting and breathing heavily, but no longer a wild creature.

Once I deemed the mare safe, I handed the reins to Ilana. She was white as a sheet but took them. I didn't know what to expect as she stared, at me, open-mouthed.

"You're riding astride," she finally said.

Really? I thought, anger suddenly flaring up in me. *I just risked my neck for this girl, and all she can do is insult my riding?* Without saying anything, I turned Charm back to the palace and set him at a gallop. I didn't look back.

Chapter Twenty-Seven

"Oh, milady, you'll catch cold." Annabeth piled another blanket on me. The first few had been nice, but I was starting to feel smothered.

"Really, I am fine. I only got a bit wet," I said, carefully extricating myself from the mountain of blankets.

I was helping myself to a second cup of tea and a butter cookie when there was a knock at my door. I nodded to Annabeth, who opened the door.

Standing there was the ice queen herself, Lady Ilana Oleshin. She had also changed, now wearing an elegant but simple dress of deep blue. Her hair was still wet but had been pulled back into a simple braid. She looked acutely uncomfortable.

"What do you want?" I snapped. I took a savage bite of my cookie and turned my attention to the fire, refusing to look at her. "If you want to berate my riding style some more, please just go away."

"No, not at all." Ilana sounded pained. "I wanted to apologize."

"Excuse me?" I said, my head snapping up to look at her.

"May I come in?"

"I guess so," I replied, confused. Annabeth gave Ilana a quick curtsey before running off to busy herself somewhere else. I wished I could leave too, but I sat immobile in my chair, waiting for Ilana to explain herself.

"I am sorry about my comment on your riding. I had not meant offense. I was merely so surprised."

"Surprised that I wasn't sitting like a lady or surprised that I could actually ride a horse?"

"Both, actually. But most unexpected is that you risked your own safety to help me." Ilana sounded genuinely astonished, and it hurt.

"I am sorry you think so little of me." Though I thought of the night I sent her the fake letter, and knew she had good reason to think poorly of me.

"No, it's not that. I'm not saying this right." For the first time since I had met her at the faire, Ilana seemed flustered. "We have been cruel to each other, and it is I who started it." Ilana stared at her feet, unable to meet my eyes. "And yet, you risked your safety to help me. It's not a kindness I'm used to."

"I wasn't being kind. Just because I don't like you doesn't mean I wanted to see you thrown from a horse and break your neck."

Ilana looked uncomfortable, but she nodded. "I am sorry."

"Why do you hate me?" I asked. "I mean before I sent you the letter," I quickly added. "I had done nothing to you, and you set me up and humiliated me in front of half the ladies of court. And for Aloisia's sake, that powder is wretched stuff." I shivered thinking about the terrible itching from the vermillion bean.

"I didn't want Casper to marry you," she said bluntly. Her answer wasn't entirely unexpected, but I was astonished at her brutal honesty.

"Do you still love him?" I had been so relieved Ilana had left me alone after the night I forged Casper's letter, I guiltily wondered if I had caused her more heartbreak than I realized.

"No," she said with a sad laugh. "I've only loved one person, and he's dead. But love has nothing to do with it. My family hopes for a royal marriage, and I will be disappointing them greatly. And with Christopher's death, my only other option was Casper."

Things slowly clicked into place. Constance's pointed remark about someone angling for a crown no matter who they had to marry and Ilana's pointed remark, *you know nothing about my love,* suddenly made sense. "King Christopher, was he the one you loved?"

Ilana nodded slowly, her eyes gleaming. For a moment I thought she might cry, but she pulled herself together. "We were going to be engaged," she said softly. "I wanted to leave Reynallis after he died, but my father told me that my entire family was still depending on me to secure a royal marriage. They had already planned on it when Christopher and I . . ." she trailed off, probably not wishing to speak about her dead love.

"I had no idea," I admitted, not sure what else to say. Ilana had done so much to vex me, but now I felt sympathy for her. "Our situations are vastly different, but I know what it's like to have your family depend on you."

Ilana gave me a weak smile. "Well, mine will simply have to adjust to disappointment. I never relished the idea of marrying

Christopher's brother. The night you sent me that letter, I cried, knowing I would have to marry Casper.

"Of course, I was furious you had made a fool of me, but I was also relieved. And I've seen the way Casper looks at you. Christopher used to look at me like that." She sniffled, but quickly composed herself.

I didn't know what to say but was saved from coming up with an answer by another knock at my door. *Who is it now?* I wasn't sure where Annabeth had run off to, so I went and opened the door to see Casper standing on the other side. My face flushed as Ilana's words repeated themselves in my head. Did he look at me a certain way? I couldn't tell.

"Nor, I heard what happened and wanted to make sure you were all right," he said, breathlessly, and I realized he had been running. "I was told one of the horses spooked in the storm and you went galloping after it!" He paused, seeing Ilana. "Lady Ilana," he said courteously, though he couldn't completely hide his curiosity at seeing her here. He might not have all the details, but he was as aware of our rivalry as the rest of the court.

"Your Highness," Ilana said, giving Casper a curtsey. "I should let you two talk. I was about to leave." With that, she quickly made her way to the door.

"Wait, Ilana," I said. When Ilana turned, I added, "I'm sorry too." Ilana gave me a quick smile, the first I had ever seen her direct at me that was not dripping with disdain. When she left the room, Casper threw me a questioning look.

"It's a long story, but I might have made a new friend."

"Glad to hear you are playing nice for a change." Casper smiled and I pouted in mock irritation.

"I am always nice."

Casper wrapped his arms around me, his bright smile erasing all the worry in his face. "I am just so relieved it was not you thrown off a horse."

I squirmed in his embrace, freeing one of my arms so I could playfully punch him in shoulder. "It would take a lot more than a horse to fell me," I joked.

"I have no doubt, Nor. You are the bravest, cleverest woman I know. I think nothing short of the entire fay army could stop you."

I had to bite back a sting of guilt, his words conjuring up images of Pel in the dungeon. I knew I owed Pel, that I had to save my friend, but I hated keeping such a secret from Casper. I wished I was brave enough to confess, but my nerves failed. Instead, I burrowed my head into his shoulder, and as he stroked my hair, I pretended that I had done nothing wrong.

Chapter Twenty-Eight

Almost before I knew it, the morning of Casper's coronation had arrived. I had been up since sunrise, my nerves jangling. I was excited for Casper, but there was also a jittery energy in me. Once he was officially crowned king of Reynallis, we would be able to set out and tour the country. I longed to leave the palace walls, even if only temporarily. I had not been much help to Casper lately, too preoccupied assisting Constance with the coronation details, and, to be honest, avoiding him. Having Pel help me transform straw into gold had been a dangerous secret, but having freed Pel after Casper gave specific orders to imprison him felt even more treasonous, as if I was personally betraying Casper, which probably I was. Traveling the country would be a welcome distraction. If I could help enough people, I would not feel quite so guilty knowing I had lied to Casper. *I did not have a choice,* I told myself, justifying my duplicity.

I was pacing around my bed chamber, deep in thought, when Annabeth arrived. I did not hear her enter and jumped when she opened the door.

"Annabeth," I said breathlessly, trying to control my nerves. "You startled me."

"My apologies, milady," Annabeth said. She dropped into a curtsey; awkward due to the large items she was holding.

"It's fine," I reassured her. I had to stop myself from assisting her as she lay out the packages she had been carrying. A stunning red and gold dress with oversized sleeves and full skirts now lay on the bed. I admired the creation, gently running my fingers along the fine embroidery of climbing roses and large circles patterned throughout. *Spinning wheels,* I realized. Casper wanted to make sure I felt fully included as a new almost-member of the royal family.

Annabeth laced me up and helped me into the delicate golden slippers. I remembered with a trace of amusement how awkwardly I tottered about on the small heels my first night at the palace. Much had happened since then, the least of which was that I could now easily walk, and even dance, in such delicate shoes, even if I still preferred sturdy boots.

Annabeth carefully combed my hair before creating intricate braids, woven through with strands of gold and set with the same ruby hairpins I had worn on the night of our engagement ball. The same ones I had used to pick the lock and free Pel. I was careful not to give anything away, as I stared at myself in the large silver mirror. My hair gleamed, almost golden in the morning light. The girl in the mirror looked far more regal than I imagined I could ever feel.

"Milady, you look so beautiful," Annabeth gushed when she had finished styling my hair.

"Thank you," I said, trying to sound confident.

"You will make a lovely queen. I am sure of it."

I didn't say anything, but rose, careful not the wrinkle the lavish skirts. Annabeth curtseyed again and I made sure I was smiling as I headed for the door. Sir Yanis was there to escort me to Casper's rooms, where I would be meeting up with him and Constance so we could enter the royal cathedral together. It would only be the three of us, as my brothers and Flora would be waiting for us at the cathedral, seated near the front in places of honor.

"My lady," Sir Yanis said when he saw me and dropped into a low bow.

Most of the court was already at the cathedral, but the servants we passed all bowed or curtsied as I walked by. I hoped I looked like a majestic leader, but I felt my stomach roiling with nerves. *Stop being foolish,* I chided myself. I wasn't the one being crowned today. I simply had to arrive with Casper, sit in the front pew, and watch him become king. Despite telling myself that, I could not force the butterflies from my stomach.

In front of Casper's door, I took a deep breath as Sir Yanis knocked and announced me. When Casper saw me, he just stared.

"Do I look presentable?" I asked, suddenly self-conscious.

"You look absolutely stunning," he said and pulled me into a tight embrace.

"You are going to wrinkle my . . ." I started but was cut off by his lips on mine. They were warm and soft, his kiss brief but passionate. And when he pulled away, I felt dazed.

"Sorry, I could not help myself."

"No," I said weakly, smiling. "That was nice."

"Constance should be here soon."

"Are you nervous?" I asked. Casper appeared every bit the king in his red and gold velvet tunic and embroidered cape. And he looked so incredibly handsome that I had to fight the urge to kiss him again.

"Perhaps a bit," he confessed, and for a moment looked adorably sheepish.

I slipped my hand into his and gave it a squeeze. "I know you will make an excellent king."

"How can someone this good looking not make an excellent king?" Casper joked. We stood there for a few minutes, hand in hand. It was a nice moment, and I could almost forget my anxieties. "Nor, I would like to give you a present," Casper said, suddenly breaking the silence.

"You don't need to give me anything. This is your day." *And you've given me so much,* I thought.

"But I want to." Casper turned to face me, all kidding replaced by a serious sincerity. "Without you, this day would be but a painful reminder of my brother's death. With you, this day holds hope. Hope that his death was not in vain, that I can be a king worthy of his sacrifice, that I can save Reynallis from the fay." He beamed at me. "You give me that hope, Nor. Name something, anything you want, and I shall give it to you."

"Oh, so you want to give me a present, but not have to pick it out?" I said, trying to tease, but my throat felt thick, guilt making it hard to get the words out. I knew if I asked for lands or jewels or titles, Casper would grant them all, but there was only one thing I wanted. His forgiveness would be the richest gift I could ever wish for, and more that I deserved. "I want a boon."

"A boon?" Casper's eyes raised in confusion.

"Yes, I want one royal favor. A future promise for forgiveness, or whatever I might ask." I added the last part quickly and held my breath, waiting for his reply.

Casper's brow softened, and he smiled, as though my request was odd, but charming. "Nor, I don't think you will ever need my forgiveness—"

"Just in case," I pleaded.

"Very well, Nor. If it pleases you, I shall grant you a boon. Though I thought you would ask for a horse or a garden or something."

"It is all I want," I said, stepping in closer to him, close enough to inhale the spices of his soap. "After all, I have you." And after his coronation, I could truly be honest with him. The thought lifted a heavy weight from my chest.

"I believe it's time to make my little brother a king," Constance said as she entered the room. She was stunning in a red silk dress, embroidered with gold and black roses. Her black hair was elegantly styled and a golden tiara set with rubies adorned her dark locks.

"You are radiant dear sister," Casper said. "Good looks must run in the family."

"And you are presentable, I guess," Constance said, but her voice was unusually warm.

"Shall we go and make your presentable little brother king?" Casper asked, an impish look in his dark eyes.

But Constance remained motionless, her eyes suddenly glossy. "Actually, you look the very image of Christopher."

Casper froze, uncertain.

"I know I will never be as great as him. But I will do everything in my power to live up to his legacy."

"He would be so proud of you." Constance's words were soft as she appraised him.

Casper's lips twitched up in a smile, and something strikingly familial passed between the royal siblings. "It means a lot to hear you say that."

"I'm sorry, Casper." A tear rolled down Constance's face.

"What is the matter?" Casper's smile immediately made way for anxious concern.

"I should have written. All those years ago." For the first time since I arrived at the palace, Constance was crying. I had never seen her so vulnerable.

A brief look of pain flashed over Casper's face before he smoothed it away. "Water under the bridge, dear sister."

"No, it was truly wretched of me." Casper started to interject, but Constance waved him to stop. "It hurt so much to lose you. I thought it would be easier to try to forget you. And then Flora came, and I was afraid that if you returned, she would be taken from me. I was selfish, terribly selfish. I should have been a better sister to you. But you have always been so responsible, so dutiful to your family and your country. I know Christopher would have been pleased to see you become king."

Constance deflated after her speech, as though her haughty airs were only in place to hide the vulnerable young woman beneath them, and I was reminded how tiny she was. I waited for Casper's response, hardly daring to breathe myself. But Casper needed only a moment to take in his sister's words before he threw his arms around her, embracing her tightly. Constance's arms stuck to her side and she stiffened, unfamiliar with such affection, before she melted into her brother's embrace, hugging him back with equal intensity.

"I love you Constance. And I forgive you." Casper's words were muffled by Constance's hair, but I could still hear them. I blinked back a happy pressure behind my own eyes. "And we will find a way to keep Flora at court."

"Thank you, Casper."

After a long time, Casper let go of his sister. I studiously stared out the window, pretending I had not witnessed such an intimate family moment as Constance wiped her eyes with the palms of her hands and took several steadying breaths. Finally, she turned to me. Her eyes were a touch watery, but her smile was genuine. "You," she said, turning to me, "look magical."

I smiled and could not help but give a twirl in my gown, the skirts fluttering out. I imagined that they would glitter under the chandeliers when Casper and I danced after the feast tonight.

The royal cathedral was a massive structure with vast, ivory walls that swept up into large, golden-domed ceilings. As with the rest of the palace, green vines of climbing roses decorated the walls. The front of the cathedral consisted of an enormous wall of stained-glass roses, their red and pink panels throwing colored light onto the waiting crowd.

As the wide doors were flung open, the sound of hundreds of voices crashed over me. In addition to the many rows of pews on the main level, there was a balcony level where local peasants were allowed to attend the ceremony, and every seat was taken. The nobles of the court were there, dressed in their finest outfits of silk, velvet and lace. Foreign dignitaries and various visiting lords and ladies I did not recognize also filled the immense space. My stomach lurched, and I was glad I had only eaten a few bites of toast this morning. I squeezed tighter on Casper's arm.

Casper turned to me, and for just a moment he looked like a frightened boy, not a man about to be crowned king. Somehow, that actually relaxed me a bit, making me feel like I wasn't the only one feeling apprehensive. I forced myself to smile at him, trying to pour my support for him into that small gesture, and he smiled back, suddenly the confident future king again.

"Ready to be crowned?" I asked.

Casper took a deep breath and led me down the center aisle. Everyone stood at the sight of us and a rush of fabrics against the polished wood pews filled the hallowed place. The noise of the crowd grew in anticipation as we passed, and I focused on keeping my head up and looking forward. At the end of the long aisle was an altar, from which Father Geoffroi, a priest from the Order of The Divine Mother, stood, his red robes bright against the white walls.

As we reached the front of the cathedral, I removed my arm from Casper. He gave me a quick kiss, sweet and swift, like a feather blown across my lips. I knew it was not remotely part of the etiquette for a king, and that made it delightful. Without a word, Casper turned to the altar and I crossed the short distance to the pew in the front row. It was reserved for myself and Constance, who was only a few steps behind me. Devon, Finn, Jacobie, Duke Arnette, and Flora were all seated on the pew behind us. I flashed them a quick smile before sitting down next to Constance. We settled our skirts and stared up at Casper.

Casper carefully knelt before the priest, his red velvet cape flowing behind him. Father Geoffroi began with a lengthy prayer, asking for the blessing of the Father, the Mother and the twins, Aloisia and Chace.

"May the Mother watch over you," the priest said as he anointed Casper with rose oil, roses being sacred to the Mother as a sign of renewing life.

"I beg the Mother to show kindness on me as she is the mother of all creation. I pray she guides me to protect my people," Casper said, reciting the required lines. I couldn't see his face as his back was toward the congregation, but his voice rang strong and clear.

"May the Father grant you long life for your reign," the priest said. This time he handed Casper a tall, white candle that Casper lit from one of the nearby candles. Fire was sacred to the Father, and a sign of eternal life.

"I beg the Father to provide me with a long reign so that I may serve my people well." I was impressed that Casper could recite his part so smoothly. I was sure I would be stumbling on my words with so many watching me. I had no idea how I'd manage reciting wedding vows in front of the entire court when the time came. I wondered if I could get away with writing them on the inside of my hand.

Father Geoffroi then took a soft, brown object off the altar. "May the sister Aloisia grant you wisdom during your reign." The priest slipped the object around Casper's neck. I realized it was a garland of owl feathers.

"I beg Aloisia deems my intentions pure and grants my wish to rule as a just and wise king with order in my kingdom," Casper recited. Aloisia was the goddess of wisdom and order, and thus highly respected by kings and religious rulers. I was less sure how her brother, the god of chaos, would be included in the ceremony.

"And finally, may the brother Chace inspire you to solve the problems in the kingdom and outwit its enemies." With that, Father Geoffroi handed Casper a silver chalice, one I knew must be filled with honeyed mead, a drink sacred to Chace. With one gulp, Casper had drained the cup.

"I beg Chace to allow me to be a clever ruler in times of peace and times of war."

The main tributes to the gods over, Father Geoffroi continued with a long prayer followed by an even longer sermon on the importance of a king to his country. I was trying hard not to fidget. Finally, the royal crown was brought out, and even I gasped as it was pulled from a polished chest.

A maid of the Mother presented the priest with the ornately carved wooden box, richly inlaid with mother of pearl and silver. The box gleamed in the light from the stained-glass windows. Father Geoffroi carefully withdrew a key from around his neck and put it in the lock at the front of the box. With a click, the lid opened, and he reached inside to pull out the king's crown.

A murmur of excitement rose in the crowd as Father Geoffroi held the crown aloft, ensuring everyone got a good look at the headpiece before he placed it on Casper's head. It was an ornate thing, far more jeweled and sculptured than the simple golden band Casper had been wearing.

Wrought out of gold, domed arches converged in the center, from which rose a large ruby. Underneath the domes rich, red velvet lined a gold frame that was encrusted with pearls, diamonds and emeralds. With so many gems, it had to weigh a ton, but to his credit, Casper never so much as flinched when the crown was place on his head.

Father Geoffroi gave Casper a final blessing before nodding at him. "May the Holy Family keep you safe, smile down on Reynallis, and grant you a long reign. Please rise, King Casper."

With that, Casper rose, graceful, even with the weight of the crown. He turned to face us, and I gasped along with the crowd. Something about the crown or the ceremony had given him an air of authority, and there could be no doubt in anyone's mind that Casper was now the one and rightful ruler of Reynallis. He stood tall, a commanding presence. As his eyes swept the pews of the cathedral, he silently declared himself king to everyone in attendance. He radiated power, and I shivered for a moment, not sure why.

"Bow down before your king," Father Geoffroi called out, breaking into the awe that was rippling through the crowd. "Long live the king!"

As everyone rose to their feet, the words turned into a rhythmic chant, growing in intensity as everyone from the great nobles to the peasants in the balcony repeated them: "Long live the king!" I joined in, swept away in the presence of greatness that was Reynallis's new king. It did not matter the boy in front of me was Casper, my friend and betrothed who was charming, with eyes that lit up with new ideas and cracked jokes to make anyone feel at ease. Right now, he was our strong and imposing king.

With complete certainty, I knew I had requested the right gift. I would be able to tell Casper the truth about Pel, about the straw, and use the boon to ask for forgiveness. I owed him the truth as both my king and my betrothed. And since he loved me, he would understand why I did what I'd done. I would wait till the ceremonies and feast were over, but afterwards, I would speak the truth. A thrill of nerves went through me, but also a new lightness, knowing that soon, I would no longer need to hold the burden of my secrets.

Chapter Twenty-Nine

"Long live the king! Long live the king!"

The chant grew louder as pews were pushed back, scraping against the stone floor. Lords and ladies rose, a great wave of silks and velvets that peaked as everyone got to their feet, and then slowly sank down as everyone fell into deep bows and curtseys. I did the same, dropping into a curtsey, though I continued to stare up at Casper through my lashes.

He looked commanding, and so strikingly handsome, like the best version of someone a portrait painter would create, leaving out the flaws. Casper's strong jaw was set and his eyes were dark and intense as he surveyed the crowd. He still held the lit candle and it made the owl garland shine and the crown sparkle.

I sent my own silent prayer to the Mother. *After tonight, no more secrets.*

"Arise, my subjects, subjects of Reynallis." Though Casper didn't yell, his voice was powerful, radiating through the room. A hush fell over the crowd as everyone stood, eyes proudly fixed on their new king. If anyone was concerned that a younger brother was taking the crown, their doubts had been crushed. In that moment, with the light from the stained-glass window illuminating him in a warm halo, Casper looked every bit a legendary king.

The chanting resumed.

Casper briefly bowed his head in acknowledgement, then stepped away from the altar and proceeded down the center aisle.

He stopped right next to where I was standing. All around, people had begun to bow and curtsey again. I dropped into a curtsey before Constance whispered to me, "He's waiting for you Elenora. Go."

Right. I rose, trying to maintain a dignified air, and stood next to Casper, taking his proffered arm. He gave a quick wink, which made my heart flutter. I smiled, and together we slowly made our way out of the cathedral, giving everyone the opportunity to gaze upon their new king. Constance and Father Geofroi fell in step behind us, and my brothers and Flora followed behind them.

We only made it a few steps before the doors crashed open. A swarm of stunningly beautiful men, and even some women, rushed into the cathedral, bright silver swords drawn and glittering. A blast of arrows hit the crowd. I looked up to see that archers had invaded the balcony level. Screams of surprise arose around me, and I just stood, dumbfounded, trying to take it all in.

Casper reacted on instinct, pulling me behind him. I nearly tripped on his long velvet cape.

"We're being attacked by the fay!" I screamed as my senses returned. Our assailants were vicious, cutting down the frightened nobles who were not quick enough to move away. Some of the lords and knights had swords, but everyone was packed so tightly into the pews, it was hard for anyone to maneuver. Cries of fright and pain filled the air as people tried to fend off the fay or hide under pews.

I pulled out the dagger hidden around my leg. Constance would be horrified to see me pull up my skirts, but having a weapon was worth it—though a small dagger would be little defense against so many swords and arrows. Where were the royal guards? The guards who had been in the cathedral rushed to our defense, but I did not see any reinforcements coming from the outside.

I almost didn't notice that a faerie had leapt from the balcony, gliding on silver wings to land right behind me. He raised his silver sword with ease, and I was nearly struck by the broad side of his sword.

I whirled around and jumped out of the way, less agile with all my skirts, but I missed the brunt of the blow, getting nothing more than a scrape that ran along my arm. I held out my dagger, which looked especially insignificant against my foe's long silver sword. The faerie was tall and lean, but stronger than he appeared, as he maneuvered the sword with an inhuman grace. He wore silver mail over forest-green leathers, and like Pel, he had pale, luminous skin, but his eyes were a crystal ice blue, pure as the sky, and his hair a shining onyx black. Unlike Pel, there was no warmth in his eyes, and he stared at me coldly. His gaze reminded me of Elrik. I shuddered, terror freezing my veins.

"Are you going to fight me with that?" the fay scoffed. His voice was smooth, but deep and deadly, and I felt like I was slipping into a nest of vipers.

The blue-eyed fay lunged for me again. It broke me out of immobility like a dunking in cold water. I tried to back up, but Casper was still standing behind me. A quick glance told me he was fighting off another fay, but I couldn't get a good look as I needed to stay focused on the one trying to kill me. I kept on the balls of my feet, waiting for the fay to attack. As he brought up the sword again, ready to deal a killing blow, I leapt toward him, grabbing his arm and pulled. I would not have had enough leverage to change the direction of his swing, so instead I pulled down, the same way he was going, giving him so much force that he swung down, missing me and stumbling to the ground. As he did so, he quickly turned it into a roll.

I had few precious seconds to come up with a plan for when the faerie got back up and continued his attack. I looked around, desperate for a more substantial weapon. There was nothing. So I rushed to the faerie, who was almost on his feet, and jabbed my dagger into his sword arm. He dropped his sword and let out a scream, the sound blending with all the other screams in the room. His hands swung out and clamped on my arms, pinning them to my sides with surprising force. I tried to kick out, but he lifted me and threw me across the room.

I crashed into one of the pews. My shoulder took most of the impact, but my head followed closely after with a hard crack that sent black spots floating into my vision. Pain ripped up my shoulder and into my head. I fought an intense wave of dizziness and sudden nausea, afraid I would vomit or faint. Forcing myself to take a few breaths from the slight cover of the pew, I cautiously peered around.

The cathedral was pure chaos. Bodies lay strewn around the floor and slumped over pews. It was mostly nobles, dark crimson blood from arrows or sword wounds staining their bright silks. A few of the faeries were also down, golden blood pooling around them. I couldn't tell if they were injured or killed. I didn't even know if fay could be killed. But there were still too many of them still attacking. They were so graceful and beautiful, so strong and deadly, like angels of death summoned to the cathedral.

I desperately searched for my friends and my brothers amidst the fray. Casper was easy to spot, still in the aisle, his dark hair slicked against his head, his crown lost. He was fighting hard, hampered by his cape. Some of the royal guards had finally come to assist him.

I wanted to go and help, but I had to find my brothers. They had been right behind us when we began to exit the cathedral, but I had lost them in ensuing chaos. I scanned the room, desperate to find them, when I heard my name called.

"Nor!" I bobbed up from the pews to risk a glance and saw Finn. He was crouched near a bench close to the front and gestured frantically for me to come over. I felt a wave of relief at the sight of him and prayed Jacobie and Devon were with him.

I was about to move when I saw Duke Arnette, fighting a fierce-looking faerie, cross in front of the aisle. The faerie had silver hair and a cruel smile that chilled my blood. The duke, despite his older years, kept pace with the faerie, blow for blow. He parried a strike from the faerie and returned one of his own. Gold-silver blood spurted from a gash on the faerie's arm, as the creature screeched with anger and pain. The duke took the opportunity to raise his sword in a killing blow, but before he could make the final strike, an arrow hit him in the eye. I screamed as blood came pouring out of the socket. He gurgled, mouth spewing foamy blood as he fell backward, his good eye staring straight ahead, not seeing anything.

A sick sense of horror washed over me. I tasted bile and had to fight the urge to vomit. I could still hear Finn calling to me, even above the din of the fighting. I had to get to him, make sure he and Jacobie and Devon were all safe, but the idea of moving seemed impossible. I wanted to curl up under the pew and close my eyes, hiding, pretending that this was all a bad dream. I saw several other people doing just that, trying to make themselves small and unseen.

But Finn kept calling to me, yelling my name. I had to get to him. Clamping down on my own terror, I forced myself to move, crawling down the aisle, praying I would be overlooked in the chaos that surrounded me. I tried not to look at the bodies that lay across my path, moving around them as carefully as I could. I desperately wished I were in tunic and trousers. My voluptuous skirts were heavy, dragging me down and picking up every bit of gore and blood from the floor. I wished I had time to cut off some of my massive skirts, but I refused to stop. I kept low, but an arrow found me anyway and hit my hem. It missed my leg, but I was unable to move forward till I pulled the shaft out of the thick material.

"Finn," I cried, as I got closer to my brother. "Keep your head down." When I finally reached him, Finn was huddled low in the pew, with Jacobie in his arms. I could have wept with relief to see them. Next to him were Flora, Ilana, and another young lady of the court. She had chestnut hair and was about my age. I had seen her around but couldn't remember her name. Everyone looked fearful, but seemed unharmed.

"Elenora," Flora cried, and crawled toward me, giving me a tight embrace. I saw tears in her eyes. "You're bleeding," she said, gesturing to the place where my head had hit the pew.

"It's nothing," I said, hoping that was true.

"Where is Constance? And Casper?"

"I don't know," I confessed, feeling a terrible stab of guilt. "I didn't see Constance once the fighting started. I was with Casper, but I got thrown to the side. I saw the royal guards go to aid him," I added. I prayed they were keeping him safe. I *needed* him to be safe. "Are you all right?" I asked, knowing it was inadequate. "Is anyone hurt?"

"No, we found cover right when the attack started," Finn said. I felt proud of his quick action. "But Devon . . ."

"Where is he?"

"I was attacked," Ilana said, her voice a sob. "He defended me and attacked the vile thing that had gone after me. He got lost in the melee," she added gesturing to the fight going on.

"Flora, is there another exit?" I asked.

"No, the only way in is through the back," Flora said. Her eyes were wide and scared, but her voice stayed steady.

I looked around, forcing myself to breathe and to think. So far, the fay army had not reached the front of the cathedral, but it would not take long, especially if the fighting went poorly for us. The exit in the back was blocked by the battle. The clashing of swords and screams were so loud my head rattled, increasing the pain from where I'd hit the pew. Blood from the cut on my forehead was running down my face, and I had to wipe it out of my eyes. The midday light from the stained-glass wall made my head pound harder.

The stained-glass wall.

I swiveled my head to look at it. There were iron inlays that framed the pieces of colored glass, but they did not look very thick. I told the group to stay put and made for the altar. I didn't make it more than a step before I felt a pull on my skirt.

"Nor, don't go!" Jacobie was gripping my skirt so tightly, his tiny hand was white with effort. His tear-stained face was more panicked than I had ever seen it.

"I'll be right back," I reassured him, as I pried his fingers from my dress.

"No!" he screamed. "You'll leave and never come back. Just like Mama and Papa!"

"Jacobie, stop!" I snapped. My stomach twisted as he let go of me, a look of shock and hurt on his face. "I need to do this so we can get away. I need you to protect Finn and these ladies," I said, gesturing to Flora and Ilana. "I promise, I will be back for you."

I tucked Jacobie back into Finn's care and made my way toward the pulpit, moving quickly. As I approached, I began to push the heavy altar. The deeply polished wooden alter reached my shoulders. I heaved at it, pain shooting up my injured shoulder. I sucked in air, forcing myself to keep going and it finally moved, but only a few inches.

"Here, I'll help." I looked over to see Flora had followed me. I wanted to send her back with the others, but I needed the assistance.

"Now," I said, and both of us pushed at the wooden structure. It moved a few more inches, and I looked toward the window. Only a few more feet, I thought desperately. At least the cathedral was on the ground level, and the drop out the window would not be far. That was if we could smash through the window first.

We had pushed the altar about halfway to the window when I saw movement in the periphery of my vision. I whirled in time to see a faerie, strikingly beautiful with white curls and silver armor, swing down a sword at me. I had just enough time to push Flora and myself out of the way. The fay's sword went crashing into the altar, making a deep cut in the wood.

"What do you want?" I screamed, not knowing what else to do. This faerie was a good head taller than me. He approached again, dancer-like in his grace. I brandished my dagger, but he just laughed as he moved toward me.

"You kill ours so we kill yours," he said, almost conversationally before raising his sword for another swing.

I was confused by his words, but certainly wasn't going to get myself killed, not if I could help it. I jumped to the side, his blade missing my torso, but catching my arm. His silver sword cut through my red velvet sleeves and sliced into my arm. I gasped from the pain but kept my eyes on the faerie.

"We didn't kill any fay," I said. Maybe if I could keep him talking, he'd be slower on his next attack. "We can find out if anyone is hunting the fay. Stop them." I was rambling and I knew it, but I felt desperate, manic.

"Violence is the only language humans know. So, we've learned your language," he said taking another step toward me. I took a quick step back but tripped on my torn skirts and fell down hard. I tried to scramble backward as the fay raised his sword yet again, but my movements were hampered by the layers of skirts and petticoats under my dress. I thought I heard a nearby scream but couldn't be sure if it was Flora or myself. I flung up my arms, trying to protect my face.

The blow never came. Instead, another sword—one of simple iron—clanged against the silver blade. I looked up to see Sir Yanis battling furiously with the fay. The pair was surprisingly well matched. The white-haired fay was swift, his movements almost a blur of motion. But Sir Yanis was built like an ox, and all those muscles gave him great power, which he expertly used to his advantage, even forcing the faerie onto the defensive.

I didn't watch the battle for long, scrambling up to my feet and returning to the altar. Flora was visibly shaking, and I worried she would go into shock.

"Flora," I said sharply. "We have to get this moved. Now!"

Flora looked like she might be sick, but her resolve hardened, and she nodded. We resumed pushing the altar. It was awful to have the fight behind us, to not even see what was going on, knowing that Yanis was the only barrier between myself and the faerie warrior. I kept my attention on moving the heavy wood, despite the clashing of blades to my back.

It seemed to take forever to get the altar close to the window. The girl with the chestnut hair came to help us. We heaved a final time, forcing the altar to topple down on the shining glass wall. With a great crash it smashed through images of red-glass roses and transparent, green vines. The sound reverberated through the cathedral, echoing off the walls. The shattering glass and cracking iron mountings added a strangely musical quality to the cacophony in the room. Heavy wood fell through the window and onto the grass outside. A rainbow of colored glass sparkled as tiny pieces flew through the air, casting rosy hues on the floor as the light shone through them. I shielded my eyes to protect them from stray shards. When the glass settled, there was a large hole in the stained-glass wall, and the altar lay covered in glass fragments just outside.

"Go," I yelled at Flora and the new girl. "Get out. Find the guards. Watch the glass."

The girl with the chestnut hair quickly obeyed, stepping cautiously through the shattered glass. Once out of the building, she took off running, and I hoped it was to find help.

"What about you?" Flora asked. She looked uncertain about leaving me in the cathedral.

"I need to get my brothers out and find Constance and Casper. We'll meet you outside." Too late I realized that mentioning Constance was not going to get Flora out of the cathedral. She looked wide-eyed and worried, but she didn't move.

"You need to go," I repeated, urgency building in my voice. "You can't help Constance by staying here, but you can alert the rest of the royal guard. Get them to come," I told her. *What I was really wondering was why they hadn't already been alerted to this attack.* Flora remained mute but nodded before she made her way out of the cathedral.

Yanis was still fighting my faerie attacker, but they both looked exhausted. I scurried back to the pew where I had left my brothers and Ilana. I was deeply worried that Devon was still not with them, but I had to get Finn and Jacobie to safety before I could look for him.

"What about Devon?" Finn asked, as if he were reading my thoughts.

"Hopefully he's safe, but we're no good to him in the middle of the fighting."

I feared that he would fight me, but he solemnly followed Ilana as I carried Jacobie outside. A few feet away, I set Jacobie down on the grass. He had stopped crying, but tear tracks were fresh on his face.

"Go get help, and make sure you stay far away from the cathedral. Be careful of any path leading to the forest, they must have gotten here somehow. I have to go back."

"What?" Finn cried at the same moment Jacobie wailed for me to stay, making my heart twist in my chest.

"You just said we were no good in there. Please, Nor, don't go back." Now Finn looked truly terrified.

"I meant *you* aren't good in there. I need you to go spread the alarm. I need to get people out of the cathedral."

"I will come too, then," said Ilana. Surprised, I looked at her. There was nothing false in her expression.

"Fine," I relented, "but don't come back inside. Wait until I've gotten people out, then tell them where to go or lead them somewhere you think will be safe."

Unfortunately, Finn and Jacobie followed Ilana and me back to the cathedral. I conceded to let them help people once they were outside, but not to come any closer to the palace. There was no time to linger and argue. Every moment spent out here, someone was dying inside the cathedral. I prayed Casper wouldn't be amongst them.

Chapter Thirty

I slipped back into the cathedral, the noise and smell hitting me like a wall. The crash of swords still reverberated through the room, and the metallic smell of blood drenched the air. Littered on the floor were bodies of both fay and humans, and I wondered how many were injured and how many were . . . worse.

My eyes were drawn to a red dress behind a pew close to the front. Careful to stay against the back walls to avoid drawing attention to myself, I scurried over to the prone figure. It was Constance, slumped against the wall.

She had been partially hidden by a pew, but not hidden enough. An arrow stuck out of her side and there was a dark wet spot surrounding it.

I forced myself forward, desperate to see her chest rise, her eyes open, any sign of life.

"Constance," I said, as I got close to her. Her eyes were closed. "Constance!" I repeated.

"Flora?" Her eyes slipped open and I could have cried with joy. "Oh, no." They slid shut again.

"Come on, Constance, I need you to help me here. I'm going to get you out of here." As carefully as I could, I draped one of her arms around me. I struggled to get to my feet, her weight on me making it difficult. But she was a delicate princess and I had spent my life living in the wilds, which had made me tough. As I slowly rose, I hoped no one would notice us. Constance screamed in pain, and I used my free hand to cover her mouth.

"I know it hurts, Constance, but you have to be quiet." I had both our backs to a wall to get a moment of support.

"I'm dying," Constance said. It came out as a moan, draining the little energy left in her.

"You're not dead yet," I grunted, trying to summon some fight in her. "Casper and Flora need you. And I need you to help me get you out of here."

At the mention of the others, Constance opened her eyes. Tears streamed down her face and she looked dangerously pale, the dark bloodstain on her waist growing. But she pressed her lips together into a tight, white line, to keep quiet, swallowing her pain. I braced her between the wall and myself, and slowly walked toward the opening in the window.

"Nor, look out!" I heard Devon scream.

I turned in time to see a faerie dancing up to me. His sword was bloody, and he smiled at me with sharp teeth. I tried to get in front of Constance, but she slumped to the floor. I had nothing to defend us against this new threat but my small dagger. The faerie raised his sword.

An iron sword crashed against the fay silver. Devon had appeared, putting himself in between me and the faerie.

"Nor, get out of here!"

I was rooted to the floor, terrified this strange warrior would kill my brother.

Their swords continued to meet, the faerie attacking and Devon defending blow after blow. Devon had stopped yelling at me, focusing all his attention on his opponent. Sweat beaded on my brother's forehead, and my stranglehold on my panic weakened. The faerie was tiring him out. Devon had not spent his life training to be a knight. He was no match for this warrior. Dread washed over me with every sword blow.

A final sword thrust from the faerie sent my brother backward, barely dodging the attack. He landed on his knees, rolling away just before the faerie struck again, almost taking off my brother's head.

"Devon!" I screamed, unable to stop myself.

The faerie rushed towards my prone brother, his back towards me. Seeing an opportunity, I sprinted towards the faerie, plunging my dagger into its back, just below his ribcage. The faerie cried in pain, reeling around even as my blade stayed stuck in his side, golden blood staining his leather tunic. In the moment the faerie was distracted, Devon sprang up, slicing his sword across the faerie's neck. The scream morphed into a sick gurgle as the faerie fell back, golden blood pouring from the slash across his neck. He toppled to the ground, an expression of frozen agony on his face.

Devon whirled to face me. "Get out of here!"

"Help me with Constance," I cried, and rushed back to the princess. She was unconscious, and for a horrible moment I feared the worst. But then her chest rose for a shallow breath. I draped one of her arms around me and struggled to stand. The pain in my shoulder and the cuts burned but I refused to let her go. Suddenly, she felt lighter. Devon picked her up as easily as if she were a ragdoll. I gestured for him to go out the window.

"Stabbing someone in the back. You fight dirty," he said as we made our way through the broken glass, but I heard the relief in his voice.

"And thank Chace for that." But there was no pride in my words. All I felt was horror and terror at the massacre happening before us.

Flora was standing outside as I had commanded her. Her eyes grew wide as she took in the sight of Constance. She rushed over with a few other nobles who had made an escape. With their help, Devon passed Constance through the gap in the window and into their waiting hands. I staggered after them, almost collapsing the moment I was on the grass outside. Tiny glass shards bit my hands, but I didn't care.

"Is she?" Flora asked, pure fear in her voice.

"No," I said. "But she was badly hurt. There is an arrow in her side. She needs a physician."

I swallowed. "Has Casper come out?" I asked, praying he was safe. Flora shook her head sadly before going back to attend Constance. The fighting was still raging on. I risked a look back, into the cathedral. Sir Yanis was engaged in battle with a different fay, but I forced my eyes away. I had to find Casper.

Not wanting to go into the battle completely defenseless now that I was without my dagger, I looked for a weapon. A young fay lay a few feet inside the cathedral. His eyes stared up, sightless. Though he was the enemy, he looked barely older than Finn, with burnished brown curls and a bit of baby roundness to his face. I felt sick all over.

I picked up the sword next to the dead faerie boy. The sword, a bright silver weapon, was surprisingly light in my hand, and the hilt, richly engraved, was still warm. There was no blood on the sword. The faerie boy had accomplished nothing but his death today. I whispered the quickest prayer to Chace that the chaos would be in my favor, and then plunged ahead.

I was not skilled with a sword, so I tried to stick to the sides of the cathedral, caring more about finding Casper, though I didn't know what I would do if I found him. *When,* I corrected myself, *when I find him.* I silently made my way around the side wall. The fighting had died down and I thanked Chace for my luck, as none of the faeries took much notice of me, too busy in their own battles. There was a thick cluster of fay standing in the aisle. They did not seem to be actively fighting. *Were they guarding something?* I drew closer to see.

Casper was in the center of the circle, his cape gone, fighting a faerie. Casper did not appear severely injured, but there was a gash along his cheek that was bleeding down the side of his face. He was putting up a good fight, but his opponent was clearly a master swordsman. The faerie's back was to me, and I could only see the dragonfly-like wings and hair the color of true gold. I knew two faeries with golden hair, but only one who served Queen Marasina.

For a moment, I was back in the Biawood, everything smelling of ash from the burned village. I tasted dirt as I was pressed into the ground, Elrik's knee holding me down while he casually slowed my blood and sang his twisted lullaby.

I'll lock your heart in a crystal jar
So never again shall you go far.

As I gasped, Casper raised his sword to Elrik's, an impressive creation of sharp silver and a hilt that glittered from encrusted crystals. The two swords met with a deafening clash that rang out clearly, despite the rest of the battle in the cathedral. The faerie swung up from below and sliced Casper's arm. I was sure the cut was deep despite the thick velvet Casper wore.

"Casper!" I screamed. Eluding the fay guards, I rushed forward to swing my sword at Elrik with more fury than skill. Too late, I realized my mistake.

In unison, Casper and Elrik turned to looked at me.

"Nor, get away from here!" Casper yelled.

But shock froze me in place. When Casper's golden-haired opponent turned around, I saw that it wasn't Elrik.

Chapter Thirty-One

I t was Pel.

Blood drained from my face.

"I'm sorry Nor."

My vision narrowed to Pel as anger rose in me, fast and scorching hot. I raised the sword, ready to strike at Pel, but he easily deflected my blow with a halfhearted block before sending my sword flying to the ground.

Casper stepped between us. "Leave her alone!" he said to Pel, his blade raised, ready for an attack.

I stood for a moment, trying to figure out a plan, when slender fingers with an iron grip grabbed me. I flailed wildly, trying to free myself as Pel raised his own sword, his eyes now locked on Casper.

"I need you to behave," my captor whispered in my ear. My blood iced as I twisted around to see Elrik, the *real* Elrik, leaning towards me as his hands held me fast. His amber, cat-eyes glittered as he licked his lips. I tried harder to free myself, but it was no use. It was all I could do to stop from screaming, afraid I would distract Casper, making him an easy target for Pel. Already, the two of them were back to fighting, one sword coming down for a hit only to be parried by the other.

"My dear Elenora, you're hurt," Elrik said, sounding almost disappointed. I had so many cuts on my arms. I remembered what Elrik could do with blood and my stomach flipped in fear. I thrashed, but Elrik had already pinned my wrists behind me with one hand and grabbed my arm with his other hand, right where I had been cut by the faerie's sword. He squeezed the slice on my arm hard, blinding hot pain seared up and I let out an involuntary scream of pain before clamping my mouth closed, biting my lip hard to prevent another scream. I tasted blood. "I did warn you to behave," Elrik chided, holding my arms tight.

Through tears, I saw Casper look over at me. It was only for the briefest of moments, but it was enough of a distraction for his opponent. Pel knocked him backward, kicking out his legs.

Pel's boot connected, and Casper was thrown backward to the floor. In a flash, the faerie was standing over him, Pel's sword mere inches from Casper's throat. One small jab and Casper would be dead.

"No!" I yelled, my voice raw and jagged. Pel didn't even look at me. Despite the pain in my arm, I struggled wildly against Elrik's grip, but his grip remained firm.

"Nor," Casper said, but his voice was cut off as Pel dug his sword into Casper's neck. Not a deep cut, just enough so a trickle of ruby blood slowly slid down his throat, pooling on the floor. Time stood still.

"Enough." A new voice came from the entrance of the cathedral. One strong, commanding and female. Everyone looked over and all of the fay bowed. An imperious woman entered the cathedral and made her way toward us. She was the tallest women I had ever seen. She was also the most beautiful with pure silver hair that fell down her back in cascading waves. She moved with the grace of a dancer and the deadly intent of a trained assassin. Her sapphire-blue eyes radiated fire and triumph as she made her way up the center aisle. Her opal skin glowed in the light and her intricately embroidered tunic, trousers, and chain-mail shirt were all stained with both red blood and golden blood.

"Drop your weapons or your new king dies," the woman commanded. Her voice was musical, but strong enough that the entire cathedral heard, the sound echoing off the white walls. Throughout the room, the humans realized what had happened, staring at Casper; defeated and at the mercy of the fay.

Slowly, the knights and guards and anyone else who had been fighting lowered their swords in surrender. Surrounding fay were quick to collect the weapons. I wondered if the fay would kill us all now, but I didn't see another option. Not one that would leave Casper alive.

"This is where it gets interesting," Elrik gleefully whispered in my ear. He was no longer squeezing the cut on my arm, but his grip was unyielding. Not that I could risk any movement, lest Pel decide to do something to Casper. I tried to catch my breath. Elrik had not worked any blood magic on me, but the realization brought little relief. Maybe he was biding his time. Or maybe there was too much iron in the room. I looked at all the iron swords the fay were collecting. It didn't seem to harm them, though they weren't doing any magic. They had won this battle with strength, not magic.

"I am Queen Marasina, and I demand your surrender."

A gasp went up from the crowd as her words sank in. The queen of the fay was here, standing before us.

"So, this is the little kingling," the queen said, as she approached Pel and Casper. "He hardly looks dangerous." Fay laughter rippled through the room, musical and deadly.

"Your Majesty," Casper said, looking up at Queen Marasina from his position on the floor, but not daring to move with Pel's sword still at his throat, "why are you doing this? Your attack was unprovoked."

"Unprovoked?" the queen scoffed. "You humans murdered my son. The fact that I do not kill the entire royal family is more mercy than you deserve."

"We have not killed any faerie prince," Casper said, his words almost an echo of what I had told the faerie that had been attacking me.

"Don't lie to me, human," Queen Marasina snapped. "My eldest son came to your lands. My disappointment was great, but I believed he would be safe enough until he tired of the charade and came back home. Then I learned that my noble boy died fighting in a war, a *human* war. One your father started with another human king. Six years too late, I understood the true dangers of living with humans. And I vowed my revenge. In payment, I would kill the king. But King Charles was long dead by the time I found this all out, also killed by the same foolish, human, war. I was left no choice but to kill his son."

"Please don't kill him," I begged, unable to stop myself. Elrik hissed and tightened his grip, but I managed to continue, despite the pain, adrenaline coursing through my veins, the terror keeping me alert. "Casper had nothing to do with the Southern War."

The fay queen turned to me, a dark laugh issuing from her lips even as her eyes remained icy. "He is not the son I had killed."

"Christopher. That's why you sent an assassin after my brother." The realization and rage read plainly across Casper's face, only Pel's sword at his throat keeping him still.

"You are a smart little kingling, smarter than your brother." Queen Marasina stared down at Casper. "I indeed had your brother killed." She gave a small nod towards Elrik that turned my stomach. "But then I learned he had a brother, another king to take his place and start new wars. And I knew I had to step in. If I took away this new king, there could be no more wars. The humans I leave today will know to be careful, because I will have their little king. So now I win."

"Please let Elenora go. I'm the one you want."

Queen Marasina studied Casper, as though he were some strange animal she was trying to understand. "So kingling, you want me to show mercy. Where is this Elenora?"

"I have her here for you, my queen," Elrik called out proudly. I tried to struggle, but he squeezed the cut on my arm. The sharp pain almost brought me to my knees, but I refused to be supported by Elrik. Black spots bloomed before me and it was all I could do to remain standing.

Queen Marasina turned her fierce gaze on me. Her sapphire eyes bored into me, as though she could pluck thoughts straight from my mind. The queen smiled then, which scared me even more. It was a cold, hard smile with sharp, pointed teeth.

"Ahh, so this is the Elenora Molnár I have heard so much about. You are the little commoner the kingling brought in to test your claim of gold making?" I was surprised she knew that, and she registered my expression. "You've been very helpful to my subject, isn't that right?"

I expected Elrik to respond, but instead, Pel did.

"Yes, my queen. I learned much from her." Without removing his sword, he turned and stared at me with sad, pitying eyes, but I felt myself growing hot again with rage.

"How could you, Pel? I saved you." I wanted to hurt him. But Elrik still held me. I could feel him gently shaking with laugher behind me.

Before Pel could say anything, the queen laughed, a dark and musical sound. "Which I believe he repaid with a room full of gold. Pel's been such a good spy, collecting all the information I needed to lead my army to battle, right when the most powerful humans would all be gathered together. And from what he's told me, he would not have known if not for you."

"Nor, what have you done?" The words came from the ground, and I looked down to see Casper staring at me, despite the sword at his throat. The deep hurt etched into his face was enough for me to feel as though someone was stabbing my own heart.

"I didn't . . ." I stammered, not sure what I was going to say. *I didn't mean to? I didn't know the faerie I helped was a royal spy?* Everything I had done to help Pel came crashing back to me, the guilt so much stronger now. I had been an idiot to believe Pel's story that he was trying to escape his brother and his queen. He had been working for them all along. Feeding them the information I so willingly gave him. And like the fool that I was, I had assisted in the downfall of my king and country, actively betraying them. I had betrayed Casper. "I'm so sorry," I said weakly, but my voice was barely a rasp.

"Bind him," Marasina commanded to a guard standing next to her, indicating Casper. "We'll take him and the girl." Faerie guards rushed toward Casper, and Pel removed his sword from Casper's throat so guards could haul Casper to his feet and bind his wrists.

"*Dormrir*—" Elrik started to say. I tensed, but he was cut off.

"No," Pel said.

"What?" Queen Marasina turned to Pel. He faced his queen with firm resolve.

"Why would you care what happens to me?" I spat at him. I knew it was foolish, but I was too angry to care. At the moment, I hated Pel. And I hated myself more.

"She is innocent of the humans' crimes. We should leave her be," Pel's voice was determined.

"Brother, hush," Elrik hissed. "You'll ruin everything."

The queen's look of amusement dropped and there was a deadly steel in her voice. "Pel, I gave an order. We are taking her to do with as I please. Are you disobeying a direct order from your queen?" Her voice was glacial, and for a moment I was glad that her fury wasn't directed at me.

Pel refused to look away from his queen, his bright green eyes meeting her cold blue ones.

"My queen, please, it would be my greatest honor to do your bidding," Elrik said, his voice poisoned honey.

"Leave her be," Pel was suddenly in front of me, in the way of the queen. Elrik snarled, and his grip tightened painfully on my arms.

Queen Marasina took a few steps toward us, Casper no longer a concern for her as the other guards secured his hands and legs. She leaned in so close that only Pel, Elrik and I could hear her. "*Rumpelstiltskin*, I order you to bind this girl, and ensure that she cannot escape. She is my prisoner now. You will obey me. I will decide how to punish this act of disobedience when we arrive back at court." Without a second glance at us, she turned to the doors. Pel and Elrik exchanged a look that I couldn't decipher.

"You've done it now, brother," Elrik breathed.

"Come my subjects, we leave." Queen Marasina strode out of the cathedral, her guards immediately flanking her. Two held Casper between them, his wrists and ankles bound. When she was almost out of the cathedral, she turned back. "You too, Elrik. I want your brother to manage the girl."

"But, my queen—" Elrik whined, his voice angry and petulant.

"Now!"

Elrik wiped emotions from his face, instantly serene. "Of course, my queen." Elrik released me, but Pel quickly took his place, grabbing my wrist, his grip as unyielding as his brother's, though he held my uncut arm. As he was leaving, Elrik turned to me. He gave me a dark smile that sent shivers down my spine. In a caressing voice, he said, "I will have you in the end. I promise you that. No one knows your value like I do, you sweet thing." With that, he turned to Pel. "And you, brother, don't mess this up. You've already angered her to the point of using your name." Before Pel could respond, Elrik pivoted on his heel, following Queen Marasina out of the cathedral.

"You aren't going to do this," I said to Pel, hoping that some shred of the bond I thought we had shared was real. His emerald eyes were stony, and though he seemed to be struggling greatly with himself, he nonetheless pulled out a slim, braided rope.

"I'm sorry, Nor," he said, his voice low. "She commanded me. I must obey."

"But you stood up to her," I argued, desperate to reach the boy I thought I had known.

"Not after she—" Pel said, but he stopped himself. Instead, he started wrapping the rope around my wrist of the arm he was hold.

"Was it all a lie?" I couldn't help but ask. Pel stiffened, and I got all the answer I needed. If I had thought his abandonment hurt, it was nothing compared to his betrayal.

"Put out your other wrist."

I stared at him, agog and unmoving. "You think I'll just make this easy for you?"

"Please, Nor, don't make this harder than it is."

"I didn't realize betraying me was supposed to be easy." I tried to pull away, but it was a futile effort.

"Nor, if I don't return with you, I can promise you Marasina will do terrible things to your king."

Casper. I felt my breath leave and my stomach clench as surely as if he had punched me. Whether or not Pel was lying, I realized I had to go with him.

It was the only way I could find Casper. The only way I could help him. *And I had to rescue him.* I owed him that much at least, considering all my betrayals. Resigned, I glared at Pel, but obediently offered up my free hand, and fought the urge to struggle as I let Pel bind my wrists.

He knelt, tying my ankles with additional rope. There was a length of rope between my ankles, enough so I could walk, but not run. The rope was slender, and I hoped I might be able to work my wrists free when no one was looking.

That is, until Pel touched the cut on my arm. Though his fingers were gentle, I winced. It was only a brief touch, a flutter of his fingers against my skin. I had not been thinking of his blood magic. Terror welled inside of me.

"What are you doing?" I asked, staring at my blood on his finger.

Too late, I saw he was using my blood to perform transformation magic on the rope. I struggled, but it made no difference. Where there had been slim rope binding my wrists, now there was a smooth, silver metal. It felt stronger than iron. Though I was relived he wasn't using blood magic in my veins, I had never felt so trapped, not even in the tower so many nights ago.

"May Chace bring you a fiery death," I spat. Pel ignored me, changing the rope around my ankles to metal, with a chain between them.

Pel gripped my arm, making sure I wouldn't try to escape. *Not that I would try*, I thought darkly. Not when I had to get to Casper. As he led me out of the cathedral, the humans looked on, scared and stunned. None came after me, and I didn't blame them. If something happened to me, the fay queen might retaliate on Casper. Even I knew that. I hoped my brothers were still on the other side of the cathedral, safe from the fay.

Outside, the sun was bright. It seemed out of place for a day to be so beautiful after such an ugly event. In the brilliant light, my head ached worse than ever. And though his grip never loosened, Pel refused to look at me, but kept us marching to catch up with the queen, who was already on the edge of the forest. How could I escape and rescue Casper? There had to be some way out of this.

Elrik's words came back to me. *And you brother, don't mess this up. You've already angered her to the point of using your name.*

His name.

Rumpelstiltskin. She had called him Rumpelstiltskin.

I suddenly remembered Pel telling me that someone could command him only by using his true name. *Of course. Rumpelstiltskin is his true name.* The realization was so distracting that I forgot to walk and tripped. Only Pel's grip kept me from falling. I knew Pel's true name, and I could use it. I could command him to free me now, but then I would never be able to save Casper. I would wait for a better opportunity.

Pel took me to the edge of the palace grounds and into the Biawood Forest. I could no longer see the queen and her soldiers, or even Elrik, but I was sure they were already heading back to the fay realm of Magnomel. Even if I could control Pel, he was only one fay against many.

But at least now I had a secret weapon. I knew his name. His true name.

Rumpelstiltskin.

Chapter Thirty-Two

As Pel led me deeper into the Biawood Forest, my injuries demanded to be heard. I'd been able to ignore them during the heat of battle, but my head and shoulder throbbed, and all the cuts and bruises shot with pain at every step. I looked at the blood on my clothes, wondering how much was mine.

Pel must have noticed my pain. "I can heal you," he offered, his voice soft.

"I would rather die."

Pel looked at me sadly but did not press the offer. Instead he ushered me deeper into the forest.

"Where are we going?" I demanded, trying to make my voice braver than I felt. Pel didn't answer, or even look at me again. We weren't on any path, though I could tell we were heading to the road that led to the northeast. *Towards Magnomel.* Pel's claim that he was trying to escape the fay kingdom and his brother was nothing more than a bitter lie.

I tried in vain to think of a way to use Pel's true name, *Rumpelstiltskin,* but couldn't see a way to do it now and still rescue Casper. I would have to wait till we reached Casper. I prayed they weren't planning to kill me first.

At last, I began to hear voices ahead, mostly that of Queen Marasina issuing orders. The icy fear I had felt in my stomach swelled as I was pulled into a clearing. I gasped. A fay war camp was set up with tents, small fires, and dozens of armored faeries all milling around.

They were packing up the camp, but also joking and laughing with each other, celebrating their victory. There were at least twice as many fay as had attacked the cathedral. With a sickening feeling, I realized that these forces must have taken out the royal guard, making the cathedral an exposed target. Any hope of an easy escape drained out of me.

"Pel, there you are," snapped the queen, who finally turned to see us. "Took you long enough. Put her in there," she said, gesturing past a row of tents.

"Yes, my queen." Pel's voice was flat, but he didn't hesitate. She thrust an ornate silver key on a long chain at him before leaving us.

Pel took me past a row of tents and into the center of the camp. In the middle of camp was a massive cage. Bars as thick as my wrist gleamed a shiny silver, sparkling in the sun. The cage rested on four large wheels, similar to those traveling carnivals used for their animals. It wasn't empty, but there were no animals in it. Casper was bound in the cage.

"Casper," I cried. Casper looked up to see me, and for a moment our eyes met. He opened his mouth as if to say something, but then his face darkened, and he turned away. My heart cracked.

The cage door was opened, and Pel was lifting me up and inside.

"Please, don't do this," I begged, desperation making my voice shake.

Pel grimaced, but he never stopped. "I have to." With that, he forced me into the cage and locked the door. I stared at him, anger and heartbreak warring within me. Much more than bars stood between us now.

Elrik sidled up to the cage, a dark smile on his face. "I think I like you tied up and behind bars." He gave me a hungry look.

"Get away from her," Pel growled at his brother, but his indignant tone only amused Elrik.

"You can't keep her all to yourself, big brother," Elrik mocked. "She belongs to the queen. Unfortunately, you are on Marasina's bad side now. We'll see who gets her soon enough." With that, Elrik departed, slipping between tents.

Soon after Elrik left, Queen Marasina called Pel away, leaving another fay in his place to guard Casper and me, not that any escape was possible in a locked cage, our wrists and ankles bound with strange fay metal. I tried rubbing the metal bonds against the cage walls, to test how strong they were, and if the bonds might scratch, but they remained intact, gleaming and impervious.

All around us, the faeries were busy, bundling up supplies and putting out cooking fires. Many of them would stop to stare at us, mouths curved up in sharp, smug smiles, but none approached the cage.

Casper refused to even acknowledge me, staring out of the bars, his face a stony mask. Eventually, the entire camp was dismantled, and the fay began to march back toward Magnomel. A pair of faeries hooked up the cage to a waiting horse. I knew this was coming, but it didn't stop the swell of fear I felt as the horse started walking, pulling us behind him. I glanced over at Casper. He was still staring straight ahead but now his face was wet with tears.

Casper, I wanted to whisper, *I will find a way to get us out of this. I know something that will help us.* Before I had the chance, he turned to face me. I had never seen such hatred in his eyes, not even when he first thought I was a thief and a liar.

"How could you do this, Elenora? Betray your country? How could you betray me?"

"I didn't mean to," I said, hot tears threatening to explode out of me. "I thought I was helping a friend." My words were a poor excuse, even to me.

"Everything you've told me has been a lie. I don't know you."

"I was going to tell you."

"That you were in league with my enemy?"

"I wasn't in league with them," I cried. "If I was, do you think I would be in a cage now?"

For a moment, Casper didn't respond, and I thought maybe he was realizing that I spoke the truth. But then he snorted, disgusted. "Perhaps you are simply terrible at playing both sides." With that, he turned away from me, staring out through the bars of the cage. "Don't speak to me again."

"We have to figure out a way out of this."

"There is no way out of this."

"What do you mean? You're just planning to do nothing? And stay a prisoner?"

"Yes," he spat, finally looking back at me. His eyes were red, and I saw a terrible sadness in them. "For the sake of my country, that's exactly what I plan to do. If they have me, then perhaps they will leave Constance alone to rule. She'll probably do a better job than I could anyway. I spent five years as a royal hostage in Faradisia, so I have plenty of practice."

I stared at Casper. It wasn't at all what I expected him to say. "This isn't the same."

"No? It was a gilded cage back then, and this one is simply more literal." For a moment, he looked wistful. "When I left Faradisia, I thought I might actually be free. But thanks to your friends, that will never happen." He turned away from me, and this time, I didn't press him.

It was my fault we were prisoners of the fay. So, it fell to me to save us. "I will see you freed," I whispered. I couldn't tell if he heard me or not. It didn't matter. He would believe me when I got us out of here. As soon as I figured out how.

For five days we traveled through the Biawood, getting ever closer to Magnomel, and whatever the queen had planned for us there. My wrists and ankles chafed in their metal bindings, which were never removed.

Unable to wash, the blood from my cuts caked into my heavy, ruined dress; the hard, crusty fabric sticking to wounds on my skin and smelling rankly of copper and dirt. Every bump and start on the journey sent new waves of pain through me, but I forced myself to remain quiet.

I refused to give the fay that satisfaction. In the beginning, they would gawk at us—their human prisoners—but after a few days that seemed to lose appeal as excitement grew in the camp.

I overheard small snatches of conversation, and the soldiers were eager to get home. The idea made me ill.

After the first day, Casper had stopped speaking to me, and none of my pleading could change his mind. He wrinkled his nose in disgust, telling me, "You stink," before resuming his silence. Though he smelled as ripe and bloody as myself, and despite the far greater dangers we were about to face, my face flushed hot in shame. I remembered his similar comment the first day we met at the Spring Faire. We traveled in silence; two animals locked in a cage. Each evening, the fay army would stop once the sun was low in the sky and set up camp. A fay solider, but never Pel or Elrik, would individually let us out of the cage to relieve ourselves before locking us back in the cage with a small ration of food and water. It was the only time we could fully stand or walk, and my limbs ached from confinement.

The first night, I had tried to pick the lock with one of the golden hairpins that Annabeth had used to arrange my hair for the coronation. Miraculously, it had had stayed in my hair despite the battle. I pulled it out like a hidden treasure. Working the lock with it failed, as my movements were awkward and clumsy with my wrists still bound in the fay metal. I ended up dropping the pin. It fell to the ground next to the cage. With it went any sense that I could free us.

Late on the fifth night, I sat against the bars, unable to sleep. Though the cage was on the far end of the fay encampment, I could see their cooking fires, bright against the dark forest. Most of the fay crowded around the fires, eating and talking. And though I had barely seen Pel at all on the journey, he approached the cage now. He looked tired, dark copper circles under his eyes and his shoulders slumped. But I had no pity for him.

"We'll reach the Forest Court tomorrow," Pel said. "I can heal you before we get there. You'll need your strength."

For a moment I couldn't respond, still offended by his offer. He took another step. Rage washed over me.

"Don't even think of touching me," I hissed. He stopped, still. "We aren't friends and never have been. I've been a pawn to you this whole time. Don't pretend you care what happens to me now."

"Nor, it wasn't like that." Pel sounded hurt, but now I knew what a skilled actor he was.

"Stop it, Pel. Just stop. No need to lie to me anymore."

"I wasn't lying. I was serious about wanting to take you away from all this, Nor. I wanted to find a place for us where you and I could be safe from humans. But you turned me down, and I could not disobey my queen."

"So, this is my fault?" I spat, infusing venom into my words.

"I'm sorry, Nor."

"And when you didn't come when I called to you? Everything you said about running away from your brother and your queen— more lies?" I couldn't help but ask, though I knew the answer in my heart, should have known it from the beginning.

"My queen wanted the little king. And if Elrik brought you to Magnomel, I could have kept you safe there." Pel's words were flat. He offered no apology.

I felt like I had been punched. I recalled the smell of smoke, of dirt and fear from those terrible moments under Elrik's control. All while Pel knew. All while he wanted it to happen. Fury warred with hurt in my chest, and I had to fight the urge to scream at him, to cry, to do anything that would hurt him even a fraction as much as he had hurt me. And I might have, if I hadn't looked over to see Casper, sleeping fitfully on the other side of the cage.

I had to choose between Casper and revenge.

"I have one thing to say to you before we reach your home." I lowered my voice to a whisper, forcing him to lean close to the bars of the cage.

"What is that?"

"*Rumpelstiltskin*, I command you release Casper and me."

Pel's eyes grew wide.

"You will release us from this cage and remove our bindings."

From the anger that flashed in Pel's eyes, I knew I had done well.

"Nor, you don't know what you're demanding." Pel tried to keep his hands still, but they were starting to shake, and he looked like he was fighting a battle of wills, one he was losing.

"I know exactly what I'm doing. And you, *Rumpelstiltskin*, will release us." The command seemed to overcome him as his hand flew to the lock on the cage. His other hand went to a chain around his neck and I saw him pull out the key Queen Marasina had given him.

"Nor, you will make this worse for all of us," Pel said, heat in his voice, grudgingly unlocking the cage.

I ignored him. "Casper, you have to wake up," I whispered as loud as I dared and pulled on his sleeve.

Casper's eyes flew open. As soon as they focused on me, they furrowed in disgust. He closed them without a word.

"Casper, the cage is open. We're getting out of here." I shoved him, hard. He opened his eyes again and saw what was happening. Now, he was alert.

"What's going on?" he hissed.

"We're getting out of here. The cage is near the outskirt of the camp, so we can slip away without alerting the fay."

As soon as Pel lifted the cage door open, I thrust my shackled wrists in front of him. "Don't make me do this, Nor," he said, sounding more anxious than I'd ever heard him. His eyes darted around the camp, but I ignored him, waiting for my bonds to be released. Unable to stop himself, he grabbed my hand, reopening a small cut on it with his nail. It barely hurt, and he deftly smeared the blood on my bindings, first on my wrists, then my ankles. Under his concentration, the metal melted back into a simple rope, which he unwillingly untied. I rubbed feeling into my wrists and ankles, feeling giddy with my new freedom.

"Let that be enough," he said, though he was already reaching out for Casper's bonds. "It will be worse for you if you take your king with you."

"Nor, what in the Mother's name is going on?" Casper asked, instinctively pulling back from Pel.

"We're getting out of here. I'll explain later. Let Pel remove your binds." After a tense moment, Casper warily extended his wrists to the faerie.

"Is he an ally now?" Casper asked, as Pel removed his binding with another smear of blood from my cut.

"I would never assist you, kingling," Pel muttered at the same time I said, "Not exactly."

Free of our bindings, we climbed out of the cage. Casper glanced warily around, but none of the other fay were near this side of camp.

"Come on," I said to Casper, as soon as the stiffness from the confinement had eased enough that I could walk without stumbling, "We need to leave." Casper looked like he was about to argue, so I continued, "This is our one chance to get away. You can hate me later." For a moment Casper seemed unsure, but then nodded, and turned away from the camp.

Chapter Thirty-Three

"Prisoners escaping! Prisoners escaping!"

Pel's loud cries pierced the quiet of the night. Soon, fay solders would be rushing to the alarm. I cursed myself for not commanding Pel's silence.

"Nor, we have to run, now!" Casper grabbed my hand. "Come on," he yelled, fear and urgency in his voice. We had only seconds before the entire fay army was upon us. There wasn't enough time. We'd be captured again. I could already see movement around the campfires. *I need more time.*

"Come on, Nor!"

We could never outrun the fay on our own, they were faster and stronger than Casper and me, even at our best. I frantically looked around. Faerie soldiers were rising from their places around the campfires, I saw the gleam of metal reflecting the fires as they grabbed their weapons. There had to be some sort of diversion. My mind felt slow and sticky, filling with a hopeless panic. All I saw were faeries, tents, the cage and cooking fires. *The cooking fires.* I could only think of one thing to distract the fay. But I remembered Chelle. The ash in the air and smoking husk of a village. I thought of my own home burned to the ground. I stood frozen. I couldn't do it.

"Nor, now!" Casper yelled at me. The desperation in his plea, the terror I had never before heard in his voice broke me. For him, I would do this terrible thing.

I pulled away from Casper and faced Pel once again. "I wish there was another way," I said to Pel. His brows knit in confusion, but I forced myself to harden my resolve. Pel had given me no choice. I didn't quiet my voice this time, making it strong and full of intention. "*Rumpelstiltskin*, I command you to torch this camp. Set the tents aflame." I took a quick breath, knowing what this would cost. "Watch them burn."

The confusion on Pel's face was replaced by pure horror. I felt sick.

"Now!" I commanded. Then I took Casper's hand and we ran. The weight and bulk of my thick velvet skirts and tight corset were so cumbersome, I gathered the skirts in one hand, ripping the fabric where my blood had dried it to my skin. A wheeze started in my chest as we raced into the dark forest, far from the camp.

We never saw the ravine in the forest floor, a drop of about fifteen feet. My foot slipped on dead leaves and both of us went crashing down, rolling into bushes and slamming into trees. When we finally stopped, we both sat gasping for air. Every part of me felt bruised, and my chest was close to exploding from lack of air. I took shallow breaths, wishing I could remove the cursed corset.

I started to rise but Casper pulled me back down, gesturing frantically for me to be silent. He pointed up toward the top of the ravine. If the fay were chasing us, this would be the best chance to lose them. He gestured to a large bush and crept into it, making sure not to be visible from above. Huddling next to him, we waited in a tense silence. After a few minutes, urgent voices sounded far above us. They were the fay solders, and the sound of them sent a stab of dread through me. I stared up at the top of the ravine, trying to make out the figures by moonlight.

Not long after, I could smell smoke, faint but distinguishable. It meant Pel had let the fire rage, just as I had commanded. As if on cue, a new fay voice was heard above us yelling about a fire back in camp. There was a hurried commotion, and soon all the voices were gone. Casper and I didn't speak, but for the first time since the fay attacked, the silence didn't feel completely hostile. I tried to push what I had done from my mind, but every time I inhaled the scent of smoke, I was reminded.

Hours later, as the sky was starting to lighten in the east, we got up. My limbs screamed in protest. I looked around, trying to detect any hint of iridescent wings or glowing skin. But it seemed Casper and I were alone amidst the trees and shrubs.

"We need to head southwest," I said. "Wait, no. The fay will probably assume we are heading straight back to the Sterling. If we go due south, that should throw them off, and then we can circle back toward Sterling. I can get us through several days in the Biawood, so long as we don't run into the fay again." I started to walk, but Casper stopped me.

"Will you tell me what just happened?" His eyes were serious, but I couldn't tell if he was angry.

"We escaped," I said, trying to make my voice light.

"That's not what I mean. How can I trust you, Elenora? You lied to me about everything." I began to argue, but he raised his hand, gesturing for me to stop. "Your ability to create gold was a lie. You lied to me about the fay—you *worked* with the fay! My kingdom was attacked because of what you did. But now you just had their camp set aflame? Are you still working with that one?"

I shook my head.

"Then why did he help you? Elenora, I thought I knew you. I thought I loved you."

I felt a fresh stab of pain at his words, though I more than deserved them.

"I was going to tell you everything, right after your coronation. I wanted to be honest with you, and then we could have had a fresh start, a life together. That's why I asked for the boon, so I could use it to ask for your forgiveness."

"That's why? You can't expect that I'd forgive your deceit because I promised you a favor. You can't pay for lies like they are debts."

"I thought Pel was my friend," I began. Casper huffed, clearly thinking this was another lie, but I continued. "I saved him from bandits in the woods. I overheard them talking about how they captured a faerie and were considering turning him in to the crown for the reward money. Or killing him."

"You should have let them."

"But he looked so helpless. I felt sorry for him. I knew fay were dangerous, but he was all alone. I know what it's like trying to survive on your own."

I left out the part about setting a small fire in Acel's and Garin's camp, lest Casper thought I did this regularly.

"But you were never on your own. You had your brothers. At least Devon should have taken care of you."

"And he did. He does everything he can to take care of us," I shot back, feeling a surge of defensiveness about my brothers. "They all do. But they aren't clever the way I am. Or maybe not as deceitful. They're smart, by Chace's chaos, Finn is probably the smartest boy I know. But they were never as good at deceiving people as I was, *as I am*." My cheeks burned hot, as I felt a sick mix of shame and pride. I had never confessed this to anyone, not even myself.

"And that's a good thing?"

"Only when you want to survive. When my parents died and my village was torched by Faradisian soldiers, we were only children. And there was no one, and I mean *no one*, to take care of us. And my sister, who was far kinder and sweeter than I'll ever be, she died because she was weak and gentle. She got sick and we couldn't even pay for food, much less a healer. Then I lost her, too, and it was *your family's* war that took them from me. I don't know what being a royal hostage was like for you, but you didn't look starved when you returned to Reynallis. I have been. My brothers have been. When Rilla died, I promised I would do whatever it took to keep my brothers alive. I was willing to steal or cheat if that meant we'd survive. It has always been up to me to make sure we have a plan. If I had started that sooner, maybe I could have saved Rilla." Hot tears streamed down my face, my nose running. But I didn't care. This guilt was my private pain, one I had never shared, not even with my brothers.

Casper stepped toward me, whether to comfort or berate me I couldn't tell, but I waved him back. I wiped my sleeve across my face, rubbing my eyes and nose, getting dirtier for my troubles.

"So, I felt sympathy for Pel, and I freed him. In return, he gave me a golden thread." I pulled up my sleeve, showing the cursed golden bracelet that was still locked around my wrist. I continued as briskly as possible, trying to simply relay the facts, lest I got too emotional again. I told Casper about my idea for the straw. About Pel's aide in the tower. I told him everything.

Once I finished, I dropped to the ground, too emotionally and physically drained to stand. I waited for Casper's next move.

He sat down across from me, and for a long time we sat in silence. His face, normally so expressive, was a closed mask, his thoughts secrets.

"I don't even know what to say to you, Nor." The fire was gone from his voice, replaced by a deep sadness. In some ways, it hurt worse. "I don't know if I can ever forgive you."

"I don't expect you to." I felt like my cracked heart was splintering into tiny, sharp, broken pieces. I stared down at my hands, afraid that if I looked at him, I'd have to see how I'd killed his love for me.

"What you did goes beyond selfish or stupid. It was deceitful, maybe even traitorous."

I focused on breathing in and out. I wished I had a knife to cut the stupid corset strings.

"But I see now that it wasn't cruel." Casper's voice was as flat as before, but I whipped my head up in surprise. "I don't think I ever really understood what you needed to do to survive."

"I'm sorry," was all I managed to say.

"Me too."

I looked at him questioningly. "For what?"

"My family is supposed to protect our people, not destroy them. I was told I was too young to be involved in the Southern War, but you lived through it."

"It wasn't your fault." I burned remembering how I had snapped that it was his war.

"But it is my responsibility."

"You can't save everyone. Look at me. I'm failing miserably, and I'm only trying to take care of my brothers." *Please let them be all right,* I thought. Even if Casper wanted nothing more to do with me, I would still make it back to the Rose Place to get my brothers.

"I really believed your familiarity with the common people would have made you a great queen."

I fought back the stinging behind my eyes. "What do we do now?" I forced myself to continue to look at him. There was pain in his handsome, dark eyes, and it burned me to know it was because of me.

Casper stood, dusting himself off. For a moment, I was simply amazed at how regal he managed to look. Despite being filthy and injured, he stood tall, looking every bit a king. "We head back to Sterling. We fix this."

"We?" I hardly dared to breathe the question.

"We," Casper confirmed, extending his hand to me. I took it, and he helped me to my feet. I felt a jolt at this small gesture, this touch, but I was afraid to read into it. He pulled his hand back as soon as I was standing.

"I don't know if I can ever trust you again, Nor. Not after all this. But I'm not going to leave you in the middle of the Biawood with a fay army so close. We need to get home. Then we'll figure out what to do next."

I stepped in line with Casper and we slowly made our way south, heading back toward Reynallis. We didn't talk much, and the silence felt ripe with unsaid things. But I would deal with those when we were back at the Rose Palace. I didn't know what I could do to win back Casper, *if* I could win him back. But I knew I would try. I would do anything to convince Casper to give me another chance. Half my heart died when Pel betrayed me. I would find a way to save the half I had given to Casper. I would find a way to win back his love.

Epilogue

There was nothing worse than a fay being commanded by his true name, forced against his will to follow the command, no matter how much he loathed to do so. It is why faeries kept their true names so close, often only confiding in their monarchs and the most intimate family members. When the queen ordered Pel to personally handle Nor's capture, he thought he had reached the height of humiliation.

But he was so very wrong.

Nor was not the kind creature Pel had taken her for, the one Pel had wanted to keep safe from the war he knew was brewing, the war he had helped to begin. He had even made plans to take her where she'd be safe from his queen, willing to keep her hidden from his queen. He would have been willing, eager even, to live that double life if Nor had chosen him. But Nor did not want a life with him. *No.* She was hungry for power and destruction, choosing her golden prince over the freedom he had offered, destroying everything in her path. The helplessness, the unrequited rage he felt as he was unable to stop himself from freeing her and her damn king. And then to set fire to camp, unable to resist as though he were nothing more than a marionette. Pel cursed himself for ever letting his guard down with a human, even one with sun-colored hair and clever eyes.

"Explain yourself," Queen Marasina demanded after the fires had been put out. Several tents had burned to ash before soldiers had been able to fully smoother the flames. Only a dozen soldiers sustained minor burns from the fire, as the soldiers had still been eating. It would have been so much worse had his comrades been asleep in their tents. But the damage went much deeper. Too many eyes saw Pel with the torch, and now he stood before his queen, two of her fiercest guards by her side. Even his family's place in court would not save him. "My prize prisoner has made an impossible escape along with the human girl. They could not have done this without help. And then you set fire to our camp." Her sky-blue eyes grew cold. "You defied me after the battle and now this. Do I need to question where your loyalties lie?"

Pel swallowed hard, fighting the fear and anger that came with her threat. Once upon a time, he had believed he could be loyal to his queen and devoted to a human. But that was like trying to hold fire and ice. Twice he had been commanded by the use of his true name, and now he had to beg forgiveness from his queen, even though she was the one who used his name, careless enough to let Nor hear it. But this was somehow his fault. Treason was a serious offense. It was suicide, and a painful one, as his queen could force her subjects to do anything. Pel could be commanded to cut himself till he bled to death or remain in place as he slowly starved. Pel swallowed again. "No, my queen. I would never."

"Then explain yourself," she repeated, ice in her words.

Pel stood, trying to form words that would appease his queen and spare his life. All he had to do was tell her that Nor had heard and used his name, that it had been beyond his control. He would be punished, but surely not so severely, but for a moment, his tongue stuck in his mouth.

"The girl figured out his name." Pel turned to see Elrik by his side, showing a veneer of brotherly devotion that Pel knew was an act, albeit a convincing one.

"What are you doing?" Pel whispered.

"Saving our family from disgrace," Elrik hissed before addressing the queen. "Pel had no way to resist when she commanded him."

Queen Marasina advanced on the brothers, her brows knitting together in scrutiny. "Is this true, Pel?"

Looking into her eyes, Pel knew he could not lie, even if he had a convincing lie that could save both Nor and himself. And Nor had chosen her king over him. So Pel chose his queen over Nor. "It is true, my queen. Please forgive me." He bowed low in supplication.

To his surprise, Queen Marasina laughed, a quiet sound that lacked all mirth. "That human is cleverer than I gave her credit. Perhaps we shall be best served by killing her."

"No." Pel was surprised that his silent hope was echoed out loud by Elrik's interjection. Queen Marasina's laugher died abruptly, her eyes narrowing in on Elrik.

"Would you dare defy me, too?" The cutting edge was back in her voice.

Elrik elbowed Pel hard before he could speak, the sharp pain taking away Pel's breath. "I would never deny you anything, my queen," Elrik said easily. "If you demand that we kill her, I will stab her through her heart myself. But you yourself stated how clever she is, and I am intrigued. She must have learned a great deal more about the human royals than she has already divulged, secrets that could be useful. I would like to pry those secrets from her."

Elrik's words were smooth and convincing, but Pel could see the greed in his brother's eyes. He wondered why his brother wanted Nor so badly, sure it had nothing to do with aiding the queen. Likely, he wanted to take her merely because he saw that Pel had wanted her, and Elrik had always coveted whatever Pel possessed. But Pel kept his mouth shut. He would find out his brother's true objectives later. Elrik would be disappointed to know that Pel now wanted nothing to do with the girl.

But the queen smiled then, as though reaching a conclusion. "You make a point, Elrik. Perhaps I was too hasty, and she may prove useful. Very well. Find the kingling and the girl, bring them back to me." Elrik bowed low in thanks as Queen Marasina focused again on Pel. "And to prove your loyalty Pel, you shall aid your brother in tracking them down. Can you do that without allowing the human to ensnare you again?" There was mockery in her voice, but her meaning was clear. His blunder would be forgiven if he proved himself with this task. All he had to do was retrieve Nor and her king.

Before he could allow any sympathy to cloud his resolve, Pel focused on remembering the feel of the torch in his hands, the destruction Nor had forced him to commit, against his will, even after all the chances he had offered her. Pel allowed the anger to bubble up within himself, pushing everything else aside. She thought he was an idiot, a tool to be used and thrown away. But that was the last time Pel would let her take advantage of him. Pel would no longer be her fool. He walled up the piece of his heart that still ached for Nor, pretending that piece of himself was dead. He remembered the string of gold, still snug around her wrist. It was only a matter of time before even the smallest drop of her blood would touch the gold. He would be able to find her. And there was one final obstacle she would face, leaving Magnomel, that would help him.

Pel bowed low before meeting his queen's eyes. "Of course, my queen."

Acknowledgments

Thanks first to the beautiful tradition of oral storytelling and to the Grimm brothers, for writing them down. I've loved the dark, old versions of fairytales for as long as I can remember, but also felt it was past time the miller's daughter got some agency. And a name. For names are powerful things.

I've dreamed of this day so long that it feels like my own fairytale coming true now that it's finally here. And there are so many people who have helped me on my journey of sharing Nor's story. Many, many thanks to Sue and her fantastic team at CamCat Books. I couldn't have asked for a more enthusiastic group of book lovers to bring my debut to life. Maryann, this cover is so pretty it brought me to tears. Laura, thanks for answering my million marketing questions. And special thanks to my own fairy god-editor Cassandra for holding my hand during this publishing process.

Thanks to Elena and Brianna of the wonderful Wunderkind PR. Thanks to my agent, Steve, and his wife Ruth, for taking a chance on me. Seeing this book in print is even more exciting than tea with the queen. Thanks to Elaine, whose sense of story is stellar. And my immense appreciation to everyone in my own writing tribe. The Greater Los Angeles Writers Society and WestWords have been not only places I go to learn and write but build friendships that have gotten me through rejections and celebrated victories. Thanks to NaNoWriMo for giving me a safe place to try my hand at a novel and later to create the first draft of this story. My gratitude to all my beta readers and critique partners for their feedback to make *Gold Spun* a stronger story. Thanks to Jenna and Sheri for their early endorsements when Steve was pitching Gold Spun to publishers.

Thank you to my friends and family who have supported me during my writing adventures. Erica, these costumes are stunning. You totally rock, and I owe you so many lamps. Thanks to Craig for giving me support when I needed it and space to write. Much love to my pups Buttercup and Nor, who are always happy to snuggle with me while I write. Even now, Nor is curled up next to me in bed under the covers as I write this. It's very cute.

And finally, my eternal gratitude goes to you, my readers, for whom I tell my stories.

About the Author

Brandie June spent most of her childhood onstage or reading, as both activities let her live in fantastic stories. She moved to Los Angeles to study acting at UCLA, and eventually branched out into costume design and playwriting. While she spends most of her free time writing, she will still take any excuse to play dress-up, especially if it involves wearing a crown. She happily promotes more stories as a marketing director for kids' films and anime. She lives with her husband, two spoiled rescue pups, a spoiled cat, six fish tanks, and five bookshelves.

You can find out more about Brandie at
www.brandiejune.com

More from CamCat Books

An excerpt from

Shadows Over London

by Christian Klaver

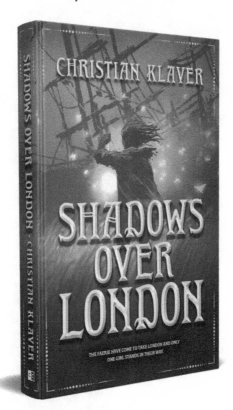

Prologue:
The Faerie King

Some dreams are so true that it doesn't matter if they actually happened that way or not. They're so true that they've happened more than once. My dreams about the Faerie were like that. Most of the rest of England got their first glimpse of the Faerie on the night London fell. But not me. I saw my first Faerie ten years before that, on my sixth birthday.

My name is Justice Kasric and my family was all tangled up with the Faerie even before the invasion.

Because I'd been born on Boxing Day, the day after Christmas, Father always made a grand affair of my birthday so that it wasn't all swallowed up by the other holidays. That's why, long after Christmas supper had come and gone, I stood at the frosted window of my room looking out into the darkness trying to guess what kind of surprise Father had in store for my sixth birthday. I was sure that something wonderful was coming. Maybe a pony ... or even *ponies*.

I crept quietly out of my room. I didn't want to wake Faith, my older sister. I didn't see or hear anyone on the top floors, but then I heard movement from down in the front hall. Father. He clicked his pocket watch closed, tucked it back into his dark waistcoat and pulled the heavy black naval coat off the hook by the door. I was sure he'd turn around and see me crouched on the stairs, but he only stood a moment in the shrouded half-moonlight before opening the front door. A cool mist rolled noiselessly past his ankles as he went out.

I was in luck! Where else would Father be going except to feed the ponies? I drew on my rubber boots and threw my heavy blue woolen coat on over my nightgown, determined to follow.

When I opened the door and looked out into the front garden, the mist hung everywhere in soft carpets of moonlit fleece. Father was nowhere in sight, but I could hear him crunching ahead of me.

I paused, sensing even then that some steps took you further than others. The enormity of my actions lay heavily on me. The comforting, warm interior of the house called for me to come back inside. It was not too late to go back. I could return to the rest of my family, content with a life filled with tea settings, mantelpiece clocks, antimacassars and other normal, sensible notions. The proper thing would have been to go back inside, to bed. I remember shaking my head, sending my braids dancing.

I followed Father outside into the still and misty night.

We went across the front garden, past shrubs and frozen pools, and descended the hill into the snow-laden pines. His crunching footsteps carried back to me in the still air. I followed by stepping in the holes he'd left in the snow to make less noise, jumping to match his long stride. The stables lay behind the house, but clearly, we weren't heading there. We lived in the country then, amidst a great deal of farmland with clumps of forest around.

The silence grew heavier, deeper, as we descended into the trees and a curious lassitude swept over me as I followed Father through the tangled woods. The air was sharp and filled with the clean smell of ice and pine. On the other side of a dip in the land, we *should* have emerged into a large and open field. Only we didn't. The field wasn't there. Instead, we kept going down through more and more snow-laden trees.

The treetops formed a nearly solid canopy sixty or seventy feet above us, but with a vast and open space underneath. The thick shafts of moonlight slanted down through silvered air into emerald shadows, each tree a stately pillar in that wide-open space.

I worried about Father catching me following him, but he never even turned around. Always, he went down. Down, down into the forest into what felt like another world entirely. Even I knew we couldn't still be in the English countryside. You could just feel it. I also knew that following him wasn't about ponies anymore and I might have given up and gone home, only I had no idea how to find my way back.

After a short time, we came to an open green hollow where I crouched at the edge of a ring of trees and blinked my eyes at the sudden brightness. The canopy opened up to the nighttime sky and moonlight filled the empty hollow like cream poured into a cup. This place had a planned feel, the circle of trees shaped just so, the long black trunk lying neatly in the exact center of a field of green grass like a long table, and all of it inexplicably free of snow. Two pale boulders sat on either side like chairs. The silence felt deeper here, older, expectant. The place was waiting.

Father lit a cigarette and stood smoking. The thin wisp of smoke curled up and into the night sky.

Then, the Faerie King arrived.

First, there was emptiness, and then, without any sign of motion, a hulking, towering figure stood on the other side of the log, standing as if he'd always been there waiting. I'd read enough of the right kinds of books to recognize him as a Faerie King right off and I shivered.

The Faerie King looked like a shambling beast on its back legs, with huge tined antlers that rose from his massive skull. He wore a wooden crown nearly buried by a black mane thick as lamb's fleece that flowed into a forked beard. His long face was a gaunt wooden mask, with blackened slits for eyes and a harsh, narrow opening for a mouth.

Except it wasn't a mask, because it moved. The mouth twitched and the jaw muscles clenched as he regarded the man in front of him. Finally, he inclined his head in a graceless welcome. He wore a cloak like a swath of forest laid across his back, made entirely of thick wild grass, weeds, and brambles, with a rich black undercoat of loam where a silk lining would show. Underneath the cloak, he wore armor that might once have been bright copper, but was now rampant with verdigris. He leaned on the pommel of a wide-bladed, granite sword.

The Faerie King and Father regarded each other for a long time before they each sat down. A chessboard with pieces of carved wood and bone sat suddenly between them. Again, there was no sense of movement, only a sudden understanding that the board must have always been there, waiting.

They began to play.

The Faerie King hesitated, reached to advance his white king's pawn, then stopped. His leathery right hand was massive, nearly the size of the board, far too large for this task. He shifted awkwardly and used his more normal-sized left hand. Father advanced a pawn immediately in response. The Faerie King sat and viewed the board with greater deliberation. He finally reached out with his left hand to make his move, and then stopped. He shifted in his seat, uncertain, then finally advanced his knight.

I could feel others watching with me. Invisible ghosts hidden in the trees. The weight of their interest hung palpably in the air. Whatever the outcome of this game, it was important in a way you couldn't help but feel. However long it took, this timeless shuffling of pieces, the watchers would wait and I waited with them. With only a nightgown on under my coat, crouching in the snow, I should have been freezing. But I didn't feel the cold. I only felt the waiting, and the waiting consumed me.

Father and the Faerie King had each moved their forces into the center of the board, aligning and realigning in constant readiness for the inevitable clash. Now Father sliced into the black pawns with surgical precision, starting an escalating series of exchanges. Around us, it began to snow.

As the game went on, Father and the Faerie King lined their captures neatly on the side of the board. Father looked to be considerably better off. The Faerie King grew more and more angry, and he squeezed and kneaded the log with his massive right hand so that the wood cracked and popped. Occasional bursts of wood fragments flew to either side.

Father's only reaction to this violent display was a long, slow smile. He took another Turkish cigarette calmly from a cigarette case and lit it. I was suddenly very chilled. That kind of calm wasn't natural. The smoke from Father's cigarette drifted placidly upwards. His moves were immediate, decisive, while the Faerie King's became more and more hesitant as the game went on. The smile on Father's face grew. I watched, and the forest watched with me.

Then the Faerie King snarled, jumped up, and brought his massive fist down on the board like a mallet. Bits of the board, chess pieces, and wood splinters flew out into the snow. Twice more he mauled the log, gouging out huge hunks of wood in his fury. Then he spun with a swiftness shocking in so large a person and yanked his huge sword out of the snow. He brought it down in a deadly arc that splintered the log like a lightning strike. Debris and splinters had flown around Father like a ship's deck hit by a full broadside of cannonballs, but Father didn't even flinch. Two broken halves of smoldering log lay in the clearing.

"Perhaps next time," Father said, standing up, the first words either of them had spoken. He brushed a few splinters from his coat.

The Faerie King stared, quivering, his wooden face twisted suddenly with grief. Then his legs gave out and he collapsed in the snow, all his impotent rage spent. He sat, slumped with his mismatched hands on his knees, the perfect picture of abject defeat. He didn't so much as stir when Father turned his back and left.

I couldn't tear my gaze away from the rough and powerful shape slouched heavily and immobile in the snow. White clumps were already starting to gather on his arms, shoulders, head and antlers, as if he might never move again.

Father climbed directly to my hiding place and stood, looking down at me with amusement in his glacial-blue eyes. I'd forgotten all about hiding.

He warned me to keep silent with a gloved finger to his lips, then put a hand on my shoulder and steered me away from the hollow. Father fished his watch out of the waistcoat pocket and checked the time as we climbed back up the slope. We walked for a bit, surrounded only by the sound of crunching snow and the spiced scent of Father's smoke.

"Well," he said finally. "I've always encouraged you to be curious, little Justice, but *this* is a surprise. Did you follow me all the way from home?" He didn't sound cross at all, only curious. So it was a family trait.

"Yes." I looked back the way we'd come. It was hard to imagine that *I* was the biggest surprise of this night.

"You must be cold," he said, "yes?"

I *was* cold, suddenly. Father draped his coat around me, then picked me up and carried me like a princess. The soft wool of his coat was warm and comforting, as were the familiar scents that clung to it. The Turkish tobacco with cloves and ginger. Ordinary, familiar smells that sluiced away the strangeness of the night.

"Father, what was that horrible thing?" I asked

"Oh, not so horrible, Justice. Not really. Though I suppose the church might not agree. But then, you'll learn to think for yourself and not take *their* word, eh?"

"Yes, Father," I said. I knew exactly what the church would have to say about a creature like that, but maybe that wasn't so important.

"Well," he said after a time, "now I have a problem. This needs to be a secret, you see? But I know how little girls talk. Perhaps a bribe? What would it take to keep this our secret?"

He didn't need the bribe and we both knew it. I would have done anything for him.

But he'd asked, so I said, "A pony?"

He laughed. "Well, I don't have a pony on me, but . . . here, hang on tight." He shifted my weight a little so that he could fish around in his coat pocket.

He handed me a chess piece from the game, one of his knights. At least it *looked* like one of the wooden pieces from the game back in the hollow, but how could it be? The Faerie King had bashed them all to bits and I hadn't seen Father pick anything up when he left. Still, there it was.

"Would this horsie do?" he said.

I looked closer.

The piece wasn't just a horse's head, but an entire stallion carved in loving detail. It reared up, riderless, wild and beautiful. More than beautiful. The dark wood gleamed, reminding me of the glossy flank of a living horse.

"It's wonderful," I said, taking it in both hands. It was warm to the touch. "I couldn't feed a regular horse, anyway."

"You are very wise for such a small child," Father said.

"Does it have a name, Father?"

"Why, of course it does. All important things have names. Remember your promise here not to tell a soul about what you saw, and I'm sure we'll discover her name together."

A sudden sleepiness overcame me. It felt impossibly late, near morning. He must have carried me all the way home because my next memory was Father climbing the steps inside our house and then lowering me into bed. He moved carefully so as to not wake Faith, my older sister.

Moments or hours later—I could never be sure—I sat up.

Father was gone. I was in my nightdress only, with no sign of my coat. In the bed across the room, Faith was in the deepest kind of sleep, immobile, as if it would take a prince to wake her.

But the sweet smell of Father's Turkish cigarette still lingered in the air.

I looked for the chess piece, but to my disappointment there was nothing in the bed, nothing on the dresser. There was no sign of the chess piece anywhere.

So, for many years I discounted the memory of that night in the forest, believing it only a lovely and somewhat frightening dream. I didn't find out how wrong that idea was until much later.

CamCat Books

VISIT US ONLINE FOR
MORE BOOKS TO LIVE IN:
CAMCATBOOKS.COM

FOLLOW US

CamCatBooks   @CamCatBooks   @CamCat_Books

CPSIA information can be obtained
at www.ICGtesting.com
Printed in the USA
LVHW091655210521
688147LV00010B/338/J